0340

Winter Music

Winter

Music

KAREN RILE

LITTLE, BROWN AND COMPANY — BOSTON–TORONTO

FIRST EDITION

LIBRARY OF CONGRESS CATALOGING IN PUBLICATION DATA

Rile, Karen.
    Winter music.

    I. Title.
PS3568.I3774W5   1983   813'.54   83-7984
ISBN 0-316-74657-6

VB
Designed by Susan Windheim

Published simultaneously in Canada
by Little, Brown & Company (Canada) Limited

PRINTED IN THE UNITED STATES OF AMERICA

For both J.R.'s, L.S.,
and in memory of James B. McDade

Winter Music

Chapter 1

I

Sunday afternoon
October 22, 1978

James, you know my rule. You know I refuse to accept any student who is younger than fifteen or who has been playing for less than three years. Anyone. No one gets past this, yes? Well, this week I auditioned a boy who has just turned eleven, and has studied for less than a year. His mother is on the Board of the school, but she wasn't the one who convinced me to hear him (although she thinks so herself). It was actually Samantha, my former pupil, his teacher. He has been taking lessons with her at Germantown and she came to me and said, in her embarrassed whisper, "He is too much for me. In nine months I have taught him everything that I have to teach."

So I told them to come to my apartment, the mother, the teacher and the boy, Gabriel. I wanted to intimidate them, you know. They would have been more comfortable in the surroundings of the school, all of them, even the boy, who isn't enrolled yet, though I'm sure his mother takes him there often. So I had them come here. I watched them from the bay window as they arrived and argued with the doorman about parking. I could see them looking at the red carpets and the gargoyle pots outside, and before they came in the mother was pushing the boy's loose curls behind his ears while Samantha was brushing off the shoulders of his school blazer. You can picture it. They vanished beneath the awning and soon they were knocking at my door.

James, he is a translucent, fragile child, as beautiful as a girl. I could see the blue veins beneath the skin of his throat and his temples. His fingers were relaxed about the handle of his case. Imagine, no tension in his fingers. At first their thinness disturbed me. I thought: he cannot possibly have enough wind for this instrument.

Gabriel. *There has been an Angel Gabriel in my past. A faint recollection, maybe, from the catechisms I learned the year I spent in a Catholic school; or perhaps from some poem I was made to memorize and have forgotten. The Archangel.*

Gabriel the angel; Gabriel the faun. William Kinkaid used to wear a tie clip with the theme from L'Après-*midi d'un* faune *engraved on it. Tiny musical scratches in the gold. Gabriel, then. I would ask him to play the chromatic scale.*

No one spoke. They were waiting for me to begin. I considered leaving them there in the doorway, telling them that the boy was still too small for the flute, to bring him back when his chest was larger. But I liked his name, Gabriel. I ushered them in, brightly. His calm hands intrigued me.

The mother was aggressive, quick, and at once the room was cluttered with her conversation. Samantha, nervous as usual in my presence, introduced us loudly. I had met the mother already several times, at benefit concerts and whatnot. The redness of her hair, the cold blue of her eyes, irritated me. I stared at the child. He was still, his knuckles loose on the handle of the case. He smiled politely, did not speak. I told him to warm up.

The mother talked relentlessly of school matters, making clear to me again and again her influential position on the Board of Trustees. (She's only there, James, because of her ex-husband, and I happen to know that she won't be reappointed.) I pretended to ignore her. Samantha was panting a little, breathless with her tension. The boy unzipped the canvas cover, unlocked the case. So many students fumble when they prepare for an audition. But he assembled the instrument in a single, swift, I would say, acrobatic motion.

And Samantha was right: he is good. He has more talent than most, a better feel for the instrument than children years older than he. He is too much for Samantha to handle. He does need a teacher like me — but my roster is already full of the best. I don't need another one. What I need is time, time to write, not another prodigy to worry over. And there are other teachers in the city, Philadelphia Orchestra members, for instance, who would be perfectly suitable. His father can afford to pay any teacher, and his mother would take him to New York twice a week if she had to.

So why, James, do you think I took him? I'm not certain what draws me to him, but I think it is his serenity. And James, I did it. I showed him (rudely) my mangled hand. I have tried this on other children, to test them, and even the ones who I know have been warned (most are prepared already by their parents, or their teachers), even the oldest, the bravest, they all flinch. It's a sight that brings horror upon a musician, especially a child musician. You know how serious and unplayful these children are. My maimed hand.

I cannot impress you with the importance of his reaction. Let me try. Even you, James, even you who have lived through all of this with me, are disquieted by the sight of my left hand, if it wanders to the table when we are eating, if it taps out an enthusiastic rhythm during a concert. Think of it. But this boy was not alarmed or disgusted, and he did not look away quickly. Instead he stared at my hand for the amount of time one would take to examine an unusual brooch on a woman's breast. Then he looked me in the eye, lifted the embouchure to his lips, and ran through a few scales. I was struck; but neither Samantha nor the mother noticed my amazement or the situation that caused it. They were paying so close attention. You'd think they would have caught on.

I will teach him on Tuesdays at seven. He has soccer practice until six, his mother says, an hour to change and to be driven to my apartment. I did not want to teach him at the school. He is special.

I told him to buy all the usual books of études and exercises. He has some already — Samantha's good work. He does all the scales, can switch from one key to another without hesitation. All of his audition pieces were done without music, and he played for over half an hour. I think he may have an exceptional memory, or else he was exquisitely prepared. We shall see.

It is Sunday afternoon now, late Sunday: out the bay window the street is orange from the sunset. His first lesson is in two weeks. I wonder if he really is all that I have made him in my mind. I would like for you to see him. I think that I am right; I usually am in such

*cases. If he does quite well I will bring him to meet you, maybe
backstage at a concert. Of course, it is premature to say this, but I
have not been so excited about a student since I was coaching you.
(Don't think that I am comparing him to you. It's nothing like that.) I
have a hunch about his genius, though, and genius is the word here.
Like you. Not like these students who win competitions and then join
some orchestra or chamber ensemble, or go to law school. Something
makes me think he will be a soloist. We shall see. Perhaps I will bring
him to meet you.* Gabriel . . .

Lawrence had been writing for forty-five minutes. The sunset
was heavy on his closed window and the room had grown hot.
Droplets of sweat were forming on his forehead and the back of his
neck. He could feel a wetness under his arms. He capped his fountain pen, and with his right hand he pulled his sweater off over his
head. Instantly he was damp and chilled. Five o'clock. Time to
put on the tea. During the week he had a girl to do the cooking,
but on weekends he took care of it himself. Unless he went to a
restaurant, his meals were light. English muffins and soft-boiled
eggs. Years ago he'd learned how to crack the top off and scoop out
the soft inside without getting shell splinters inside the bowl. He
hated the gritty crunch of eggshell in his mouth.

The telephone rang. It was James, from Chicago. A break during rehearsal.

"I was just writing you a letter. I was going to give it to you
when you get back. How is it there?"

He chose a fork and began to mash the eggs into a lump of salty
feta cheese. This mixture he spread on a toasted muffin. He cut the
conversation short since he did not like to chew while he was talking. He did not mention Gabriel.

II In his own kitchen, Gabriel was making Kool-Aid,
from a tiny foil packet with a drawing of a grinning glass pitcher
on the front. He added half again as much sugar as the directions
said. He liked it sweet. He stirred fast, making purple puddles on
the counter. His mom would be complaining about that.

She was upstairs right now calling him about something. He didn't answer. Instead he tried to guess what she wanted. It could be: one, his sweaty soccer clothes, which he'd stuffed into his underwear drawer after practice on Friday (they were probably dried out and smelly by now); or two, he hadn't practiced yet and it was already five o'clock; or three, she knew he was drinking Kool-Aid again, and would spoil his dinner.

He drank a big glass, as fast as he could. It took five gulps; and he remembered to put the pitcher back into the refrigerator, and he remembered to shut the refrigerator door (but he didn't wipe off the counter top) before he went upstairs to see what was wrong. She noticed his purple mustache immediately.

"You've been drinking Kool-Aid again," she began.

In two days he was going to start with a new teacher. He wasn't nervous yet, though everyone was trying to make him be. Mr. Chattarjee. He could pronounce it, but it was hard to spell. There was something wrong with Mr. Chattarjee's hand, fingers missing. His mother said something about an accident. He would have to find out about that.

She was holding his stiff ball of soccer clothes and some of his clean undershirts, which were now smelly. She was still yelling. Gabriel looked at his fingertips. They had turned purple when he licked them and touched the pinkish dust on the inside of the Kool-Aid packet. He licked them again, but the sour grape taste was gone. He rubbed them against his jeans, but the skin was stained. The purple wouldn't come off. His mother was emptying everything in his underwear drawer into a laundry basket.

"Wait," he said. He kept his best baseball cards in a sweat sock that didn't have a mate. This he rescued from the basket.

"Go practice," said his mother. "Now."

III Lawrence took the dustcover off his Selectric. The scrap paper he had used when he changed the ribbon yesterday was still there.

hjkl; THE GREAT GOD KRISHNA PLAYED THE TRANSVERSE
FLUTE....XXXXXXX Every good boy does fine. All cows eat grass.

He ripped the paper out of the carriage and it tore in half on its
way out of the typewriter, before he could ball it up in his hand.
His editor wanted to see chapter ten by the end of the week. He
opened his notes and took a fresh sheet of erasable bond from the
top drawer.

IV

I told you about Strawberry Fields,
You know the place where nothing is real . . .

Gabriel's mother wanted him to listen to classical music only,
but he loved the Beatles. For his eleventh birthday, Toby had
given him *The White Album*, and Gabriel played it whenever his
mother was out of the house. Right now she was driving around
trying to buy a Sunday *Times*, even though it was almost night
and any store that would have been open would have sold out
hours ago. Theirs had never been delivered, and his mother
wanted to read the music reviews. All she ever read was the
reviews and the Arts & Leisure section. Gabriel read the *Magazine*, the Sports section, and sometimes parts of the *Book Review*.
Neither of them liked to look at the news.

He was getting ready to practice, assembling his wire music
stand, and the stacks of études and exercises he had to play
through by the end of the evening. Samantha was crazy about
exercises. She let him call her by her first name, even though he felt
more comfortable saying "Miss Engs." But she wasn't his teacher
anymore. He didn't know when he would see her again. He did
know for sure that, no matter what, he wasn't going to call his new
teacher by his first name. Mr. Chattarjee. His mother said, "He
has a Ph.D., but he doesn't like to be called 'Doctor.' "

Gabriel turned off the stereo and struck an A. His mother kept
the Steinway tuned perfectly, even after Elise died. No one played

it anymore, except at parties, but still she paid a tuner to come to look at it every two months. Gabriel didn't really need the piano. He had, according to Samantha, perfect pitch. He always knew when he or anyone else was off. He used the Steinway partly out of habit and partly just so that it would be used. (His mother always said "Steinway," never "piano." That was her way of telling everyone what a fine instrument they had, without actually saying so.)

It was a used piano, anyway. His mom had bought it from the music school, for Elise to practice on. They used to have a better one, a firsthand one, but his dad had taken that when he moved out. This was a good instrument, though. Every time Toby said they should sell it Mom got furious. Gabriel didn't want to sell it, either. It didn't seem fair to do that to Elise, even if she was dead.

He did the major scales first. B-flat was his favorite.

Two and a half miles down the road, Elizabeth, Gabriel's mother, switched into first and rattled up the hill. She hadn't been able to find a *Times* anywhere, but Gabriel was right, what could she expect at a quarter of six on a Sunday? She should have gone to get one this morning. The car was making unhealthy noises again. She'd have to take it back to the dealer for the third time this month. Never buy a foreign car.

At least Toby was home. Elizabeth rarely dropped by without calling first. She was afraid of finding his house empty, or finding him with someone else.

"I was in the neighborhood," she told him. "Do you have a copy of the *New York Times*?"

His house was a mess, as usual. The living room was swimming with smoke, something was burning in the kitchen. Elizabeth choked. The television was loud.

"Eagles are winning," said Toby. Newspapers, clothes, and half-empty cups were all over the floor.

"I'm reheating a pizza," said Toby. "I think it's ready. Excuse me." While she waited she scavenged through the newspapers for the Arts & Leisure pages.

Toby came from the kitchen and offered her a can of beer. As usual she refused. He kissed her.

"My pizza burnt," he explained. "Ruined, ruined. Have you eaten yet?"

"Oh God, I forgot," she said. "I haven't defrosted anything. I haven't even thought about what to make. And it's quarter to seven. I'm a lousy mother."

"A great mother. Lousy housewife."

"You have a way with words."

"I make that my business."

V If Lawrence could have picked up his typewriter he might have tossed it out the bay window. The hell with the chapter. The hell with the boyhood of William Kinkaid.

A beach in Hawaii? Who cares?

Time to escape, like a real writer. He put on one side of his Rampal recording of *Handel's Complete Flute Sonatas*. Largo, B minor.

He poured half an inch of Rémy Martin into one of his larger snifters.

James, where are you when I need you?

Lawrence was beginning to doze, which was bad. It was too early to go to sleep, and when he slept sitting up he always had nightmares. He had set aside the evening to work on that chapter. It had to be done. He had already finished the research, the interviewing. That alone had taken a lot of September and half of October. Now he had to put it all together and make it interesting reading. But he had already solved all the puzzles for himself. He didn't feel like writing it all out, for other people. A waste of time, it reminded him of some university research paper.

The deadline is Friday, he kept thinking. The commitment he'd made to his editor. He'd given his word, now he had to get to work.

The record ended and he wanted more Handel. He put on side two.

VI It was seven and his mom still wasn't home. Gabriel was getting hungry, but he didn't smell anything in the oven. Great, she probably hadn't even started dinner before she left. She was probably at Toby's again. Things were always better when Toby came over here.

He put his flute down and went to the kitchen for another Kool-Aid. When he was there he remembered to feed the goldfish. That was his responsibility. His mother didn't like animals. She had made him get rid of the gerbil, and after Elise died, she had sold the cat. Gabriel hadn't liked the cat much; it was always trying to eat Mr. Gerbil. What Gabriel objected to was this: why had she sold the cat, but kept the piano, which was worth more and nobody used? Of course it had to do with the fact that Dad had given the cat to Elise, and Toby was allergic to cats.

He put his second Kool-Aid glass in the sink next to the first. His mother better come home soon because if he got much hungrier he wouldn't be able to concentrate on practicing.

Elizabeth was telling Toby, "I'm hungry. Sort of."

Toby said, "The solution to our joint hunger must be that we should all — meaning you, me, and your progeny, whom we will pick up on the way in our separate cars — should all go to Roy's." There was an angry flicker in Elizabeth's eye when he said "separate cars."

"No, Toby. He has to practice. He has his first lesson in two days and once he sees you he'll be all riled up. I won't be able to calm him down all evening."

Toby said, "This little maestro must eat, however."

"Howdy, pardners. Welcome to the Old West. What can I do you for?"

"Two Double R Burgers. Two large fries. Two milk shakes, chocolate."

"Condiments behind you to the left."

"Just the salad bar, please, and a medium Tab," said Elizabeth.

Gabriel grinned at his mother. "Chicken. You're chicken."

The girl at the register had rings on all fingers, including both thumbs. She wore an artificial red-felt cowgirl hat. "Thanks, pardners, come again."

"Elizabeth, you smoke too much."

"I'm down to two packs a day, now."

The man at the table next to them put six sugars in his coffee. He pulled a half-smoked cigar from his trouser pocket and asked Elizabeth for a light. She gave him a box of wooden matches. He asked for a quarter.

Elizabeth's eyes flashed with anger.

Gabriel loved the feeling you get when you just start to unwrap the foil from your Double R Burger and the smell of it goes right up your nose and suddenly your stomach aches with the biggest hunger you could ever feel, but it doesn't matter at all because you're just about to take a bite and then your hunger'll melt away slowly with each bite until it's gone and you feel slightly stuffed.

Except it's not like that, not exactly, he thought; there are french fries, too, with catsup and horseradish sauce. They're for the bites in between the other bites, to clean the hamburger taste out of your mouth and to make you want it more.

Gabriel finished the whole hamburger, but not his fries. He had swirled the red catsup and the white horseradish together over them so that the whole mess reminded him of the insides of the frog they were dissecting in science. If he told his mother this she would be mad. It's bad manners to talk about disgusting subjects at the table. When she got up to get more croutons he told Toby, who said to remember it, it might make a good metaphor to use someday.

"Write it down in case you need it later," he said.

Gabriel took the lid off his milk shake, which he always saved for last. Milk shakes were his favorite food, next to Kool-Aid. But he only liked the kind of shakes you get when you are out. When his mother tried to mix them in the kitchen, out of milk and ice and bananas and brewer's yeast, they tasted terrible, and the straws never stood up like the straws in the ones you get from Roy's.

His mother was telling Toby that the neighborhood was going downhill. She was upset by the man who'd asked her for a quarter. After she'd gotten the manager (in a cowboy hat with a cowboy checkered shirt and his name tag, MR. WHITEHEAD, MANAGER) to throw him out (he hadn't used a gun or a lasso, the costume wasn't for real), she hadn't been able to eat her salad. She smoked three cigarettes, and the whole time, Toby kept telling her not to. Gabriel didn't like smoke in his face either, and he said so. Finally she got interested in her salad again, and realized she didn't have enough croutons.

The problem with the neighborhood wasn't that blacks were moving in — and even if that was a problem, which it might be, partially, because more blacks than ever *were* moving in, even then you couldn't say so just to anyone, Gabriel knew; you had to be careful who you offended. Why, their street had been half-full of black people, professionals, for fifty years or more. His mother said she'd read all about this somewhere. She'd done research on the neighborhood when they'd moved there. Professionals and artists. A good neighborhood for children. But the bad black people, the ones who were poor and lived in the houses on the other side of Germantown Avenue, they were the ones who robbed houses, and they had gangs. That's why it's not safe to walk outside at night, even in their beautiful neighborhood. And now these people even come into a restaurant and bother you when you're eating. That's why you couldn't go to a public school. The school district was zoned funny, and those kids from the poor neighborhoods went to the same school as Gabriel should have gone to. All the kids on Gabriel's street went to private schools, and two of his neighbors went to his school, and three kids on the block after school went to his old music school where Samantha teaches, only they all take piano and no one takes the flute in his whole school besides him. (The other flute players in his old school were all girls.) Gabriel didn't know anyone who went to the new music school, which he was sort of enrolled in, and which was Elise's old school, but he wasn't going to go there anyway, because for some reason he was going to be taking lessons in his new teacher's house, which was downtown.

Toby was trying to change the subject. Elizabeth kept talking about moving, selling the house and buying a condominium somewhere. She talked about this when she was upset about gangs or break-ins, but she never read the For Sale column in the paper, and she never visited the real-estate offices.

"How 'bout a movie? I'll bet neither of you've seen *Annie Hall*, and I've only seen it twice, so it's perfect! And it's playing at the Eric, and I know because I looked it up before we left. It starts in twenty minutes. So! We have just enough time. Let's go."

"No. Gabriel hasn't touched his flute today. As it is, he'll only get about two hours of practicing done before bed, and he has his first lesson on Tuesday."

"That's not true, Mom — I did practice when you were gone. I did all the scales and arpeggios and half the études."

"Oh, great, and I suppose you didn't even touch the Vivaldi. You've had it for over a week now and you've only read it through once. What's Mr. Chattarjee going to think?"

"We don't have to tell him I have the Vivaldi. Then what difference will it make?"

"Don't you think Samantha told him all the pieces she gave you? She probably typed out a list for him. Think, Gabriel. You don't want to embarrass yourself for your first lesson with him, do you?"

"Why is he such a big deal? So what? Who cares?" Gabriel caught the look in his mother's eye. "All right, all right, the Vivaldi."

VII   The record was finished. Lawrence was dozing in the chair next to the piano. His sweater, which he'd spread across his knees, had fallen to his feet.

He had to use the phone. He had to get help. But one by one, as he tried to turn the dial, each finger telescoped into his hand, leaving not even a stump, just a vague, useless paw. He tried dialing with his mouth, but when his teeth touched the telephone they shattered, filling his mouth with tiny splinters. The receiver hung at his knees, but he couldn't pick it up with his useless hands. The operator had come on the line.

"Hello? Is someone there?"

He wanted to cry, "Help me! Help me!" but he couldn't answer with his mouth all full of crumbled teeth.

Whatever was coming was getting closer. He screamed and his sharp, jagged teeth flew out of his mouth, landing on his leg, piercing his flesh. Suddenly he knew that it was his own teeth he'd been afraid of. A cool pool of blood soaked through his trouser leg.

Lawrence sat up. He had dropped the brandy snifter in his lap and soaked one leg with cognac. The record had ended long ago, but the turntable and amplifier were still uselessly lit up, waiting. It was chilly in the apartment, time to turn the thermostat up. His teeth did hurt, from the caps to the roots. He'd been grinding them in his sleep again. How depressing that he hadn't done any work tonight — and it was clearly time to go to bed since he couldn't seem to stay awake. Tomorrow was Monday. He didn't have to teach, so he could work all day. And he'd make sure to call James just to wish him luck before the concert, as he always did, before every major concert in the Western Hemisphere.

There was some cognac on the upholstery of the chair. He tried to soak it up with a napkin, but the faint brown stain remained. He hoped the girl knew how to clean it. There was probably some perfectly simple trick, like rubbing in seltzer water or mayonnaise. If not, well, he could move the chair into the kitchen, or get it reupholstered, or forget about it. He switched off the stereo, replaced the dustcover, and put away the albums. The apartment wasn't warming up very fast. He went into the bathroom and turned the shower on hot. With the door closed it would be nice and steamy. He put his clothes on the chair for the time being, an expert at one-handed folding.

In the warm, warm water his muscles relaxed, tingled. He could feel himself thawing. The warm soap smell rose around him. When he stepped out he noted that the room was filled with a pleasant white fog. He rubbed his body dry and wrapped himself in his terry-cloth bathrobe.

The air in his bedroom was sudden and cool. He pulled the blinds shut, closing out the twinkling cityscape below. His racket lay on the chair beside the bed. Perhaps if he got enough work done by tomorrow afternoon, perhaps he would play. Tomorrow night was Monday, and James would be playing in Chicago.

James would be back when? Tuesday. The electric blanket was set for five. He raised it a notch to six. His glasses he put on a chair, beside the racket. He could reach them there when he first woke up, before he got out of bed.

VIII   By eleven-thirty Gabriel hadn't even started the third page of the Vivaldi. His mom and Toby were talking in the next room. Every time he started to put the flute down for a break, Elizabeth's voice would come sailing through the wall: "We're listening to you, Gabriel," or, "Sounds good in there." That meant, "Don't stop." She wasn't really listening. If she were she'd be shouting things like, "A little slower [or faster] at that last passage, please," or "Don't you think your legato tonguing needs more work?" Not that she knew anything about music, or the flute in particular. That was just her way of being bossy. Sometimes she would force Gabriel to play a passage one way and then Samantha would make him relearn the entire thing. And Mom was always messing with his phrasing. That was her way of showing off to people how she knew what phrasing was. That way other people would think she knew a lot about music, when she really didn't understand it at all, except what she'd learned in ballet school, and that was mostly all about rhythm. And Gabriel had an even better sense of rhythm than she did, so she could hardly ever correct him on that. Still, she was always telling him, "Tongue this measure, slur this passage," for no reason. Gabriel did what she said to avoid a fight. But lately he'd learned the trick of practicing it both ways: hers when she was home and his when she wasn't. And his at the lessons. Now she wasn't listening so he was playing it his way: the way the music was marked by the publisher, exactly. Gabriel wondered if Mr. Chattarjee would write all over the music, changing all the printer's marks, everything from the trills to the slurs to the metronome beats. Samantha did, and she probably learned it from him, since he'd been her teacher. She would take a fresh new sheet of music that he'd just bought, and cross out half of it and cover it with marks from her purple felt-tip pen. She did it so fast that Gabriel wondered whether she had it memorized or if she was just making it up.

"*Gabriel*. What are you doing in there?"

"I'm too thirsty. I can't play anymore without a drink."

"It's almost midnight. I want you to finish up. You have school tomorrow."

"So what? I'm thirsty. Why can't I have just a little bit of Kool-Aid? Just a juice-glass full. Not even a whole cup. Six ounces."

"That stuff is full of sugar. It'll make you salivate and you won't be able to finish practicing."

"Oh, Mom, you're not fair."

Toby's voice went *bzzz, bzzz*, too low for Gabriel to understand what he was saying.

"All right. You've had enough for tonight. Put your flute away, get some Kool-Aid, and go upstairs to bed. And don't forget to clean up if you make a mess in the kitchen."

"Yah! Okay."

"And you have to make up the practice time tomorrow."

"Okay."

"And for God's sake, brush your teeth." Gabriel didn't bother to wipe out his flute with the cleaning wand. Besides, he was intrigued by the wet green residue that always formed when he didn't clean it for several days. He snapped the case shut, zipped it into the cloth case, and laid it on top of the piano. He left the music out on the stand, opened to where he would begin tomorrow, and he ran into the kitchen. As he passed the room he could hear his mother saying, "I don't understand why he craves that stuff. Why can't he just drink water?"

When Gabriel was in the kitchen, out of earshot, Elizabeth said, "I bought a copy of *Musical America* yesterday. It has a list of all the agents, and I can tell what kind of rosters they have by the ads in the front. I'm going to start writing letters to New York."

Toby said, "Let it wait awhile, Elizabeth. Let's see what happens with the new teacher."

Elizabeth said, "This has nothing to do with the teacher. This is the other end of his career. My end."

Toby said, "You realize you could be making a mistake." Elizabeth flushed a little and lit a cigarette.

Toby said, "No, I'm not telling you how to raise your kid. It's just that I care about him and, well, give me a little credit for being able to see a few things which might elude you since you're so close to him. Even a mother can miss things."

"Such as?"

"Such as that Gabriel is eleven years old. A little boy. When I was eleven I spent my time playing street hockey and collecting baseball cards."

"And look how you turned out. Oh, damn it, Toby. He *has* baseball cards. Hundreds of them. I don't know where they come from. He keeps them in his socks. I'm not pushing him. I'm not some self-serving old cliché of a stage mother. But I take his career seriously, and I know with his kind of talent you have to act early. There's only so much room for solo flutists in this world. I'm doing something for him that could make his concert career. How many soloists can you think of who got to the top without someone behind them the whole time, struggling?"

"Eleven-year-olds don't have careers."

"In music they do. Yes they do. This time counts very much. This is the head start that could get him there. I could never forgive myself if I didn't give it to him. Failure . . . that would be so terrible for an . . . artist." Elizabeth exhaled slowly through her nose, like a dragon. Toby fanned the smoke away from his face.

He leaned back in the sofa, propping a throw pillow behind his neck. He was smiling.

"What I'm trying to say is, let him grow up. Let him go to school and play in orchestras with the other students, and give student recitals. Let him grow up awhile, and then, when he's eighteen or twenty, or however old he'll be when he's ready to be a professional, let him get an agent then."

"You're wrong. He's a prodigy. He's not just an artist. He's a genius. He is capable of an early start and he deserves one."

"Listen, kiddo, do you think that, regardless of how note-perfect his playing is, that it's going to hold much interest for a serious listener when he's twelve, when he doesn't have anything called experience to prop him up? Children make cute, but boring, uninterpretive musicians, even prodigies. That's a fact. They get audiences because they're curiosities, not because of their musicianship. Prodigies can ape adults, but that's it. They're special attractions. Not quite freaks, but not artists either. Let Gabriel mature first, in a normal environment, in a school. You know the list of prodigies that get famous overnight, and then fade away. They don't make it. You never hear from them again."

"And you know the list of prodigies who do make it."

Toby was on his feet, walking out of the room.

"Where are you going?"

She heard the refrigerator door open, the snap of a beer can, giggles, prancing feet on the tile floor. They were clowning in the kitchen. Playing football. Elizabeth gathered up her cigarettes, lighter, ashtray, and carried them carefully out of the room. Gabriel had wrestled Toby down to the floor and neither looked up as she emptied the ashtray, washed it carefully, washed Gabriel's Kool-Aid glass, and the empty pitcher, and scrubbed the grape stains off the counter top. The digital clock said 11:52.

"It's past someone's bedtime," she said. They didn't hear her. Gabriel was chasing Toby around the kitchen table. Toby knocked over a chair. He let Gabriel catch him. He scooped Gabriel up and held him upside down. Gabriel shrieked and thrashed his arms. His curls bobbed wildly and his face turned deep purple.

"It's *bedtime*," said Elizabeth.

"Yes, ma'am," said Toby. He carried the upside-down boy out of the kitchen.

"Up the wooden hill, up the wooden hill," she heard him singing, thumping up the steps. Elizabeth took a sip from Toby's beer, made a face, and rinsed out her mouth with water. She never had gotten used to the taste of beer.

IX   Elizabeth's mind had collapsed into a murky, drowsy half-dream. It was about Elise, her piano, music that was familiar, or had she composed it herself for the dream? No, it was something that Elise always played. No, Gabriel played it. What was it?

"The Vivaldi."

"What?" said Toby. He was awake, putting his watch on. Elizabeth sat up, slowly.

"I had a dream. About music. What are you doing?"

"I'm getting dressed, of course."

She sank back into the pillow. "Don't go. Stay just this once."

"Now," he said, waving his finger, "don't start."

"You don't want Gabriel to find you here in the morning. Do you think he doesn't know you're here now? Oh, Toby, what's the difference? Gabriel loves you." Toby had found Gabriel's hat, the one with the silver wings sewn on it. He put it on.

"Sahry, dahling. Ah have to flah home and wahter mah apartment. Ah think the carpet must be gettin' a little drah these days."

Elizabeth rolled over, into the warm spot he'd left in the bed, and groaned. "Come over tomorrow night for dinner," she said. She felt his kiss on the back of her neck and his footfalls vibrating down the hallway, down the stairs, as he left. The front door closed gently.

In his bed Gabriel stirred awake for a moment, shivering. That must be Toby going home. He hugged his teddy closer and sighed, again, in his sleep.

Outside, Toby's car, parked behind Elizabeth's in the driveway, sputtered awake. Somewhere a dog was barking, and the ground sparkled with the year's first frost.

Chapter 2

I Marina took the express bus from Thirtieth Street Station. It was crowded with people, duffel bags, real suitcases. Some businessmen carried only briefcases. She sat next to a fat man in a gray overcoat. His face was red and sweaty and he fanned himself with a copy of *Time* magazine. She unbuttoned her blazer. It was warm on the bus, for October.

Everything was uncertain; for instance, she didn't have a plane ticket. James had said that one would be waiting for her at the flight counter, but how could she know it would be there? All she had was a slip of paper, in his handwriting, with the address of the hotel, the Front Royale. Could she trust that? Was she crazy? Was she really flying to Chicago to be with James Rosen, or was this a fantasy?

No one on that bus could have known she was scared. Marina was so calm and tall with her back straight against the seat and her left knee firmly crossed against the right. She did not fidget, twist the straps of her backpack, or scrape her fingernails across the canvas grain of the flute-case cover. The bus pulled into the airport terminal.

It was huge, but not confusing. She followed the signs. She asked for her ticket at the United counter, and the woman gave it to her, just like that, without asking for identification. She bought a *New Yorker* from the stand. On the cover was a watercolor drawing of a news vendor selling pumpkins along with newspapers and magazines, on a New York street corner. She was half an hour early. She found a Life Saver in her pocket and popped it into her mouth without looking at it. She guessed the flavor: mango. From the window of the waiting area she could watch the planes landing and taking off.

There were vending machines in the aisle. Should she buy a pack of cigarettes? Maybe not. Her usual debate: should she risk a scratchy throat? She needed her wind, but she also craved that calm long stream of menthol, which would relax her. Her mouth watered. In anticipation she chewed up the Life Saver. She searched her pocket for quarters. The takeoff was delayed by forty minutes, the TV screen in the waiting room said, and she would be sitting there, waiting, alone.

At the hotel Marina stood alone in line behind all those businessmen going to the same convention, all friends, laughing. People looked at her curiously. A schoolgirl alone in a hotel? She tried to be arrogant and the clerk was so rude.

"I have a double room booked in the name of James Rosen," she announced.

"Are you Mrs. Rosen?"

"No."

"You'll have to leave your own credit-card number, then." Credit card? James hadn't prepared her for anything like this.

"Look, Mr. Rosen will be arriving this evening. Can't you give me a key to the room just till then?"

"If you don't have any credit cards" — (pause) — "you'll have to pay for the first night in cash. Now." He stamped ADVANCE PAYMENT ONLY — $75.00 on the reservation card. Finally she convinced him to take thirty dollars, all she had, plus her flute. He promised to lock the instrument safely in a vault.

The room was small and dingy, with one window, which faced an alley, and two single beds.

"This costs seventy-five dollars a night?" she asked the porter who had led her down a maze of corridors. She would have never found it on her own: it was about a quarter mile from the elevator. He didn't answer, just turned around and left.

What was she going to do with herself while she was waiting for James? She didn't have her flute. She tried the television and it didn't work. She undressed and, careful not to wet her hair, took a shower in the enormous cracked bathtub. She dressed again, the same clothes she'd been wearing, but with fresh underwear and her best perfume. She lay down stiffly on one of the beds and tried to close her eyes. Everything was so silent: no street sounds, no neighbors.

Was there anybody on this floor besides her? It was four in the afternoon; James was due to arrive at eight. She was too afraid to leave, too distracted to read her magazine.

How safe was this fleabag? What if someone raped her or murdered her? She hadn't told anyone that she was going to Chicago. Wouldn't her parents be surprised to get a call from the Illinois police? She hadn't called her mother in three weeks. They thought she was at school, and at school they thought she was home sick with a strep throat.

There was a hammering sound in the hallway. Bang! Bang! What was that? A shout? Again! Closer!

Who had a key to this room besides her? There was one for James waiting at the reception desk and —

Her door slammed open. It was an old black woman in a uniform. Crazed. She was out of breath from running. Marina gasped.

"Maid service, just checking!" the woman screamed. She pulled the door shut. Bang! She was gone. Bang, bang, down the hallway. The sound grew fainter and disappeared. When Marina's heartbeat slowed she got up and chain-locked the door. What kind of hotel lets its cleaning staff do that? She pulled the pillow out from under the bedspread and pressed her face against the scratchy linen, waiting for James, replaying her memory of last week's invitation.

"Marina, do you want to come to Chicago?"

She had opened one eye. Those were disembodied words. Who'd said them? James.

James had silk socks. He put them on carefully in the half-dark, folding each till it was almost inside out, fitting it exactly on the toes, and then pulling it gently over the heel, the ankle, the shin. Such perfectly kept feet.

"Chicago?"

"I'm flying to Montreal for two days, then Chicago. I could arrange for a ticket and you could meet me there."

"Why?" She was drowsy, weak. She hadn't eaten since breakfast.

"Why not? Take a few days off."

She sat up. Her neck ached from sleeping wrong. Her hair was loose, everywhere.

"No," she said, at once thinking that she would like to go.

It was dusk and the temperature had gone down with the sun. She switched on the light, went to her closet and found her coarsest, bulkiest sweater, and shivered as she pulled it over her head. She had never been west of Harrisburg.

"We should get something to eat. I don't keep much food here," she said. Outside it would be night already, and chilly, and the air would smell like autumn. She followed his clean profile across the room as he gathered his necktie, jacket, shoes.

On Saturday afternoon she left. She had to skip orchestra rehearsal and wind quintet — she called the school with a raspy voice and told them she was ill. She brought her flute and an orange nylon backpack, the only piece of luggage she owned, and she kept thinking, I look like a kid running away from home.

Now, in Chicago, she was alone with the ticking of the clock, the two blue-curtained rooms, and the ninth-story view of Lake Michigan. James had left for rehearsal at eight A.M., and at eight-thirty she crawled out of bed, dressed, and went down to the coffee shop. She sat at the counter, ordered coffee, and smoked two of her Salem Lights. She had a craving for yogurt and granola, but neither was on the menu. She asked the waitress if they served fresh fruit. They had canned fruit cup and melon, $2.50 per slice. Too expensive. Everything in the hotel was expensive. Marina left a dime tip on the counter and paid for the coffee, taking a handful of mints and a toothpick from beside the cash register. What did she want with the toothpick? Toothpicks are repulsive. She threw it, unused, into the sand-filled ashtray in the lobby.

She peered into the windows of the gift shop, the pharmacy, the liquor store. None of these were open, only the magazine stand was selling things: a lot of newspapers from Chicago, some from New York, one from San Francisco, the *Washington Post*. No Philadelphia papers. They had the same issue of the *New Yorker* that she had bought yesterday and still hadn't read. Gum, cough drops, candy bars, Life Savers. She bought a pack of Tropical Fruits, and some Halloween candy corn in a plastic bag. These she would put in James's tuxedo pocket before the concert, for good luck.

She strolled through the red lobby, where the flags of many countries were draped from the ceiling. *Plush*, she thought. What an ugly, sloppy, red hotel. The clerk who had embarrassed her yesterday was sitting at the reservations desk. He wasn't much older than she was. She stared at him, trying to look haughty. He did not respond.

She watched the street from the side exit. It was windy outside. A man lost his hat, just like in an old movie. The doorman caught it and handed it to him. There were rows of taxicabs parked along the curb, waiting to take hotel customers to their conventions and their businesses. The doorman wore a uniform like a theater usher's, and a hat like a train conductor's. She must have stood too long next to the exit.

"Can I help you, miss? Get you a taxi?"

She jumped. "No thank you!" She walked briskly back to the elevator, back to the suite. Nine forty-five A.M. James wasn't due until three. What would she do with herself? Practice? No, she should see the sights of this new city. But James had given her no suggestions.

She found a map in one of the drawers. The Art Institute. That she'd heard of. And it was on the same street as her hotel, many blocks to the left. How many? A mile? She examined the legend printed in the corner, measuring the distance with her index finger. Not quite a mile. Walking distance. She got her wool blazer from the closet. Good thing she had brought it along; Chicago was cold. She double-checked for her wallet, her suite key, wound her watch, and left.

She walked with long, precisely spaced steps, and no one bothered her.

She passed several small restaurants — cafés, according to their signs. Card shops, drugstores, and some kind of Jewish cultural museum. Across the street was a big park. Was it safe to walk in? Anyway, it was too cold for a park. She moved faster, trying to increase her body temperature. Should she have brought her parka along on this trip? No one else was dressed more warmly than she, and no one else looked painfully cold. Two little boys in shirt sleeves chased past her, screaming.

She was glad to get away from that hotel.

When she saw the building she knew must be the Art Institute, she grinned. She joined a flock of people trying to cross the street. In her mind she was replaying last night's pillow talk. It was like a radio script, everything in darkness.

"Kazakov; that's fantastic. A Russian who grew up in Trenton."

"My mother's Ukrainian. There happens to be a fair-sized community of ethnic Ukrainians in Trenton."

"Do your parents play?"

"My father conducted a little orchestra in Kiev. Now he drives a bus."

"I see. Why did he leave the Soviet Union?"

"Just because. Because he was married to a Ukrainian."

"Have you ever gone back to Russia?"

"I was born here. In Trenton."

"Your family is very European? Close-knit?"

"Uh-uh." (Pause.) "I don't go home much."

II Eric Fish, watching her in the crowd approaching the Institute, ran a narrative, a story he was telling himself, through his head:

If, on Sunday morning, you were sitting on the steps of the Art Institute, waiting for it to open up, you would have seen this girl marching down Michigan Avenue. Once you saw her you wouldn't be able to take your eyes off her thick brown-black hair — so long that if it wasn't flying out straight in back of her in the wind, it would hang down past her waist, down to her hips. And once you noticed that wild hair you'd have to look at her face. Man, what a face, out of another century. You've seen her face before. Where? — in a painting, but not in Chicago. It was in Paris, at the Louvre. The Virgin of the Rocks, *your second-favorite Leonardo. She's the angel in the lower right corner. (Your favorite Leonardo is the one with you in it, the* Saint John the Baptist, *the Paraclete.) Just think, the two of you, straight out of the Louvre. You sitting on the steps and her stamping up the steps of the Art Institute of Chicago.*

She tries the door, but it's locked. You see her reading the sign that says it's open at eleven. She's looking at her watch. That hair of hers is covering her shoulders, her back, rippling a little in the wind, rippling all the way down to her ass.

You'd probably want to start a conversation. You could ask her for the time. That's what Eric Fish did.

She told him to look at his watch, which he'd forgotten to conceal. He could tell by her accent that she was an American, East Coast, North, like him. He was disappointed. She had seemed to have a foreign feeling about her. He asked her did she know she looked like a fifteenth-century angel. She said she knew, and then she walked away and sat down on the cold stone. She fished through her pocketbook for a cigarette. In a flash he was beside her with his lighter. When he looked into her face he thought she was going to slap him, but she just lit her cigarette, which was difficult in the wind. He asked her did she want to get high, but she did not answer.

When the guard opened the doors, Marina was the first one

inside. Fish started to follow her, but after she'd bought her ticket, the first place she went was the women's room.

III   James was four hours late coming back from rehearsal. Marina wasn't nervous anymore, since he'd called an hour ago to say he was meeting some people and would be back soon to take her to dinner. Now she was just annoyed. She had spent the entire day alone in a strange city. And after he'd practically pleaded for her to come with him. What did he want her for if he wasn't going to spend any time with her?

She took out her flute. She had been taking it out, practicing for half an hour, putting it away for half an hour, and then taking it out again, ever since she'd gotten back from the museum. That creep who'd followed her all the way back! She kept thinking about him. What nerve! Good thing the doorman had rescued her.

At least she had her flute back. James had retrieved it for her from the desk when he got in last night from Montreal. He had made a scene at the reservations desk because they'd been so rude and given her the wrong room, not the suite he'd asked for. He'd also gotten her money back. She only wished the clerk who'd embarrassed her had still been on duty.

She ran through her warm-up exercises for the fourth time that day, then stopped. She should take a shower, she decided. He would probably take her someplace nice. She put down the flute, on the bed, thinking: rule one, never leave your instrument anywhere where someone may sit on it.

Ten minutes later, when her hair was soaking wet from the washing she'd given it — she'd used one of James's shampoos, Pantène — she realized that she had forgotten to pack her blow dryer. If she let her hair drip-dry it would be all curly, which would be fine, but it would take two hours, even with no humidity, to dry. She'd end up in a fancy restaurant with a wet head. Well, maybe James had brought a hair dryer. She thought she'd heard him using one in the bathroom that morning while she was trying to sleep. Or was it an electric razor?

None in the bathroom, or in the "hers" closet, or "his." It wasn't in any of the drawers, but it might be in his suitcase. He had three of them, a big one for suits, a smaller one, and one that was really a flight bag, which matched the rest of his luggage. She looked in the flight bag first.

No hair dryer. Just a razor, after-shave lotion, two bottles of shampoo (he must have a shampoo fetish, she thought — two more bottles were in the shower), soap, cologne, and some bottles of prescription drugs. She picked one up to read the label.

Rrrrrrr! The phone was ringing! Startled, she dropped the bottle and it rolled across the rug, under the bed.

IV After the museum closed, Fish had gone back to the hotel and hung around, hoping that girl would come outside again. He knew she must really be staying there because the doorman wouldn't have gotten so rough with him if she weren't a customer.

He waited at the bar, where he could see everyone coming in or leaving the building. He was drinking Heineken, a toast to the girl he was waiting for. And besides, this place was too classy to sit around drinking Bud. He was beginning to itch for a toke, but he was afraid to leave his post. Afraid the girl might come in or leave while he was in the men's room. So he bought a pack of Camels and started going through them, one after another. The waitress, in her black fishnet stockings and miniskirt — Fish hadn't seen one of those since he was about ten — kept serving him mugs. He was running up a tab, hoping the girl would show up before he ran out of money and ended up having to wash dishes in the back.

His luck, as usual, was good. After two hours and seven beers she came strolling out of the elevator with this older guy, whom Fish thought to be about forty. She was dressed like Fish could hardly believe, in black satin a few shades darker than her hair. She had black spiked heels and a silver shawl. Fish swallowed hard with approval. Man, what that black dress did for her body!

She had her arm around the guy and she was talking, and smiling and laughing. Fish didn't get a good look at his face, but he was dressed really slick, in an expensive European suit, the kind you'd see in a high-class Paris disco. His shoes were definitely Italian. Fish thought to himself, Well, the woman has taste.

The man had an overcoat draped over his arm, but the girl didn't have one. They were headed toward the door. Fish thought, It's cold out there. She's going to freeze.

They got into the cab and Fish could see her arms folded across her chest before the cabby shut the door and drove away.

She didn't see him.

He managed to split without paying the bill, and then he hopped a bus over to Ben's.

V   Since she hadn't found a dryer, she had braided her hair and swirled it into a bun, thinking how kinky it would be when she took it down later, dry.

She'd put on the black silk dress and the black shoes that she wore for her most important concerts. And her onyx earrings and necklace her father had given her when she graduated from eighth grade. She rummaged through her backpack till she found the little compact of plum blush that she'd bought once and hardly ever used.

Then she thought, I look ridiculous. I'm too dressed up. She took off the dress and put on the oversized T-shirt she used as a nightgown.

And just then James came in with his coat all cold from the autumn wind and said, "Hurry and get dressed. I'm late, I know, but I made reservations at my favorite restaurant in town and we'll lose the table if you don't hurry. Wear that black thing hanging in your closet. I like that."

She'd unfolded her silver shawl, which she'd brought along, just in case.

"What about a coat, Marina? It's cold outside."

"I forgot to pack one." That was a lie. All she owned besides her wool blazer was a snorkel parka. No dress coat.

James was on the phone, ordering a cab from the desk.

So, this is what it's like, she thought. I'll make a caption for this moment: Marina Kazakov makes her Chicago debut.

She concentrated on the smell of her perfume and the smell of James's cologne. It was so cold. She had to distract herself . . . His and Hers, those were the only smells in the cab. First she separated them, she knew each so well. Hers was familiar and his was intense. She had been smelling it for over a week now, but she felt she had smelled it somewhere before, too. It was French, in a strange, violet-colored glass bottle, with a name she didn't remember. What was it, L'homme? No, more complicated. L'hommage? No, that's not it.

"What's the name of your cologne?"

"Oh, is that what you were thinking about? I was wondering about that profound look of concentration. Guess."

"I don't remember. L'hom — something."

"L'homard."

"Oh — wait, that doesn't sound right, either. Are you sure?"

"Is it *my* cologne?"

Smells are like music. She hadn't thought of that before, but it was true. Her smell and his smell were like counterpoint. They made their own separate statements, and together they made a different one. She tried to think of other smells, like when she went home to her house in Trenton. Those smells. The first thing she noticed every time was the smell of whatever her mother was cooking: the meat would be the main theme and the other foods, the vegetables, cakes, coffee, the smoke of her father's cigar and her brother's incense, would be like interwoven harmonies. Various instrumental sections. The name of her perfume was Echo. It came in a tiny bottle that held only three-quarters of an ounce. Uncle Franz had bought it for her three years ago on his way home from a trip to Europe. It was French, like James's cologne, and though she didn't know how much it cost Uncle Franz, she had an idea it was expensive. She only used it for holidays and special events — like now. The smell reminded her of Indian tea and incense. Jasmine. James's cologne smelled like men's things.

Hardwood hairbrushes, leather shoehorns, gold cuff links. But cuff links have no smell . . .

The cab stopped, finally, in front of a giant office building. James was giving the cabby some bills, telling him to keep the change. The door opened with a whoosh of freezing air and Marina hopped out. Every pore of her body felt exposed to the wind. Quick! Inside!

The restaurant was on the roof, and they were alone in the elevator going up. Marina caught a glimpse of herself in one of the floor-length mirrors as they stepped out. Good, her hair was somehow still in place. The maître d' seemed to recognize James, and he led them past tables and tables to the only empty one in the place: right in the center of the room. A white tapered candle in a crystal candlestick was lit already, flickering.

"My favorite spot," said James. "A good place to be seen."

Everyone was watching them. Marina sat down, opened her pocketbook, and found a cigarette. James was giving his overcoat to a waiter.

"I'm sorry," said the waiter. "I did not know that the lady wishes to smoke. We have arranged for Mr. Rosen to have his favorite table, but this is the nonsmoking section. If you like we can arrange another table."

There are no other tables, thought Marina quickly. She shoved the cigarette back into her purse.

"No, that's all right. I'm fine," she said.

"I didn't know you smoked," said James.

"I don't. Much."

"You're nervous?"

"Why? No. Just hungry."

There were no prices on Marina's menu. She checked the back of it to see if there was a fixed price. No, nothing about that. Strange. Well, in that case she would just order anything and not feel guilty about the price. Besides, he could afford it, she was sure. Unfortunately, she didn't know how to read the French names. She'd had French back in grade school, but somehow she didn't remember any vocabulary lists about food. *Champignon* is mushroom, she knew, *poulet* is chicken, milk is *lait*. Otherwise nothing on the menu made sense.

"What is '*ris de veau*'?"

"Sweetbread."

"Oh?"

"That's the pancreas of a calf."

The waiter arrived. "Madam, today's special is *l'homard aux truffes. Très délicieux, je vous assure.*"

"Yes, but what is . . ."

"Ah, *bien*, madam, you desire translation. It is the lobster broiled in a delicate sauce of herbs and white wine and simmered with the truffles. Is quite tasty, *n'est-ce pas, monsieur?*"

"Oh, it's fine." James coughed into his napkin.

"*Homard?* It's a lobster? A lobster. I'll have the lobster."

"*Bien. Deux, monsieur? Bien.*" James ordered wine, appetizers.

He wears a cologne named after a lobster? Bullshit. He'd been putting her on and she hadn't even known it. Well, she'd just ignore the whole thing. At least lobster sounds more romantic in French than in English. She was starving, and there was an aesthetically slim *baguette*, sliced into neat little sections, sitting in the breadbasket, which seemed to be lined with white satin. She glanced at the other tables. Of course no one, whether he had been served yet or not, no one was eating the bread. Marina was dying to eat just one or two of those sections, but she didn't dare touch a crust, let alone break off a piece, let alone deface the perfect butter sculpture beside her. James had ordered drinks: Pernod and water. It tasted like licorice, like the ouzo her grandfather liked to drink. It was exactly the same color as the tablecloth, as though the bartender had practiced adding the right amount of water to make the color match. She checked the level of her drink against James's. Hers was lower. Already she had drunk too quickly and she'd only just had one taste. It was going to be a long evening.

James was staring into her face.

"Do you think I could get a glass of water?" she asked. He snapped his finger and told the waiter to bring her one, which he did, instantly.

Now I have two vessels of liquid in front of me, she thought. When he brings me the wine I will have three.

The music was a recording of a string quartet. She couldn't recognize the piece, but she thought it was probably Haydn. The other tables were full of people as well-dressed as she, and relaxed, as if they did this every day. Good thing she had decided to bring the black dress along on this trip. None of her other clothes would have been appropriate for this place.

They probably all know who James is. Everyone knows who he is, even the waiters. They all wonder who I am.

She scanned the room for reporters with cameras. None, so far. Maybe they aren't allowed into the restaurant. The waiter brought her goose-liver pâté, with tiny slices of rye bread. She knew she would have to leave two-thirds of it on the plate, and the part that she ate would have to go very slowly.

Halfway through dinner the couple sitting next to Marina and James finished and went away. Marina felt a little more comfortable with no one to overhear her on the left. In a few minutes the waiter (this place did not seem to have busboys) came to clear away the vacant table. He put the dirty dishes on a silver platter, which rested on a silver cart. He also took away the candles, flower arrangement, and saltshakers. Then he bundled up the whole yellow linen tablecloth and took that away, too. The table underneath was an ordinary cafeteria table, a hideous color pink. A huge scratch ran from one side to the other. One corner was chipped. Marina stared at the table, surprised. In seconds the waiter was back, with a fresh tablecloth and new candles. He replaced the flower arrangement and the shakers, laid out new utensils and napkins and, *voilà*, a new couple appeared, trailing behind the maître d'.

"They're all like that underneath," said James. He was grinning at her.

"What?"

"All the tables. They're all like that. You can't expect them to buy good wooden ones if they're just going to cover them with a tablecloth, can you? It's expensive to run a restaurant."

Marina allowed herself to taste another bite of lobster. Judging from the state of other people's plates, it was bad manners to eat the vegetables that came with the meal. But Marina loved scalloped potatoes, and it was such a shame to waste them . . . she liked them better than she liked this *homard*. She sliced a piece of potato with her fork and bit into it quickly. Well, none of the other dinner guests gasped in horror. How long could she get away with this? Would she dare attempt another bite of potato? James, of course, had barely touched his dinner.

Isn't he even hungry? she wondered. Marina had already finished her water and was discreetly sucking on ice cubes to keep busy. She was ravenous.

James had a habit of staring. He was looking at her now, as he refilled their wineglasses. Tonight he was not in a conversational mood. Marina tried, for the umpteenth time, to start one. She'd tried: "How was the rehearsal?" hoping for an insider's view, some good gossip or information, some name-dropping. She'd gotten: "It went well enough," a little nod, lips curling into a smile. This time she said, "Mr. Chattarjee called this afternoon."

James straightened his back and leaned forward in his chair. At once a veil seemed to lift from behind his eyes. He looked concerned. "Lawrence Chattarjee? What did he want?"

"He said he wanted to wish you luck. He said he'd talked to you earlier, but he had to hang up then and he was just wanting to finish the conversation."

"That's all?"

"That's all."

Marina played with her parsley. This restaurant probably buys a ton of parsley every week, and none of it ever gets eaten. Parsley is the last priority on the plate, lower than the vegetables. Unless the waiters take it back and eat it in the kitchen, or take it home with them, all of it gets thrown out. Marina wondered how much of the untouched bread and vegetables was eaten by kitchen help.

"It scared me to death when the phone rang," said Marina. "And when I found out it wasn't you I was really uptight. I'm still nervous about being here in the first place. I keep imagining that my father's going to find out and come club us both to death with his Ukrainian bear-stick."

"His what?"

"Oh, it's this big polished wood stick we have hanging over our fireplace at home. My grandfather says they used to use them for protection against bears, and it's a family joke that if anyone's bad my father will beat us with it. Never mind."

"I see."

"And then when I found out it was Mr. Chattarjee I was so embarrassed. Do you know what he said to me? He said, 'Is this Marina?' Obviously you told him I was going with you. I don't appreciate that. I'm so embarrassed. I don't think I'll ever be able to look at him again."

"He doesn't teach you now, does he?"

"No. Next year he's supposed to."

"But he knew quite well who you were when I described you to him."

"It's a small school."

"You don't know Lawrence. He doesn't remember anyone unless he finds a reason to. Intrigue. He doesn't even know the name of the housekeeper he's had for six months. I'm serious. I don't think he knows the names of all his students."

"So what are you trying to tell me?" said Marina. Her face felt warm around the cheeks and ears. Was she blushing?

"I don't know." James smiled into his dinner.

The trip from the restaurant back to the hotel was warmer . . . or at least it seemed that way. Marina was drunk, not enough to feel warm, but enough so that she didn't mind the cold. She snuggled beside James in the cab and he put his arm, his cold sleeve, around her. Gradually his coat felt warm against her body. Her mouth tasted like the last thing James had ordered: cognac. It had burned her throat going down. She grew drowsier and drowsier until, when the cab pulled up in front of the hotel, she was almost asleep. Inside, the main floor of the hotel was alive with convention people wearing cowboy hats and name tags. In the dark, red-upholstered bar, a female singer was bellowing, "What are you doing the rest of your life . . ." Dazed, Marina followed James into an elevator, where a tiny loudspeaker was playing a familiar tune she couldn't name. Electric violins.

"Do you think our flutes are safe in the room?" she yawned.

"I checked mine in downstairs," said James, unlocking the door.

"You did?" Why hadn't he suggested that she do the same? She glanced over to the chair where she'd left her instrument. There it was. She picked up the case, to test its weight, because what if . . . no, it was fine. Still there. James was in the other room hanging up his coat. Marina looked in the mirror. She studied the way her bracelets hung on her wrists. A fifteenth-century angel, that guy had said. Hmmmm. Which angel, though? She took down her hair, unbraided it, and brushed it out. It was still a little damp, but it fell over her shoulders in glossy, perfect kinks. She wished that she didn't have to sleep on it now, that it would look like this tomorrow. James's face appeared behind her in the mirror. He looked into her eyes, but he did not touch her. She reached for her bag of soaps and toothpaste and went into the bathroom.

Over the running water she heard him ask, "Marina, did you go through my shaving bag?"

"What?" Marina stopped in horror, mouth full of toothpaste. She spat into the sink. "Why? Oh, I was looking to see if you had a hair dryer." She stepped into the doorway holding her toothbrush. He was turning the bag upside down, shaking everything onto the bed.

"I had some medicine, some pills, in this bag. I'm sure I packed them. I had them in Montreal."

"What did they look like?" said Marina, remembering a bottle. What had she done with it?

"I need those pills. I can't sleep without them."

"I don't remember seeing any pills," said Marina.

"Oh, Christ," said James, throwing the shaving case down on the bed. He pulled out another suitcase and began to rummage through it.

"I had one in my wallet. That I took last night. The rest were in a plastic bottle, which I packed, goddamn it."

"You're upset," said Marina stupidly. He was more nearing hysteria. He must really need that medicine. If only she could remember what she'd done with it. She went back to the sink and rinsed off her toothbrush.

"Maybe there's a drugstore open and we can get some more," she said.

"Without a goddamn prescription?"

Marina began to put the scattered items back into the shaving bag: soap (Safeguard), toothbrush case, five bottles of prescription drugs, razor case, cologne (L'honneur — so that was it), a box of Band-Aids, a sewing kit with tiny spools of black and white threads, and a jar of Vaseline.

James slammed the suitcase shut and sat on the bed.

"I'm sorry," he said. "Sorry to act like this." He swallowed. "But listen, are your sure you didn't see another bottle of pills when you were looking for a hair dryer?"

"Pretty sure." Oh, what had she done with it?

James went into the next room and came back with his coat on.

"Where are you going?"

"For a walk."

"Can I come with you?"

"Stay here. Go to sleep." He was gone. It was midnight, Chicago time.

VI   Fish was making his way down Michigan Ave., trying to find the dorms of Roosevelt University, where his brother lived, where he was spending the weekend. He had to leave on a ten-A.M. flight tomorrow and he really needed to crash. But where the hell had Roosevelt College or University or whatever it was gone? It had been here just this afternoon. Fish found himself outside of the Front Royale again. What was he doing here? Was he on the right street? He wondered if the bar was still open, the one where he'd stiffed the cocktail waitress. That seemed like days ago, but it was really only a few hours. What a night! When he got back to school he'd have to stop partying for a week to get his head together. Oooo. Maybe two weeks. He sat down on the curb outside the hotel. What time was it? He had no idea. All he knew was he needed sleep, lots of sleep, and unless he could find his brother's place he wouldn't be getting any. It was freezing outside, too. He'd be lucky if he got home without pneumonia. The doorman stepped outside. Fish thought he was going to shoo him away, but no, he was flagging down a cab. A cab. What a good idea. A cab could take him to his brother's place. And what the hell, it couldn't be that far away. How much could a cab ride to Roosevelt College cost? Fish felt for his wallet. Oh, shit, it was gone. No, that's right. As a precaution, he hadn't brought a wallet. His money was in his shirt pocket. Five, seven dollars. Enough. Plenty. A cab was rounding the corner, pulling up in front of the hotel. Fish put on his dark glasses, to hide his eyes, just in case.

"Are you going anywhere near Roosevelt College?" asked Fish. A man from the hotel got into the cab. The cabby shrugged and looked at the passenger, who said tersely, "It's on the way. Get in."

The man in the cab looked familiar. Where had he seen him before? Of course. That's the dude who was with the girl he'd followed from the museum that afternoon. He was on his way home now. Must've been a hot date. Fish wondered if the girl lived in the hotel or if she was just visiting the city. As the cab pulled away he looked at the hundreds of windows in the hotel. Which one was hers, or was hers on some other side of the building? Was she watching her man leave, from the window? Wouldn't she be shocked to see Fish getting into the cab with her man? His head ached. He massaged his temples, hoping to ease the pain a little. The man beside him was drumming his fingertips on the door handle. Tappity-tap. Tappity-tap. Fish needed an aspirin.

The cab stopped. He looked up. The cabby and the man were both staring at him.

"*Well*," said the cabby. "This is it. Roosevelt."

"Short ride," said Fish.

The cabby blinked.

"How much do I owe you?"

"The meter says one-sixty right now."

"Never mind," said the man. "I'll get it."

"Thanks," said Fish. "Thanks a lot." But what was it to that guy anyway? The way he was dressed, he surely could afford it. Fish slid out of the cab, and after some trouble, found the entrance to the dorms. The guard at the desk said, "What room, please?" Fish couldn't remember the number.

"The name is Fish, Nathan Fish." The guard looked it up in the index and dialed the intercom.

"Tell him it's his brother Eric."

Nate and his roommate had been asleep, already. Two skinny, pimply college freshmen tucked in at midnight on a Sunday. Eric had to make as little noise as possible and didn't turn on the lights. They were already annoyed at him for waking them up. Both had a midterm tomorrow. The same midterm in the same economics course that all freshmen seemed to take in their first semesters at every college. Eric himself, though, had never taken any economics in the three years he'd been at college. At least someone was a little sane in this world, still. He kicked off his shoes, took off his glasses, threw his jacket over a chair, and flopped into the sleeping bag that was still spread across the floor from last night. Nate and his roommate were breathing deeply again. Poor dumb shits. Eric decided to leave his brother a few decent joints as a present. Maybe that would help loosen him up a little. He shut his eyes, hoping sleep would ease the headache. If not, there was always that half a Quāālude in his jeans pocket.

VII   Marina pulled off her dress and hung it carefully in the closet. She would have to wear it again tomorrow, to the concert. She put on her T-shirt/nightgown and went into the bathroom. First she washed her face with the hotel soap. Then she slowly rubbed in her own moisturizer. She brushed her teeth again and flossed them. She lay down on the floor and exercised until her legs ached. It was quarter to one. No James. She propped up some pillows and climbed onto the bed. The *New Yorker* was waiting for her beside the bed. She began to flip through it, reading only the cartoons: two large monsters looking at a little monster. One big monster says to the other, "How cute." Some bears in an automobile showroom, looking at campers. She put the magazine down. She was sleepy. She should just go to sleep. She turned out the light and slid under the covers. Where had James gone, anyway? Was it fair, or even safe, to leave her alone in the room like this? What if the creep who followed her came back and found her here? Marina climbed out of bed and chain-locked the door. Then she unlocked it, and hung on the doorknob outside the little sign that said in four languages, Do Not Disturb. She locked the door again, and replaced the chain lock. She was safe. And if James couldn't get in, it just served him right.

In Philadelphia, under the clear sky of the first autumn frost, Lawrence slept restlessly, dreaming of the subway rail slowly, slowly, crashing down on him as he raised his hand to cover his head.

Toby slept, fully dressed, in a fully lit room in front of a loud television set, upright in a chair, his neck in a bad position, growing stiff for the morning. Elizabeth slept alone, clutching a pillow beside her, and in the room next to hers, after the bathroom and the linen closet, slept her son, in a tangle of blankets that smelled faintly of bubble gum. On the floor beside his bed lay his teddies.

And in Chicago, on the floor of a strange room, Eric was slowly sobering in his sleep. In his dreams he called himself Fish, his last name, a better name, a more nasal, more appropriate sound than "Eric."

Marina slept alone, in the bedroom of a suite on the ninth floor of the Front Royale Hotel, but in her sleep she thought she was home, not in her Philadelphia apartment at Seventeenth and Spruce, but in Trenton, in the row house, in the pink-and-white bedroom that her parents saved for her and kept the same, always.

Only James was awake at this hour, somewhere in Chicago, in the apartment of friends he had not meant to visit so soon. He was there to borrow Valium, but one does not appear at midnight after a silence of many months, just to borrow Valium. He had to be charming.

It was Monday already. The morning of the day of his concert with the Chicago Symphony.

Chapter 3

I   Freddy and Maur had had a quiet candlelight dinner that Freddy had cooked himself, working all day in the kitchen with James Beard and a broken disposal and two burners out of commission — it was so hard to get the super to do anything these days! But when it was all done and ready and the lights were down low and the wine now uncorked and chilled just right, then, they both had to agree that it was well worth Freddy's aggravation, and what aggravation was not well worth the trouble it'd been in the end when you had the finished product, which was so excellent in this case? They'd put on one of Maur's tapes when they were just about ready to sit down. It was an audition tape, a live recording of a concert, and the applause sections hadn't been edited out completely. Freddy's face flushed with pleasure, as always, when the applause came on.

"Don't mind it," Maur had said. "I should've put on a record."

"No, I like it," said Freddy. "I really do." Maur knew Freddy liked to listen to the applauding. It was as though he thought they were applauding both of them, not just Maur. In fact Freddy often said how he wished applause sections weren't edited out of commercial recordings.

"It's a good, cleansing break between sections of a recording.

Better, psychologically, than jumping from one piece into another," he would say.

They had before them such an exquisite spread: A delicate cream-of-watercress soup, sprinkled with flecks of marjoram, in the silver tureen that Maur had picked up in Genoa in '66, on the European tour. The salad was avocado on romaine lettuce, drenched in Freddy's special vinaigrette, the one he'd never ever give the recipe for to anyone, no matter who was asking. That was served in the finely worked Egyptian-mosaic bowl that'd been a gift from Sadat when Maur conducted at the Kennedy Center last August. In the glass-covered dish was — no, not pheasant, as you'd expect from the elegance of it all — for Freddy knew that Maur should be watching his cholesterol, and like so many other black men of middle age, Maur had a problem with his pressure. It was sea bass, baked in parchment paper, on a bed of wild Persian rice, all garnished with delicate sprigs of parsley and four perfect pea pods. And their favorite Pinot Grigio absolutely glittered in the cut-crystal Irish glasses. All surrounding that charming little arrangement of fall flowers that Freddy had remembered to stop for on his way home from the market.

They sat in their soft-backed chairs in the center of the room, with their cool, blue, English linen napkins unfolded neatly across their laps. The candlelight flickered in the glass frames of the Picasso print behind Maur and of the Warhol portrait of Maur behind Freddy.

When the tape ended Freddy jumped up to get another.

"No," said Maur, "never mind. It puts knots in my stomach, anyway, to listen to myself conduct while I'm eating. It gives me a little gas. I prefer the silence. It's so lovely in here; I just want to savor the atmosphere, with no distractions."

Yes, they were truly alone. The city and its noises were so many flights below them, and it was so peaceful in the soundless room, it was as though they'd escaped into a world of their own. A world of beauty. Beautiful smells, beautiful tastes, beautiful, beautiful surroundings and beautiful thoughts.

And after they'd eaten and cleared the things back into the

kitchen — Freddy'd said that he'd do them later — they brought their glasses over to the sofa and sat back to enjoy the rest of their wine, while they waited for Cleveland.

By the time he got there, and wasn't that like him to be always just a little bit late, they had already got out the cognac and the chocolates. Freddy had a bottle of V.S.O.P. Napoleon that he'd found at the duty-free shop in Amsterdam for half the price of what it was here in Chicago. He served it in his finest, thinnest, lead crystal brandy-snifters, the smaller ones. The Napoleon was smooth and the taste blended so well with the Italian chocolates. (Oh, how Maur loved those chocolates! Freddy had to watch him to be sure that he didn't eat too many.)

Neither Maur nor Freddy approved of the way Cleveland dressed. His pants were always too tight. He wore silk blouses and unbuttoned them too far, enough so that you could see the red-brown coils of his chest hair. The angle of his haircut was too sharp, too flamboyant. He wore three gold chains at his throat and three on his left wrist, and on his left index finger he wore a two-carat diamond.

They had tried and tried to tell him in as many subtle ways as they could think of, and when they finally spelled it out for him he still wouldn't understand: he should tone it down, in public at least. Cleveland was so young, so impetuous. He just wouldn't listen. But then, he was doing rather well for himself now, even if you didn't count Freddy's help and Maur's influence, and what a talent! Perhaps there was no harm in this kind of independence. Times were changing and who says you can't have your own style these days? No one could say that Cleveland didn't have flair, that was for sure.

He arrived at nine-thirty. His cheeks were blushing with the healthy cold night air, and his eyes were sparkling with excitement.

"I had dinner tonight at L'Oeuf d'Or, and as I was leaving James came in," he began. (Of course! James was in town for tomorrow's concert. Both Freddy and Maur had been thinking about it all evening, but neither had said it aloud.)

"Oh, was he?" said Freddy.

"Hmmm?" said Maur.

"He was with a *girl*."

James with a girl? James Rosen?

"He didn't see me, I don't *think*," continued Cleveland. He took the snifter of cognac that Freddy handed him and sat down. Of course they would all talk about James tonight, now.

Even after he'd moved back to Philadelphia to be with Lawrence, after Oxford, James had kept in regular contact with Freddy and Maur. It was they who had introduced him to Cleveland in the first place. (How well they remembered his first remark, before he'd even been introduced: "A violinist named Cleveland? If he forms a chamber group, just think, he can call it the Cleveland Quartet.") But suddenly all of that was in the past, as of last year, and no one knew why, at least Freddy and Maur didn't know why and if Cleveland did he wasn't telling.

How strange it was not to hear from him for almost a year, since that last concert he'd had in Chicago. How puzzled and anxious they'd been. And how hurt that he hadn't called to tell them his travel arrangements for this concert. They'd known for sure he'd be in Chicago at least on Sunday, which was the day before the concert, but no word from him at all.

And now what was this? Cleveland had seen him in a restaurant (wasn't that just like Cleveland to go to James's favorite restaurant on the night he knew James had to be in town) and he was with a girl? Well, under normal circumstances it wasn't odd to see James, or anyone for that matter, out with a woman. There were wives and daughters of patrons, the ladies of society, and women musicians to entertain (and of course so many agents were women, as well). But under these conditions it was strange. Why would James not call them all year and then turn up in an obvious spot, his favorite restaurant, and with a girl. What was he trying to do, anyway? Suddenly they were reduced to following his career through newspaper-review clippings, album covers, and hearsay, and he was taking a strange girl out to dinner.

"What did the girl look like?"

Cleveland laughed and poured himself another cognac. A stray wisp of hair had fallen across his forehead.

"Just a child. She couldn't have been older than seventeen. She must be a *musician*. She had on a black outfit that looked like it just fell out of a chamber orchestra."

"Maybe someone from the orchestra, then?"

"Not a chance. I can recognize anyone who's *anything* in Chicago. She's definitely not from *here*."

"A Philadelphia Orchestra member, maybe?"

"*My* guess is she's a student. Some kind of *groupie*. I'll bet she plays the flute. *Cute*, of James."

"Is she pretty?"

"Who knows? She was dark, probably Jewish, lots of hair, strange Eastern-looking eyes. *Interesting*. Yes, I'd say she was 'pretty.' Thin, like a dancer."

Freddy chuckled. "An ingenue."

Maur bit into another chocolate. Freddy put on a tape of Cleveland's and they settled back in their chairs to listen. The warmth of the cognac and the glow of the room surrounded them as the evening slowly melted into night.

Suddenly, hours later, the intercom phone rang, startling them awake from their state of drowsy comfort. It was after midnight. James was downstairs in the lobby.

Freddy, who had answered the phone, repeated the startling news into the receiver. Maur jerked awake and sat up stiff on the sofa. Cleveland laughed softly. Freddy said to the night guard, "Send him right up."

James looked pale and agitated. One side of his shirt collar was sticking out of his overcoat. They could tell he was disturbed.

Nevertheless he was smiling, though it was a tired sort of smile. He shook hands and hugged Freddy and Maur. He turned toward Cleveland, who made no motion to get out of his chair.

"Cleveland," said James. Cleveland nodded and sipped his drink.

"Well, well, sit down, James, sit down." Freddy was pouring

another round of cognac and handed James a snifter. James tossed his coat over an empty chair and sat on the sofa, next to Maur. He began to drum his fingers on his knee. Freddy hung the coat in the closet.

"It's been," said Maur, "a while."

"Yes," said Freddy, "quite a while."

James swallowed his cognac in one gulp. "Nice," he said, nodding at the glass. Freddy poured him another.

"How is the business world?" said James. He took a sip.

"It's fine," said Freddy. "Just fine." James nodded and drummed some more on his knee.

"We bought a salt mine in Central Africa," said Freddy. "I'm going there next month."

"How nice," said James. Freddy nodded.

"In September," he said, "I had to go to Hong Kong. Two of our factories burned down."

"I'm sorry," said James.

"No, it's quite all right," said Freddy. James turned to Maur, who was sitting stiffly beside him.

"Maur, I hear you're conducting in Atlanta next week."

"That's right," said Freddy. "With André Watts!"

"Mmmm," said James.

No one said anything for a while. Then Cleveland said, "Who's the nymphette?" (Aha! James had thought he'd seen Cleveland leaving the restaurant.) Freddy leaned forward and closed his eyes. Maur cleared his throat.

"Look," said James, standing up. "The truth is, I came here to borrow a Valium. That's all I want from you. I don't want an interrogation."

No one moved except Cleveland, who crossed his legs. "You drop by after *midnight* on a Sunday to borrow a *Valium?* This isn't a social visit? Come, *come*, what kind of friend are you?"

Freddy said, "I have some Valium in the medicine cabinet." He left the room.

Cleveland said, "You knew if you came *here*, to this apartment, at this hour, you'd find us all awake. You know us very *well*."

James said, "Look . . ."

"You know us *very*, very well, don't you? Well enough to know *exactly* what we're doing at any time. Well enough not to call us for a year, and to feel free to just drop by when you happen to run out of drugs." Cleveland swirled the brandy around in the bottom of his glass.

James said, "I'm not up to this, Cleveland. I have a concert tomorrow and I have to get some sleep. We can talk about this later."

"*Poor baby*," said Cleveland.

"Cut it out, Cleveland," said Maur.

"And when, may I ask, will *later* be?" said Cleveland. "The next time you need a Valium?"

Freddy came back into the room with an envelope. "Here's five," he said. "That should hold you over till you get back to Philadelphia."

"I can see you after the concert tomorrow night," said James to Cleveland. "We can go somewhere for drinks. I have a one-A.M. flight."

"Will *she* be coming along with us?" said Cleveland.

"No."

"And what will *she* be doing in our absence? Have you hired a baby-sitter?"

"Cleveland," said Maur.

"I think James is tired," said Freddy. "He needs to get his sleep before the big day."

"I'll call a cab," said James.

"No need," said Cleveland. "*My* car's downstairs. I'll give you a ride."

"No," said James.

"No?" said Cleveland. Freddy handed James the envelope.

"Oh, all right," said James. At once Freddy was at the closet getting their coats.

"We'll be there tomorrow," said Freddy as they walked to the door.

"You bought tickets?" said James.

"We didn't choose it," said Maur. "We have a subscription." Cleveland swung open the door and led the way to the elevator.

"I have a new townhouse," he whispered to James. "It's on the lake."

At five A.M., when James arrived back at the hotel room, he could not open the door more than four inches. Marina had put the chain lock on. He could see her reflection in the mirror as she slept. She had left on all the lights in the suite, except the one next to her side of the bed. Resting on his pillow was a copy of the *New Yorker*. He knocked softly for her to waken and let him in.

II After she drove Gabriel to school, and then made a second trip because he'd forgotten his soccer clothes and his lunch, Elizabeth washed all the breakfast things. It was amazing how one boy's breakfast could dirty two cups, two plates, a bowl, a frying pan, two forks, three spoons, one knife, and every surface in the kitchen.

She was going to have to take the car back to the dealer. It had stalled twice this morning, already.

At eight-thirty she ran upstairs and changed into her warm-up clothes. She did her stretches on the living-room floor. One, two, pull! pull! She bounced a little, cheating, trying to loosen up. She was so stiff. One, one, one, one-two. She could see the kitchen digital clock from where she was. Her routine took exactly thirty-five minutes if she was careful not to rush through it.

Today, two-three, she was going, two-three, to write, two-three, to the agents, two-three. She had a good, one-push, idea, one-push, of where, one-push, to start, one-push. She'd been talking, two-push, to the mother, two-push, of a girl, three-push, a pianist, three-push, who'd been performing, three-push, in New York, four-push. Nine years old.

She slid into a split. Aaah. She was so tight, a good way to pull something; she was lucky she hadn't. She should have warmed up a little longer. Eight fifty-five. Pull, pull, she pressed her nose against her knee. Easy. Something in her back ached a little.

What was the name of that girl in New York? She doesn't go to school at all. Just concertizes. Of course, at this point, what could you teach her?

The name of the management was Argot. *A*, at the front of the alphabet. Fine, it would be one of the first on her list to write to. The mother said they did such an excellent job for, what was her name, Natalie, Natasha, Nadine, something with an *N*.

She was doing sit-ups. She'd write twenty-five letters today, the first twenty-five to New York, only she'd pick ones with impressive rosters. Twenty-five letters, well maybe fifteen. This would take forever to type. She should be borrowing that word-processor memory typewriter in Toby's newsroom that he was always talking about. No, she should make Max get his secretary to do it, for God's sake — wasn't this his kid, too? But Toby, Max, it was all useless. She was the one who took all the responsibility here. She was the one. (Forty-eight, forty-nine, fifty.) She was the one, but Max would have to pay for it. The agent's fees, the publicity notices, the brochures. Fine with her. She would do the work, do the worrying, show the concern; and he would pay for it. And they deserved that much from him, didn't they? Especially now that there was one less of them than when he left. One less to have expensive lessons, coaching, trips to New York (she had been ready to enroll Elise in Juilliard; that would have started in September of last year). And then there was the cost of an even better instrument, to replace the used Steinway that Elizabeth had gotten when Max moved out with the good one.

So it was all quite a bargain for Max, with only one agent to pay for. One blossoming talent to support. One career. And Max was just famous for supporting careers in the arts. (It was sixteen years ago that he'd promised to take her away from all the competition, the pain of the ballet. He was going to take care of her, make it easy, give her her own little studio to manage, if she wanted. She'd protect her children from that kind of defeat. She never let Elise approach a barre, even when she asked for lessons. Let her have another art. And let her have a sport. Riding lessons. Great. Ideal exercise for a child. Just watch out for her head near low-hanging tree branches.) Ninety-seven, ninety-eight, ninety-nine, a hundred. Nine o'clock.

She began to run in place.

Sometimes she put on her track shoes, drove over to Gabriel's school, and accompanied him on his two miles. In fact, she could run faster than most of the junior-varsity soccer team, discounting that they'd just finished practice and might be a little tired. The coach, some college kid, threw her puzzled looks, but she ignored him. As long as he didn't ask her to leave she might as well stay. Gabriel didn't say he minded having his mother beside him, asking him questions about his day, for eight laps around a soccer field, but he didn't seem enthusiastic about her either. She wondered if he was embarrassed in front of his friends to have her there, but he never said so. When they were finished, she, trying hard to appear less out of breath than he, drove him home. (Where he would go straight to the kitchen and leave a mess before beginning to practice.)

Sometimes she went to his soccer games. They were after school, or on Saturday mornings. The junior varsity didn't play till after the varsity, so she couldn't predict when the games would begin. Most of the spectators went home after the varsity was through, so Elizabeth usually found herself alone in the bleachers with a few other mothers, some of them yelling encouraging slogans to their sons, some of them trying to comfort and distract their younger children, and some of them sitting quietly like herself. Occasionally she tried to talk to the quiet mothers. Not about soccer; she neither liked nor understood the game. She was glad Gabriel was getting his exercise, but she was afraid he'd slip on the wet ground. One boy had broken his ankle during a game. She'd seen it happen. And any game where you bounced the ball off the top of your head couldn't be too safe. At least she knew he wouldn't hurt his fingers playing soccer. That made it better than football, basketball, and baseball, which were Gabriel's favorite sports, which he shouldn't play, at least not now, because he was so small.

At the last soccer game she'd been to she'd met a woman

younger than herself, whose son, on Gabriel's team, was her first and only child. The woman was sitting in the bleachers with a stack of papers in her lap, a manuscript. She was making corrections on it with a red pencil. Elizabeth, curious, introduced herself. The woman's name was Hannah. Her last name was Russian and complicated. Her son, Peter, running across the field, the star of the junior varsity, was the fastest one on the team.

"We picked out this school for academics," Hannah said, "but all Peter cares about is the soccer. Next year he'll be on varsity. I wonder what that'll do for his math grade."

Gabriel's grades are just fine, Elizabeth thought but did not say. Soccer, flute, and everything. He still gets the best marks in the sixth grade.

Hannah wanted to know how Elizabeth had come to choose the Wolfe School. She was from out of town, she said, and her husband, too. They had no idea of where to send Peter until a friend, who had graduated from the school himself, recommended it.

"It wasn't exactly a choice for us," Elizabeth explained. "My husband went here, and his father before him, and his grandfather, too. In fact" — she didn't know if she should admit this or not — "the new gym is named after Gabriel's grandfather. Van Allen Hall — he gave them the money to build it."

"Oh!" Hannah smiled enough to expose the chip in her front tooth. "Your husband must be our friend Maxwell Van Allen, my husband's employer! I had no idea he had a son Peter's age. I thought his children were just babies."

"Some of his children are," Elizabeth said dryly. "I'm his first wife. We're divorced." (So Max didn't even tell his friends that Gabriel existed. Even when he was recommending Gabriel's school to them. His school. Their school. The Van Allens' school. Some proud father. Gabriel the afterthought. The twice-yearly tuition bill and athletic fee.)

Hannah, who should have been embarrassed, Elizabeth thought, continued to chat. As though she'd found a new friend. Peter had gotten that soccer fever from his father, who'd gone to boarding school in France, though he was actually a Russian. Elizabeth pretended not to be interested, though she was.

Hannah's husband was a translator. Russian, French, and English. Into and out of those three languages. Hannah said she knew Russian and French, though not nearly so well as English. She was from Brooklyn, could you tell? And she did her husband's copyediting, for English translations only. Which was what she was doing right now. She offered to let Elizabeth examine the manuscript.

"No, thank you."

It was a biography of Shostakovich, the only one to be written in the Soviet Union. It had been smuggled out by Hannah's husband, and now he had finished the English translation. The Van Allen Press was going to publish it on next fall's list. "It should create quite a stir. It should get international notice."

"How very nice," Elizabeth said. So, Maxwell was getting into the music business himself. Funny how he hadn't mentioned it to her. No, he probably hadn't even thought about it. It wouldn't have occurred to him that he was in a position to make connections to help his only son.

Gabriel's team lost. In the car on the way home Elizabeth asked him about Peter.

"He's all right."

"All right? Is that all you know about him?"

"He's the best player on the jayvee, but he's not that good." Gabriel grinned. "We stink. He think's he's a lot better than he is. He says his dad's going to send him to soccer camp this summer." Gabriel paused to look at his mother, who was looking straight ahead at the road. "His dad knows Dad. Dad's the one who told him about the Wolfe School when they came here from New York." Elizabeth didn't blink.

"Does he do well in school?" she asked.

"Not well. Not bad."

"But how does he do?"

"He's in the middle group. I guess he gets B's mostly. I don't know."

Elizabeth's knuckles tightened on the wheel. "Does he play an instrument?"

"God! Who cares? How do I know? I think he plays the violin. God, why do you care?"

"Don't say *God*."

Thump, thump, thump, thump, thump. Elizabeth looked at the clock. Five minutes was up. Her calves were feeling just the right amount of exhaustion and she was perspiring lightly. She jogged to her bedroom and hung her sweat clothes in the closet. Max's closet. She kept her regular clothes in her own closet and her sweat clothes and dance clothes in Max's. Let his old empty closet be the one that smelled bad.

Time to take a shower, she thought, reaching up to finger lovingly the never-used pair of pointe shoes suspended from the tie rack. The last ones she'd bought. Perfect pink satin with perfect uncreased laces. She'd thought to stuff some new lamb's-wool in the toes. Size 7½, unadulterated and pink. That color, on any other article, would have been garish. Only a dancer can wear pink satin and remain in good taste. These should be yellow and faded after all these years, but she kept them in the closet, where they never got light. She slid the closet shut and stepped in front of the mirror. In sixteen years she had gained only five pounds, no more. Her back (she turned to study it) was still laced with the same muscles that had amazed Maxwell when they first met. Only her face had aged — reddened, wrinkled slightly at the eyes, around the mouth. The ravages of too many cigarettes.

She wanted a cigarette. "No, I smoke too much." She'd take the shower first, then let herself have a cigarette. One cigarette. With coffee. Then she'd write those letters.

III A bar of sunlight, escaping through a tear in the black window-shade, moved slowly across the floor, across the tangle of socks and shoes and sleeping bag, till it landed on Eric's face, prying open his eyes. Fish sat up, sweating. The room was too warm. There were clothes and bedsheets everywhere. Nathan and his roommate were gone. To breakfast? To the midterm?

What time is it? Eric had a dull, insistent headache and his right nostril was clogged. He found his watch under some socks and focused slowly. Holy shit: 9:30. There was absolutely *no way* he could get to the airport in time. He'd have to call Dad. Dad wasn't going to like this at all. Eric stumbled down the hall, into the bathroom to take a leak in one of the many empty stalls. No one was around. Probably everyone in this dorm, which was for freshmen, had the same midterm this morning. Eric shuddered as his bare left foot landed in a small puddle by the sink. The bathroom was freezing. Someone had opened a window and all three shower curtains were flapping. Eric considered taking a shower: too strenuous? But Fishes love water. Blowing his nose on a piece of toilet paper, he went back down the hall to Nathan's room for a towel and some soap.

On the bathroom mirror over the sinks someone had written in chalky green toothpaste: ECON SUCKS. Very freshman. In between the loops of the letters Eric saw his face, which was shiny from not washing and from a night of overheated sleep. He was growing a new pimple next to his nose. Wonderful. He shut the offending window and chose the cleanest-looking shower stall. As he had hoped, there was hot water. Perfect. Ah, but he'd forgotten to bring shampoo. Was it worth going back to his brother's room, now that he was wet? Never mind; he rubbed the bar of soap directly on his head. This would probably give him dandruff. He hummed a little as he soaped himself, a jazz melody, Bob James? Just as he was soaping his chest (what little hair there was provided the friction he needed for a really fine, thick lather), the bathroom door opened. Eric heard another guy come in, put his things down at the sink, go into the stall and take a leak. The flush took the cold water away from the shower and Eric was suddenly scalded. He resisted the temptation to scream, instead held his breath until the cold came back on and he was fine. He could hear the other guy coming out of the stall, running water at the sink. Maybe this guy had some cream rinse he could borrow, to save his hair from the soaping he'd just given it. Eric stepped out without turning off the water and stepped around the corner, toward the sinks. He stopped suddenly. This was no guy. It was a girl with long blond braids, which she was unbraiding. Her fingers froze midbraid. In back of her the mirror read ECON SUCKS. Her eyes widened, then she giggled.

"Oh, I'm sorry," she said.

Eric stepped backward around the corner, back into the shelter of the shower. He could feel his body blushing from the waist up. What should he say?

"I thought this was a men's room," he shouted above the water.

"It is," came the reply. "I'm just visiting" (another giggle).

Eric stood under the water waiting for her to finish whatever she was doing and leave. But she kept banging things around, turning the sink on and off, making little noises. Eric was getting impatient, he was already very clean and rinsed and the water kept tapping down on his shoulders. Maybe in a minute the girl would go into one of the showers and he could escape. All this water couldn't be good for him. His skin would get chapped, or he would catch a cold. And his headache, which had almost disappeared, was coming back stronger than ever. Finally he couldn't stand it any longer. He turned off the water.

"Are you almost through?" he said. His voice cracked on the word *through*. He cleared his throat.

"What?" came the female voice. "Well, in a few minutes. Why?" Eric could feel his blush start up again.

"Do you think you could hand me my towel?" This time, at least, his voice didn't crack. The girl turned off the water.

"Where is it?" she said. Her voice was flat. She's annoyed, he thought.

He began to say, "On the towel rack," but before he could finish, five red-painted fingertips were thrusting his towel and his clothes through the curtain. His underpants fell next to the drain, into a pile of suds.

"Thanks," he said. He pulled his clothes on over his wet body and draped the towel over his head. The shower curtain screeched when he pulled it open, and droplets of water flew into his face. The girl was still at the sink, brushing her hair, which was kinky from the braids, and the color of spun gold (Eric imagined the angel hair, gold leaf, of a thirteenth-century painting). He nodded to the girl, who watched him, unsmiling, as he opened the door. She ran the brush through her hair again and it crackled with static electricity.

Back in Nate's room Eric stripped and dried himself with another towel. He put on fresh underwear, fresh jeans, and a shirt that he'd only worn once before (white Mexican muslin with embroidery by his sister Sylvie); he rolled his dirty clothes up in the sleeping bag and sat on Nathan's bed. He remembered his headache. Where would Nate keep his aspirin? There was none in his desk, none on his dresser, none on the shelf with his bathroom supplies. Eric remembered the piece of Quāālude in yesterday's jeans pocket. Too much trouble to unroll the sleeping bag. Probably a very bad idea to take a lude, anyway. What he should have was some coffee. He found a jar of instant Maxwell House, but no method of boiling water. Maybe he should just eat a spoonful of instant-coffee crystals. The phone rang. It was his father's secretary, who put him on hold. Eric waited for his father's voice.

"You missed the plane" was the first thing his father said. Just like Dad not even to say hello.

"I couldn't get a cab —," Eric began.

"Never mind. I'll have to get Agnes to book another flight. What do you think I'm made of, anyway? 'Oh, don't worry, Dad'll pay for it.' Not a thought for anyone else. You're all the same. You, your brother, Sylvia. That's right, go ahead. Take, take, take."

"Dad."

"Don't Dad me. Wait, here's Agnes. Hold on."

Eric whistled softly into the phone waiting for his father to come back on the line.

"Agnes has booked you a flight already. The next one she could get . . . it's . . . one A.M. Arrives in Philadelphia four A.M., our time."

"Thanks, Dad."

"All I can say is you'd better not miss it."

"I won't."

"And take a cab from the airport. You're nuts if you think I'll pick you up at that time of night." Click. The line was dead. Eric hung up slowly and put on his shoes and coat. He might as well get some breakfast if he had a whole day to kill.

He paid cash to get into the student cafeteria, where a fat woman with a mean look in her eye pushed a plate of runny eggs in his direction. He served himself a bagel, which was barely thawed, and two cups of coffee with lots of sugar. He carried his tray over to the nearest empty table and sat down. As he was salting the eggs he noticed Nathan and his roommate sitting at a table across the room. They must have just finished their midterm. Eric carried his tray over toward them — Oh. Sitting at their table was the girl with the kinky golden hair. Eric stood still. Too late, Nate had seen him and was waving. Eric swallowed hard and continued to walk.

"This is my brother," Nathan was saying to the girl and a tall bearded boy who must be her boyfriend. "His name is Eric, but he calls himself Fish."

The girl let out a high-pitched scream of laughter. "We already met," she said, glancing at her boyfriend, who was grinning at Eric.

"This is Harold," said Nathan, "and his girlfriend Cynthia. Hey, did I miss something?" (Cynthia and Harold were still smiling.) Eric put down his eggs.

"We met already, in the shower," he said. His eyes met Harold's, and Harold looked away. Cynthia was eating bacon and her red, pointed fingernails were shiny with grease. Eric sipped his acid-sweet coffee and pushed away his tray. He still had no appetite, effects of last night's cocaine.

He chatted with Cynthia. Where did she go? Smith. What year was he? Third. What year was she? Second. And how did he like Penn? Her sister had graduated from there in '75. Fine. Just fine. He was in art history.

Nathan and his roommate were comparing what they'd written on the midterm. Eric felt an oncoming nausea, and the return of his headache.

"Dad called this morning," he said, looking away from Cynthia's glistening fingers, to Nathan's orange juice. "Checking up on me. He knew I'd miss the plane this morning."

"What did he say?" said Nathan.

"He was pissed. How come you didn't wake me up, schmuck?"

"You were into some heavy partying last night. I figured you'd probably kill me if I tried to. Anyway, since when are you in a hurry to get back to school?"

"Thanks."

"There's always a later flight."

"He was pissed as hell."

"So, what else is new?"

"He booked me a one-A.M. flight from here and told me to take a cab from the Philly airport."

"So, he'll pay for it."

"Wanna bet."

Eric stood up and put on his coat. "Give me a key. I'm going back to your room." He glanced at bearded Harold. "I forgot to shave."

Nathan dug into his pocket. "If you go out," he said, "don't forget to leave the key at the desk downstairs."

There was a chorus of good-byes from Nathan, his roommate, and Harold.

"See you later, Eric," said Cynthia, waving her polished nails.

"Call me Fish," he said.

Outside, Fish saw a bus stopping at the corner. He forgot about shaving, about his brother's key in his pocket, and ran toward it. The door parted and he hopped on. He would see Ben again before he left.

The bus rolled past the Front Royale, past where the beautiful girl he'd followed yesterday was staying. Fish imagined that she would be waiting there on the corner for the bus, and climb on glancing mysteriously from side to side, and then sit down beside him. No. Only an old black man got on. He sat across from Fish and immediately fell asleep.

Fish closed his eyes and pictured Ben's little apartment above the drugstore. It was cramped and there wasn't much light, but Ben called it his loft just the same. Fish had expected a real loft from the letters. Did it make a difference, though, just as long as Ben was happy? Fish pictured the room, lit artificially with many lamps; a hammock for a bed; three large easels, each with a different painting; palettes resting on the chairs, and hanging from nails on the wall; tubes of paint, and paint rags on the floor; everything heavy with the smell of turpentine and hashish.

It was eleven, so Ben would be asleep now with the stereo on. He had the best record collection of anyone Fish knew. Classical, jazz, important rock albums, and now punk music, which he said he didn't like much but collected for sociological reasons. He always slept with an album on, playing one side over and over again on automatic in order to memorize the music in his sleep. Ben painted all night, slept all morning, and was a waiter with a phony French accent in a French restaurant in the afternoons and evenings. No college, no courses — just his friends, his painting, his music, and his drugs.

Ben answered the door shirtless, in the same pair of baggy trousers he'd been wearing yesterday. The wind rustled the green surgical pants and whipped through his curly hair.

"You *must* come in," said Ben, through a yawn. "Cold."

"I didn't leave yet."

"You didn't leave yet. I can see that."

"I missed the plane."

"Yeah?"

"Uh-huh." They were up the steps, to Ben's open door. String music on the stereo.

"Bartók?" said Fish.

"Shostakovich," said Ben. "Quartet in C Minor, his last. Very interesting. He uses his initials to form the notes for a theme. Heavy borrowing from himself, of course. You might notice that."

"I wouldn't." Fish had a poor memory for music.

Fish cleared a place on the floor to drop his coat. He kicked off his shoes and flopped onto the hammock.

"First you wake me up," said Ben, "after I just got to sleep an hour ago. Then you come park yourself in my bed." Ben opened the paint-spattered refrigerator door and pulled out a gallon bottle of burgundy.

"Breakfast?" said Ben. Fish shook his head no.

"I always drink wine with my vitamins," said Ben. Fish stared at the ceiling, on which Ben had painted a huge pink rose. Probably he had painted it while tripping. The petals of the rose swirled inward to the center almost like a spiral.

"I was up all night working," said Ben. "I finished a canvas." As a rule Fish didn't really like Ben's painting. He liked the idea of Ben's being a painter, but he didn't think much of his work. Too ill disciplined. Too untrained. He would have been better if he'd gone to art school, at least. Fish sat up to see the canvas Ben was showing him, the one on his biggest easel. It was an enormous, sloppy, fat blond nude, sitting on a crooked couch, holding a rose by its stem in her long red-tipped fingers.

"The perspective is off," said Fish.

"That's intentional," said Ben.

"It's disturbing," said Fish.

"It's supposed to be," said Ben.

Fish looked at Ben, who was sitting calmly on a stool, wineglass at his lips, considering his painting.

"Did you ever try painting from life?" said Fish carefully. "A live model. It could really help. I mean, there's something just screwy about her anatomy."

Ben smiled and finished his wine. "Don't you think I did that on purpose?" he said. The record ended and started again.

Ben put his glass on the floor and sat beside Fish on the hammock. His weight made Fish slide down a little so that his shoulder and knee touched Ben, who was holding a piece of wood and a little knife, carving something. Slices of wood fluttered to the floor, landing at their feet.

If he stretched things he could say that the girl in the painting looked a bit like the girl in the bathroom this morning, Cynthia. Of course the only real resemblance was the blondish hair and the painted nails, and Cynthia wasn't fat at all, or at least he couldn't tell since she'd been wearing a long blue robe at the sink, and at the table she'd been sitting down. It was stretching things to say that they were alike, and still what a temptation to look for a repetition of themes in his morning, the way he'd look for them in a book or in a painting: Eric was desperately trying to distract himself from thinking that Ben's thigh was uncomfortably close to his own.

And yet as kids, or even in high school, they'd thought nothing of wrestling for hours on his bedroom floor or else Ben's. And they'd shared the same tent or the same bed a hundred times, and they were always using the same pipe or the same joint or the same glass to drink from, without even thinking about it. Without even thinking about germs or touching. And who else was he like this with, like himself, Fish, without trying to be cool or thinking "image." He was more Fish with Ben than with Nathan or any girl, or anyone. So why did the touching of their thighs, their knees, their elbows bother him, especially now, when they were reunited for a short time? Was it so intense? Was it that their friendship was condensed into a few days, every few months. Was that what made the physical . . . but he forced himself to remember that last night Ben's hand had rested, for a moment only but very calmly, at his waist. Frustration from following the beautiful girl had caused his discomfort, he decided. That was it, and the drugs, and what was a kiss between friends? What was it but nothing, nothing to mention or even remember. Nothing to remember but the flicking of wood chips to the floor, wood chips landing on his socks. Fish shook his feet, but a few pieces remained, clinging.

"What time is your plane?" said Ben slowly, whittling. Fish told him.

"So come with me to a concert tonight. I have a ticket and I know someone who can get you one. I'm leaving work early just to hear this."

"What concert?" said Fish, inching himself away, then finding his weight pulling Ben's shoulder down tighter next to his.

"James Rosen. It's a solo performance with the symphony."

"I think he played with the Philly Orchestra last week," said Fish. "I didn't go."

"Here's your chance. I'll call my friend." Ben stood up and Fish was alone again on the hammock. With the receiver in one hand and the telephone in the other, Ben paused.

"I saw him last night. He came into the restaurant, and the headwaiter was sick so I pleaded with them and they let me do his table." Ben tucked the receiver under his chin and dialed. "Hello, Cleveland," he said. "This is Ben. I have a friend who's in town for the day and is dying to come to the concert with us. Do you think you could manage? His name is Fish. Eric Fish. Right, as in flounder. Thanks a mil, see you then, right."

"Cleveland plays violin in the symphony," said Ben, "but he wants to be a soloist. He's a regular at the restaurant and he gets me tickets to anything." Eric nodded, feeling sick but happy to be alone on the hammock.

"Do you have anything to eat besides wine and vitamins?" he asked. Ben shook his head.

Eric took the bus back. Fishing through his pocket for change, he found his brother's room key. Poor Nathan, locked out of his room, and Eric still hadn't shaved. All seven of his chin hairs were probably sprouting. He'd get off at the Art Institute for another look around. He'd shave before the concert, and Nathan's roommate must have another key, anyway. He put on his dark glasses before getting off the bus. He'd stroll up the steps real slow, scanning the people outside the museum for the Front Royale girl. Maybe she'd be back again today. (But what had Ben meant last night, what had he been doing, a long slow caress between the best of friends, what, what, what, he felt as though he weren't even there. It was someone else, someone in a dream, another person there and he in the wrong place, watching. What was it?) Eric moved toward the Institute, his back very straight.

IV   Gabriel was the first one in his group to solve the math problem. He had a new copybook today because yesterday he'd finished the last page in his old one. This problem was the first one on the first page, and he had written it very neatly, and he knew it was the right solution because he'd already checked the answer in the back of the textbook. Everyone else was still working so he shut the copybook and took out his Magic Marker to write on the cover, which was a plain green (his favorite color).

GABRIEL VAN ALLEN
GRADE 6, GROUP A
THE WOLFE SCHOOL
CHESTNUT HILL
PHILADELPHIA, PENNSYLVANIA, 19118
AMERICA

Next to this he drew a spider. He wrote: DO NOT OPEN. PRIVATE PROPERTY. CONTAINS SPIDER EGGS. And under this, in letters an inch high, he wrote MATH.

Peter Kazakov was in a lower group, but his circle was next to Gabriel's circle and their desks just happened to be back to back. Today after lunch their class was putting on a talent show for their parents and for the seventh- and eighth-graders. Gabriel and Peter had both brought their instruments. They were the only boys who played anything besides piano in their class. Gabriel's flute had been resting on his lap all morning, because his mom had warned him not to put it in his locker. "Someone might steal it, and imagine what we'd have to go through to get your father to buy another one." Peter's mother must have said the same thing; his violin was lying on the floor, under his chair, and if Gabriel slouched down far enough (holding on carefully to his flute), he could touch it with his heels. The violin case was larger and more impressive than the flute case, and that morning, before school started, everyone had wanted to look inside. But Peter hadn't opened it.

"It's very antique," he'd said. "The only people I let touch it are my teacher and my dad. Even my mom can't pick it up." Gabriel would have let anyone hold his flute who wanted to, as long as he was careful and didn't drop it. But no one asked, so he just sat down and kept it on his lap all morning.

Finally everyone in the group had finished the problem and someone was putting it on the board.

"Gabriel," said Miss Hahn, "are you paying attention?" No, Gabriel was not. He opened his copybook and checked his solution against the one on the board, which Miss Hahn was praising. They were exactly the same.

"How many others got this one right?" said Miss Hahn. Only Gabriel raised his hand.

After they finished eating, the sixth grade skipped recess and went to the auditorium to get ready for the show. The taller boys moved around props and bleachers for the singers to stand on. Miss Hahn told Gabriel and Peter, and George, who was going to do magic tricks, to wait quietly backstage till it was time to go on. Peter began to whine. He stomped his foot and slumped in his chair.

"Yes, Peter?" said Miss Hahn.

Peter said that he needed a private room to warm up in and tune his instrument, and that he also needed to tune to the piano because his mother was coming to accompany him. Gabriel, who had been planning to play solo, looked at Peter suspiciously.

Miss Hahn threw her arms up in the air and asked Peter where he would like to warm up.

"The faculty lounge," said Peter. Normally no boys were *ever* allowed in the faculty lounge. Miss Hahn told him to go ahead and looked at her wristwatch.

"Do you boys need to warm up too?" she asked Gabriel and George. They both shook their heads, and Miss Hahn ran onto the stage to look at the props. In the distance Gabriel heard the squeaks of a violin being tuned. He opened his flute case. The silver was especially shiny this week because his mom had polished it in honor of his audition with Mr. Chattarjee. He examined the head joint: there were some fingerprints from yesterday's practice, but his finger stuck inside the hollow came out clean. No green slime had formed overnight. He screwed the flute together and ran his fingers up and down the keys. The metal was cold. If he played it like this he'd be way too flat. What he really needed was to warm up, so why had he said no to Miss Hahn? Something about Peter asking for the faculty lounge and getting it had made him uncomfortable. Maybe he'd wanted to seem like he didn't need to warm up. Remembering a trick that Samantha had taught him, he stuck the flute up the sleeve of his blazer, so that the embouchure rested snugly under his armpit. His right hand closed up the flute case and his left arm, like the stiff wooden arm of a toy soldier (he had an army of them at the bottom of his old toy-box), hung at his side.

"Why did you do that?" said George, who'd been watching him. George was stuffing a toy rabbit into the false bottom of a plastic top hat. Gabriel started to tell him, but Miss Hahn ran up, clapping her hands for quiet. The parents and the other grades were assembling in the auditorium now and there must be complete silence backstage. Now everyone heard the sounds of pitch pipe and violin.

"Go tell Peter to stop warming up and come out here," Miss Hahn told George, who left his hat and wand on the chair and skipped away.

First was the singing. They had to get in line according to height, which meant that Gabriel was next to Peter, and they were both in the front row. The class sang in two-part harmony, alto and soprano, with Miss Hahn conducting and Henry Oppenheimer playing piano. Some of the tallest-boys' voices were changing already, so Miss Hahn had instructed them to mouth the words but not to sing. Peter and Gabriel were both sopranos, but Peter was much louder and whenever he hit a wrong note he threw Gabriel off.

Miss Hahn pulled the lever and the curtains opened. Gabriel saw his mom in the front of the parents' section. She was smiling right at him. When she saw him look at her she lifted her hand and gave him a little wave. He looked away and kept singing: *It's a world of laughter, a world of tears. It's a world of hopes and a*

*world of fears. There's so much that we share that it's time we're
aware it's a small, small world. It's a small world after all, it's a
small world after all* . . . Gabriel was glad to be a soprano. The
altos had some kind of weird harmony Miss Hahn had written,
and most of them couldn't remember the notes.

There was a little commotion at the back of the auditorium as
the door opened — Peter's mom was sneaking in, late. With her
was a man who was very tall, with a long black beard, and who
must be Peter's dad. They were pushing their way through a row
of people, saying something, probably "Excuse me, excuse me,"
making their way toward two empty seats. Gabriel glanced
sideways at Peter, who was blushing. Peter stopped singing long
enough to say "Oh, hell" in Gabriel's ear.

Next they sang a song about a bridge in French. Lawrence
White (who was black) sang the alto solo and Gabriel sang the
soprano one. He kept his eyes on Miss Hahn as he sang (it was only
a few measures long), and his voice quivered a little out of nervousness. When the song was finished, during the clapping, Peter whispered to him, "You sounded just like a girl." Gabriel could see his
mother, with her hands raised high in the air, clapping extra hard.

They marched off the stage the way Miss Hahn had showed
them at rehearsal: Peter leading half of them off stage left, and
Gabriel leading the rest off stage right.

Lawrence White did a singing solo with Miss Hahn at the piano.
Henry Oppenheimer did a piano solo, and then it was time for
Peter's piece. Gabriel could see everything from backstage: Peter
walking out importantly, holding his bow like a sword, Peter's
mom tripping as she ran up the stage steps, sliding onto the piano
bench. She gave him an A and he tried three times before getting it
right, almost. In all fairness, though, Gabriel considered, the
piano was badly out of tune.

Peter played the same Vivaldi A-minor Concerto that every
beginning violinist played at every recital at Gabriel's old music
school. Cripes, Gabriel had heard six-year-olds play it better. He
was taking it much too slowly and he and his mom had trouble
staying together. Gabriel smiled and wondered why he was happy

that Peter was doing such a bad job. For some reason he'd been afraid that Peter would be as good a musician as he pretended to be. His playing was plain boring. He looked at Peter's mom, who was wearing a jeans skirt and sneakers. She had a scarf tied around her head, hiding her hair, and ever time she lifted her arm you could see a huge hole in her sweater. Gabriel smiled again. One thing his own mom would never do, she would never dress like that. *Especially* if she had to go on a stage.

Peter was taking forever to finish the piece. He did all the repeats and Gabriel suspected that he even invented a few repeats of his own. The whole audience was probably asleep by now, but Gabriel couldn't see them from his place backstage. He even felt a little sorry for Peter. He was so bad, and even though he didn't know it yet, the audience was sure to let him know. Miss Hahn, who was back again from leading the rest of the class out, around, and back into the auditorium, into reserved seats where they could watch the solo acts with the audience, stood there staring, smiling at Peter and his mother. Her faced looked like a mask, Gabriel thought. Her smile was so stiff. He didn't know what it meant. Was she laughing at Peter or what? He couldn't read her expression at all.

Finally, finally Peter was through. The clapping started timidly (a few people had tried to clap in between movements and Peter had hushed them with an angry look), then grew louder and louder. Gabriel was confused: people were cheering. Peter took a magnificent bow, then nodded to his mother, who curtsied. They both walked offstage. Gabriel heard chairs screeching on the linoleum floor. The audience must be standing up. A standing ovation? For that performance? Then Miss Hahn was in back of Gabriel, whispering in his ear, "Isn't he talented? Isn't he wonderful?" Gabriel looked up into her face. She was serious. He nodded, thinking that his mouth was feeling very dry. Peter was coming onto the stage for the third time, and only then was the clapping dying out. His mother stumbled out in back of him, bowing and curtsying. Gabriel put his hand on his stomach. Lunch had been peanut butter and Fritos, and he didn't feel so good. Too late, though; it was his time to play.

"Go ahead," Miss Hahn was saying, giving him a little push. "Go. Go."

Suddenly Gabriel found himself on the stage, pulling his flute out of his blazer sleeve. Peter had left his music on the stand, which Gabriel moved out of the way. His music, as always, was memorized. He carefully adjusted the head joint, tried a note, adjusted some more. The warming trick had worked; he wasn't the least bit flat. He took a deep breath and began to play, the same Telemann piece he'd played for Mr. Chattarjee, his most impressive piece technically. He found himself going a little extra fast, just to show off, knowing somewhere in the back of his mind that his mom wouldn't approve. But his eyes were unfocused, blurred with concentration, and he couldn't see her face. He was flying with the music: faster, more precisely, each note perfectly as written. At each pause the silence of the room seemed to crush him like a heavy stone — and then he would leap back into the music, his fingers performing on their own, from their memories, and his breath struggling to support them. As he neared the end of the piece, he began to wonder what to do next. He did not know what he should do when his fingers ran out of music, when he had to stop playing. For a second he thought he could not imagine the world without these sounds he was making . . . and just then it was over. He stopped. The applause started with a crash. Gabriel looked up but he couldn't see his mom's face in the audience: everyone was standing up. It was odd to see the seventh- and eighth-graders on their feet clapping for him. He looked backstage to Miss Hahn. She was bowing over and over again. She waved her arms at him and bowed again. Gabriel realized she wanted him to bow. Of course. Everyone bows at recitals. He bent his head low, the way he'd been taught, bringing his nose as close to his knees as possible. Oh, he was sick. His stomach twisted with that particular pain that told him he was going to vomit. He must *not* throw up on the stage in front of everyone. Clutching his flute he ran offstage, past surprised Miss Hahn, out the door, down the hall, straight to the bathroom. He didn't bother to lock the stall door, or even close it. There was no time. He held his flute tightly as he choked and retched, his face close to the toilet. He was sick one peanut-butter sandwich, a bag of Fritos, one apricot fruit roll, and a carton of chocolate milk's worth. He flushed the toilet and leaned against the wall of the stall to rest. His mouth tasted horrible and he was sweating.

The door opened and in burst Peter.

"Miss Hahn says to see if you're okay." Gabriel didn't answer. He balanced his flute on the sink and rinsed out his mouth.

"That was really queer the way you ran off stage," said Peter.

"I threw up just now."

"Wow."

Gabriel washed his hands, careful not to splash water on his flute, but wetting his shirt cuffs. "Is it over?" he asked.

"Almost. You should see the way George screwed up his magic act. He couldn't get the dumb rabbit out of the hat. Everybody laughed at him, even his mom. I saw her."

Gabriel played a scale. The notes echoed, bouncing off the fixtures.

"That sounds cool," said Peter. "You'd better come back. Miss Hahn says you hafta." Gabriel played the opening bars of the Telemann. He liked the way flutes sound in bathrooms.

"No," he said. "I'm staying here."

"You hafta come or else."

"Else what?"

"Else she'll come and get you herself, dope."

Everyone looked at them as they snuck into the auditorium. Gabriel caught his mom's worried eye and looked away. There were no seats left, so they had to stand in the back with the teachers. Gabriel could feel Miss Hahn watching him.

The headmaster was up on the stage talking the way he always did at assemblies. He was saying how wonderful America really was, after all, and that American youth was something to be proud of. Gabriel could not stop thinking that his flute case was backstage and that he would have to go afterward to get it. He could not remember where he'd left it exactly. Was it on the chair that he'd waited on beside Peter and George, or was it on the floor by the spot where he'd watched Peter and his mother? Someone could have kicked it away by now or put it somewhere. Most people wouldn't even know for sure what it was. As soon as this was over he'd have to go right back there and rescue it. Thinking about this made him warm and sweaty.

Mr. Shaffee kept talking and talking. Gabriel could see the top of his mother's head. Her red hair made her easy to pick out in a crowd. George was sitting directly in front of him, in one of the last seats. Poor George, whose mother laughed at him along with everyone else. Gabriel wondered if people laughed when he ran off the stage. No, probably not. Peter would've told him, for sure.

Now Mr. Shaffee had said something that made everybody clap. He was going to establish an award, an award for the best solo performance at every grade's talent show. In fact, he and the teachers had already voted on the award for this afternoon's recital. Would Miss Hahn please bring up the envelope with the vote tally? Gabriel leaned back against the wall. Please God, he thought, confused, don't let it be me.

Well, this is unusual, Mr. Shaffee was saying. Today there was a tie. The judges had cast equal votes for two of the performers. The Wolfe School was just so brimming with talent, think of that. Gabriel's eyes smarted with tears that he would not allow to escape. He knew exactly what was going to happen. He held his breath and tried not to listen to his name being announced along with Peter's. He should never have played at this show. Music should be kept at music school and never at regular school, where no one understood the first thing about it except him and his mom. Even Miss Hahn, who was supposed to know about music, couldn't tell the difference between Peter and him. But he had to march up the aisle beside Peter. He had to take the award and he had to stand there on the stage while everyone smiled at them both. At least his mom would understand.

Elizabeth was furious. The Kazakov boy had been so vulgarly mediocre, and he had received a longer applause than Gabriel (of course, that was Gabriel's fault, since he hadn't come back onto the stage for curtain calls). And there they were, awarding both boys equally with school ties from the school shop. Didn't Gabriel already have four ties just like that, three in his closet and one around his neck right now? What kind of school was this that couldn't differentiate between the less-than-average and the excellent? It was Max's school, that's what it was.

"Isn't it clever," the woman next to her was saying. "They're giving them ties for a tie. Oh, your boy is so cute." Elizabeth gritted her teeth and smiled. If Max weren't paying the tuition, she'd take Gabriel out of the Wolfe School tomorrow. And now the assembly was over and she had to shake hands with all the moronic teachers and face Hannah Kazakov and her husband.

Chapter 4

I James ordered nothing but tea and an English muffin, but Marina didn't care. No one else was having late breakfast in the fancy dining room — no coffee shops for James. No one there but them and the waitress, who had a peculiar bumpy rash creeping down her forearm, past her shirt sleeve. Marina was planning to eat everything possible and she refused to be embarrassed. Orange juice, grapefruit pieces, two croissants, scrambled eggs (not too dry), four pieces of bacon, cinnamon toast, three cups of black coffee, and a glass of water. All this, barely looking at James except to say, "Are you sure you don't?" and "Well, just try a piece of this, it's really delicious." But he wouldn't taste a thing. He was silent and Marina refused to notice this, thinking instead of the emptiness she was filling in her stomach. Why had he left her alone so much? She didn't ask him where he'd gone last night. She waited, saying nothing, all the time her fork going from plate to mouth. He wasn't going to tell her? Hm. It must be a regular thing for him to disappear on women for most of the night, and to leave them sitting around in hotel rooms in strange cities for whole days, showing up hours later than he said he'd be. In the time she took to gobble up everything except half a croissant and the fatty ends of the bacon, he drank one cup of tea, with milk, and had a muffin, which he didn't even finish. She was too full and if she sat there much longer she'd get drowsy. Marina tapped her feet restlessly. What were they going to do today before the concert? she asked him.

James sighed, closing his eyes as he inhaled. Blink. He opened them. Marina was still there, across the table. He had a short rehearsal with the orchestra at one. That was it. He thought they'd just relax. Marina's color deepened. Was she angry or was that just her body trying to digest? He'd watched her eat all those things. When had she gotten so greedy? How could such a slender body hold all that food? Her eyebrows grew more pronounced when she flushed. She should consider plucking them. He told her so, and she said, "I *like* my eyebrows."

Her eyebrows? Ouch! She'd tweezed them once when she was thirteen, and they'd been sore and swollen all day. But then she'd grown to like their fullness, which was comfortable and familiar in the mirror. Who was James to make a personal comment like that, anyway?

"I thought we'd do something more interesting," said Marina. "Remember me? I've been sitting in this hotel room all the time, pretty much, since we got here."

"I'm here to do a concert. I have to relax before I play."

"Then why did you bring me here in the first place?"

"Not to amuse you, if that's what you expect. Go take a bus tour of the city if you want to be entertained. Go to the zoo or something. I'll give you money. Just tell me what you want to do."

"I have my own money, thank you."

"Fine." The waitress left the check on a small silver tray. James took out his wallet. Marina folded her napkin into a square and placed it over her plate. Was that all he was going to say?

The waitress was making her way around the empty tables, across the room to pick up the money. Sigh, blink. Marina was still there. He couldn't erase her by shutting his eyes. Sitting there watching him, a reproachful black kitten. She'd been fed, but she was being denied her playtime. He repeated the word, *concert*. "We're here for the concert." Marina folded her hands on the crumb-speckled tablecloth. She had the lean fingers of a musician. Fingernails shapely, short, and clean, like James's own.

Upstairs she sat cross-legged on the bed and watched him getting ready to go to the rehearsal. He took a Valium, just in case. The maid hadn't fixed the room up yet and Marina sat silent and catlike in the confusion of the pillows, bedsheets, and blankets. They spoke of the weather: neither of them had any idea about it. James called; forty-two degrees at eleven A.M., colder than yesterday. He suggested that she stay in, since she hadn't brought a winter coat. Stay in the room and practice till he came back; she needed to practice anyway if she was missing school today.

Marina didn't move from the bed, not while he tightened his ascot around his neck, not as he dabbed just a little extra aftershave (L'homard?) on his cheeks, buttoned his jacket, pulled on his overcoat, then his gloves, fine thin leather. Flute case in hand he turned at the door and smiled at her. Why was he smiling? He stopped. She was sitting straight, like a yogi, left foot hidden under the blankets. Once again he thought of a cat. Back beside the bed he touched her cheek, then her lips with his lips. She did not respond. She had good control of her facial muscles, which remained perfectly taut.

She is sulking. I have brought a child with me, he thought, and when he clicked the door shut behind him he considered Marina only for the instant it took to walk to the elevator and board. Then she was gone from his mind.

Five minutes after noon. Marina lay back on the bed and did bicycles with her feet in the air. Her stomach was so crammed with food. She needed to, but couldn't, burp.

Upside down, she could see her flute case, which was lying on the chair where she'd left it yesterday. But who could work on a full stomach? Wasn't discipline created from leanness? The plump face of Rampal passed through her mind as she lay still on the bed imagining herself as a famous fat flutist, ten years later, eating huge breakfasts and cutting records every morning. She giggled and closed her eyes, switching to her favorite private daydream of herself in a huge metropolitan symphony orchestra, meeting so many soloists, so many guest conductors. Perhaps she would live for a while with a handsome concertmeister. She would buy three new black concert gowns each season . . . She yawned.

When she woke it was after one and the maid was knocking at the door. This lady was slow and fat, a different one from yesterday. After one and the rehearsal would have already started. Why hadn't he invited her to come along and listen? She took her *New Yorker* and her cigarettes and went downstairs to the lobby to wait for the maid to finish.

At five-fifteen he was back. Marina loved the smell of the wool in the coat of a man coming back in from the evening cold, but she didn't hug him. She was at the window watching the pinkness descend around everything, sparkling on the lake, which was big enough to be an ocean. She couldn't see the other side, even from way up in the hotel. She turned to look at him. He'd been gone for five hours for a "short rehearsal." On the night table beside his side of the bed was a small bottle of pills. The maid must've found them when cleaning.

"I don't know," said Marina when she saw James staring at the bottle. "They were here when I got back."

They had room service right away, cake and tea. James couldn't eat much before a concert. Marina had said that she wouldn't eat. It was too early for her to be hungry. But Black Forest was her favorite, and eventually she ate all of hers and the cherries he'd picked out of his. She took the first shower because her hair had to dry, and dressed slowly. It took a long time to get ready, each waiting for the other, both in each other's way.

James in his perfect-fitting tails and Marina in her smooth black dress emerged from the elevator at seven. Everyone in the lobby watched them as they walked through the front entrance, under the flags of many countries, out the huge double doors and into the limousine sent by the orchestra. Everybody watched James and Marina, her breath shallow, her arm loosely looped through James's. She was so slight to be going into the cold without a coat.

Eric stepped off the bus in front of the theatre and zipped up. He was glad he'd brought his parka. It was still sweater weather in Philadelphia, but here tonight it wasn't much above freezing. He was supposed to meet Ben on the street. Why hadn't they said inside? He should have thought of that, since he knew Ben was rarely on time. At the box office there was already a line of people picking up their reserved seats. Maybe he should get in line, but were the tickets in Ben's name or his friend's? What was that guy's name? Something odd like Cincinnati. A musician in an orchestra. Just like Ben to know someone like that.

Oh, there he is, over there, less than five minutes late. His coat was half unbuttoned and so was his shirt underneath. His hair flapped about his face in the wind.

"Just left the restaurant," he said, "barely had time to change." All at once they were in line and Ben was pulling out of his pocket a black necktie, which he was looping around his neck. His shirt, which was collarless, was also black. He began to do the buttons. On his feet he wore black Adidas sneakers. Eric stared at them.

"When I get some cash together," said Ben, "I plan to buy black snakeskin leather boots. I have in mind exactly the pair I want." They moved up in the ticket line. At the window a woman was arguing with the clerk.

"If the concert's sold out, then why do you advertise it in today's paper?" she was screaming. "I came all the way from Evanston in an old Chevy without heat for nothing!" Behind the glass, the clerk mouthed something, gesticulating.

They gave their coats to a girl in a booth with a sign, CHECK HERE. Ben made a joke to her about Poles and Hungarians. "Czech here," he explained to her when she didn't smile. She was busy. She had a hundred coats to hang up with her nail-bitten fingers. She pushed her glasses up her nose and took another pair of coats. Ben pulled Eric through the crowd, to the section on their tickets, the middle front of the ground section. Excellent seats, the best in the house, Ben was saying. Eric did not tell him that he preferred to sit up high where he could watch everything that was going on. You can't argue when someone claims you have the best seats in the house. A girl at the entrance was giving them programs. She thinks that we paid for these good seats, thought Eric. All he noticed about her was the flick of yellow hair at her waist and the thinness of her wrists. Another girl, an usher, a bulky Oriental, led them to their seats.

Eric had lied to Ben about the girl in the bathroom that morning. "We walked in on each other in the shower. I mean she was a *big* lady. All this wet long blond hair. A really *big* woman, if you know what I mean." Eric was embarrassed to say *tit* or *boob*, even to Ben. He let Ben guess the rest.

"So you screwed her right there, huh?"

"Of course, but she locked the door first. You can lock the main door to the whole bathroom if you want."

"Can you?"

"Yeah, and she was afraid her boyfriend would knock on the door."

"So you got it on right in the shower?"

"Of course." Had Ben believed him? There was no way to tell. There he was, sitting beside him, chewing on the corner of his program; his long, black-sneakered right foot running across his left knee, gazing at the empty stage. What was Ben thinking? Eric used to be able to tell, but no more.

It was much harder to figure him out now. For instance, Ben had the skinniest legs of anyone Eric could think of and he used to wear his old blue-jeans all the time. But this morning he'd been dressed in those baggy trousers that made him look like a guru, and now he was wearing the tightest shiny black jeans Eric had ever seen. How he had found pants that fit that tightly over his thin legs was anyone's guess. He looked almost *dangerous* with his long curly hair, his tight black clothes. On his left index finger he wore a silver ring in the shape of a snake swallowing its own tail, and, something Eric hadn't noticed until they'd taken their coats off, on his breast pocket was pinned a small metallic rose.

Fish wanted to ask Ben what the rose was all about, but something told him not to.

Backstage, James reached into his tuxedo pocket and pulled

out a small packet of orange-and-yellow-and-white candy corn.

"What's this?" he said.

"I put it there yesterday," Marina looked away, smiling. "For good luck, sort of." She looked at her feet.

They were alone for a moment, finally. Everyone else had left the dressing room. James put the candy on the table and kissed Marina's forehead.

"You have fifteen minutes," he said. "Go out front and find your seat. Some old friends of mine rent the same box I always sit in, and that's where the symphony put you." He reached in his pocket for her ticket.

"Go on, I'll see you at intermission."

"Okay. Good luck."

"Who needs luck?"

Marina wanted him to put the candy back into his pocket, to keep it there while he was playing; the way knights carry souvenirs of their ladies into battle. Please, please put it in your pocket, don't leave it there on the table, she wanted to say.

She turned to leave as his manager stormed in, fresh from the airport, in time for the concert.

"Bernie!" said James. He started to talk excitedly. He did not introduce her. Marina walked out into the hall.

She was slightly lost backstage in the maze of corridors and dressing rooms until a man carrying music stands pointed her way to the exit. She walked tall and carefully into the crowd. She was important tonight, even if her position was not a musical one, but a social one.

Freddy had brought along a quarter-pound box of Godiva chocolates for the concert. He gave Maur the ones with the nuts in them, because they were his favorites. Freddy was letting a luscious truffle dissolve on his tongue when they saw her climbing the steps to the box. They knew it was she from Cleveland's description. Oh, how clever of Cleveland to convince his friend in the box office to put James's comps in the box with them so they could get a look at her. There was a seat in the box for Bernie, too, but he always sat backstage when James played. So they would have her all to themselves.

She *was* pretty. They could recognize that from Cleveland's description, too. Small and slender, but long in the limbs. She would have been graceful if she were just a bit more relaxed. Poor girl, she seemed so tense; she held the small of her back so straight. Her black hair rippled down past her hips and it was true, she was dressed a bit like a student musician in recital. But her sandals were quite tasteful. Freddy guessed they were Brazilian, or possibly Portuguese. And black stockings with seams. Freddy liked to see those on women.

She hesitated, almost imperceptibly, upon entering the box. She looked at them as though thinking she should perhaps introduce herself, but instead she sat down in the seat that was farther away and looked at the stage. Freddy noted her profile, her nose, which was graceful but strong, and her strong eyebrows. Her lips had a sensitive pout.

Maur broke the ice by saying, "Good evening." The girl turned to him and her eyes let out a spark of recognition. Maur said, "My name is Maurice D'Artoit. Pleased to meet you."

The girl said, "Oh yes, I know, you conducted us in Philadelphia last year. I go to Curtis.' So Cleveland was right. She was a music student. Philadelphia last November. That was the last time they'd seen James there, and Lawrence, who so seldom traveled.

"My name is Marina Kazakov," she added, remembering her manners.

"This is my companion," said Maur, "Alfred Weinburg."

The three of them sat there smiling, Marina wondering if she should have sat closer, or if it was all right to have skipped the seat that separated them. She wondered if she should mention James. She was nervous, being thrown into this world, to be sitting there with Maurice D'Artoit, the conductor from the Dominican Republic, to be connected with James Rosen, to know these people who should have been her idols. Who *were* her idols. They were her teachers and she felt small and young. Marina makes a social debut, she thought, before her music debut. If only her heart could stop beating so fast, if only she could be sure not to betray her nervousness. If she could be as cool as she'd been when she first approached James after the master class and somehow she'd been the last student in the room with him before they closed the building. He'd said, "Want to get some coffee?" and she'd said, "All right." And she'd felt fine right then, excited but not even scared.

How deeply she was in all of this. It was only a game at first, going from his hotel room to school that next morning, and feeling that big, important secret all day. Now she was here and she didn't know what she was supposed to do. What was expected of her? Should she be using all this somehow, to help her career? She didn't know. She didn't know. If only there were someone to ask.

The two men sitting beside her in the box — one of them important-sounding, the other she knew was important — were eating chocolates out of a gold-foil box. Mr. Weinburg offered her the box. There were two pieces left. Should she accept or refuse? Not to insult him she took one, not to be greedy she took the smaller one, which, however, was not the closest to her, so she was not sure if she hadn't been rude after all. It was a caramel, her favorite. She dreaded butter crèmes, could barely bring herself to swallow them.

Mercifully the lights flickered, then began to dim. The orchestra was assembling on stage.

"That's Cleveland out there now," Ben was saying as a youngish man emerged from the curtains and slid into place, fourth among the first violins. Eric couldn't see too well from where he sat. His glasses were still rolled up in the sleeping bag. But he sensed, or imagined, that there was something attractive, no, attracting about Cleveland. Perhaps it was the way he moved across the stage. He didn't just walk. He glided, as though his feet weren't touching the floor. His hair was cut like the pictures of men's haircuts displayed in hairdressers' windows: angular. He was tucking his instrument under his chin, tuning up, like the others.

"They tune to an A, to the violin," Ben was explaining. "I have perfect pitch."

Marina, too, had perfect pitch. She couldn't help but hum that A whenever she heard an orchestra tuning. Subconsciously the index finger of her left hand pressed together on her thumb, all others relaxed: she fingered an imaginary flute.

The applause began, like the sound of a wire brush being dropped, and continued mechanically, as Sir Georg Solti appeared. Marina had shaken hands with him backstage. And now he bowed, and the applause thinned almost to a stop, until James walked out. He seemed so tiny, so far removed and in the spotlights, but he walked with dignity. The audience belonged to him — his mood and stance were infectious — and they began to clap with dignity, not rigidly, but with a certain rhythm. Marina thought for a second that they were clapping in triplets, anticipating the high strings that were going to accompany the flute obbligato in the development of the first movement. Of course that was silly. Hardly anyone else in the audience would know the piece about to be played as well as she did. It was the one the school orchestra had done with James last week. The one they'd prepared for weeks, just to get ready for him to come and solo. She knew every measure, every trick of the piece, and she knew the solo itself so well. She had gotten to do it at one of the rehearsals when all three of the senior flutists hadn't shown up. She'd listened to the Rampal recording over and over. She knew exactly how Rampal did it and she had a good idea of James's interpretation. It was not radically different: he barely even changed the cadenza in the first movement — how could you improve much on Rampal? But every little flourish, every slightly different tempo, everything that was James's own, Marina had noticed and remembered.

James was bowing and the applause was quieting, so the piece could begin. Marina could not allow herself to breathe as she waited for the burst of strings, the orchestra's introduction, the greeting of the solo flute. Her fingers gripped the velvet-padded railing and she leaned forward.

Fish was reading his program. First there was a flute concerto by Aram Khachaturian. (How do you pronounce that? Ben must know.) Next, intermission, then two works just for orchestra — something by Bartók and Mozart's *Jupiter.*

Concerto for Flute and Orchestra, transcribed and with a cadenza by Jean-Pierre Rampal. I — Allegro Con Fermezza. Fermezza? Fish wondered if this would be one of those modern pieces where he couldn't tell the end of one movement from the beginning of another. *II — Andante Sostenuto. III — Allegro Vivace.* He had a better idea of what those meant.

The piece started abruptly and every time an interesting Eastern-sounding melody started it would cut itself short, or some annoying-sounding other melody from the other instruments would interrupt. Fish leaned back against the soft velvet seat and glanced at Ben, who stared at the stage, unblinking. There was something familiar about James Rosen and Eric couldn't figure it out. He'd probably seen his face on a poster or a record somewhere. Maybe on an album in Ben's apartment. Still, the stage was too far away to study him very closely. Why did he think he'd seen him before?

Theme I: Marina's fingertips responded to the rhythm of the peasant melody. Barely aware, her muscles played along in countersubject to the orchestra. But his clarity and precision of tone was something she could not produce on an instrument herself, something she would never produce, except in such a trance, where she could feel that these sounds were her sounds, coming from her . . . the solo flute began to alternate with orchestral statements: a small conversation that would lead to the discovery of the second theme. She felt a small, vague discomfort in the back of her neck, in her spine, each time a note fell differently than she had anticipated it. Each variation of tonality and texture pricked her consciousness, a tiny spark, but then the movement grew slow, *poco meno mosso,* and she exhaled with relief, waiting, and there it was, the lyrical solo, the second theme.

Her eyes focused, slowly, on the string section. Like dancers in motion with the music, the violins moved, bowing in unison with each other and with the music . . . Ah! the short flute cadenza, the hushed orchestra: rhapsody! quickly, ended, and now the development was ready . . .

Freddy had always said that James was an artist who could only grow finer with the years. His was a talent that deepened, became rich, mellow, mature, and this was just further proof of that. Why in the year since they'd last heard him, his tone had taken on even more of that classical polish, the master's touch, the ageless, timeless quality. James Rosen (Freddy would note in his journal that night), James Rosen was not merely a musician. He was music. What heights he had attained! He was a peer of the greatest flutists, of Rampal, of Kinkaid! And all this time they'd worried that he was in a slump. They thought he was slipping downward, into a regression, a depression. He took a quick glimpse of the girl, Marina, beside them. She sat in a state of stiff transfixion. How she idolizes him! And perhaps, though it would be unlikely, she is good for him — for how excellently he plays.

Eric thought suddenly that James Rosen looked an awful lot like the guy he'd seen on the arm of the beautiful girl from the hotel. Wait a minute. The guy he'd seen going out the door or the hotel, and later in the cab . . . was it possible? Well. No, it couldn't be, he couldn't have ridden in a cab with such a famous person and not have known it, could he? Where had that cab gone after it had dropped him at his brother's place? Hmmm. Could it be? Eric watched the performance with new interest. He decided that the beautiful girl was somewhere in the audience and that James Rosen was playing to her. After that the piece didn't seem as boring to him . . . at least the melodies were a little more sustained.

Marina's eyes settled on one of the violinists, the fourth chair. There was something unusual about the cut of his tuxedo; for one thing, he wore it very tight, and the collar was different in some way. He had sharp, high cheekbones; she could tell this from so far away in her box. His reddish hair, unusual in the orchestra of so many brown, black, and gray heads, bounced in time with the music, dramatically. His bowing wrist cocked at a delicate angle, he rippled through the triplets. And now, as the long cadenza began, Marina watched him as he, with his instrument placed carefully on his knees, watched James. The whole hushed orchestra was watching James. Sir Georg Solti, everyone in the entire theater was watching James, except Marina who watched this violinist, who, watching James, seemed to her to be changing, inside, gathering strength and power, growing huge, like a giant bird, about to take off, fly after James. Marina thought, this is a concerto originally for violin, so it is his piece, too. He must feel that. He must want to take it, have it be his own. No, but he hears how James uses it, how he handles it and how much that silent waiting orchestra is anticipating him. No, he could never take the piece away from James, not while he is part of that orchestra. Not while he hears James's music, his incredible cadenza. If only there were a way for their instruments to mingle, to become the same, and then they could take this cadenza together. Impossible, of course, impossible. Marina found herself leaning too close to the velvet rail; Alfred Weinburg was staring at her with a faint smile. Of course, she looked like a silly schoolgirl so entranced with the music. She sat back a little, but not all the way, because if she did the velvet rod would block her view of the young violinist. How differently he gazed at James — all the other musicians watching him with a dull stare, counting the rhythms, remembering the notes, understanding only the mathematics of his music. They were technicians, mechanics, but this violinist was an artist. Something moved in Marina's abdomen and a chill raised goosebumps on her arms, under her black satin sleeves. She shuddered, and for a second remembered how cold it was outside: how she and James had had to walk with dignity, slowly, from the limousine to the stage-door entrance, and how she had wanted to bolt from him, to escape instantly into the warmth of the building. (Flashbulbs had popped. Where, she wondered, would those photos appear?)

When that particularly long flute solo ended, Fish half expected the audience to break into applause, the way they would at a jazz concert, after an instrumental solo; after all, everyone had seemed so into the playing. James Rosen had gone on and on (was he improvising?) higher and higher. It was the best flute playing Fish could remember hearing. At one point Ben had reached over and gripped his wrist.

"Listen to this," he'd hissed, squeezing, and Fish had listened carefully, though not quite sure he was understanding it completely. When the flute stopped and there was a pause before the orchestra started up again, the audience seemed to sigh, "Aaah," but nobody clapped. Ben shifted position, crossing his other knee. Fish took the opportunity to bend down and scratch his ankle, which had been bothering him. The orchestra was playing music that sounded a little familiar — was that material they'd already done? Fish wanted to ask Ben, but he was afraid to whisper just yet. Wait until in between movements to ask questions, he thought . . . but wait, how many movements had gone by? He wasn't sure, but he thought they were still on the first. He glanced at his watch; eleven minutes had passed since the piece began. That's about right for one movement, about to end, isn't it? He waited, to see if he was right.

Freddy took particular pleasure in the structure of this movement; it was so good to hear a twentieth-century work with a traditional form. He would have liked to hum along a little with the recapitulation. Oh, and he would have if he were at home and this were a radio broadcast, for he permitted himself to do that in such circumstances, even if there was someone else in the room. Maur hated to hear him humming, though. Freddy always restrained himself from such indulgences when he was at a public concert, even if Maur or anyone else hadn't come along and he was quite alone in the box, because there was the outside chance that someone else would be able to hear him — you could never tell with the acoustics of these places, you never could be sure where your voice might carry. So he just sat there and enjoyed it in silence. Maur was conducting with his finger, as usual, but as Bernie had suggested, he kept his hand at his side, and conducted to the ground. It was too embarrassing to be spotted doing this in public; it would be so awful to be thought of as one who finds Sir Georg's work inadequate. Yes indeed, one must always think of the image if one is leading a public life. One must always be so conscious of the hostile press, or the manager of a rival. Freddy and Maur called them enemy agents for a joke. Good thing that Maur was such a disciplined man, so controlled, so able to keep his sense of decorum, such a perfect gentleman at all times, the gentleman artist. Maur was a true creator, of *refined* masterpieces.

Oh, and now for the coda (a few glimpses of that precious first theme!), and Freddy looked to Marina, who was gazing so blissfully at the stage. Did she love James? It was quite possible, no probable, for who so young, so inexperienced, and in the privileged presence of such magnanimity, such excellence, such greatness — who could not? No, there was no doubt that she loved him. That was for sure. The real question was, Did he love her? How could he? It was true she was beautiful; those long white fingers entwined, resting on her lap, and she was young. James was young himself and yet he had an appreciation, a true passion for youth. But the truth was, she was very different from anything he could have ever known, and he'd been so happy before. Why had he wanted someone like her? How long had they been together? Six months? The whole year he'd stayed away from them? A woman. She was not quite a woman, but then she was a woman. Would be one soon, at least. How could this be what James would choose or want after all these years? Was she right for him? Did James know? Could he know himself well enough to know? *Oh!* The coda ended with a flourish and the movement was finished, followed by the creaks and coughs of the audience shuffling. Marina turned toward Freddy and Maur. Maur, still staring down at the stage, did not notice. Marina smiled, lips parted slightly, then lowered her eyes (gleaming with shyness, Freddy would note later in his journal) and gave her attention to the stage.

Eric turned and whispered — one of Ben's curls tickled his cheek — "which movement are we up to?" and Ben pointed his bony waiter/painter's finger to *Andante Sostenuto*. Eric strained his eyes in the half-dark to read the program book.

He turned the pages, careful not to make them crackle too loudly. There was a description of the music he was listening to:

This work was originally composed in 1940 as a concerto for violin and orchestra, but in 1960, with the composer's permission, flutist Jean-Pierre Rampal began to transcribe it, adhering closely to the original score, with the notable exception of the long cadenza in the first movement, which he completely rewrote, the range of which, in the original, being quite often below that of the flute. The transcription was completed in 1968. This is the debut of the work with the Chicago Symphony.

On the next page was a list of orchestra members. Eric checked the violins and found the name of Cleveland Arms fourth on the list. Sounds like the name of an apartment building, he thought. He looked up at the orchestra, at the corresponding person, who was playing languidly, not looking at the conductor as was the violinist next to him.

Next there were lists of sponsors of the orchestra, rich people who probably gave away millions of dollars just to get their names on the page. There were lots of ads for restaurants, including the place where Ben worked, L'Oeuf d'Or, which had a line drawing of a bottle of wine next to a lobster and a wineglass and some grapes. Eric hadn't had time to visit Ben at the restaurant. Probably it was such a ritzy place they wouldn't let him inside, anyway. On the inside back cover was a glossy photo of some fancy liquor in a green bottle: Rémy Martin. Ben was probably learning all about the expensive drinks and gourmet foods from working at that place. Well, if he ever got so rich and famous — which Fish couldn't see how, since his paintings were so crummy — he'd know how to live.

Toward the middle of the third movement, Marina started to wonder: Was she supposed to go backstage as soon as the piece was over, or should she sit here until the end of the concert? What was she expected to do? She should have checked with James before she came out here. She twisted a piece of hair between her finger and thumb. Probably the best thing to do would be to go back and congratulate James right away and listen to the rest of it back there with him. But what if he didn't want her; he was so strange about the time he spent with her. If only she'd had time to ask before his noisy fat old manager had come in. But it was too late to wonder what to do anymore because the clapping was starting, and the curtain was closing and Alfred Weinburg was leaning over the railing shouting, "Bravo! Bravissimo!"

She pushed her way through the crowd, toward the backstage door, followed at some distance by chubby Mr. Weinburg, who had a hard time squeezing around people, and Maurice D'Artoit, who was having even greater trouble because he was recognized by people who knew him and people who wanted his autograph. Everyone else was headed the opposite way, out into the hall, toward the bathrooms or the champagne bar. By the time Marina reached the door, she'd lost them. She talked her way past the guard, her heart beating faster than she would have liked it to. Why did she feel like a bad little girl sneaking where she shouldn't when she had a perfect right to be there?

There was already a crowd of people at James's dressing-room door. How had they all managed to get there so quickly? The door was open but she couldn't see inside, there were too many bodies blocking her path. Her heart palpitated slightly when she thought, for a second, that the violinist who had absorbed her attention during the cadenza, and part of the second movement, and even during parts of the finale, might be there in the crowd in James's dressing room. It would seem appropriate: the violinist had seemed so *in contact* with James — as though it were just the two of them playing a duet, as though the orchestra and the audience and Sir Georg Solti didn't even exist. But of course, the violinist couldn't be here, he'd be backstage in another area, with the other orchestra members, preparing to go back onstage for the second half of the program. Marina was tempted to go back to her seat and watch him again to see how he responded to an orchestral performance without a soloist. Yes, she would like to watch him again, before the evening ended, and that would be that, until she might perhaps years later meet him by chance at some musical happening, after she had graduated and was traveling in orchestral circles. She sighed. She had to go into the dressing room right now, but she couldn't get by. Obviously none of these people had any idea who she was or else they'd step aside and let her through. She didn't recognize a single face.

"Excuse me," she said. No, that sounds too timid and little-girl. "Excuse me," louder. She wedged herself in a little. Here comes Alfred Weinburg and Maurice D'Artoit. Finally. Would they have better luck getting through this mess? Excuse me, excuse me, excuse me! Daringly loud that time. Plunk! She was through the doorway, suddenly in a clearing. Everyone in the room was clustered around James, who was sweaty and handsome with his bow tie unfastened and loose and his damp hair shaggy on his forehead. His hand was being shaken vigorously by everyone and he was signing his name again and again with his gold fountain pen, right across his photograph on the program. Bernie was beside him, holding his flute case, and they introduced each other to the congratulators they knew personally.

Bernie said, "This is Mr. and Mrs. Silver of Central Illinois Art Exchange. You're going to be on their recital series next season, isn't that right, Mrs. Silver?"

Mrs. Silver said, "We're so pleased to meet you. It's thrilling to meet you." James signed his name in the book she handed him.

There was a small sleepy girl sitting on the love seat in the corner. Marina sat down beside her. The little girl's white-stockinged legs dangled above the floor — her thumb was in her mouth and she swung her feet restlessly. Marina knew she should probably be standing beside James, being introduced to people, but something weary or nervous inside of her kept her on the sofa. She tried to talk to the little girl. "What's your name? How old are you?" But the child covered her face with her free hand, one thumb still in her mouth, and said nothing.

Alfred Weinburg and Maurice D'Artoit were barely in the door by now. Mr. Weinburg looked at Marina curiously, perhaps jealously, because she was sitting down and he was in that long line.

Then she could hear the faint strains of the Bartók being played onstage and she thought once more of her violinist.

After the concert was finally over, Ben insisted on dragging Fish to something he called "The Green Room," which turned out to be hardly green at all and filled with people. Everyone was waiting for Sir Georg Solti and James Rosen to appear, to congratulate them.

Ben said, "Cleveland knows Rosen real well, so we'll get introduced personally." Eric's eyes kept searching the room. He knew, if James Rosen was really who he looked like, that the beautiful girl would be somewhere in this room. This was too much. It was almost embarrassing. He did want to see her, but he'd made such a jerk of himself yesterday. How could he have known he'd run into her today?

"Ben, let's go. We can go out for a drink, get something to eat. Let's not hang out around here?"

"Are you crazy? Don't you want to be introduced to James Rosen?"

"I know, but he might not show for a while."

"Besides, you have to meet Cleveland. He'll be here any second."

An usher came into James's dressing room and made everyone except Bernie and Mr. D'Artoit, Mr. Weinburg and Marina clear out.

"Please wait for Mr. Rosen and Mr. Solti in the greenroom."

I don't belong here, thought Marina, as Mr. Weinburg handed her a plastic cup of champagne. He'd brought a bottle and the cups along with him, in a shopping bag. No one seemed at ease except Bernie, who was talking rapidly about travel arrangements for James's Japan tour in April. "I mean, if you wanna go first-class and travel American it's up to you but I think you oughtta take advantage of their offers to put you up in their homes, that is if you don't mind takin' off your shoes all the time, joke haha, you know paper houses, but it's up to you and it would save you a bundle, remember you won't be making that much with all their taxes, which brings me to the point that you might be wanting to spend as much as you can while you're in the country so you're not being taxed on what you take back to the U.S. — that's double taxes, and you know what that does to your pocketbook — and I don't know how we're going to handle this but I think we both better sit down with the accountant real soon so we can make a good game plan . . ."

"Bern," said James, "we're going to have to talk about this later."

"It'll have to be soon," said Bernie. "We don't have all year."

Mr. Weinburg was refilling Marina's glass when the usher entered saying, "Mr. Rosen, your well-wishers are assembled in the greenroom, if you'd like to greet them now."

How could he be here, in this very room, that creep who'd followed her from the museum. Jesus! Marina stepped in back of Mr. Weinburg. This was too much. How could that guy possibly have known that she'd be here tonight. He must have seen her with James, or maybe some Chicago gossip column had printed a picture of her and James together. However he found out, he was here now in this very room with her. Would he have the nerve to talk to her? Of course he would. He's probably dangerous. He probably cuts up girls and keeps them in his basement. Wonderful — and here he was. At least the room was diluted with a lot of people. As long as she didn't go anywhere alone she was safe — for the time being. Who knows? She flicked her hair behind her shoulders. Now was a good time to act arrogant.

"Don't turn around," said Eric to Ben, "but remember yesterday I told you I followed some girl from the Art Institute to her hotel?"

"The one who set the doorman on you?"

"Right. In a minute turn around real slow and look over there in the corner behind Rosen. She's right there."

"No shit!"

Ben saw Marina, their eyes met, she looked away.

"She must have something to do with Rosen," said Ben. "She's standing right in back of him."

"I know," said Eric. "I'm so embarrassed."
Ben was laughing at him.

There are too many things going on in this room, thought
Marina. First the creep and his awful friend and now this: her
violinist had just come in. He walked like a dancer, quickly, and
his heels barely grazed the carpet. Marina could see his face clearly
now. His pointy nose, the hollows of his cheeks. His hair sparkled a
little, as though it had just been brushed. And now he was walking
over to the creep and his friend and they were all talking. (He
knows the creep?)

Cleveland's eyes met Fish's as Ben introduced them. Up close,
Fish thought, there is something evil — no, devilish — about this
guy. He has a look that is very familiar. Wait a minute. It's the
John the Baptist again. The Leonardo painting I saw in the
Louvre, the one I always wanted to look like. This guy really is
John the Baptist. The Baptist smiled and Eric's stomach muscles
tightened. Ben and Cleveland were talking. If you added Ben's
hair to Cleveland's face you would have the Paraclete exactly.
John the Baptist. Hmmm.

There, thought Freddy, is Cleveland in all his faunlike beauty.
Remember that for the journal. He has a couple of young boys
with him tonight. He nudged Maur and they went over to be
introduced. James was still busy, being congratulated, and they
had already talked to Sir Georg.
Marina stood alone in the corner and watched.

II The stewardess brought James a glass of water and he
used it to swallow a pill. Marina settled back against the pillow
and fixed her eyes on the headrest in front of her. She could feel the
length of James's arm against hers. They were sharing an armrest.
His shoulder started up higher than hers, and his wrist only began
where the tips of her fingers ended, but their elbows met, side by

side. He was moving the right side of his body, trying to put the pill bottle back into his jacket pocket, and she looked out the window at the blue metal wing of the plane.

"Want one?" he said. Marina looked down. He was holding her tiny bag of candy corn, the one she was sure he'd left there on the table in his dressing room. The one that had made her so embarrassed after she'd given it to him: the silly, childish present. Automatically she took one and pressed it to her lips. It was smooth like plastic, the texture of wax. She had eaten thousands of these in the recess yard when she was little. They'd gone on sale every autumn and disappeared from the candy stores before Christmas. Automatically she bit off the orange-and-yellow sections and swallowed it. She examined the little white imitation tooth. They'd used that trick so often to fool each other and their mothers, and the tooth fairy. This part she held on her fingertip. James was watching, wondering what she would do with it.

"A pearl?" he said, guessing wrong.

"No, when we were kids we used to pretend they were teeth." She held her fingertip to his mouth and he kissed it, taking the candy with his tongue.

She was glad to have the inside seat, protected from the aisle by James's body. She didn't want to have to talk to that guy, the creep, the one who'd followed her. She didn't even want to look at him if she could help it.

The five of them had gone out to a bar, after the greenroom finally cleared out. By then it was already late — eleven-thirty — and they had to be on a plane at one, so it was just a place around the corner, where they all knew Cleveland. That was his name, her violinist. A table was cleared for them instantly, even though the place was crowded. It was all so short: forty-five minutes before they rushed away — they had already packed their things and the hotel was sending them to the airport, no need to pick them up. Marina was worrying, vaguely, the whole time, about her flute, how it was being handled by bellboys and porters. As soon as they sat down, the waitress was bringing them cognacs, all of them, without even asking what they wanted, and no one else even objected or seemed to think it was unusual, so Marina thought this was the way they do things here, and she sipped hers slowly: it burned as it trickled through her mouth, down her throat. She was next to James, snug on the inside bench beside the wall, and across from her was Cleveland, her violinist. She was afraid to look at him, afraid to look nervous, and afraid that he would notice something in her eyes that he should not. The creep was sitting on a chair in the aisle, since the benches were not long enough, and when Mr. Weinburg and Mr. D'Artoit came in he suddenly gave Mr. Weinburg his chair and said he had to leave, had to catch a one-o'clock flight to Philadelphia. And then Marina gasped out loud, but nobody noticed (there was a jazz band in the back of the place, they were playing furiously).

What made her gasp was not only the travel plans of the creep, whose name became Eric when he was introduced to her, but the sensation of Cleveland's (was it his?) stockinged foot — he must have slipped off his shoe under the table — pressing its way up her shin and then resting for a moment on her knee. He was leaning back against the bench. His eyes narrowed and he smiled. Marina's heart raced. Had anyone noticed? Her mouth was dry. She took another sip of cognac — her palms were moist. All of this was like being in seventh grade and having the high-school boy, whom you love secretly when you are alone in your room, smile at you in the supermarket. The warm foot was prying her knees apart . . . Marina concentrated on the commotion in the bar. A chair was being brought for Mr. D'Artoit. The creep's friend Ben was asking James something about the Khachaturian. James's hand lay relaxed on the tablecloth. Cleveland's hand (he wore a silver ring in the shape of a snake) reached across and covered James's. They were whispering something together, a small private conversation in the middle of the noise. The foot did not hesitate on its journey. Marina sat motionless, allowing this, all the while smiling at Mr. D'Artoit or Mr. Weinburg or swirling the liquid in her glass.

And suddenly, just when she was beginning to feel comfortable there with all of them, and beginning to think that Alfred

Weinburg — Freddy — was the kind of adult she would like to have for a friend, and beginning to joke a little with Ben, who wasn't really even that much older than she was and was pretending to know all about music, and who had a look in his face that seemed honest and a little astonished to be in the presence of James Rosen, and just as she was adjusting to the excitement of those toes . . . her temperature had risen, her heart was still beating fast, but evenly, suddenly it was time for them to rush off, to get into a taxi and be driven to meet their suitcases at the airport. The foot withdrew, stroking her thigh as it left, and everyone was standing up, putting on coats (except Marina, who had to explain to everyone that she'd forgotten hers), and saying good-bye to them. There was a lot of kissing, and Cleveland was telling them that he would come to Philadelphia in the spring. He gave her a special look: they had a secret now, didn't they?

Now, with her cheek pressed against the cold glass, she tried to remember him exactly. James was reading her *New Yorker*. The No Smoking sign above them was still lit. She reached into her blazer pocket and found her cigarettes. She fondled them with her hand, thinking of Cleveland, not taking the pack out of her pocket. Cleveland had been smoking in the bar. Turkish cigarettes, with an ivory holder. She reached into the other pocket and dislodged a Life Saver: tangerine. She did not offer one to James. She wondered whether he would come back with her when they landed. He'd told her already that he was embarrassed to be seen going into the building, past the nosy desk-lady who made him sign in and out. (For reasons of security all males entering the building had to do this.) Maybe he would just go back to his hotel and that would be that. She wouldn't go with him because she had school tomorrow, she had to get ready. She had to check to see if there were any messages for her at the desk; her parents might have called. No, she couldn't go home with him tonight. And when they went in different directions, what would happen to them then? Would he call her again, and how soon? She remembered for a painful second that he was her only connection to Cleveland.

Chapter 5

I It was the day before his first Chattarjee recital and
outside everything smelled like fresh thawed mud: soon it would
be spring and baseball season was not far away. Already in the
drugstores and at the 7-Eleven checkout there was a new line of
baseball cards: this season's. Gabriel had forgotten his catcher's
mitt on the porch all winter, so it had frozen and unfrozen with
the weather and was understandably a little stiff.

Mom was in New York all day until late tonight and he had
promised her that he would start practicing the minute he came
home from school and only stop when Toby came over to give him
dinner. Toby had promised pizza. After that he was supposed to
practice until bedtime, which was very early, ten. He was supposed to be well rested and alert for the concert. But who could
have known that the temperature was going to rise to fifty-four
this afternoon when it had been in the thirties all week long? The
last pieces of dirty gray ice had disappeared from the curb and
washed themselves right up against the leafy clogged gutters.
Gabriel had leapt over these puddles on his way home from the
bus stop, and then when he got almost to his front door, he'd seen
that Steven and Selby were waiting for him on their front porch
with their ball and bat. Could it hurt to play for just a little while?

Steven and his sister Selby lived next door. They were black and
they were twins and went to the Catholic school down the street

from Wolfe School. Wolfe School kids didn't talk to Saint Joseph Academy kids, because they were queer and they wore uniforms. Saint Joseph kids said Wolfe School kids were snobs. Gabriel didn't play with Steven and Selby Watkins much in the winter, except when it snowed enough for a school holiday and they all went sledding. But all spring and summer and during the fall when it was warm enough they played baseball. Steven and Selby were a year younger than Gabriel, but they were taller than he was and Selby was tallest. She was also the fastest pitcher he had ever met of kids their age. All three of them were on the neighborhood Little League team and Selby was one of the stars. Gabriel was also on the Wolfe School junior-varsity team, but there he didn't get to play his favorite position, which was catcher. Last Christmas Toby had given him a complete set of catcher's equipment, all brand-new. Before he'd only had a mitt. He had tried everything on in front of the long mirror in his mom's room many times during the winter, but today was his first chance to use it all outside.

So when he saw Steven and Selby waiting there for him, already changed out of their school uniforms, sitting on their porch with their bat and balls and arguing with each other over a certain Pete Rose card, Gabriel could hardly say no. He thought of his new equipment, still in the bag from the sporting-goods store, lying there under his bed, never used before, and he thought of how warm it was out. On the bus he'd taken off his snow jacket and stuffed it into his schoolbag. It was warm enough for just his blazer. He told the twins to wait for him right there, he'd be out in a minute. He let himself in with the key he kept on a string around his neck and dumped his books all over the hallway. Upstairs he was out of his school clothes and into his jeans fast. Everything landed on the floor. He could hang them up later. He put on the catcher's things and stopped only long enough to admire them in his mom's mirror. Out back Steven and Selby were already deciding where to put the bases, arguing about which bald patch in the lawn had been first base last summer.

As usual they started this way: Selby pitching, Steven hitting, and Gabriel catching. They had a rule among them that the batter was allowed five strikes for every out and five outs before they switched. That way it took a little longer before they had to switch positions. Usually nobody but Gabriel wanted to be catcher: the Watkins kids just liked to pitch and bat, but today Gabriel knew that they were dying to use his new catcher equipment. He also knew that if he made up some excuse, like his mom said for them not to, that they would just get mad and go inside. So when Steven struck out (screaming that Selby had cheated) and his time at bat was up, Gabriel had to unfasten everything and let him wear it.

The ground was soft and when Gabriel hit the ball way off into the bushes in the Weiss's yard and slid home, he got mud all over himself, even in his socks. It was getting dark out and Toby would be coming over soon with the takeout pizza. Steven couldn't find the ball in the bushes and Selby called him a moron. Steven shoved her and Selby punched him on the arm. Steven went inside to tell on her to his mom, and Gabriel and Selby looked for the ball in the bushes. They found a broken water-pistol and a dirty, naked, chocolate-colored doll with no hair and no legs that used to belong to Selby, but no ball. Mrs. Watkins was at their back door calling for Selby to come inside right this minute. Steven was standing behind her, staring at them, picking his nose.

"I bet he told on you," said Gabriel.

"He's such a retard," said Selby, putting the accent on the first syllable of *retard* the way everyone in the neighborhood did. She stomped up the steps to her back porch, and the Watkins family went inside. Gabriel, too, went inside. It was almost sunset and before he noticed what he was doing he tracked mud all over the kitchen floor. He took off his sneakers and ran downstairs to the laundry room. He threw everything, his clothes, his sneakers, socks, mask, mitt, pads, everything into a laundry basket and ran upstairs in his underwear. He still had mud on his arms and legs, but there was no time to take a bath. He washed up a little at the sink and now there were dirty puddles all over the bathroom. Just as he was squirming into a big clean sweat-shirt he heard Toby letting himself in with his key. Gabriel pulled on his school pants and a pair of sweat socks and ran downstairs.

Toby brought two cans of beer for himself and a can of Mountain Dew for Gabriel. They had pepperoni pizza with extra cheese and they split a bag of Fritos. For dessert they each had one of the orange Popsicles that Gabriel's mom had put in the freezer for them. They watched part of a 76ers game on the living-room TV, which Toby had carried into the kitchen just for this reason. But after they finished eating, Toby made Gabriel turn off the TV and take out his flute. Gabriel wondered if Toby could tell that he hadn't been practicing that afternoon, but Toby didn't say anything about it.

Gabriel first went through the scales and exercises, which took more than half an hour, now that he was with Mr. Chattarjee. He couldn't skip scales or fake études like he had sometimes done with Samantha; Mr. Chattarjee could somehow always tell how much he had practiced each part of the lesson and how much attention he had paid to everything.

Midway through the harmonic minors he heard Toby going outside. Was he leaving? No, he wouldn't go without saying goodbye. He heard a car door slam and then Toby was back inside the house, his footsteps going toward the kitchen. *Clack-clack.* What was that? Oh, Toby must have brought his typewriter. He was planning to stay the whole evening until Gabriel's mom got back from New York.

Gabriel had been with Mr. Chattarjee for nearly five months now. The lessons with him were very different from the ones with Samantha or with his piano teachers before her. He'd had so many piano teachers, four of them, from the time he was five till when he switched to flute last year. He'd started piano with Mr. Gordon, who'd taught all the music at the Wolfe School when Gabriel was little, before Mr. Gordon got married and went away and Miss Hahn took over. But he'd only taken lessons with her for a month before his mom realized that he needed someone better. So then it was Mrs. Godunov at the Germantown School, the tiny hunchbacked woman who reminded Gabriel of a witch and who'd hit him on the knuckles with her pointing baton whenever he made a mistake. Sometimes in her heavy accent, which Gabriel could not always understand, she called him a stupid, stupid boy, and she often told him about her girlhood in Vienna when children had taken lessons three times a week and had practiced each night for hours. Gabriel was afraid of Mrs. Godunov and hated to go to lessons or to practice. One Saturday morning he'd come out of his lesson crying, with sore knuckles, and his mom found him a new teacher the next week. Pale thin Miss McElroy had been Elise's first teacher. With her, Gabriel, who was six by then, first began to love music. He knew that he could never be as good as Elise, who played whole Beethoven sonatas and Chopin waltzes, but he learned his Clementi sonatinas and his scales and his Hanon exercises perfectly, and Miss McElroy would sigh and smile at him and say how much he reminded her of his sister. Gabriel knew that Miss McElroy missed Elise, who was now studying with a famous pianist who taught at Curtis.

"Your sister was my first prodigy," she would tell him, "and if you keep practicing like this you may be my second." Then she would sigh again and they would both know that if Gabriel became very good his mom would find him a famous teacher, too. When Gabriel was eight Miss McElroy died, no one would tell him how, and he and Elise and his mom, and Dad, who was just moving out of the house with the Steinway, all went to the funeral. There was no one else there but Miss McElroy's mother, who was crying, and her brother who'd flown in from California and was not crying, and two other students and their mothers, and a woman, whom no one else knew, with short gray hair, red lipstick, a red dress, and men's shoes. Gabriel remembered her red dress and lipstick and how his mother had said it was inappropriate for a funeral. Last year Gabriel had asked Toby, who'd never even met Miss McElroy, but knew her story, and Toby'd told him that she had one morning taken too many pills, enough to fall asleep for a long time and never wake up, in other words, die.

Gabriel had studied for two years after that with Elise's teacher, Mr. Grainger, who was related to the composer Percy Grainger, and who had played with famous orchestras all over the world. Elise was four years older than Gabriel, and she was as near to perfect as he could imagine anyone would ever be, except when she was mean to him and wouldn't let him into her room when her friends were over, or when she was grouchy when she first woke up, or when she always made him play shortstop because he was so small he could hardly pitch or catch anything. But she had beautiful hair, which was red like their mom's and long, and she was the smartest girl in her class, and she played the piano so well that sometimes when she was practicing and guests were in the house they thought they were listening to a record of Rubinstein. Mr. Grainger wanted Elise to leave high school and go to Curtis full-time, and Mom was beginning to think this might be a good idea. But then a teacher from New York, from Juilliard, had heard Elise playing at a recital and he had offered to be her teacher there. Mom had thought about this for a while and she and Elise had had many quiet talks discussing what they should do.

Finally it was decided: Mom and Elise went up to New York every Wednesday for a lesson, and next year Elise would enroll in Juilliard full-time. They might even have to move to New York, or otherwise Elise would have to live up there with Aunt Jane, Dad's sister, who had an apartment near Lincoln Center. Wednesday nights Gabriel ate dinner with Toby, who was Mom's boyfriend by then. Gabriel still had his Saturday-morning lessons with Mr. Grainger, who he was afraid might be mad at them for taking Elise away to New York. Gabriel knew he was no replacement for Elise. Mr. Grainger never suggested that *he* should leave the Wolfe School and go to Curtis full-time. Mom never mentioned this, either, and by then she was spending all her time talking about New York, worrying about New York, wondering if Elise should have an even better teacher, wondering if Elise should be starting a career soon, maybe get an agent. Meanwhile Gabriel learned all his music by heart. If he could never be as wonderful a pianist as Elise was, at least he would do something she couldn't: it was easy for him to memorize music. He learned everything in all the books that they kept inside the piano bench.

On Saturdays when Gabriel had his piano lesson Elise had her riding lesson. She was at the age, fourteen, when all girls love horses and want to own one. Dad refused to pay for a horse of her own but he did let her have the lessons and he said if she got to be a good, responsible rider then maybe, when she was sixteen, he would buy her a horse. Mom didn't like her to be so horse-crazy when she should be practicing, but she let her go anyway, saying that Elise needed her exercise, plus, if she didn't learn to ride now when she had the opportunity, she might never do it. So on Saturdays Dad came by and drove her to the stables and Gabriel and Mom went to Mr. Grainger's house for a lesson. Sometimes Mom sat in on the lesson and sometimes she waited in the living room reading magazines.

One Saturday morning Gabriel was playing the Liszt piece that Mr. Grainger said was too hard for him but that he'd begged and begged to play because Elise did it so wonderfully, but he was struggling through, trying to make his fingers do the same work that Elise's did so easily. The phone rang and Mr. Grainger got up to answer it. It was Gabriel's dad, and he was at a hospital. Elise had hurt herself falling off a horse, and they should leave the lesson immediately.

Actually, Elise was dead. She had died instantly, but Gabriel's dad hadn't wanted to tell them that over the phone. She had been riding along, looking the wrong way, and she'd struck her head on a tree branch. By the time she slid off the horse to the ground she had already stopped breathing. She had broken her neck. Just like that she was dead. Gabriel remembered that on that morning she had called him a retard and chased him out of her room and later he had snuck in and put a fake hairy spider the size of his fist under her pillow. Dad went home with him and Mom that afternoon and the three of them sat together on the sofa hugging each other and crying. At night after Dad left and Toby and Mom were talking softly in the kitchen, Gabriel had gone to Elise's room and taken his spider out of her bed. He put the spider on the top shelf of his room and didn't touch it again till the summer.

That was Gabriel's last piano lesson. He'd always thought of the Steinway as really belonging to Elise, and he could not bring himself to play it. He'd thought his mom would be mad when he told her he didn't want to play the piano anymore, but she'd only said, "Fine, I understand. We'll find you another instrument." For a month Gabriel had no instrument, and he wondered which one he would learn to play. He liked the shape of the tuba and the sound of the oboe. His mom was trying to talk him into violin. They went together to student recitals at Curtis, where his mom was on the Board of Trustees, and Gabriel heard organs, violas, trumpets, cellos . . . and a flute. It was a rainy Monday night and they almost didn't go to that recital because the car was having trouble starting: stalling every few blocks on the way up. The flute piece was the second on the program, which was lucky, because they were late enough to have missed the first piece. It was a girl playing. Her first student recital — she was fifteen, which was how old Elise would have turned on her next birthday. The girl had a long black braid down her back and tiny pearl earrings, just like a pair Elise had. She was nervous. Her fingers trembled before she started to play and she didn't look at the audience at all, even when she finished. Gabriel's mom told him later that she was not even very good. But from the minute she started to play Gabriel knew, instinctively and more certainly than he'd ever known anything, that this was his instrument. The sound made him shiver. He'd heard flutes before, but always on the radio or in the middle of orchestras. He'd never listened to one like this. The music was like a human voice. It touched him somewhere in the back of his head. When he told his mom on the way out of the recital he expected her to argue with him, try to promote the violin instead. But she only said, "Yes, I know. I could see it in your eyes." The next week they bought him a flute (his dad had to pay for it), a nice Italian one with open holes. Silver-plated. ("When you get good we'll buy you a sterling silver one.") After that the Steinway was used only for tuning.

Gabriel did not realize how quickly he learned flute technique: he had no one to gauge himself against, and Samantha was not one for giving compliments to children. He knew something was odd when Samantha kept talking to his mother for as long as half an hour after each lesson. They spoke in low whispers while Gabriel and her next student, a fat high-school girl whose name he didn't know, waited outside the room, on the wooden music-school waiting bench. His mom wouldn't tell him what Samantha said in those talks other than, "She's happy with your progress," or "She thinks you're a really bright boy." And then one day they got in the car and his mom said, "Samantha thinks it's time you found another teacher." Gabriel's heart sank. He'd thought that Samantha liked him. He'd thought that he was practicing well enough. But when he looked at his mother he saw that she was smiling at him.

"Gabriel, you've gotten so good she doesn't think she can teach you any more."

Gabriel thought of this whenever he was frustrated with his practicing, whenever he was in a rut, making the same mistakes over and over, not getting anywhere. It was a good cure for little problems like that. It made him think he could do anything.

As Gabriel was running through the Vivaldi, he heard Toby's clack-clack stop in the kitchen. The television was on for a minute, then Toby switched if off and groaned loudly.

"The Sixers are getting creamed," he reported. Gabriel groaned too, and continued playing. Soon the clack-clack started again.

Everything about the flute was right. For example, it fit in his hand so naturally, like it was an extension of his body. He could think on the flute — he could think right *into* it, and his thoughts would come out in music, something he had never done on the piano. On the piano he'd felt cramped and uneasy, but on the flute he was always comfortable. Is this the way it was for Elise when she played the piano? Had it been like this for her? Or what if she'd been given a flute? Would she have been like Gabriel had been on the piano, or would she be like Gabriel on the flute, but better, ten times better, because she was so much better than he was in every way?

Or Mom, look at Mom, she couldn't play anything but she could dance and she had long thin hard muscles in her legs. When he was very little he used to go with her to her dance class and watch her (she was better than anyone there, even the teacher) and think that he would want to lift his legs so high and fly so quickly around the room someday. But she had never let Elise or him take dance lessons. She said the whole dance world was bad for children . . . but what if they had? The might have become real dancers, like in the Pennsylvania Ballet that Mom used to belong to. They might have danced as well as Elise played the piano or Gabriel played the flute. Or his dancing might have been as bad as his soccer game, who knows? Mom never let them find out, not even when Elise begged for ballet lessons, when she was nine and everyone was taking them. Gabriel's dad had once said to Mom, "No son of mine is ever going to study ballet." He said that just because Gabriel had said he might like to — his mom had just taken them to see Baryshnikov. This made Gabriel want to learn even more, but Mom just said no. No. Children should not have to go through that. No. Go through what?

Mom was in New York tonight and she would be home after Gabriel was already in bed. She was up there meeting with managers from three different agencies, trying to decide which one would be best for Gabriel, and if he should have one at all. Mr. Chattarjee had said he shouldn't turn professional for another eight or ten years. Toby was dead against it too, and Dad said it was ridiculous for eleven-year-olds to have professions. But Mom wasn't sure, and she'd had some offers from agents. She said they were very impressed that Mr. Chattarjee was teaching Gabriel and by Gabriel's demonstration tape, which she had played for them. He might even have to go up to New York to audition later on.

At ten to ten Toby came down and told him it was time for bed. Gabriel ran through the last passage two, three times more, just to make certain he had it. He did have it. It was his, it was even part of his memory now. He undid his flute and, in honor of the recital tomorrow, wiped it out carefully.

Toby had tossed crumpled paper balls all over the kitchen floor, and the table had a fine cover of eraser crumbs. His hair was all messy — as though he'd just woken up, and his sleeves were rolled up to his biceps. Gabriel followed him into the kitchen and Toby sat down and began typing at once, not even looking up to notice Gabriel taking a pitcher of Kool-Aid out of the refrigerator. He poured himself a large glass and put it on a tray, with a napkin and six peanut-butter cookies. This he carried carefully.

"Good night," he called on his way out.

"Mmmmf," said Toby, who did not stop typing.

Gabriel put the tray down on his desk, careful not to knock off any of the baseball cards. He liked carrying things on trays instead of in his hands. It was something his dad used to do. Now his mom got furious if she ever saw him taking food into his room, let alone on a tray. Today was a good opportunity because Toby was here and he never minded this kind of thing. Gabriel just had to remember to take the tray downstairs sometime before his mom saw it. He searched through his desk drawer for matches and lit his candle. That was another thing he couldn't do when Mom was around: light matches. She was always afraid of him catching the curtains on fire. He thought of putting his Beatles album on his little record player, but no, Toby would hear that and know he wasn't asleep, and besides, he already had the last page of the Vivaldi repeating in his mind: it was much more beautiful than "While My Guitar Gently Weeps," and he wanted to keep it there.

Gabriel had a special felt-tip Magic Marker pen that wrote skinny if you held it one way and fat if you held it the other. Toby had shown him how to work it so that the lines of letters were fat on the way down and thin on the way up, just like ancient Roman lettering carved in stone. He was using this pen to write his name in the front of all his books.

He'd seen it in the library in his father's new house. All the books said in the front of them, in nice black ink, Ex Libris Maxwell Van Allen, except for a few that said *Sylvia Fish* in blue or green and after the word *Fish* there was written, in black ink, *Van Allen*. That was Dad's new wife. He was allowed to call her by her first name, Sylvie. Mom called her Silverfish behind her back.

Gabriel was sipping his Kool-Aid and writing his name carefully. It was his project to write his name in all his books, eventually. He did ten books a night, every night before bed.

Some of his books had been Elise's. He'd taken them for himself the day he and Mom had cleared out her room. He'd kept her paperback Bible, her dictionary, her catalogue of Northeast American rocks, her horse books, and anything else that could be a boy's book. He'd let Mom give away all the books with pictures of teen-aged girls on the cover. They'd also given away all her clothes, except the T-shirts and sweat shirts, which Gabriel had kept; and all her things: old toys, dolls, funny hats. Gabriel had kept her records, her baseball cards, and her rock collection. They'd sold her riding equipment. Her stacks and stacks of piano music were in the closet of her bedroom, which was now a combination guest room–television room–Mom's sewing room. For a while they'd felt funny using the room, Mom and Gabriel had both cried when they went in there, but Toby had helped them paint it a different color, white instead of blue, and Mom had sewn new curtains. They changed around the furniture, took out her chest of drawers, put in a sofa and a TV, and soon it was a different place, not like Elise at all. Mom had suggested that it would be a good quiet room for Gabriel to practice in, but no, somehow he never did get used to it. He preferred to do his playing downstairs, in the music room, next to the Steinway.

He finished the last book. It was Elise's old copy of *Gulliver's Travels*, which she was supposed to be reading in her English class in high school the year she died. Gabriel had read it last year: he'd thought it was so funny that he'd read it again. He aways read his favorite books twice. Houyhnhnm, he thought. Whinny, whinny. If Elise had had the time to read the book, she'd have loved it. She loved all jokes that had to do with horses.

Thinking about Elise made him a little sad. He decided to go to sleep. It was a quarter to eleven and Mom might be coming home soon. Where should he hide the tray and the empty glass? Under his bed. He kicked his baseball cards under there, too. His school clothes were still on the floor. These he carried into the bathroom and stuffed into the hamper. As he got into his pajamas he noticed that his leg was still muddy from the slide home in the afternoon. He scraped some of the dry mud off with his fingernail. Too late for taking a shower. Oh well, maybe Mom would be changing the sheets on his bed tomorrow anyway. He remembered to brush his teeth, and then surrounded himself in bed with his four teddies.

Downstairs, Toby was starting the paragraph again for the fourth time. When the sound of Elizabeth's car appeared in the driveway, he waited for the predictable click of her heels and the sound of her key in the lock. What would her mood be? He braced himself. In the doorway, under the bright bulb of the Japanese ceiling lamp, she was taking off her gloves. Her hair was very red. She looked up at Toby as he came through the kitchen door. She was smiling.

A minute later they were in the kitchen fixing coffee and she was talking excitedly, can of ground coffee in one hand, percolator in the other. He closed his arms around her waist and squeezed. He found with his tongue the little corner where her earlobe joined her jaw, right in back of her earring stud; he bit gently her earlobe. She struggled away from him, busy with coffee things. She was telling him that she'd done it: she hadn't gotten an agent for Gabriel, but she'd found the next best thing, a publicist. She'd signed the papers. It was done, finally. This woman knew everyone, even the agent for James Rosen. She knew Lawrence Chattarjee personally, and that had probably helped, but she also knew several agents who just happened to be looking for a prodigy, maybe a pianist or violinist, but flute was fine, different, something she knew could probably sell. What luck on their part! She knew an agent whose last prodigy, a pianist, was eighteen now, still a wunderkind, but too old to be cute. It was time for another one. That agent had tried again last year, with a girl cellist, but it hadn't worked out. The girl had been unstable.

"Wait a minute," Toby interrupted. "What kind of papers did you sign?"

"Oh, nothing long-term," said Elizabeth. "Don't look at me like that. When it comes to Gabriel I'm very cautious. I know what I'm doing. All I promised is that we'd pay her to 'package' Gabriel for one year and that we would pay her a regular monthly fee of two hundred dollars till Gabriel gets an agent, plus printing costs for publicity materials. Max'll take care of the money, I'll make sure of that. And when the year's up we'll reassess the situation and see if we want to continue with her. It's a good firm, Toby, I checked it out. They've gotten agents for some pretty important names." The coffee was ready. Toby got out the mugs, and the sugar for himself.

"Where's my good wooden tray?" said Elizabeth. "Oh, never mind" — she got out a plastic one — "this'll do."

They carried everything into the living room: coffee and peanut-butter cookies (there was nothing else to eat in the house, except Fritos and cold pizza).

Sitting there on the sofa, they saw the sleepy figure of a little boy taking himself to the bathroom. He emerged for a second into the hallway light and disappeared behind the closed door — running water, the sound of flushing.

"Oh, let's tell him!" said Elizabeth. "He's half awake anyway — let's bring him down here."

"How do you think he's going to feel about all this? Have you ever asked him if he *wants* a manager?"

"Toby, he's a *child*. Don't make me mad. Let's not get into that. Come on, let's get him down here." The bathroom door opened and she called his name. He stood in the hallway, surrounded by light, squinting.

"Mom?"

"Come downstairs, we have something to tell you." Gabriel came down, his legs still shaky from his half-dream. His pajama bottoms were on backwards, inside-out; the little slit was on the wrong side, the tag at his waist. He was slipperless on the cool wood floor. He climbed onto the sofa between them. His mom took a bite from a peanut-butter cookie. She never ate stuff like that. What was going on?

Elizabeth pushed Gabriel's curls out of his eyes. He should have had a haircut before tomorrow's recital, she knew, but she could hardly bear to have it trimmed; it was so curly and perfect.

"We're celebrating, Gabriel," she said. "Today I found a woman who might be able to get you an agent."

"Oh," said Gabriel. "Good." An agent was something he needed, he knew, if he was going to be able to play for real audiences and with orchestras.

"Aren't you happy, honey?" said Mom. "Oh, this could be the best thing I've done all year."

"Yesss," said Gabriel, concentrating on drawing out the *ssss* sound. He thought for a second of his recital tomorrow, and his stomach felt tight.

"You should go back to bed," said Toby. "Tomorrow's a big day."

"Can I have a cookie?"

"Not after you've brushed your teeth," said Mom.

"Climb on my back," said Toby. "Come on, I'll give you a ride."

"Up the wooden hill, up the wooden hill," sang Toby slowly, thumping up the steps.

Elizabeth wandered into the kitchen and began picking up the scattered paper balls. What was Toby working on tonight? She unraveled one:

Michael spent his afternoons in the company of his grandmother, who was deaf, anyway, so he often took his cello upstairs, past her, into his locked bedroom, where he cautiously lowered himself out his window and scampered off to play baseball until it was almost dark, the approximate returning time of his father, and he had just enough time to climb back up the trellis, comb his hair, and find himself some easy spot right in middle of a Haydn concerto. His father would soon come by, knocking on the door, praising him for his hard work.

That was all that was on the page. Elizabeth dropped it into the trash.

II   Mary March was alone. The Sibelius record ended and she wouldn't be able to change it until she was finished with these prints. No matter, silence was nice, too. She hummed the last few measures to herself. Her darkroom was the kitchen — with the right shades and lightproof curtains she'd been able to engineer it, the perfect workspace with running water and lots of counters.

The only drawback was that there was no music in the room — she'd had a good Sony radio, but she'd discovered that the light from the dial was affecting her prints. With the stereo in the next room, she couldn't switch radio stations or change records. When she got frustrated with this she'd just remind herself of all the years she'd been bombarded ceaselessly by noise, never a moment of quiet, not even when she was sleeping, not with Dick snoring all night long every single night for thirty years. There'd been babies crying and children screaming and laughing and shouting, fighting, yelling for her attention, yelling for her to come, dogs barking, cats crying like children, television commercials, telephones ringing, rock 'n' roll records, Toby's Beatles, Joan's piano lessons, Allison's Rolling Stones, Grateful Dead, Blood, Sweat, Tears, Earth, Wind, Fire, Arlo Guthrie, what else? Ben's electric guitar, God, that was loud, alarm clocks, motorcycles pulling into the drive at three A.M., Toby's typewriter clacking away till sunrise, Joan's Irish country folk music, Allison's screaming shouting bad trip, sirens, Dick screaming shouting, Ben screaming shouting, slamming doors, stomping feet, telephones ringing, splinters of glass, and dogs barking. God, she could hear it all over again in her head! Just to think about all that noise, all those migraines she'd fought off with aspirin and Valium, God, Dr. Schultz had given her that stuff and she'd taken it for so long without even knowing, God, the numbness and the pain, and the noise. So that was all over now for her, and she cultivated silence — she liked to think of it like that — she cultivated silence, like the plants, like a taste for good wine, which of course she could never have developed while she was married to Dick. She sighed happily. It was nine o'clock in the morning and *no one* was going to disturb her, make her stop what she was doing. It had taken her so long to get used to the luxury of living like this, she'd been so jittery with the knowledge that she could have whole days to herself, doing what she wanted to do, it didn't seem right, she was cheating someone, she kept imagining, *I should be somewhere else*, it's wrong for me to be doing this. But no, this was her whole day. Hers. And she wasn't going to waste a second.

She pressed the blank paper into the tub of developer. At the Franklin Institute, where she'd taken a course in technique, they'd taught her to use tongs, but she didn't mind putting her hands into the chemicals, she liked it, she got better control this way, could get the paper out more efficiently, it seemed, besides, she liked getting her hands into what she was doing. First it was a pattern, background and subject appearing simultaneously, faintly, a pattern of trees and the pale, now darker, darker, figure of the black woman, enormously pregnant, in a cheap, torn, hugely patterned shift. Swollen bare feet. The woman was smiling, talking, teeth missing, at someone in back of the photographer. She had sparse, wind-tossed, nappy hair.

Mary bit her lip with excitement. This one had turned out as she'd wanted it: compositionally it was interesting, but most important she'd captured the spirit of the woman. She'd try a few different exposures, she thought, sticking it into the stop bath, then turn the lights on and look it over. Oh! she was so happy!

She'd taken the photo yesterday in Fairmount Park. The woman was part of a black family picnic, the kind where there are hundreds of people, ranging from shriveled oldsters to babies, and hampers and hampers of fried chicken, potato salad, ribs, corn bread, cake, watermelon, Pepsi, beer, everything. She'd photographed whole families, groups of children, the oldest grandmother holding the youngest baby, some athletic-looking teenage boys, some little girls holding little black dolls. They had all wanted their pictures taken — they thought she was from some magazine or newspaper — and she'd gotten their names and addresses in case she needed them to sign release forms. She'd been printing from the negatives all morning, but this was the best so far. Probably the best work she could do. This should be able to at least place in a contest. Or sell to a good magazine. Her heart beat fast and happy.

The phone rang, smashing her cocoon of silence. Her print was safe in the stop bath. She covered up the package of paper and reached her arm out through the curtain, pulling the receiver into the darkroom with her. It was Toby.

"Hi, Mom, I'm at the paper. I can't talk long 'cause I have a deadline, but this is important. Remember when I told you I knew the photo day-editor to say hello to, but not much more? Well, last week I took Gabriel over to a soccer game and it turns out his kid's on the opposing team, and we both stayed to watch, we were cheering on opposite sides, but we got into a conversation and I managed to work in that you do these human-interest-human-condition photos and he said if you'd like him to see your portfolio you should bring it down and tell him who you are, and he gave me his home number here, let's see, what did I do with it, so if you don't reach him at the office, here it is, Victor 7-9914, his name's Charlie McCoy, did you write that down? Good. I've got to go, but I thought you might want to give him a ring really soon, he has a rep for being a little absentminded . . ."

Mary told her son about the pictures she'd taken yesterday, how well they were turning out, how she'd had the presence of mind to get her subjects names and addresses.

"Great, sounds like you're doing just great — well, I have to get this thing handed in by noon —"

"Toby?"

"Mmm hmmm?"

"Which team won?"

"What? Oh, the other guys. Gabriel's team lost, always do, it seems. He's a mean little kicker, though."

Families, strange things, at least hers had been. Had that black family, what was their name — most of them were Washingtons, some had names like Stoner and Teak — had they had the same battles, fights, alliances? Why were Toby and Joan such good friends, ever since they were little, ever since Joan was born and Toby had been so happy for a little sister, but Joan and Allison, just four years apart, were from different planets, practically, well no one had spoken to Allison for years, not since she moved to California when she was just nineteen, and that was the end of her, maybe she talked to her father but not to them, maybe Ben heard from her, but he wasn't telling, and Toby and Joan had such cool disregard for Ben, talking about his lack of discipline behind his back and probably jealous of his good looks, but they were right, he was lazy, they hadn't been able to make him go to college even though Dick was supposed to pay for it, it was in the agreement: Allison's and Ben's tuitions, what a waste since neither of them had gone, Allison all high on drugs somewhere and Ben claiming to be an Artist with a capital A, you had to smile when you thought of it, you really did. He'd been there for a year now, in Chicago, but he called so regularly, not like Allison, you didn't have to wonder all the time if Ben was dead or alive, and of course she had this secret fantasy, what mother wouldn't, that Ben would move back to Philadelphia and go to a decent art school, there were so many in the city. He could live at home for free and Dick would pay for it, and he'd have the proper training he needed, because, what could you expect, his work *was* rather naive, but he was just a boy still, and he'd realize all this soon and he'd come home to discuss it, maybe that's what he'd discuss with her after Easter dinner. She loved Toby, she loved the girls, but she loved Ben the best and he knew it and she knew he wouldn't let her down. He'd come home, she was sure of it. He'd come home with all his energy and vibrance, and he'd fill up this empty house. Ben would.

III Lawrence has risen at six, as he had planned, and washed quickly. He'd set to work immediately on the chapter, knowing that Max would be sending someone over in the afternoon to pick it up. The copyeditor was rewriting everything so he didn't know why he was bothering. He knew his prose was clear enough — maybe a little old-fashioned, but it was correct and pleasant-sounding. Yet every chapter he sent in came back disfigured by thousands of red pencil markings. The typesetter's galleys would read like copy from *Time* magazine. They might as well print on the cover of the book, *The Life of William Kinkaid* by Lawrence Chattarjee *as told to* whatever her name was, that girl, the thin little free-lancer he'd been introduced to once when he visited the Press. She couldn't have been older than twenty-five and she was rewriting the entire book. Bah, it wasn't worth getting upset over. He was an historian, a scholar. He was no copywriter. If the Van Allen Press wanted to water down the language of his book so it would sell better, let them. Maybe the average musician would have problems understanding his style, though it did seem clear enough to him; but what mattered was the message behind what he was writing and that it remain unaltered by the copywriter's purge of jargon and polysyllables. Max was probably right: this was no monograph. It was for the reading public, so it should be readable. But why should he go to all the trouble of writing it if it was only going to be changed? He might as well give that girl his notes and let her put the book together.

Which, of course, was an exaggeration, he admitted. He was being grumpy because of the early hour. Really, she did a good job; she was careful not to damage any of his ideas when she corrected his language. She must be a bright girl to do that so well.

At seven-thirty the maid brought his breakfast. He had been working so hard he hadn't even heard her come in. She was putting a pot of tea and a plate of English muffins beside him on a standing tray. She asked if he wanted tomato juice or orange.

"Which would be easier for you?"

"Don't make no difference — whatever you like."

"Tomato, then." She was gone, shutting the door behind her. She wore a uniform to work every day, Monday through Friday, even though he'd never asked her to. Where did she get that uniform? Was there some kind of store that sold them? It seemed peculiar for someone not connected with an institution to wear one. The girl was terribly pleasant, enough so that he sometimes suspected her of being condescending. Nothing seemed to be too much trouble for her — she even ran his bathwater if he asked, and she got him all his meals and cleaned up after him. All he had to do was shop for the food and pay her on Friday afternoons. She even did his laundry.

She'd been with him for several months already and she seemed happy. Maybe she would stay for a while, which would be good. She

Last year he'd gone through five housekeepers in a row, one after another they had left him: one getting married, one getting divorced, one going back to nursing school, one leaving for no reason, one leaving because she never could get used to the sight of his hand.

Here she was, back with the tomato juice, in a tall glass, with a slice of lemon and flecks of pepper floating on the top: just the way he liked it.

"Thank you so much, dear." He always called her "dear." He was too embarrassed to admit to her that he couldn't remember her name. He had it written down on the flap of his checkbook so he could pay her each Friday without problem. From week to week, however, her name would slip through his memory. He was always tempted to call her Edna, but that had been the name of his last maid, the one who'd gone back to school. He knew that he'd always been tempted to call Edna "Adele," which was the name of one of the maids before her. It was so embarrassing getting their names wrong. Surely it must have insulted them each time he did it.

She was telling him that she was going to do the laundry now and that next Tuesday was her cousin's birthday and he was flying up from Atlanta so could she please have that day off. He told her of course, and if she wanted to take more than one day to be with her cousin then she should feel free.

"Fine," she said, "then I'll be gone Wednesday, too." He wondered vaguely if he would have to pay her for those days. What had he done in the past in such circumstances? He would have to ask someone if it was proper to pay your maid when she hadn't worked, if she had told you in advance.

She gathered up his pajamas and sheets from the still-unmade bed and left.

When he was little they'd had a maid, a little Indian girl named Sujita. His father had shipped her in from a village near his hometown in the Punjab. Sujita (why could he still remember *her* name?) must have been about sixteen when she came to live with them, but she'd seemed older, almost a grown-up. She was a peasant girl, from a low caste; his father had explained this all to him when his mother wasn't listening. His father told him that he must be kind to Sujita and obey her when his mother left her to watch after him, but never to be too friendly. Sujita had come to them with a huge suitcase filled with saris. For the first two years she dressed Indian every day, in spite of his mother's offers of her old clothing, or trips to stores. She wore enormous jingling silver earrings and on her forehead was a red Hindu dot. One of her eyes was crossed and Lawrence had never known which one to stare at when he was talking to her. She learned English slowly. Lawrence's mother could say nothing in Punjabi but "I love you," and Lawrence knew only the few useless words his father had taught him ("train" was pronounced something like *geddi*, "car" was what, *topi?*) Only his father could speak to the girl in her language and he had refused to, except when absolutely necessary. Sujita cleaned their house and did their wash. Lawrence's mother let her cook sometimes, but not too often — she was afraid Sujita would burn the kitchen down with the gas pilot since she wasn't used to American kitchen equipment. Also, Lawrence's mother hadn't liked curry enough to eat it every single day. Sujita had cried herself to sleep almost every night — Lawrence could hear her through the walls, since his room was next to hers. Finally she left them to go to England and marry an Indian street-sweeper she'd never met. Her father had arranged it with her huband's father, and Lawrence's father had lent her the money for the boat ticket, which, as far as Lawrence knew, she'd never paid back. That was the only maid they'd had. When she left, Lawrence's mother had to do all the housework along with her teaching. Again Lawrence spent his afternoons after school alone, waiting for his parents to come home. In a year his father was gone, and he and his mother moved to a smaller apartment, closer to the city. That was the year she bought him his first flute: he was eight.

"And now," he said aloud to himself, "I am forty-eight and I am writing a book that has nothing to do with any of that." Time to start thinking once again of William Kinkaid. He put down his tomato juice and resumed typing.

Lawrence was a fast typist, even though he was missing fingers on his left hand. In fact, he typed nearly sixty words a minute, not counting mistakes. That was pretty good for a man, apparently. Both Max and Freddy had told him they had a hard time finding secretaries who could type at all, unless offered outrageous salaries.

He could think far faster on the typewriter than he could in longhand. His left hand had only a middle finger, an index finger, and a thumb, but it wasn't so bad because the index finger controls more keys than any other finger on the typewriter. The ring finger and the pinky had their functions taken over by the remaining two hyperactive ones. It was no trouble at all. He hadn't known how to type before the accident, so this was the way he'd learned.

By ten he had finished the rough draft and was ready to settle into the rewrite. Really, he could give the girl the rough draft, for all the changes he knew she was going to make in it. But somehow he couldn't stand the thought of handing her something that wasn't finished sounding, at least to his own taste. He had also considered writing the whole thing in the copyeditor's style to begin with: why not save them the trouble? But he just wasn't able. His own language was precise and unalterable. It was part of him. And if his book wasn't to come out the way he'd written it, then it would have to be revised in this roundabout way, by someone else.

By noon he was finished with the second draft, which he proofread quickly. It didn't really matter if he'd made typographical errors — that girl would catch them right away. He wandered over to his stereo and selected a record James had cut only recently — it hadn't been released yet, but James had given him one of the promotional copies. It was the Khachaturian concerto he had played with the Chicago Symphony last fall. Neither Lawrence nor James was tremendously fond of that particular piece, but they agreed it did have its moments, especially the flute cadenza in the first movement, modified by James with Lawrence's help. It was precisely at this point that the intercom buzzed to tell him that the copyeditor was downstairs. He turned the volume down a bit and waited for her to come up.

She was followed out of the elevator by the maid with her laundry basket full of Lawrence's clean shirts, socks, and underpants. Since he could not remember either woman's name he did not introduce them, and felt bad.

"I'm Joan, from the Press," (so that was her name) said the girl in a nervous, defensive voice. Her eyes swept across the apartment, critically. She had never been there before.

"Yes, of course, come in, Joan, sit down," said Lawrence, stepping aside so she could pass. Joan remained planted in the doorway. She was standing stiff in her oversized parka, clutching a battered manila folder.

"That's okay, I'm just here to pick up the chapter." But Lawrence insisted that she stay for lunch, which the maid would be preparing in the kitchen right now. Joan, who must have been instructed to humor the Press's more distinguished authors, finally agreed, removing her huge army-green coat and draping it uncertainly over the piano bench. The coat slid to the floor, and Joan quickly picked it up.

"Yes, you can leave it there," said Lawrence, answering her nervous, questioning glance. She was wearing a black sweater, black boots, and faded blue-jeans. She must be a feminist or something, thought Lawrence.

Joan sat tense in her chair. Lawrence knew personally that the chair was quite relaxing, but every muscle in her body was rigid. Her shaggy brown bangs were hanging in her eyes, so he could not judge exactly her expression. Her jaw was motionless, clamped shut.

"Do you like classical music at all?" asked Lawrence. The second movement of the Khachaturian was ending.

"Oh, yes. Yes," said Joan. Lawrence felt a flood of guilt. This girl didn't want to be here and he had trapped her into having lunch with him. It was as though he'd caught a bird from outdoors and forced it into a cage. She'd only stayed to be polite, or because she thought she'd lose her job if she didn't. She probably had other things to do at this very minute — in fact, he was probably using up her precious lunch hour. She might have errands to run or someone to meet — a boyfriend or a woman friend.

"Really, Joan," he began, "I didn't mean to keep you . . ."

"No," she said, "it's fine. I was just going back to the Press anyway. I would have skipped lunch." She shook her head enough for her bangs to resettle, revealing her eyes, which were brown, and clear like a child's.

The maid came back into the room, this time wearing her kitchen apron over her uniform.

"This is Joan," said Lawrence, first smiling and then wincing because he could not complete the introduction. "What would you like to drink with lunch, Joan? We have spring water, tomato juice. Do you take wine? We could open a bottle."

"I'd just like coffee," said Joan, glancing carefully at the maid.

"Well, then fine!" said Lawrence, and the maid disappeared. "So, Joan," he continued, consciously repeating her name in order to memorize it, "what do you think of the book — no honestly, is my drivel boring you to death?"

"No, not at all — I'm interested in music and yours is the kind of book I like to edit, much more than the usual things we do at the Press. Right now I'm also working on a monograph about the architecture of Independence Hall, and a sort of demographical-statistical analysis of the records of achievement scores of Philadelphia schoolchildren from 1964 to 1974." She grinned. Her face was unusually soft for one so thin. Lawrence smiled back.

"How can you stand it?" he asked. Joan shrugged and laughed.

The maid arrived with turkey sandwiches, tea for Lawrence, and coffee for Joan.

"You could move to New York, get a publishing job there?"

"I don't think my husband would appreciate that."

"You're married?"

"I'm older than I look."

"What does your husband do?"

"He's a composer and a conductor."

"What orchestra?"

"No orchestra right now. He's a conductor on the Paoli Local."
Joan smiled once again. "But he really is a composer. He writes all the time."

"Has he had any success?"

"Not really. Well, sometimes a small chamber group will get together and play his stuff, or maybe a friend will give a recital of his music, but he hasn't had any real breaks."

"Why don't you get your Press to print his music?"

Joan laughed.

"I guess that's not the way it works," said Lawrence.

When lunch was finished and Joan was once again wrapped in her ugly coat, they shook hands (he had never once caught her glancing at his damaged hand).

"There's going to be a recital at Curtis tomorrow, a small one," he said. "It's a flutist, a little boy prodigy. Why don't you and your husband come if you're not busy. I'll leave your names at the door."

"Gabriel Van Allen?" said Joan.

"Yes, how did you know that? — oh, of course, he's Max's son. Your boss."

"Right," said Joan.

"I've been teaching the Van Allen boy for several months, you know."

"Right," said Joan.

"So will I see you at the recital?"

"Sure, okay. See you tomorrow."

"Odd girl," Lawrence remarked to the maid when the elevator doors closed behind her. But he was happy inside: he'd made a friend. It was two P.M., too late to do any writing. He decided to change into his sweat suit and go to the club.

Lawrence was a fair enough squash player: it was one of his passions. He'd picked it up sometime after the accident, during his rehabilitation. He liked the blank white room. He liked standing next to his opponent, not far out of speaking range, as on a tennis court. His club was exclusive enough: for one thing women had only been allowed to join since last year. Everyone there knew who he was — their token artist, a bit of an oddity, for they were mostly lawyers and brokers: rich sons of rich Philadelphia sons.

He was somewhere near the middle of the men's ladder, but it was a tough ladder, and he'd held his place there, give or take a few notches up or down for nearly ten years. A one-handed man was at no disadvantage in this game.

It was midafternoon and the club was at its empty stage: it never got crowded until about five when members dropped by after work. He hadn't scheduled a game and there was no one around in the locker room or the lounge to play with him, so he stripped down to his shorts and T-shirt and began a solitaire practice session.

Lawrence loved the whack-whack-whack sound of the volley. He did fifty fast hard forehands, fifty backhands. It was the sound, he knew, that was most satisfying, like the lovely sound of a sheet of paper, covered with words, as he pulled it from the typewriter. Like the clink of a teacup as he set it onto a saucer. Pleasure in the music *things* give us. Found sounds, he called them. Thump! He'd hit a bad one into the tin. He scurried after the ball.

Lawrence did a lot of his thinking when he played alone. It was in the squash court that he'd first been able to think — when he was finally alone, after the accident and the long rehabilitation that followed. It was excellent exercise; it gave him back so much of the physical grace he'd lost after spending four months in bed, weeks in traction, trapped and confined. After the therapist who'd taught him to play finally left him alone, he'd gone almost every day to the courts, alone at first, then forming friendships with other men who would volley with him, give him advice on his serve or his swing. At Oxford he'd played with his tutor, a nervous, heavy man who Lawrence would not have guessed would be able to handle the game — but he was one of the liveliest opponents he'd ever met. At the end of the first match they played, Lawrence had noted his puffing red face and heaving shoulders with concern, and found that likewise the tutor was staring worriedly at Lawrence's mangled hand (the scars were fresher, pinker then), and the pale white seam that ran up his leg and disappeared into his gym shorts. But, no, I'm fine, they had assured each other and they had remained partners for the length of Lawrence's stay in England. When he visited the tutor at his home he discovered in the man's record collection all of the albums, all fourteen that he'd ever cut. Much later, before Lawrence left to return to the U.S., the tutor confided that he and his wife had been following Lawrence's career for as long as he'd been prominent in the music world. They'd once written to Lawrence for an autograph (Lawrence could remember nothing of this), and not received one, but they'd forgiven him anyway: the creator of such sounds as Lawrence had put forth would always be forgiven. When news reached the college that Lawrence was coming to Oxford for an advanced degree, the tutor had clamored to be Lawrence's personal instructor, and since he had some influence with the president of the college, he'd been allowed the privilege.

But this was nothing new for Lawrence. Everywhere he went, even now, twenty-two years after the accident, he always ran into people who remembered him, who had followed his career and never forgotten. These were the people who still played his albums, the ones who still, today, wanted his signature for their scrapbooks (but didn't they sneak an embarrassed peek at his left hand, the one that supported the album cover, or old program book, or scrap of paper, as his right hand held the pen, making his signature?). Few people that he actually dealt with from day to day had any idea who he had been. His maids, for example, were generally unaware of music, and would never have known the name Lawrence Chattarjee, even if he'd been able to continue his career. He was thankful for that. All they knew was that he was some rich semi-cripple in his late middle-age, and they expected nothing from him but good humor and a weekly paycheck. He'd had a friend at Oxford, a Hindu chap, the son of a Brahman doctor from Bombay, who had seen Lawrence only in his racial context: the half-Indian American. For Arjit's benefit, Lawrence had pretended that his father had been a Hindu, not a Sikh, and though there was never any outright mention of caste between them, Lawrence, who'd never considered himself to be a true

Indian, and had never found himself affected by values other than those Western ones he'd grown up with, sometimes found himself uncomfortable under the Brahman's pure and priestly sneer.

Arjit had lived in England since he was eight, attending British public school and speaking the King's English. He'd gone back to India only for his holidays. He was a great drinker of whiskey and eater of beef, and his favorite pastime, he claimed, since the age of fourteen, was seducing British women, blonds only. Arjit was both fascinated and repelled by Lawrence's racial composition, by the hint of fairness in the hair at his temples and his odd smoke-blue eyes. Arjit was a medical student, unaware of and insensitive to music, and until he'd heard the rumor from someone else, he'd had no idea that Lawrence had once played the flute, or had been an internationally prominent concert artist. And once he learned this he'd seemed to forget it almost immediately: music to him was an impractical endeavor, suitable mostly for the entertainment of peasants. Arjit was a powerful and ruthless squash player, far above Lawrence's level in the sport. The few times they'd played, Arjit had been simultaneously merciless and bored, and Lawrence had felt strangely humiliated in front of him by his own pale, scarred, hairless, and suddenly graceless body. Arjit had clung to Lawrence, nonetheless, for a time, as a confidant and drinking companion. In spite of his impeccable British accent, his attendance at the best of public schools, his soccer playing, his squash, and his success with blond British women, Arjit always remained on the outside of the crowd he so desperately wanted to belong to: nothing could make him British, no amount of trying. He was destined always to be a Hindu, and he would always be inferior in the estimation of the boys he'd grown up with. He would never be fair and blue-eyed. He would never leave the periphery, he could never be one of them. And worst of all he was bound to return to his father's house, in Bombay, after he received his honours degree, leaving behind everything: the weather, the people, the pubs, the women, the lovely tea things, everything. This he could explain only to Lawrence, who in his ridiculous American accent would try to console him. He enjoyed being with Lawrence, the miscegenate, who would always be inferior to both the Britons and to Arjit himself. At least Arjit was pure, and at least, as a Brahman, he was on the most superior level of his own race. Lawrence was the freakish fusion of the Oriental and the Aryan, the same possibility that Arjit himself had spread, with his own semen, among the plethora of girlfriends that he boasted of to Lawrence. How odd that Lawrence existed, and what a coincidence to have met him.

Arjit had also thought it strange that Lawrence gave him no competition, or even friendly rivalry, in the conquest of the English nurses, students, and wives of professors. This he'd at first attributed to Lawrence's shyness and politeness, but soon it had become apparent that Lawrence was actually more interested in his studies and his friendships than in women. This was at first a source of relief, for Arjit secretly believed that in spite of Lawrence's frailness (it was barely over a year since his convalescence), that he was far more attractive than himself. Lawrence had the same Oriental facial charm: slanted eyes, high cheekbones, but with a mysterious and delicate occidental coloring . . . how would the women resist him if he tried? Then one day the peculiar rumor reached Arjit (and it came to him last, as always, though he tried so hard to keep on top of things): Lawrence's reputation in the United States had been, well . . . it was common knowledge over there that he'd been living for two years with a young boy, a flutist, who was only now about twenty years old, and with whom he still kept in close correspondence (the boy was beginning to have some success in the musical world in his own right) and it was this boy with whom he stayed when he went back to the U.S. on holiday. Shocking. And the rumor also had it that Lawrence's relationship with his tutor, with whom he also played a mediocre game of squash three times weekly, was more than just friendly. Amazing that Arjit had not suspected this himself. And the newest rumor was, to Arjit's horror (this was something he had happened to overhear when he was hidden behind some stacks in the medical library), that Arjit, the Hindu and infamous womanizer, had been spending an awful lot of time in the company of Lawrence Chattarjee . . . That, of course, was the end of their friendship. As far as Lawrence knew, Arjit never had listened to a single one of his recordings, nor had he known that Lawrence had soloed four years earlier with the London Symphony, the same orchestra that Arjit heard for the first time when he took a librarian's wife away for a weekend in London, the same month in which he suddenly refused to have anything to do with Lawrence.

Lawrence's friendship with his tutor, which was quite innocent, continued, and he spent many teas with him and his chubby young wife. He remained friendly with those who would have him and still frequented the regular pubs. James stopped by to visit him once, for a week, while on tour, and played a small, uncomfortable, impromptu recital in the college chapel at the request of the chaplain, a lover of the flute. Lawrence finished his degree quickly. He was too old, he decided, to live the life of a student, and flew home to a new job at Curtis. Back in Philadelphia he discovered that his apartment was empty. James had removed himself to his own luxury apartment, and who could blame him now that he was beginning to enjoy financial success? At first Lawrence had kept in contact with his old tutor, but over the years their correspondence had dwindled. Last week the yearly Christmas card he'd mailed them had been returned (it had taken five months to come back) marked: MOVED. NO FORWARDING ADDRESS.

Smash! Another one into the tin. Lawrence paused to catch his breath. Since he'd been back in this country his squash game had improved steadily. For one thing the regulations had changed: rackets were lighter now and balls were not as hard. But he had also had a lot of practice, a lot of solo afternoons on the court, banging forehand after backhand, and thinking.

He knew a left-handed man, a lawyer, a club member who played backwards, holding the racket in his left hand. To him the problems of the court were as if in a mirror when compared to Lawrence's perception. Everything that man did was in reverse, from the way he stood when he served, to how he scooped the ball out of the backhand corner, which to Lawrence, was the forehand corner. Alone in his bedroom Lawrence sometimes tried to hold his own racket backwards: he could barely grip the thing enough to hold onto it. But somehow when he closed his eyes his phantom fingers would appear and seem to take it firmly. He would raise the instrument slowly to his lips, gingerly, careful not to disrupt the fantasy, and then he would blow softly, releasing what he knew should be his crystal, perfect tone: A-natural, G-sharp, F-sharp, E . . . nothing. No, without the left hand, the right is useless. The only notes he would ever play were A, A-sharp, B, the C above middle C and a half-step higher, C-sharp. Useless. Ruined.

Half an hour had passed since Lawrence had entered the court, and he could hear other games beginning. Soon someone was bound to come along and ask him to volley or play a game. Of course this was a pleasant prospect: a little excitement in the afternoon, but it would force him to leave his thoughts behind and pay attention to the sport.

His mind was drifting along some interesting track: what was it? Ah, yes, he was thinking about the boy Gabriel Van Allen, his newest prodigy, the child who would be giving his first recital tomorrow. Lawrence had decided not to worry about this one: he was relaxed about the idea of performing, which was a good sign. Max had mentioned to him that the boy had been jittery before a performance at his own grammar school, but Lawrence did not trust Max's opinions about his own son: he seemed to know very little about him, even less than Lawrence, who'd known him for only five months. Max, apparently, hadn't been at the school recital anyway, he had learned it secondhand from one of his authors who'd been there for some reason, who knows; the whole story seemed suspiciously worthless in light of Max's seeming disinterest in his son. Lawrence had offered to put aside tickets for Max and his second wife, assuming that they'd want to attend, and Max had been surprised by the idea. But he'd said he'd come though he didn't know if Sylvia could make it. Lawrence wondered if Max was coming to please him, a sought-after author, or to see his little boy.

The boy's talent was immense, as was his technical prowess. He had a memory for music like a computer. Lawrence's first project was to break this down a little: make Gabriel slow his pace and concentrate on phrasing, on musicality. He was too young to be an artist yet, but he must learn to feel music like an emotion. Samantha Engs and the boy's mother had been pushing him to be a whiz kid, but what an incredibly wrong approach. The boy's mind was a mathematical maze: he could understand the music intellectually better than Lawrence himself sometimes. All of that could wait for much later: what Gabriel needed now was to play like a human.

"The flute, Gabriel," he'd told him, "can be the voice of mankind. *If* you use it properly." Gabriel himself had told him that when he'd first heard a flute he'd mistaken it for an instant to be a human voice. A person singing.

"Is that the way you play?" Lawrence had asked. Gabriel, smiling all the time, had shaken his head no.

So Lawrence had kept him on the same pieces for months, adding new repertoire only occasionally, just to keep him challenged. Apparently Samantha's method had been to give him a piece for three or four weeks, each week completely changing the tonguing and the phrasing so that he'd have to relearn it and, eventually, be able to play it four different ways. Fine for polishing his technique. Disastrous for his sense of musicality. Of course, he knew where Samantha had gotten that trick — he'd used it on her to help improve her sloppy reading habits, but she must have missed his point completely. Naturally, since she was neither insightful nor bright . . . but he shouldn't be too hard on the girl, since she had brought him Gabriel.

Gabriel's sound was as pure as a boy's choir. He had the tone of an angel, Angel Gabriel. This was dangerous, however, for his purity and abstraction were too cold. It was time to bring him some warmth before he was frozen for good.

Recitals were helpful for this purpose: Gabriel must learn to respond to an audience.

"You have to *talk* to them with your flute, and they're going to talk back, without using words. It's like that. Pay attention. Don't be overwhelmed by the music." Lawrence wondered if he understood. Gabriel said that he did. There was still time.

He had a fantasy about taking Gabriel to a squash court and teaching him to play. He knew the boy was interested in sports: his mother complained about this enough. He could understand the intellectual challenge of the game immediately; he could catch on to the physical part soon enough; but there was something about companionship, about statement and reply, that Lawrence would like to show him. Perhaps, at a later time.

"Excuse me!" a man was shouting above, on the observation level. Lawrence looked up. It was Ringhold Smith, the banker, his next scheduled opponent, wanting to know if they could play their match early, since they were both there and Lawrence had a court.

"Of course!" exclaimed Lawrence, but feeling a twinge of disappointment as he waited for Ringhold to appear at the door.

Lawrence lost the match, but it was a close one and he consoled himself by knowing that he had been at a disadvantage since he'd tired himself out by playing alone for fifty-five minutes before Ringhold had arrived. Alone in the sauna, stretched out on the dry boards, he lapsed again into his daydream: Gabriel's performance tomorrow. A student's recital would not usually be the object of his thoughts for so long, but this was different. It was the first movement, the starting point of an artist's career, an artist that Lawrence would mold himself: one artist sculpting another. As he had done with James, only much, much more so, for James had been in his teens when Lawrence became his mentor, and at that point Lawrence was distracted with his own performance career.

Chapter 6

I⊤ WAS QUIET in front of the Academy of Music, where last week Philadelphians had heard de Larrocha perform Mozart's twenty-first piano concerto, with guest conductor Maurice D'Artoit of the Dominican Republic. The concert was reviewed in the two local papers: one, "*Stunning!*"; the other, "Caribbean conductor D'Artoit is losing his distinctive exotic style. He is aging rather gracelessly."

That evening there was a new stage bill posted, announcing the next performance, a special concert by the touring Chicago Symphony and Sir Georg Solti. They hadn't been to Philadelphia in years; all seats had been sold out weeks in advance. The advertisements said "All-Orchestral." A little Haydn (104), a little Mendelssohn (*Italian*), and something new and different, a piece by Ezra Laderman.

A drunk slept next to the mailbox. Two people had tripped on him in an hour and he still hadn't woken up. People began parking their cars in the high-rise lot, marching past him, past the deli and the newsstand, down the street to an elaborate old brownstone, which was once a private home: the Curtis Institute, philanthropic bastion of musical instruction. A guard stood at the door, checking the names of those who entered. This was a private recital.

In fact, the student performer was not even officially enrolled in the school, but his teacher was one of such stature that this recital was permitted.

Most of the audience had arrived by quarter of eight, but few sat down right away, most taking time to walk around and chat and to see who was who.

In the first row was a pretty girl, someone who would have been noticed anywhere, even if she weren't sitting up front: Marina. On her lap she rested her flute case, and over her chair she had draped her new camel-colored spring raincoat. The seat behind her was empty, but a coat was hung over that, as well. James walked in, well dressed, and sat down next to Marina. It was still chilly for a linen suit, but he wore one anyway: the newest style in menswear this spring. He'd had a shower just a while ago and could still smell his own cologne.

They talked quietly between themselves, but Marina's eyes kept darting to the door. She jumped. He was coming in! She recognized him immediately by his powerful, light-limbed dancer's stride. There was something erotic about him: the sharp, lean lines of his face; his hair, which was straight and thick and fine, like a baby's, and had a special not-quite-red tint.

They'd had dinner together, James and Marina, and Freddy and Maur (who were in town because of Maur's concert last week) and Cleveland, who was on tour with the Chicago. Lawrence had invited them to this recital.

Lawrence was backstage with his student and the mother. The rest of the audience was waiting for them. In the middle was Maxwell Van Allen, son of Ambler Van Allen, Jr., and grandson of Ambler Van Allen, Sr. He had the graying-blond looks of a middle-aged aristocrat, and where there might have been a small, well-kept mustache there was none. His second wife had made him shave it off. His clothes were the frayed-but-good-wool type worn by Philadelphians of high birth. Sylvia sat beside him, holding the older of their daughters. Sylvie had also brought along her brother Eric, a Penn student, because he was hanging around his parents' house that evening, bored, not studying. He was an art-history major, too smart for books, living in the Northeast with his mother and father and taking three buses to get to class every day.

Sylvie and her brother looked alike: the same Fish lips, the same bump in the same nose. But Sylvia had a delicate body, straight blue-black hair (darker even than Marina's), and large, soft eyes. She had crossed the boundary into Beauty, while Eric and his carbon-copy brother, Nathan, remained in the realm of Homely. "Thank God," their aunts often said, "the ugly ones were boys."

In the row behind them sat Toby March, his sister Joan, and her husband Douglas, who had orange hair, an orange beard, and thick-lensed glasses with plastic brown frames.

Joan, Douglas, and Toby were all slouching a little in their seats. Toby was wearing the remains of what had been a very good shirt his mother had given him for his birthday. Joan and Douglas were both wearing black turtlenecks and blue jeans. All three had outgrown their haircuts.

Through the door came Franz, Hannah, and Peter Kazakov, there by invitation of Max Van Allen.

When Marina saw her uncle, a gasp, like an inverted sigh, escaped her lips and her flute case began to slide off her lap. Cleveland, who had been talking to her, caught the instrument before it hit the hard floor, and replaced it, across her thighs. Franz saw his niece and nodded to her. The Kazakovs sat in the center back row, Peter between his parents.

Franz would not have come if Hannah hadn't insisted. She had invented some kind of personal competition between herself and Elizabeth Van Allen, between Peter and Gabriel. Besides, she seemed bent on someday enrolling Peter, whom Franz thought to be an inferior musician, in the Curtis school. Franz had had some idea that Marina might be there that night: another reason he hadn't wanted to come. His niece had changed since she'd gone away to school. He could barely recognize the skinny child turned child-woman. She was how old? Sixteen, perhaps? And living alone without adult guidance, even in the conservative Clara Armstrong Hall, must have been markedly different from the sheltered life at home with her parents in Trenton. He'd met Marina occasionally on the streets over the past year and had sometimes seen her walking hand-in-hand with adolescent boys. She'd given him quick, embarrassed introductions. These encounters had never been mentioned when they met again at family holidays in Trenton.

Her father, his older brother, had asked him to keep an eye on the girl while she was living "in town," as he called it. But the few times Franz had dropped by her apartment he had found her to be so untalkative that he hadn't bothered to go back. Now her parents were complaining to him that she seldom called them, seldom came home for weekends.

He hadn't told them the gossip he'd been hearing lately. Everybody was whispering about his niece and James Rosen. He'd kept the secret from Hannah, until now. It was confirmed. Here it was for Hannah and Peter to see. His niece, the little vamp.

"What's wrong," James asked Marina when she turned pale.
"My uncle just walked in."
At five to eight, Lawrence, Elizabeth, and Samantha Engs came through the door. Lawrence had to say hello to his friends in the front row. Marina arched her lower back, tried not to look embarrassed. She was not Lawrence's student. She had not been chosen for him because she was not good enough. Whenever she and James were with him she felt like hiding, shrinking, running away. It was hard for her to remember to call him Lawrence at these times and Mr. Chattarjee at others. She didn't belong with him. There were plenty of flute students better than she. She'd never solo. Her highest hope was to play first chair in a Class B orchestra, or third chair in a Class A. I don't belong, I don't belong, she thought. It's all a farce. I shouldn't be here.

Lawrence always tried to make Marina relax. Always a pleasant greeting for her, a smile. Marina only wondered if he was laughing.

As Lawrence went over to talk to his friends, Elizabeth found herself standing alone with Samantha. Five minutes till the curtain rose. She glanced around the audience for one confused moment and saw her ex-husband. Who invited him? Oh, it's only fair, she told herself. Gabriel is his son, too. But what nerve of him to bring that little bitch along! And their stupid baby, Carrie or Corkie or whatever the name is! Elizabeth's eyes grew narrow with anger. She didn't flush, but she grew warmer. She didn't know whether to be angry with Toby for sitting in front of Max, or Max for sitting in back of Toby, and just as she'd made up her mind to spend the minute before sitting down talking to Mr. Grainger, the former piano teacher of Gabriel and Elise, the man whom Samantha Engs had just sat down beside, just then she noticed in the back row the faces of Hannah and Peter Kazakov. Now she flushed. What the hell were they doing here at Gabriel's recital? She swallowed and pretended she hadn't seen them. Hannah had brought that stupid silent Russian husband of hers, the one who smuggled books or whatever. Oh, of course, it was Max's press. He worked for Max's press. Was this some kind of plot? Sabotage. Elizabeth, mad, sat down quickly next to Toby, not saying hello to the hurt Mr. Grainger, or to Joan or Douglas, or even to Toby, who put his arm around her shoulder. She started to pull away, but then relaxed when she remembered that Max was in the row behind her, watching.

Lawrence went backstage. It was time for the curtain to open. First an administrator appeared on stage and made a speech and everyone clapped. Next, when he was gone, appeared Gabriel's small foot, his whole leg, his whole body. The stage was close, the room was small, yet he still seemed very little. There was no music stand on the stage. What he was about to perform was committed to memory. Lawrence himself was to play the piano accompaniment, having arranged it himself, with simplified chords in the bass. He stepped out, to the vigorous applause of the audience, and seated himself at the piano, first joking out loud about a sonata for flute and eight-fingered piano. There was embarrassed laughter from most of the audience, and loud chuckles from his friends James, Freddy, Maur, and Cleveland.

Lawrence and Gabriel stood alone on the stage and nobody breathed. They nodded to each other. The A was played. Another nod and they began.

Gabriel was a clever child. Clever beyond the limits of the word; a genius. He understood the music in a way that most could not; he knew it as the composer did. With him it was a combination of instinct and analysis. He was born with a knowledge of music: it was programmed into his genes. Every cell of his body understood and had always understood. It was a world that was open for him and that the rest of the world had to break into — instinctive, pure, perfect, primary knowledge.

So how could Lawrence make him learn? The music was already in Gabriel like a machine ready to be switched on. He only had to read it and there it would come, right out of him. Presto. What could Lawrence do?

Yesterday on the squash court Lawrence had thought about the boy, what to do with him, how to form him. But it wasn't a question of formation, not when everything was already there, waiting, inside him. It was complete, the entire hierarchy of sound and shape, and all the possible colors of tonality. Every hue, tint, shade, already perfectly organized, impacted in this mind. The material was there; it was just a question of how it would ripen, how to bring it forth. It would be the listeners who would have to elicit it. It wasn't a matter of Gabriel pleasing the audience, but how the audience could extract what was embedded there in him. He was a natural musician. He didn't approach from the outside like most artists. He drew music out of himself. Lawrence knew this, yet hadn't discovered this knowledge. He had to find out by himself that Gabriel was just like himself. Lawrence, too, was a natural musician. Every note, every phrase, every idea that could ever be written — all there, all hopelessly bottled, all frustrated since his unlucky trip on the New York subway.

Lawrence was impotent. He'd lost the power to burst forth with it himself. How did he react? Not with rage . . .

The music swept through the minds of the audience. Eric, in his patient, drugged daze, could not understand it other than as a force that kept him sealed to his chair. He knew that when it finally stopped he would be able to leave the room. Sylvia tapped her feet a little whenever she could abstract a melody, and tried to keep her baby quiet. Max concentrated on Gabriel's hands, his lips. They were like his own: amazing. Then his mind slipped to Lawrence: the problem of perhaps losing one of the subsidies for the book. Would the Press have to absorb the loss? The music faded to the background. Figures leapt forward.

Hannah listened with dismay. No matter what she told herself, she could not deny that this boy was an incredible player. She would have to convince Peter to practice more hours a day. Otherwise there would be no hope of him keeping up. She was sweating with aggravation. Maybe Peter needed a better teacher. She would have to look around.

Franz listened with interest, still half-watching Marina. Now this boy was a musician, that was certain. He was one of the more talented children Franz had heard in years, far more insightful and technically competent than his niece. Perhaps his wife would finally understand and leave Peter alone. It was hopeless to force the boys to compete. What was the point? Peter was no violinist. Franz knew the boy's talents were literary, and why not? That's what he would have inherited from both parents anyway. He was tutoring Peter in Russian, and already the boy could read excerpts from Pushkin. The next language he would teach him was French. Peter would blossom late, but he would blossom. Already his school grades were improving and he had been moved into the highest reading section in the class, the "smart section," as the boys called it.

Peter had a thick stack of baseball cards in his blazer pocket. He fingered them tenderly. No one else knew he had them. He'd won them from Gabriel that morning, before school started. Gabriel could whup Peter in music, but Peter was a much better card-flipper, and he was holding right now some of the best cards that had been in Gabriel's collection. After the concert, when they were all standing around telling Gabriel how great he was, Peter planned to pull out the precious cards, just for a second, just long enough to let Gabriel see them. That would show him, Mr. Flute-Player. With the toe of one shoe, Peter played with the heel of the other, pulling it down just far enough so that his own heel peeked out. He did this too many times and his shoe suddenly fell off and flipped under the chair in front of him. Hannah elbowed him sharply in the arm and hissed, "Sit still." He slid down far enough to touch his shoe with his stockinged foot and dragged it back. Franz noticed none of this. Neither did Mr. Dinghly, the Curtis librarian, who occupied the chair in front of Peter. Hannah held Peter by the arm, tightly — too tightly — to make sure he sat still.

Toby's arm, draped around Elizabeth's shoulder, was falling asleep. It was all prickly, pins-and-needles. He pulled it down, gently, resting it at his side. Elizabeth was too absorbed in the music to notice. Released from the weight of his arm, unconsciously, she leaned forward, chin in hands, elbows on knees. Her blue wool sweater stretched forward a little, away from her gray wool skirt. Toby noticed the tiny crack in her clothing, a piece of naked pink back, and smiled to himself.

For some reason Lawrence had never told anyone that it was painful for him to play the piano. His doctor didn't know this; James didn't know; neither did any of his other friends or his students. Why? Perhaps it was his desire to protect his piano playing. If he could not make music as he was meant to, on the flute, then he would make do, become an inferior instrumentalist on the wrong instrument. The keyboard was his only musical release, excluding the cracked baritone he sometimes luxuriated in while showering. He'd once heard the story of a famous American rock guitarist who was missing one of the fingers on his left hand. But two fingers gone were too much. The best he could hope for would be a little enjoyment on the piano. And if it hurt, then he couldn't admit it for fear of being advised to stop.

The pain grew a little and Lawrence's face locked into a smile.

He had fastened himself into a small world of pleasure and hurt: he couldn't stop the music. Gabriel's music was riding on his own, his careful, guiding, following, fade-into-the-background-and-now-emerge accompaniment. No one could know there was discomfort involved. Discomfort was something he had long practiced and endured without complaint. Sometimes, when he was little, they would go to the beach, his mother, his father, and he. He would beg to take off his shoes, even when they were still in the car, the minute they'd approached the bay, the minute the smells of the New Jersey shore reached his nostrils. He'd beg to go barefoot, a privilege other children had all summer but he was never allowed at home.

His mother would say, "Ask your father." His father would say nothing, and then when asked again would say, "Yes." Off would come his oxfords, which he wore even in the summer, and his white knee-socks, and he would rub his toes delightedly over the floor carpet in the back seat of the big old black Ford sedan, imagining that the car was the beach and the floor was the sand, already. When they did reach the hotel, the slatternly room they'd arranged to rent, his parents would be out of the car, dragging suitcases out of the trunk and ordering him to follow. He would gather his shoes, socks, and whatever of his toys were in the back seat, and place his feet out the door, on the always too-hot cement, bracing himself for the first shock of the burn. He'd walk on the sides of his feet, carefully, exposing as little of them as possible to the searing sidewalk. His father would be yelling for him to hurry up, his mother telling him to put his shoes on if it was too hard for him to walk. But Lawrence would refuse to yield his privilege to them. It was too rare an occasion: to be allowed to walk barefoot. He would do so all day long, even on the broiling hot sands at the beginning of the beach, the sands so far from the water that they were filled with razor-sharp shells and cigarette butts that got caught in his toes, even all the way back up the splintery boardwalk, even on the hot tar streets and the dangerous gravel walkways. Never once would he cry or complain out loud.

At the end of their vacation trip, before they packed their suitcases back up and loaded them in the trunk of the Ford along with the buckets of clamshells Lawrence had picked up, Lawrence's father, the strange silent Indian that everyone stared at on the boardwalk, would tell him to put his shoes and socks back on. Lawrence would whine in protest and his father would repeat, "Put your shoes on," now a demand. Lawrence's mother would be there handing them to him, and sulking, he would pull on those clean scratchy white cotton socks. Though his feet would no longer be burned or cut, they would now stifle in the black oxford prisons. Family visits to the shore stopped after the summer of Lawrence's second grade. That was when his father left them: after that Lawrence could go barefoot whenever he pleased, but he had outgrown the desire to do so.

The first piece was over and the second was already halfway through. Elizabeth sat, leaning against Toby. When she first sat down she had been so angry about seeing Max and his new family and the Kazakovs here that she had forgotten what she'd been thinking about all day long: Lawrence Chattarjee had mentioned the possibility of his friend James Rosen attending the concert. James Rosen! Once, she'd been told that Rudolf Serkin might show up at a recital by Elise, but that had turned out to be a false alarm, after all the worrying she'd done. What about Rosen? Where had Lawrence gone just before the recital began? He'd been saying hello to someone. There'd been no time for introductions, he'd gone backstage almost right away.

Elizabeth tore her attention from Gabriel's playing and peered around the room. There were unfamiliar people here and there, and a whole row of them in the front. She wouldn't know Rosen by the back of his head, but that could be him over there, the man with the dark brown hair, the one sitting next to the long-haired girl and the gray-haired man. She would have liked to see his face. She knew it from so many record jackets — they must have had at least eight at home. Imagine it: James Rosen listening to to her Gabriel. Was he interested? Impressed? How did he like it? It was impossible to tell without seeing his face. Elizabeth elbowed Toby and nodded in Rosen's direction. Toby was puzzled.

"Rosen!" she half whispered, half croaked. Toby raised his eyebrows and they both stared at that group in the front row.

This could mean so, so much for Gabriel's career, Elizabeth knew. He'd already been accepted by a great teacher, and now he was being noticed by a great star. This might be crucial.

Elizabeth was trying to remember everything she had read about Rosen. She thought, he doesn't watch television. She'd read that in an interview. In another one, on television, he had said something about liking the new digital recordings. What else could she remember? In *Music Times* magazine's annual cookbook he had given a recipe for spinach quiche, which she'd thought was disappointingly unimaginative.

Her heart was beating fast. One hand's knuckles grew white clasping the rim of her chair. The other hand squeezed Toby's. He began unwrapping her tight fingers and she smiled at him, relaxing. The second piece was about to end: time for intermission.

Lawrence held the last chord until Gabriel's trill resolved and the applause began. Gabriel took his first bow and Lawrence stood behind, massaging gently his left hand with his right, smiling across the audience.

As his mother had coached him, Gabriel turned to Mr. Chattarjee and nodded gracefully. The audience clapped more loudly; in the front row Freddy and Maur bravoed and cheered. After the third curtain call, finally, the clapping stopped. Even Elizabeth's hands were tired, and it was time for cakes and tea in the lobby. Backstage, Gabriel got a hug from Mr. Chattarjee, from Samantha, from Toby, and four kisses from his mother. Everyone crowded through the door, to where the food was, and Gabriel was warned separately by Samantha, Elizabeth, and Mr. Chattarjee not to eat any cookies lest he salivate too much during the second half.

Elizabeth scanned the room for the man she had decided was James Rosen. As she looked around, her eyes met Max's and she looked away. He was standing there in his gray wool, holding a plastic cup. His wife was on the other side of the room, feeding cookies to their baby, and Max looked lost. He turned his back to Elizabeth and studied a plaque on the wall. But Elizabeth was gone already, running after Lawrence Chattarjee, whom she had seen leading Gabriel out of the lobby and back into the recital hall. Sure enough, Rosen was in there — that was Rosen, after all, he looked exactly like his photos — and Lawrence Chattarjee was bringing Gabriel to meet him. Elizabeth watched from the doorway.

"Good show," Rosen was saying, reaching for Chattarjee's right hand. Surrounding him were two older men (one of them vaguely familiar), a younger man, and a girl. The girl stood back slightly from the rest of them, who were talking excitedly and thumping Chattarjee on the back. Gabriel smiled at the girl and she said something Elizabeth couldn't hear. She stretched out her arm and shook Gabriel's hand lightly.

"So," said James Rosen suddenly, very loudly, "*this* is Gabriel. Hi, tiger, you did very well."

"Thank you. I've heard you play, too, sir," answered Gabriel in a voice so small that Elizabeth could barely hear him. Everyone laughed and Gabriel looked confused. Chattarjee was resting his left arm on the boy's shoulder.

"These are some of my friends, Gabriel. They all enjoyed your playing. This is Mr. Weinburg, and this is Mr. D'Artoit, who is a conductor" — Elizabeth shivered, hearing this — "and this is Mr. Arms, who plays violin in the Chicago Symphony, and this is Marina, who studies flute at Curtis like you will when you're a little older."

"Hi," said Gabriel. Elizabeth had the urge to step out of the shadows so that she would be introduced, too, but she controlled herself. She had a feeling her presence would be awkward. She leaned forward to hear better.

Alone in a corner of the lobby stood Maxwell Van Allen. His wife had disappeared, taking Carrie to the bathroom. He'd let his tea bag sit too long in the tea and now it was undrinkably bitter. He was wishing he had a scotch.

Joan March and her husband stood by the refreshments with Toby, all three of them gobbling cookies. Max winced, knowing that it was time that he went over and greeted them.

Joan was the best manuscript editor he'd ever had. She worked hard, long days — ten or twelve hours — and her work was excellent. But he could never manage to have a decent conversation with the girl. She always seemed to be sneering at him. Joan's husband, on the other hand, was always pleasant. He'd even gone out for a drink with him once. So that would be his approach. He'd go up and talk to Douglas.

When Joan saw him coming she bristled.

Douglas said, "Here comes the boss." Last week when Joan had asked Maxwell Van Allen about the raise he'd promised her a year ago, he'd told her sorry, it was hard times for everyone — she'd have to wait. Joan and Douglas had holes in their shoes and she was mad.

"Cool it," whispered Toby.

"Hello there, old chap," said Max, reaching for Douglas's hand. Douglas slid the cookies he'd been holding into his pocket and returned a crumb-filled handshake. Joan scowled at her husband's friendliness and she and Toby walked away.

Peter Kazakov was bored, standing next to his mom, who was talking to some old lady music teachers. He couldn't see Gabriel anywhere in the crowd, which meant he must be backstage. Where was that? He considered all the doors that might possibly lead there, but his mom had a firm hold of his forearm and it wouldn't have been easy to break away. His mom had only let him have five cookies and he was still hungry. His dad was in the bathroom somewhere, taking forever. He should have said he had to go, too. In his pocket he felt his baseball cards and a half-stick of gum. He slid it out of the wrapper and popped it into his mouth before his mom noticed what he was doing. She never approved of gum chewing, especially not in concerts. Oh, good, he thought, they're flashing the lights for it to begin again. Soon the whole thing would be over and they could go home. Tomorrow morning in the recess yard, decided Peter, I'm gonna flip away all eighty-two of Mr. Flute-Player's cards. Every single one, including his four Pete Roses. I'm gonna finish the job I started, and it'll be a cinch. What a sissy, he can't even hang onto his cards.

Franz Kazakov wore a plaid flannel shirt almost everywhere he went. His beard was long and full enough to cover most of his chest, so even if he had been wearing a necktie, no one would have noticed. He was pondering, with distaste, the back of Maxwell Van Allen's head.

Max had given him an editorship at the Press when he'd been denied tenure at NYU and moved to Philadelphia. He was always making friendly gestures, which Kazakov neither invited nor enjoyed. Max did not impress Franz: he was not intelligent, he did not understand literature, and he was barely able to keep the Van Allen Press from financial failure. He was irritated by Max's ill-timed, naive jokes, his inability to hold his liquor, and his vulgar wife, who was as loud as his own wife, but stupid.

Hannah watched the stage intensely. She was thinking, Oh, why is he so much better than Peter? Her face was filled with dismay. Peter pulled a baseball card from his pocket, examined it, and quickly put it back. Franz Kazakov wound his fingers through his beard. If only he weren't so dependent on that mediocre, bourgeois man. His gaze drifted across the room to his niece. From his seat he could see only the part in her hair, hair the same color and texture of his beard. Could she feel him staring at her? Obviously he had made her uncomfortable. She had been barely able to greet him when he came in. She was probably worried that he would report to her father about her affairs with James Rosen, but he would not. Of course he would not. She was just an irresponsible, silly girl. He resolved to do nothing about her.

Marina, unrelaxed, watched the stage, as Gabriel drifted into his final passage.

Chapter 7

LAWRENCE'S FATHER'S NAME was Rajesh Singh Chattarjee. Lawrence still has a ring of his, big enough only for a boy's finger, a finely made eighteen-carat-gold ring with flecks of paint still clinging to an ornate peacock carved on the front. The initials, in roman letters, inside are: R.S.C. As far as Lawrence knows, his father and mother met when they were students: his father, far away from home, was studying engineering at the University of Pennsylvania. His mother, of course, was studying flute. They lived together for a while in the city, despite the odd looks they received from just about everybody. Ann Frost — that was his mother's maiden name — was from Illinois, outside of Peoria, and her family had no idea of Rajesh S. Chattarjee's existence until they were told, by letter from Ann, of the marriage.

Rajesh, likewise, did not mention Ann in any of his letters to his father. He wrote home in English, a language his father could neither read nor understand. But Rajesh could not write Punjabi — he had only a rudimentary idea of the alphabet. He knew his letters had to be taken, by bicycle, into the village, where the local solicitor would, for a fee, translate them. Letters to Rajesh from his father were translated into English in the same way before they were mailed. Rajesh knew that every sentence that transpired between them would be intercepted by the solicitor, the old Hindu, Prakesh, who was famous as a gossip. Nothing could pass through his office that would not become village news. So even if Rajesh had not been too afraid of the elder Chattarjee to tell him about his real life in America, he would have been able to say nothing. Nothing was worth risking public scandal and disgrace.

Ann Frost was a thin-lipped, angular young blond, half German and half Norwegian. And like Rajesh she had grown up on a farm and was not knowledgeable about city trends and practices. She was an outcast because of her plaid jumpers and unstylish shoes, he because of his dark skin and odd headdress. With Ann, Rajesh had his first taste of the tantalizing, forbidden whiskey. Ann was used to seeing vodka and schnapps in the hands of her Norwegian father. Rajesh also swallowed his first meat (to his amazement it did not make him retch with disgust). One night when they were drunk he let Ann cut his hair — which had never before been touched by a blade. He had sobbed a little then, seeing it lying at his feet on the bedroom rug, but after that he had never worn his turban and had gotten haircuts regularly, from barbers.

Rajesh failed a few of his examinations and had to repeat the year. Ann did worse. News of her wild new life-style reached the offices of the music-school's administration and she was investigated: Yes, her teachers said, Ann's playing has only grown worse. She has not practiced, is not a serious student. She was asked to leave.

Ann found a job teaching music in a private high school and gave private lessons on the side. At least now they would have some money, a little more than the ten dollars a month that came from Rajesh's father in India. They moved to a slightly larger apartment in a secluded neighborhood, outside of the city. They were almost doing well: Rajesh was earning A's again and Ann was thinking of resuming private lessons with a Philadelphia Orchestra member, when she discovered that she was pregnant.

Rajesh didn't leave her as she'd feared he might. He stayed and they got married, informing her parents afterward. There was no written reply, only an angry telegram demanding, "Why?" — which Ann, by then with a blossoming stomach, did not answer.

In the back of her mind she wondered what Rajesh would do if his father ever learned of her.

Lawrence was a small baby. He slept poorly and seemed to catch every cold or virus that passed through the air. His first memories are of terrible earaches, Ann bending over him, giving him spoonfuls of whiskey to ease the pain and honey to ease his cough. There was hardly enough money for food and rent. Ann had to take on twice as many private students. But this wasn't enough. Rajesh was in the final stages of finishing his Ph.D. He looked after Lawrence while Ann was working, but Lawrence was difficult, constantly crying and distracting him from his work. Occasionally Rajesh would throw a violent fit, flinging his valuable drafting pens, his expensive books, half-glasses of whiskey, ashtrays, everything at hand, all over the room. Lawrence would hide from him, safe under the furniture until his mother came home. Once Rajesh hit Ann, not hard, but enough to discolor slightly the skin around her eye. She told everyone that she'd hit her eye on the bathroom towel-rack, but Lawrence had seen the fight. He knew to keep away from Rajesh when he was drunk.

In spite of the anger and the tension, there was always music in the apartment. When Ann came home from a twelve-hour teaching day, she was sometimes too tired to cook dinner — but she always turned on the phonograph immediately. Sometimes she would give Lawrence lessons on the tiny pump organ in his bedroom, the one they'd bought on a whim at a fire sale for a dollar. Rajesh demanded no talking when he was working, but music never bothered him. In fact it seemed to soothe his temper. When Ann came home and the music went on, things were better. Usually.

Rajesh demanded order. Lawrence knew, from the earliest moment, never to leave his toys on the floor. Nothing was ever to be left out of place in the apartment. But Ann was gone so much and Rajesh refused to straighten anyone's but his own things. Dirt always had a way of accumulating in all the corners. Unwashed dishes were always waiting in the sink, and piles of laundry grew, spilling out of the bathroom hamper. Rajesh could not bear it.

Finally he wrote to his father asking him to find him a housekeeper, a suitable hardworking peasant girl, who could take care of his apartment while he finished his studies. "Let her be a girl of good reputation only," he added, for the benefit of the solicitor. His father sent him Sujita, who was told immediately upon arrival that if she ever mentioned anything to her people at home about Rajesh's white wife or his little boy, an evil curse would be put on her and her children would all be born black as tar with fangs for teeth. This precaution was practically unnecessary, since Sujita could not write and had no way of communicating with her family, but Rajesh would take no chances. Sujita took care of the house well enough, but she was terriffied by Ann, whom Rajesh had told her, in Punjabi, was a witch. Ann and Lawrence never understood why Sujita would run to her room and sob each night after the dishes were washed and put away, why she refused to eat in the same room with them, and why, on nights when Ann cooked hamburgers and hot dogs, she would go to her room and eat no dinner at all. When Sujita left them, Rajesh's father wrote asking if his son would need another housekeeper, but Rajesh replied no. He had his degree by then, and a job with an American firm. Things were looking good, financially, since with his student days over he could afford a bigger apartment, maybe a small house. But something else bothered him: he knew his father was an old man now, past sixty, and even a well-fed, wealthy Punjabi landowner might not live much longer than that. His father often wrote of seeing him again. "We have had several several inquiries about marriage. One offer has caught our attention," the letters would begin, "a beautiful girl, and educated, too, the daughter of well-educated man . . ."

One Thursday afternoon when Lawrence got home from school the door was still locked. Peculiar because Rajesh was usually back from work by then to let him in . . . he waited outside on the welcome mat, quietly doing his homework problems until his mother arrived.

Some of Rajesh's clothes and one suitcase were gone. There was no note.

They took a smaller apartment, and with only the two of them to feed, Ann's salary was almost enough. Many things happened in the year after Rajesh left: they went to visit Ann's family in Illinois, his only visit with his grandparents. Ann bought him his first flute, an old nickel-plated one from a student of hers who was buying a better one. Rajesh wrote them two letters: the first was postmarked London; the second, India. The letter from London was less than a page long. Ann never let Lawrence see it. The one from India contained money, one hundred American dollars in ten-dollar bills. Half of this Ann put in the bank, in an account in Lawrence's name. The letter was even shorter than the first. Ann showed it to Lawrence and he memorized it: *Dear A and L, Enclosed is something to help you along, provided it isn't stolen through the mails first. I will not write again for a while. Please take care of yourselves, fondly, Rajesh (Daddy).*

Lawrence ran those three sentences through his mind often, trying to imagine his father saying them aloud in his peculiar accent. Quickly, however, he lost his ear for the northern-Indian pronunciation of English, and after his father had been gone for a year he could not recall his voice at all.

During summer vacation the year that Rajesh left them, Ann and Lawrence packed their things and drove for almost two days, all the way through Pennsylvania and Ohio, stopping many times to check the map, until they got to Peoria. From there Ann knew the way home well. She had driven her father's wagon through these streets every week from the time she was fourteen till she left home four years later. Now she was twenty-nine and she had a brown-skinned little boy going on eight and she was on her way home, without warning.

What could she have expected them to do? She should have known they would have hushed the whole thing up, not breathing a word of it to anyone, saying that Ann was doing very fine in Philadelphia and nothing else, not a single hint about a black man for a husband and a little black baby. But she was their only daughter, talented and beautiful, who'd won every award for promising students that the Jay Cobbs Senior High School ever offered. And any child who remembers being pulled from the floor up to her father's lap and told that she was the most special most beautiful little girl in the world, that there was nothing she could do that would ever ever . . .

They were civil. Mama fixed Lawrence hot oatmeal every morning and showed him Ann's toys, which they kept in the attic, and tried to distract him from playing in the yard, where the neighbors might notice. But it could never be the same. Something now was empty and cold. Ann wore sweaters the whole time; it was as if she just couldn't get warm. Lawrence hummed to himself and played with the toys and practiced his nickel flute, and when he was alone sometimes, in the guest room he was using (Ann slept in her old teenager's bedroom), he would shut the door and stare into the mirror, repeating, "I will not write again for a while. Please take care of yourselves. Fondly. Rajesh. Daddy," trying out different ways of twisting vowels and consonants, trying to find a satisfactory combination that sounded like his father. Ann looked up two of her best high-school friends. One was married and fat: a farm-wife. The other was divorced and ran a beauty salon, was worried about niggers buying houses on her street, and wanted to know how Ann had stayed so thin.

There was one terrible fight at the dinner table. Lawrence could not decide whether to stay or run and hide upstairs so he stayed. Chicken legs toppled to the floor and corn landed on laps. Water glasses spilled and soaked the tablecloth. It lasted a very long fifteen minutes, but when it was over, everyone was hugging and crying, and Lawrence's grandmother, who always smelled liked licorice, even when dinner was cooking, hugged him tight for the first time.

When the two weeks were up they went home and Lawrence kissed them both good-bye: the two wrinkly fat old people who were his mother's mama and papa. After that he didn't see them again, and only heard from them through cards on Christmas and birthdays. They died when he was thirteen, together, in a fire, when the old stove in the cellar exploded.

Lawrence still has the little three-inch wooden Buddha that

used to belong to his mother, which he stole from the attic where her mama and papa kept her childhood things. He keeps it, along with the ring from his father, in an obscure little box deep in the bottom drawer of his desk.

Lawrence has not heard from his father since, and to this day he wonders whether he is still alive. He always expected to receive a letter from him, perhaps on his twelfth birthday, his eighteenth, his twenty-first..., and was always careful to leave a clear trail of forwarding addresses with the post office, just in case. He would have written, but he knew no address. Ann couldn't even remember the name of the village he'd come from in the Punjab.

There is only one photograph, taken shakily by Ann with a friend's camera: Rajesh, hair wet and displaced, in wet bathing trunks by an anonymous swimming pool, around the time of Lawrence's birth. His feet and left arm are cropped out: his face, turned almost in a profile, is silhouetted by the bright sunlight, so that it is impossible to tell if he is smiling. His nose, a large, sharp, Caucasian nose, is, as far as can be told from the quality of the print, exactly like Lawrence's.

This photograph is inside Lawrence's wallet; even at this moment it rests at his hip. Occasionally, though no more often than every few weeks, Lawrence will come across it as he searches for a credit card or a receipt. But it is too vague. It does not help him recall his father's face.

The letters that never came are not so much on Lawrence's mind, not anymore, these years since the accident. But for a while they tormented him, keeping him awake at nights, chasing him while he practiced. He composed them to himself in the shower, as he walked home from the bus, while he ran through his scales. They all began: "My Dear Son," and spoke of long separation. As a young teenager Lawrence had two passions: playing the flute and all things that were Indian. He took classes at night in northern-Indian cookery, bought himself a sitar and taught himself to play. He bought a text, *Say It in Punjabi*, and taught himself a few chapters, and bought volumes of Indian paintings. He found, to his amazement, a collection of erotic Indian prints on his mother's bookshelf. Soon, however, his life became so busy with flute playing that he had no time for his other hobby: the cloves and spices sat unused in the kitchen, his books lay unthumbed on the shelf. He did, however, retain a lifelong preference for Earl Grey tea, boiled with milk and sugar and cinnamon, something he was never able to teach a maid to prepare but always had to make himself, if he wanted it right.

Where is Ann Frost Chattarjee now? She is not dead. Lawrence visits her monthly or when he can in the home he put her in after the stroke. He lost her slowly. As the months became years, she was quietly eroding, losing pieces of herself, until it was impossible to leave her alone or to keep her with him, or to put her anywhere except where they were trained to take care of her. She has aged the way true blonds do, not graying but rather fading, growing paler. Her lips, which were thin as a girl, are now two pink-gray pencil lines. She is still pretty, to Lawrence's eyes, and she calls the grown-up Lawrence "Raj." He brings her candy and bakery cookies, and books to read. Thick ones, like *Hawaii*, *The Family Moskat*, *A House for Mr. Biswas*. She turns the pages slowly, not comprehending, as he sits and watches. He doesn't know if she finishes the books or eats the food: there's never any trace of it in her room when he returns. When he asks her she smiles brightly and does not reply, but calls him Raj, "Rajesh, my dear."

When, after three edgy days, they decided that Rajesh was not coming home again, Ann had not become hysterical as Lawrence expected her to, after seeing his parents' more violent fights. She did not get drunk, as she had on the evening of the afternoon when Rajesh had given her a black eye. She had simply sat down beside her son, who was cautiously doing his arithmetic homework on the kitchen table, and opened the morning paper to the classified section: APARTMENTS FOR RENT. They moved calmly. They packed their clothes in suitcases and gave Raj's to the Salvation Army. Calmly a new school was found for Lawrence, a parochial one run by nuns. That summer they drove to Illinois and back, and when they returned she calmly sold the car.

The flute she gave Lawrence lessons on was a cheap one, but

within two months she insisted that he play on her instrument, the most valuable thing in the apartment. It was sterling silver, with a gold-plated embouchure. Her parents had bought it for her as a going-away present, on her eighteenth birthday.

In a year's time she was sure. She was absolutely positive: he was a genius. She thought about this thoroughly: what was the best thing to do? She'd arranged an audition downtown at the music school she'd been thrown out of when she was twenty, and later a hushed gentleman's voice, the registrar's, explained on the phone that Lawrence had been accepted at Curtis to study with William Kinkaid.

Lawrence needed her flute. What could she do? She couldn't have him going to Curtis with the dented old nickel one. Then she decided he should have it to keep. She really didn't need to take it along to lessons unless she was coaching a student in duets, and then the nickel one, or the piano, would suffice. She told Lawrence a story that she had recently read in *Life* magazine: Picasso's father was a painter. One day when he was gone from his studio, Picasso, who was twelve years old, sat down and made a drawing of the still life his father had been working on. When his father came home and saw what the boy had done, he gave him all of his drawing and painting equipment, told him to keep it. His father never painted again.

Lawrence practiced hard, and since music came easily to him, he progressed with phenomenal speed. When he was twelve they told him, "In a year you will be good enough to play in any major orchestra." But of course he would not. He would be a soloist.

Ann steered him carefully away from adults who might praise him too much and those who would try to spoil him. They were poor, still too poor to buy a second good flute, and Ann had only one nice dress, which she had to wear to every recital, reception, orchestra concert, and school conference she attended. On her thirtieth birthday Lawrence gave her a pure-silk Indian scarf, which he had saved for by walking instead of taking the bus to school. When she opened the box and saw what it was her eyes grew watery and red. Lawrence felt bad for making her cry and wished he hadn't bought the thing; but after that she wore it every time she wore her only good dress.

From the earliest he could remember there were always whispers about him from behind his back — mostly, it seemed, from ladies. He would overhear snatches of what they were saying, "black" or "Indian" and "you know *bssss bssss*, mother's white, *bsss bssss*." He knew he was different, but Ann told him that different was special, not bad. How many other families had so many colors to choose from? Milk chocolate Daddy, vanilla Mommy, and Lawrence, who was some days butter-pecan and other days honey-rum.

His first school was a public school: there were white kids and Negro kids and Chinese kids, but no Indians except him. In the first week of kindergarten they learned a song: *One little, two little, three little Indians, four little, five little, six little Indians, seven little, eight little, nine little Indians, ten little Indian boys, Oh! Ten little, nine little,* et cetera, and a Negro boy named Tyrone asked if this was a song about Lawrence. The teacher asked Lawrence if this was his song. Lawrence said yes. Inside he was glad to have a song about him, and he figured out how to play the melody on the little pump-organ at home.

The other mothers weren't sure about Lawrence when they saw him playing with their children in the recess yard. He was half something, but they couldn't tell what. Their children knew, though, and told them when they were asked. Oh, half that. They wouldn't have guessed. What a strange woman his mother must be.

It was a liberal neighborhood for Philadelphia at that time. Black children and white children shared the same classroom, without the white mothers panicking, saying that things were going down hill. What didn't count, though, was mixed races. It just wasn't right, the two of them living together like that. It was all very strange. Best for their children to avoid the boy, thought the black mothers and the white mothers alike. Each family began its subtle or not-so-subtle campaign: turning Lawrence's classmates slowly against him.

Even his teachers caught on to the spirit of ridicule. One afternoon the second grade was told to draw an outdoor scene. Lawrence made his apartment house, with a squirrel and his father standing outside. The clouds were outlined in green, the trees were covered with purple leaves. At first he'd been delighted when Miss So-and-So held it up in front of the class, but then the giggles began and his mood sank. Miss So-and-So could hardly get her breath for all the laughing she was doing; "Is that the color of trees in the country where you come from?" she wanted to know.

Lawrence loved a girl, the first girl he loved besides his mother. Her name was Sheila and her hair was long and blond like his mother's. When they changed seats for reading groups, Lawrence always ended up in Sheila's desk. He loved to sit there, to feel her erasers and pencils and the smooth brown paper covers on her books under the desk while he was looking at the teacher, pretending to pay attention. One day — it took all his courage, even though he was sure he'd never be discovered — he left her a note. He wrote it the night before, in brown crayon, on a page torn from his notebook, with his left hand so that no one could recognize the writing: *Dear Sheela, you are the prettiest gril in the worl. I love you. Anonymous.* He'd seen the word *anonymous* when reading through the alphabetical index of the poetry part of his reader. *Anonymous*, his mother had told him, means no one knows who wrote it. Bad luck. When they switched back to their own desks, Sheila found the paper immediately and ran with it to the front of the room, telling Miss So-and-So, "Lawrence was just in my desk last period, and look what he wrote!" How could he have been so stupid. Of course Sheila would know who had been sitting there. The teacher read it out loud and the class screamed with laughter. Then she walked down the aisle to where Lawrence was sitting with his head bent very low and said to him, "Look up." He looked up. She put her nose down low close to his. "How old are you?"

"Seven."

"What age to they get married at in the country where you come from, young man?" Lawrence humiliated himself by crying in front of everyone. Things went badly for him that year, but after his father left and he moved, he didn't have to go back to that school.

Saint Anthony's was better, but strange. Ann sent him there because she thought the Catholics would be nicer, and it was rumored that they gave a better education. Ann had never gone to church as a little girl, though her family had called itself Lutheran. Consequently whenever she filled out forms that asked for "Religion" she would check "Protestant." Rajesh was a fallen Sikh, and Lawrence, at the age of eight-and-a-half, had barely heard of religion. They celebrated Christmas, certainly, and Ann had told him about God and how God was born on this earth and the angels came to visit him, but he had never been taught to pray and had never been taken inside a church.

The Catholic kids had two advantages over Lawrence: they already knew all about this religion business, and they all knew how to write in script.

In public school you learned to print letters first, from kindergarten to third grade, and everything got printed two lines high, with a skipped line in between. No one learned to do script until after third grade, and even then the script was still giant. Catholic kids, however, seemed to do script from the beginning, and they were allowed to write in one line, one line skipped in between, so that their handwriting was much more grown-up looking.

Lawrence was far behind the rest of the class in handwriting and he wrote like a baby. The nun said nothing about this to him on his first day, but he went home nearly crying and told Ann of his embarrassment. That night they stayed up together well past midnight. They did this for a week, though it made them tired, until Lawrence had mastered the skill of writing in script. The next week the nun put a star and a little note on his homework paper saying how much his handwriting was improving already.

The big problem was the catechism. It took Lawrence a while to catch on to what they were all doing before class, standing to the right of their desks, hands folded longwise, staring ahead (it turned out at the crucifix on the wall), saying the same thing all together, strange long words that Lawrence could not understand, "*In nomine patris, et filii, et spiritus sancti . . .*" Catechism was the first class they had every morning. It was mostly a lot of questions, with answers they were supposed to memorize at night, things like, "What is a Sacrament?" and "What is the Church?" The catechism nun, who was old and lame and whose gray hair sometimes wiggled past her earflaps, called Lawrence up to see her one morning when the other kids were filing outside to the recess yard.

Lawrence was afraid of her because when she was angry at the class sometimes she would holler and wave her walking cane through the air. Some kids said that she hit kids with the cane, but no one could ever remember her actually doing it. She wore a belt of heavy wooden rosary beads at her middle and her skirts fell down, even past her ankles. Anyone would have been a little frightened to have to go up to the front of the room and talk to her all alone. Was he in trouble? What could he have done wrong?

He stood beside her waiting for her to finish writing in her book. (All nuns had the same handwriting. Long thin graceful gray-black letters with pretty loops, all written with thin silver pens.) Finally she looked at him sideways, not through her glasses, and he jumped. She told him to get a chair, sit down, and not be nervous.

"The other children are scheduled to be confirmed this spring," she told him. "Do you know what that means?" Lawrence shook his head no, wishing he knew more things than he did.

"When we are confirmed," she told him, "we become soldiers of God." Soldiers of God?

"You are not a Catholic, are you?" Lawrence shook his head again. He was a Protestant, he told her.

"Do you go to Protestant church?" He shood his head no. The only church he'd ever been inside was the one attached to this school.

"We have children of many religions coming to this school," she said. "We have Episcopals, and Presbyterians and Baptists and Unitarians and sometimes we even have a Jew, but sometimes I see a child who has no religion and I think I should tell him that if he would like to convert he will be welcome."

Lawrence nodded slowly, his hands folded in his lap.

"If you studied, Lawrence, you could become a Catholic. First you would be baptized, and since you are a big boy, not a little baby, you could have your First Communion right away, and then in the springtime you could receive your confirmation with the rest of the children. Would you like that?"

Lawrence thought that he might, and besides for some reason he was afraid to say no.

"Go home tonight and talk this over with your mother, and let her call me if she wants."

There was a shoe box on the nun's desk, covered with blue and yellow construction paper, and in green lettering the words FOR THE MISSIONS. The Missions were pagan children who were starving and were saved by Catholic priests and baptized. There were pictures of Mission children pasted on the sides of the box, and Lawrence had thought how much like himself one of the little Mission boys looked: a skinny little boy in a white undershirt. Under his picture was the word *Ceylon*. Whenever Lawrence dropped a nickel into the Mission box he would stare at that little boy's photograph wondering if he had been converted or saved yet. As he walked back down the aisle to the cloakroom to get his coat and join the rest of the class in the recess yard, he heard the nun jiggling the box.

"Look at that," she said, half to him, half to herself. "Some boys and girls have plenty of money to buy themselves candy for the recess yard, but hardly anyone thinks to give to the Missions."

Ann was furious when Lawrence told her what the nun had said, about his converting. It was the angriest she had been since before Rajesh left. She slammed pots around the kitchen (she'd been fixing them a can of soup) and used a word, *proselytizer*, that he had never heard before. She swore that she would call the nun up and tell her a thing or two — and Lawrence pleaded with her not to. What was wrong with it, he said, if he became a soldier of God? Ann told him he was too young to know what he was talking about and sent him, soupless, to his room to practice, shouting behind him that she would have to take him out of the school.

A carefully written letter from Lawrence's mother explained to the nun that she was not to mention religion to the boy privately again. The letter was mailed, to save Lawrence the pain of having to deliver it sealed, not knowing what was inside.

Lawrence wondered why the nun never called him up and spoke to him again. He thought he'd have to explain to her how his mother didn't want him to be baptized and confirmed, but she never gave him the chance. Perhaps she'd decided that he was an evil boy. Perhaps she'd found out that his father was an Indian and she thought he was a pagan. Pagan father, pagan son. The Ceylon boy remained on the Missions box on her desk, always in his white T-shirt, always holding an empty rice bowl.

In the spring when everyone else had confirmation practice, he and two Protestant girls did extra arithmetic assignments in the back of the classroom. He never talked in class, he was as good as he could be, but he always had the feeling that the nun didn't like him anymore. Pagan heathen Mission boy.

At that time he really did want to be just like them, the kids in their uniforms, boys with green ties and green pants and girls with green plaid skirts. He wanted to know the secrets to their jump-rope songs (he always missed, tripped all over the place and had to take the ends), how to play jacks, what to do when someone threw him the basketball (which was rare). But he never did anything right. Maybe it was because he spent his nights playing his flute beside his mother. Other children had brothers and sisters to practice sports with, and pets to take care of. He was better: he had a different world, where he played the flute and important grown-ups made a fuss about him. But he was inferior, too, and he knew it so, so well. He was thin and clumsy as a Mission child. He wanted so much to have strong pale fat arms that could throw a baseball hard. The smartest part of his body was his long fingers, very brown at the knuckles and the tips, which could go so fast and so precisely when they touched the flute. That was it, he was better and worse and different. He couldn't belong there and it was a relief to leave.

Chapter 8

I Years ago, on Lawrence's birthday, James had given him an electric razor, like the one he used, but Lawrence had never gotton accustomed to it. He liked to shave by hand, as he called it, with lots of foam and the tap running all the time. He had a heavy beard and the electric razor wouldn't cut through it satisfactorily. He left it on the third shelf in the bathroom, with his other shaving things.

Sometimes when Lawrence noticed it lying there he thought of donating it to the Salvation Army, or Goodwill, or whoever collects such things, but he could never bring himself to take it down, as though if he did James's visits would stop altogether and the chance of things ever being the same again would die.

Lawrence had unusually thick, dark whiskers. He shaved every morning and if he had to go anywhere in the evening he shaved again. His father had had a beard like that — this was one of the few details he remembered about his looks, the scratchy, peppery chin that he kissed hello every evening — but his father's whiskers had looked less startling against his tea-colored skin. Lawrence had inherited some of his mother's Scandinavian fairness, and unshaven after only one day he would look like a stubble-chinned derelict.

At seven A.M., the morning after Gabriel's first Curtis recital, Lawrence stood at the sink, gently scraping through the foam inside the curve in the cleft of his chin. He was a slow, patient shaver and though he rarely nicked himself, he was especially cautious here at the most curvaceous area of his face. Done! He rinsed his razor under the tap, tapped it on the porcelain, and rinsed it again. He washed the flecks of shaving cream from his face and poured some after-shave lotion on his palm — L'honneur, a French brand, also a gift from James. With his wet comb he pushed his hair into place. The clean warm bathroom smell rose around him.

Many mornings, regularly, Lawrence found himself watching himself washing himself or shaving in a bathroom mirror, and each morning when he was through he studied himself briefly and intensely, memorizing. His high forehead, pale against his hair, with the gleaming little white scar to the left, extending from his hairline; his large, weak-blue eyes, encased in their gold-framed glasses, lined with their extralong lashes (once, a grade-school teacher had proclaimed that he should have been a girl); his sharp Caucasian nose, which had grown longer even as he'd grown older; his lips — their color was graying now, he observed — interrupted in two places by small scars; and his chin, newly scraped and sensitive, a familiar rose-gray tinge.

The cold apartment air slapped him pleasantly as he left the bathroom. He slipped out of his robe and into a fresh, stiff cotton shirt, which had been prepared especially for this morning by his girl yesterday. He was meeting James for breakfast early.

James was flying to San Joachím at ten. He couldn't afford to miss the plane — he'd be arriving there in time for the orchestra rehearsal — so they'd have to be punctual. Lawrence and James hadn't been able to see each other alone at all lately, even though James had been in town for almost two weeks. It had been too hectic, first with his performance, then with Freddy and Maur's visit, and then that young boy, Cleveland, had been around also. And Marina. James still brought her along to many public events; and the last lunch they'd eaten together Marina had been there, too, untalkative as usual, eating little, smiling politely at Lawrence's conversation.

Lawrence was looking forward to their quiet breakfast alone. He chose the necktie that he knew was James's favorite, the Chinese silk one Freddy had brought him from Taiwan, and his own favorite tie clip, the one modeled after William Kinkaid's, with the theme from *L'Après-midi d'un faune* engraved on it.

On the way out of the building (seven-thirty) he passed the housekeeper on her way in. She was wearing her street clothes: an orange dress, a wig, and white boots. In the plastic Marlboro bag she swung at her hips, he knew, she carried her uniform and her floppy pink slippers. She was humming to herself, a gospel tune, and she stopped just long enough to give him an energetic, "How you doin!"

Lawrence stepped into the dazzling daylight. Rush-hour crowds whipped around him. He turned east, into the sunshine, and headed down the street to the coffee shop in James's hotel.

The woman who seated him had a piece of Scotch tape fastening down a curl on each cheek. Lawrence couldn't imagine why she had done that. It didn't seem particularly stylish. Her hair was stiffly curled, an unconvincing color of black. He ordered tea.

It was unlike James to be late, Lawrence thought as he waited. The tea water was not hot enough for the tea to steep properly. He called the waitress over and had her bring him coffee. Seven fifty-five. James had to be at the airport by nine-fifteen, which meant he had to leave in less than an hour. Lawrence studied the menu, the plants, the color of the booths and tables, the backs of the people sitting at the counter.

Ah, his familiar voice. Lawrence turned around. James was coming in through the hotel lobby entrance. Lawrence waved, and then his heart sank. James was not alone.

"Cleveland is going to give me a ride to the airport," he said, "so I invited him along for breakfast. Hope you don't mind."

"Oh, no, of course not," said Lawrence, rising out of the booth to shake their hands. James sat down and Cleveland slid into the booth beside him. Lawrence and James had identical orders: tomato juice and toast. Cleveland ordered pancakes and sausage and fried potatoes and an English muffin, with a large glass of milk.

"Cheers," said Cleveland, clinking his water glass against James's as the waitress walked away clicking her pen. Lawrence struggled, trying not to let himself resent Cleveland for being there. He had no control over the situation, so why let it ruin his morning?

He watched Cleveland carefully. Everything the boy did seemed to be for display. His movements were exaggerated, self-conscious and graceful, almost dancerly. As though he is a mime, thought Lawrence. Cleveland swung his right leg over the low arm of the booth.

His muscles were tense and obvious under the leg of his thin cotton trousers. Lawrence pursed his lips and looked away, looked at James.

Had they been sleeping together, James and Cleveland? Lawrence resolved not to think about it. Not even to consider the question. What was the point, except to make himself miserable. He had heard rumors about James's relationship with a boy in Chicago, but no. No, he wasn't going to think about it.

James's eyes were bloodshot and slightly wrinkled at the corners. His color was bad, sallow. He needs sleep, Lawrence decided. He was talking about San Joachím and about the last time he'd played there, about the coffee and the good cocaine. Lawrence raised an eyebrow and James pretended not to notice. James knew Lawrence didn't approve of his using drugs. Cleveland was watching James, drawing James's eyes away from Lawrence like a magnet.

The waitress set tomato juice in front of James, tomato juice in front of Cleveland, and milk in front of Lawrence. Instinctively, Lawrence curled his lip. The sight of plain milk disgusted him. Cleveland switched glasses deftly, eyes twinkling. Lawrence wondered, why had she given him the milk? Did he look like such a milk-fed old man? He shook some pepper into his tomato juice. There was no lemon slice to squeeze. James was drinking his plain.

There were so many things he could have said to him if they had been alone. He would have talked about Gabriel, not bothering to mask his enthusiasm, and he was anxious to know what James really thought of the boy. James was honest only when they were alone together. Lawrence caught himself about to sigh, then stopped and exhaled smoothly. So, he would have to wait two more weeks to see James. Things could be worse, he would not dwell on this any longer. He would write him a letter for now, in lieu of being able to talk with him.

James looked at his watch (it was the gold one Lawrence had given him years ago in celebration of his debut with the London Symphony) and exclaimed about the time. Cleveland ate very quickly without gobbling. Pancakes, syrup, sausage, potatoes, muffin, milk. What an extremely rich breakfast, thought Lawrence, who could eat no more than bread or dry cereal or fruit in the morning. And how slender the boy is.

"Cleveland dances," said James, guessing Lawrence's thought. "That's how he can eat like such a horse."

Cleveland finished his milk and let out a whinny. "Modern," he said.

"Pardon me?" said Lawrence.

"Modern dance," said James.

Lawrence swallowed the last bit of coffee and the waitress appeared to refill his cup.

"We'd like the check, please," said James. "We're in a hurry."

"So soon?" said Lawrence, glancing at his watch. Eight-twenty.

"Cleveland rented a car and it's parked in the high-rise garage here. You know how long it takes them to get a car out of this building."

I don't know, thought Lawrence. I don't drive a car.

"So we'd better get going," said James. The waitress put three checks down in the middle of the table. Lawrence and James both reached for their wallets.

"This is on me," said James.

"No," began Lawrence.

"I insist."

Cleveland smiled slyly at Lawrence and said he'd enjoyed the meal. On the way out, as James stopped at the cash register, Cleveland took a toothpick and placed it between his lips. Then he and James, waving good-bye, disappeared into the lobby, past the flower shop, past the candy shop, toward the sign marked GARAGE. Lawrence left the hotel from the front entrance, walking evenly between the guardian lions, down the middle of the carpet, past the doorman, and he turned left, out of the sun, toward Ritten-house Park.

The park was busy with men and women on their way to work. It was a warm morning, almost sixty degrees, and the men wore only suit jackets and the women light spring coats. Lawrence sat on a clean bench, away from the trash cans. Three benches down, a tattered old man was sleeping under a blanket of newspapers. Lawrence reached into his jacket pocket for his notebook and reread the outline for the chapter he was working on. He'd absolutely promised to finish it by Monday, and he was beginning to grow anxious. Time to get to work. A pigeon landed startlingly close to him on the bench. He looked at it, and the bird cocked its head, staring back. The pigeon, he noted, was missing part of one claw.

"Shoo!" he said softly. The pigeon did not. Lawrence stood up and waved his notebook at the bird. With a noisy flutter it was gone, this time landing on the bench with the sleeping bum, who did not awaken. Lawrence took out his pen to make some notes. A minute later he looked up, across the park to the traffic. Something had made him think of James, who by this time should be in Cleveland's rented car, on their way to the airport. Eight forty-five. Why had James brought Cleveland along to their only private meeting these whole two weeks? And why had he brought Marina along to dinner the other day? And why had Freddy and Maur come along with him for drinks the other night, when, after all, they had just seen each other the night before at Maur's reception? It was as though James was avoiding having to talk to Lawrence alone, always diluting their meetings with other people. Was something wrong or was this all just a coincidence? Or was he imagining it? Lawrence felt sweat trickle down his neck. He often felt feverish when he was sad, and he was sad from the fear of losing James.

James was the one he could talk to best, and he could explain his sadnesses only to James. But how could he tell him of his misery? He couldn't. He was alone.

He'd known James since James was a student — not his student, he'd been too busy teaching then, but he'd encountered him for the first time in a special master-class he'd given at Juilliard. James Rosen had been fifteen years old; he'd come to New York with his mother that day just to participate in the class. It was a small, elite class and Lawrence noticed him right away: a handsome slim dark-haired teenager sitting tense beside his mother, uncomfortable in his necktie and cuff links. It was 1953 and Lawrence, at twenty-three, was the undisputed star of the flute. For four years he'd been touring heavily, soloing with all the major American orchestras, and next year he'd be touring Europe for six months. He was always flying somewhere to perform. He could hardly keep his travel plans straight without constant reminders from his agent.

That afternoon he was in New York, tired after the flight back home from a performance in Colorado. When he walked in the door the phone was ringing. It was Bernie, his agent, reminding him he had to be at Juilliard in two hours for a class.

He was in a bad mood when he got there, exhausted and determined that he would be bored by the whole thing. He did not like students in general — he'd been one himself so recently that watching them reminded him of the many flaws he'd overcome, or hadn't, in his own playing. There were seven students in the class: four from Juilliard, two "professionals" whose careers Lawrence had already heard about (they were both older than he was), and this boy, James.

James played last, and though he was by no means the best technician, he played more naturally than any of them. He walked stiffly to the podium and Lawrence had expected a mechanical performance, but no, his tension fled as he raised the instrument to his mouth. He was fluid, if not precise, and emotional. When he finished, one strand of his straight hair fell loose across his forehead. He was perspiring. He smiled at Lawrence, who was also smiling, wondering how to coach him.

Lawrence saw him again, a year later, backstage in Baltimore. James was in line with the autograph-seekers.

"I met you once before," he said, as Lawrence signed his program. "At a master class in New York." Lawrence remembered him at once.

"Oh, yes, the boy with his mother."

"My mother died last month," he said.

Lawrence was puzzled. What should he say? "I'm sorry."

"She had diabetes," said James.

"I'm sorry." James was taller this year. His hair was darker, his back straighter, his smile more perfect. The line behind him was growing longer and more restless.

"I'd like to talk to you more," said Lawrence impulsively. "This is my phone number in New York." He scribbled it down. "Call me there if you're in town — and if I'm not on tour maybe we can get together." James's stunned expression made Lawrence regret having done that, but it was too late.

"Thank — thank you," James said, and walked away slowly, staring at the program.

Months later, when Lawrence arrived home from Denmark with bundles of cheeses and a copy of the first pressing of an album he'd just cut there, he found in the stack of messages taken by his secretary, Anthony, a handwritten note:

I was in New York and I called but there was no answer, so I looked up where you lived and I came here and I'm leaving this note.

Sincerely,
James Rosen

The handwriting was surprisingly fluid and self-assured for an adolescent's, Lawrence had thought. He removed the note from the rest of the messages — it had probably aroused Tony's jealousy already — and that night he called the boy's home in

Philadelphia. A man answered, gruffly. Probably James's father. Lawrence didn't identify himself, just asked to speak with James, who was not home. "I'm a friend from New York," he told the man. "Lawrence." He gave the number, speaking in a high pitch that made him sound young, like another teenager. That ought not to arouse the father's suspicion.

Lawrence and James became lovers when James visited him in New York the next week. He came up alone by train, having told his father that he had an invitation to attend a class by a famous flutist, a prospective teacher, someone he'd played for once before. Lawrence had guessed, from the way the boy signaled him, that he liked men, and he was relieved to know also that he was not James's first lover, there'd been someone else, another student, in Philadelphia.

What was it? His looks? His intelligence? His youth? Lawrence often asked himself how he grew to love James so quickly. He did not know why, but only that he had never been so infatuated with anyone before. He only hoped that James could genuinely return his love. For now, he knew, he was the boy's idol, a hero, not a real person. But he hoped James would come to love him, too, as he grew older. Lawrence became James's mentor. He convinced the boy's father that James would have to move to New York to pursue his musical career. Sam Rosen was an electrical engineer, a widower with three younger daughters. He knew little about music and building musical careers, and he was happy that a well-known flutist took an interest in his son. He could not, however, move his family and his business to New York. He was relieved when Lawrence Chattarjee offered to look after the boy when he moved to New York.

James was seventeen with he came to live with Lawrence. They traveled together and Lawrence coached him daily. Lawrence's agent, Bernie Thorn, agreed to put James on his roster the following year, so James had a head start on his career with one of the best managements in New York. Bernie had advised Lawrence this might be risky — helping James gain the spotlight might bring a little unnecessary competition — but Lawrence was adamant. He loved James and he wanted him to succeed. Besides, Lawrence was the undisputed major American flute soloist, and he'd been building momentum for years. It would be many more years before any other flutist could even begin to catch up with him.

He lived with James for a year before his accident.

It was Christmastime, 1956, and on New Year's Eve Lawrence was scheduled to fly to Japan to start his first Asian tour. James was coming, too, and he was spending much of his time studying maps of Tokyo and Hong Kong and Taipei. Lawrence had been uptown that afternoon, meeting with Bernie to discuss the trip, picking up his and James's passports, buying a Christmas present for his mother, Hanukkah presents for James's three little sisters. Usually he traveled by taxi, but it was starting to snow, and the streets were crowded with shoppers. All of the cabs seemed to be occupied already. Not to waste time Lawrence took the subway. What happened after he boarded the crowded subway car was never really part of his memory. He had an impression of the scenario, but much of it came from his wanting to recall every moment of what had so filled his life with pain. Many of the details he invented, aided by the imaginations of friends, and the newspaper reports he read. But all Lawrence really knew was that he got on the subway, found a seat right by the door, and somewhere after the Forty-second Street stop, the car derailed, toppled on its side, spilling bodies everywhere and sending a jagged panel crashing onto his left hand, severing two fingers. According to the newspaper accounts, he was the most seriously injured person on the car, except for one woman, whose spine was damaged. He remembered nothing of being rescued from the car, of the ride to the hospital in an ambulance in the middle of a rush-hour traffic jam. The ambulance attendant reported that Lawrence was awake the whole time, talking excitedly about his missing fingers, urging the attendant to turn the ambulance back so that he could collect them.

He woke up hours later, in a hospital bed, in pain, confused. His bandaged hand he could hardly comprehend. He wept silently, constantly for days, salty tears stinging his facial lacerations. A week after the accident, he asked his nurse to bring him a mirror to look at his damaged reflection. He was lucky the jag had missed his eyes, they told him. Lucky? He would be lucky to be dead, he thought. His face would be fine, they said, except for a few small scars. He pushed the mirror away. He didn't care. He also didn't care about the long gash now stitched down his left leg. He would have been glad to endure any other kind of disfigurement just to be able to play again. Some well-intentioned person told him, trying to cheer him up, of a cellist who injured his fingers while mountain climbing; the first thing the man had thought, as soon as the accident had occurred, was, thank God I'll never have to play the cello again. Lawrence did not understand how a musician could feel this way. That story must be a lie.

This whole situation must be imaginary, he decided many times. He desperately wanted to escape.

Everyone came to see him in the hospital. James was there every day. Even Tony, who'd left in a huff when James moved in, had come, offering to be his secretary again if he needed one. His mother came, daily, bringing meals she'd prepared so he wouldn't have to eat the hospital food. She would speak to him in hushed tones, tears in her eyes, and stroke his head as he drifted in and out of tranquilized consciousness.

There were cards, thousands of cards, and gifts from fans all over the world. Lawrence's disfigurement had made international headlines. James had gone to the library, photocopied the clippings from newspapers in important cities all over the world, and pasted them in a scrapbook. He had also saved most of the cards, and filled every table, every ledge, every counter top in the apartment with them. There were cut flowers and potted plants everywhere, too, and dozens and dozens of boxes of candy.

The one thing Lawrence didn't see when he was brought home from the hospital was his flute. James had hidden all the flutes somewhere, out of sight. Lawrence asked for it immediately. James hesitated, then brought it.

Lawrence tried to undo the canvas cover with his good hand, but he was clumsy and the zipper stuck.

"Take it out," he told James hoarsely. James's hands were shaking. He opened the case. The instrument glinted, reflecting the strong late-afternoon light from the west window. "Shall I assemble it?" asked James.

"No. Why? I can't practice with a bandage on my hand, can I?" James turned and ran out of the room. Lawrence could hear him in the kitchen blowing his nose. With his good hand he pushed the instrument off his lap. The head joint rolled out of the case, across the carpet, and stopped at the door, blazing gold. Lawrence closed his eyes, trying to block out the strong sunset. Why hadn't James pulled the shades? It was four-thirty, January 4th. He should have been in Tokyo.

Lawrence was well insured, and his lawyers advised him to sue the New York City Transit Authority, which he did, successfully. Money, he was told, would never be a problem. He gave his gold flute to James, but he could no longer coach him. He did not have the patience. He could not stand to listen to the instrument. He asked James not to practice in the apartment.

Bernie had two years of advance contracts for Lawrence. He asked his permission to have James substitute, claiming that losing those commissions would damage his business. Lawrence knew that James wasn't ready musically or emotionally to tour so heavily, but Bernie insisted, dramatically reciting all the good he'd done for Lawrence. Lawrence was tired. He signed the agreement without arguing. James, ecstatic and nervous, set to practicing twelve hours a day in a rented studio. Lawrence spent his mornings sleeping, his afternoons drinking Pernod, his evenings drinking cognac, his nights lying awake. He did not touch James or invite James to touch him.

For a slow, year-long trance, Lawrence lay in his room, vaguely following James's reviews, which were sometimes good. Mostly he lay idly or listened to the radio, drinking himself into a pleasant stupor by each evening and then finding himself awake each night, frightened by his terrible dreams. He knew he would never be able to escape his night terrors. They came to him unchecked, as he slept. There was no way to stop them.

James was not helpful to Lawrence then; he could not be. He was young and did not know what to do.

James was his only real friend, and that responsibility was an awesome one for the boy. Lawrence knew that James had no idea how to reassure him, no idea what to say to a man who had lost what had made him great. He knew James was repulsed by his injury. He knew James wished that he had never come to live with him. But Lawrence's accident had also given James a sudden professional advantage: by taking over Lawrence's busy concert schedule, James would have an instant career that many soloists never dare to dream of obtaining. James did not deserve this, and Lawrence didn't know if he could handle it. He was not the caliber of musician Lawrence was — there were probably a half-dozen other solo flutists who would have been better choices to replace him than James, but Lawrence had handpicked his successor. James didn't deserve it by virtue of his musicianship, but, as Bernie had argued, it is not always the music that is most important in shaping a career. The public wanted someone who was close to Lawrence, the next in line in the dynasty, and James had been his only protégé. He was the logical replacement. If he failed as an artist, he could be forgotten within one season, but if he succeeded he could be the next Lawrence Chattarjee.

Now it is only a few connoisseurs who remember Lawrence Chattarjee, the performer. His recordings are considered collector's items by those knowledgeable, but the music public has forgotten him. They all know the name of James Rosen, master of the flute.

It was after nine, and the rush-hour crowd had disappeared from the park. Nearly everyone had vanished into his or her office. The bum on the park bench wakened, slowly stretching, and scattering newspapers as he stood. The pigeon that had bothered Lawrence had anonymously joined a flock of other pigeons eating pretzel crumbs distributed by a frowzy woman. Lawrence put his notebook back into his pocket and headed home. At nine-thirty he was due to start writing. At noon he would have lunch, and at one he had to be at Curtis for a lesson. His day would be busy.

By now, he thought as he passed the doorman to his apartment building, by now Cleveland and James must surely have arrived at the airport. James must be checking in at the ticket counter. Lawrence wondered if James would call him from a phone booth to wish him good-bye.

II Late that afternoon Cleveland went to Marina's apartment and waited on the steps outside. He knew that she finished her classes around that time, and that since James was gone she would come straight home and stay there until after dinner, when it was time for orchestra rehearsal.

She saw him as she rounded the corner and her mouth grew dry. All day long she'd wondered if he'd call her or come to see her after James left. She knew Cleveland had three more days in Philadelphia, and that Mr. Weinburg and Mr. D'Artoit were going back to Chicago tonight. Why was Cleveland staying longer? She'd imagined it must have been for her, and now she knew it was true. Her heart was pounding. I feel like a character in a movie, she thought. He was staring at her, she could feel his eyes, and she was afraid to look at him. She clutched her flute and her bundle of music close to her chest. She knew he knew she knew he was waiting for her. Her breath was shallow. She would get dizzy if she breathed like that. She breathed deeper. She'd been thinking about him almost constantly ever since he arrived in Philadelphia, and had been hoping to spot him at rehearsals or in the school. She'd even wished that he'd go away so she could concentrate on what she was supposed to be doing. And every night, even when she was with James, she had fantasized about him.

She was close now, ten feet away from her building. He hadn't moved. He'd been watching her approach. She looked up, and as their eyes met, her heart leapt and she looked away. It's as though he could see into me, she thought. She wished that she could seem older and more confident.

"Hi," she said.

"Marina." He drew out the syllables slowly. Again she tried to return his steady gaze, but she couldn't. What should she say?

"I was just going upstairs," she said, stumbling slightly as she climbed past him. She could hear him getting up swiftly, following her. She stopped at her mailbox and had trouble fitting the key into the slot. Her face felt hot. No mail. Embarrassing.

At the desk she had to give them his name. "Cleveland Arms," she whispered. The woman wrote that down. "Checked in 4:45."

She took the steps up five stories. It would have been unbearable to wait with him for the elevator. She walked up ahead of him, too quickly. She was panting. He wasn't. She felt her underarms grow wet in her sweater. She had dressed too warmly today. The apartment was hot — all the windows shut. She threw her things down and began to open them. He stood in the doorway for a minute, waiting, and then she heard the door shut. She turned around. He was sitting on her sofa, one foot balanced on the coffee table.

"Can I get you anything to drink?" she asked. He nodded.

"I have coffee, Tab, orange juice. And I could make tea. And I have" — what was that stuff James had given her? — "Rémy Martin — cognac. Do you like that?" He nodded again.

She poured it the way James had shown her, into the brandy snifter he had given her. She poured in just enough so that when she tipped the glass on its side the liquid reached the lip of the glass without spilling out. She took it over to Cleveland and he held it in his palms without tasting it. She went back into the kitchen and poured herself one. She took a gulp. James had shown her how to warm it and sip very slowly, smelling it the whole time, but right now she needed a gulp.

Back in the living room she sat on the chair across from him.

"My grandfather made that," she said, motioning to the table on which Cleveland was now resting both feet. She wished she could think of something better to say.

Cleveland's nose was in his brandy glass. He nodded and said, "For you?"

"Yes, he was a cabinetmaker. The rest of this furniture came with the apartment." What a stupid thing to talk about, she thought. Her drab, ugly furniture. Why couldn't she think of anything to say. With James, at least, she could make herself seem intelligent. Cleveland didn't say much himself. He wasn't any help in getting conversation going.

"Do you have any solo performances coming up?" she attempted.

Cleveland shook his head no and made a clucking sound with his tongue. Silence, and then:

"Well, I *do* have a little recital lined up in Chicago next month. Nothing *big*."

"But you want to be a soloist?" Another silly thing to say: he had already told her so at dinner the other night when they were with James and Lawrence Chattarjee and Mr. Weinburg and Mr. D'Artoit.

"Yes," said Cleveland.

"But you're not under management?"

"No," said Cleveland.

"But you want to be?"

"*Everyone* wants to be."

"I don't. I don't want to be a soloist."

Cleveland laughed lightly, tossing his head back. Why was that funny? Marina wondered.

"Does Mr. D'Artoit help you find dates with orchestras?"

"*Hardly.* He doesn't even have an orchestra himself. Guest conductors never get to pick the soloist — and anyway he's lucky when he gets to guest conduct. Oh, he has *friends* he introduces me to, and they introduce me to somebody else, someone who might have some *influence*." Cleveland had a way of stressing certain words in a sentence, kind of underlining them with his voice. Marina liked the way he talked.

"Is that how you met James, through Mr. D'Artoit?"

Cleveland laughed again. A lock of his hair fell across his forehead and he pushed it back into place.

"What do you know about James and me?" he asked. Marina took another gulp of cognac and choked a little. She felt her face growing hot. She wasn't sure what she was supposed to know about James and Cleveland, but she thought that something was going on. It had to do with the way people talked about them and the way they looked at each other. She knew that James was gay, or that he used to be gay. He'd told her that himself, the first night he'd slept with her. He was a virgin with women, he'd said, and she was very special. But he still liked men; she knew he always would. And besides, everyone talked about James and Lawrence Chattarjee, and how James's career got started. That was history, not even gossip. But what about James and Cleveland? Marina had been afraid to ask James if there was another man because she was afraid that the answer would be yes. Really, it was none of her business, and she didn't want to step out of place. James was older and famous and his life was his own. She had no right to ask him about it, she knew, so she didn't ask and he didn't volunteer any information. She'd wondered, however, what he did on the many nights they were apart.

Often when he was in town and she called him there was no answer or the phone was busy — maybe off the hook. She was a little jealous about this and she knew she had no right to be. James might not be with someone else at all, and even if he was it was none of her business. He had never promised her anything. He had never told her he loved her, and she didn't know if she loved him. She didn't think so.

Cleveland's eyes sparkled. He is very amused by me, thought Marina. She didn't know what she should do or say. She stared into her cognac and decided to wait for him to do something.

"*Marina,*" he said finally, "why don't you want to look at me? Don't you like the way I look?"

"Oh, yes —" She was flustered. What a weird thing for him to say. "Yes, I like the way you look."

"I like the way *you* look."

"Oh — thank you." What should she say to him? He looked dangerous. He had narrowed his eyes into slits, like an Oriental. Her heartbeat was speeding up. She looked at her watch. Five-fifteen.

"Do you have to be somewhere?" he asked.

"Orchestra. I have orchestra at six."

"But *that's* not for a while."

"Yes, but — I have to eat first. I have to eat early so I don't lose my breath —"

"I didn't think you *ate* very much. You never eat much in restaurants."

"In private I eat like a monster. Really. And I don't have any food in the apartment right now. Do you want to come with me for a pizza?" She jumped up, grabbed her pocketbook, her orchestral music, her flute. "I have to go," she said.

"I'll wait for you here."

"You can't. If I leave and you don't check out downstairs... they won't allow it. Men can't be up here alone."

"Try it."

"I can't."

"Just give it a *try*. See if they notice." There was no way out of this.

"Okay," said Marina. She left, shut the door tightly, and ran all the way down the steps. She ran across the street, nearly getting hit by a car, and ran the four blocks over to Rittenhouse Park. Her head was swimming a little from the cognac. She was not hungry at all, almost nauseous. She sat down breathlessly on a park bench. The short March day was ending, and it was starting to get dark and chilly. She'd left her coat in the apartment. Well, she wasn't going back to get it.

Would Cleveland really be waiting for her when she got home from orchestra? She hoped desperately that he would and that he wouldn't. She closed her eyes and breathed slowly, deeply. The park was crowded with the evening rush-hour crowd. She wanted to be alone. She headed across the park to Curtis — maybe she could find a quiet, empty practice room.

III   That morning, the minute she got in from driving Gabriel to school, Elizabeth called Sue Levin, the woman in New York at Goldfarb Artists Services, Incorporated, who was supposed to be finding a manager for Gabriel. Elizabeth instinctively respected Sue Levin but she disliked her. She had long violet fingernails and a hook nose and perfect hair and a New York City stylishness that made Elizabeth feel pale and awkward. She trusted, from the way Sue Levin talked and moved, that she knew her way around music in New York City. Elizabeth called her at least once a week to see if she'd made any progress. She had Max paying Goldfarb $200 a month, plus he'd given them $1,500 as a deposit on a brochure for Gabriel. Sue Levin said the layout for the brochure was almost ready and that she'd have them mailed out for Elizabeth's approval soon, but that was all. It had been five months now since Elizabeth had signed the contract and still no word about a manager. Sue Levin said what Gabriel needed was reviews. He needed reviews and he needed to be heard. But how can he get reviews if he doesn't have an agent to find him engagements? When Elizabeth had brought this up, thinking it a rather obvious dilemma, Sue Levin had said, "You need a chicken before you can get an egg, right?" and then she'd suggested that Elizabeth rent a sound studio and made a better quality demonstration tape. Elizabeth hadn't mentioned this to Max yet. She knew he'd get angry and ask what was wrong with the tape Gabriel made a few months ago. She also had a feeling that once they'd made another tape of Gabriel, Sue Levin would start saying that they needed to press a record album. Sue Levin might be good at what she did, but she was also good at spending other people's money, Elizabeth had decided. She would be cautious with that woman.

She got put on hold for five minutes even though she told the secretary she was calling long distance. Finally the secretary came back and said that Ms. Levin was on another line. (Just like trying to get through to Max, thought Elizabeth.) The secretary promised to have her call back, when she was finished.

Two hours later when the telephone hadn't rung, Elizabeth tried again. In a few minutes she came on the line.

"Sue Levin."

"Good morning, Sue, this is Elizabeth Van Allen."

"I know. What is it?"

"Well, I just wanted to let you know — remember when I told

you that Gabriel was giving a recital at Curtis? That was last night. I told you there was a possibility that James Rosen might attend it."

"And?"

"And he was there. And so was the conductor Maurice D'Artoit, as a personal guest of Lawrence Chattarjee."

"And?"

"And — and well, the recital went really well. There was a standing ovation, though I wonder if it was mostly for Lawrence Chattarjee or mostly for Gabriel. They like him a lot, I know."

"And?"

"And what? I told you it went exceptionally well."

"Did you talk to Rosen or D'Artoit?"

"No, Lawrence Chattarjee didn't introduce me, but he did introduce Gabriel."

"He liked the kid's playing?"

"Yes, I'm sure of it."

"Can we get him to write a statement for the brochure? D'Artoit, too. It would be nice to have one from him."

"I don't know if I can. I hardly know Rosen."

"Okay, I'll call him up and ask. He lives in Philadelphia, doesn't he? Bernie Thorn's his manager and we don't get along, so I'll call him up direct. Where does D'Artoit live? In Philadelphia, too?"

"No, wait, Sue. I don't know if you should call him. It might look too aggressive."

"In this business you've got to be pushy if you're going to make it."

"I know but — let me try something. Let me talk to Chattarjee about it. He knows both of them really well and I know he wants to help Gabriel."

"Elizabeth, do want these quotes on the brochure?"

"Of course, but . . ."

"Then let me handle it."

"No, I'd feel like we were being overbearing if you did. I know we have to be aggressive, but I don't want to go too far. Let me be the one who calls, not a New York agency."

"You're just going to hold up the works."

"Give me a week."

"You want to hold up the brochure for a week?"

"Give me three days."

"All right. Do what you want. I'll talk to you in three days." The line went dead.

Elizabeth lit a cigarette and dialed Lawrence Chattarjee. Her heart was pounding.

His maid answered on the third ring and called him to the phone.

"Mr. Chattarjee, this is Mrs. Van Allen, Gabriel's mother."

"Yes, good morning."

"I wanted to thank you for the recital last night."

"Yes. He did well."

"You were both marvelous. You're a wonderful teacher — it shows in Gabriel."

"Why, thank you." Elizabeth wished that he would be more conversational — say something else, so she didn't have to plunge into the real reason she'd called, but Lawrence was silent, waiting.

"Mr. Chattarjee, I was wondering if you could help me with something . . ."

"Yes?"

"Mr. Chattarjee, as Gabriel's mother, you know, I'm terribly concerned with his . . . career."

"His career?"

"Well, his development."

"I can understand that. So am I."

"Well, I've taken some steps to acquire an agent for Gabriel."

"An agent!"

"I don't have one yet, but we're working with a publicist."

"My dear Mrs. Van Allen, I can't imagine that an eleven-year-old boy, no matter how prodigious, could need a commercial publicist."

"Oh, it's nothing like that — I'm just trying to cultivate a name for him so when he's ready to perform —"

"We can worry about when he's ready to perform when he *is* ready to perform."

"Really that's not what I meant, but you see, I know it's so competitive out there, what with the music world being so crowded and so many soloists. What I want for Gabriel is a head start."

"Mrs. Van Allen, what are you trying to tell me?"

"Well, actually, I called to ask a favor . . ."

"Yes?"

"Um. Last night at the recital . . . Your friend Mr. Rosen, he was there."

"Yes."

"What I'm trying to ask is, well, the publicist feels that a quote from Mr. Rosen, for the brochure, you know —"

"Mrs. Van Allen, if you wish Mr. Rosen to give you a quote about your son, you will have to ask him yourself. I will advise you, however, that he is currently on a plane en route to San Joachím, where he will spend the next two weeks. I strongly advise you to use the period of his absence to reflect on the nature and possible consequences of your request, and I hope you will decide to do otherwise."

Elizabeth felt a knot in her throat. Mr. Chattarjee sounded calm, but his words were angry. Clearly he didn't want Gabriel under any type of management. She didn't want to alienate him, but how could she give up, after she had worked so hard for this? Oh, what should she do?

IV

FROM THE DESK OF L. CHATTARJEE

March 5, 1979

> *James, good evening. I am writing this to you while you are newly arrived (or still en route?) to San Joachím, though I will not give it to you until you return to Philadelphia in two weeks' time. Good evening, then, wherever and whenever you are reading this.*

The sun set a little after five today, your favorite kind of orange-and-pink Rittenhouse Park view from my window. I was watching the sunset, drinking my cognac, as you know is my habit on afternoons when I am at home and the weather is clear. On a bench in the middle of the park, in the middle of all the rush-hour human traffic, on exactly the same bench I'd been using this morning, I saw a girl I imagined was Marina — the same strong dark hair, the same delicate limbs. And she was clutching some papers and a small case that might have held a flute. Perhaps it was your Marina. It may well have been, but I could not see her face clearly.

James, many times I find myself thinking about that girl and her dark beauty — is that what compels you? I think she must have some secret that draws you to her, and I am curious. When I am near her she is closed; she wears a mask. I do not understand her mystery. I watch her closely, but she gives me no clues.

I think that you have chosen her to be with you for a reason, but I don't know what. You never loved a woman before, and I don't imagine that you love her, or that you will ... but you want her near you. She intrigues you and I want to understand why.

I have watched her with you when she is tense and polite, and with other students. She is an ordinary girl, with ordinary talent. She is not an artist; her playing is adequate and unimpressive. I think it is her beauty that intrigues you. She is exotic, she is so different from you in ways that even I, with my almond eyes, am not. Am I right? Or do you know?

I have thought a lot about intellectual attraction to human beauty, beauty that is either different from or a reflection of ourselves. I am drawn to the beauty of Gabriel in this way — his body is a reflection of all we have had and lost. His soul is pure and his mind is untainted music. In his childishness he is perfect, the perfect human. He is an Angel. I cringe to think that he must enter adolescence.

Yesterday after the recital, when his mother and Samantha kissed him, I kissed him, too. He seemed to expect that, and to me it was quite natural. But I could not ignore the tenderness of his cheek, softer than any human skin I have felt. I will never touch him with my hands. I feel that if I even brush my fingers against him I will damage him.

I want to protect him, to keep him close where it is safe, and I am nervous for him at the hands of his mother. She is too eager to help him and her touch is indelicate. She has called me today to ask if you would write a recommendation for him, for a brochure she is having printed in New York. For some time now I have feared that she would try to push Gabriel into the professional world before he was ready, and now I know. I am not surprised that she did not mention this to me sooner. She suspected that I would disapprove, and now I have confirmed that. I told her that if she wants a quote from you, she must ask you. I will not be a part of it. I would like to do everything in my power to prevent Gabriel from being forced into a grown-up, professional, competitive world while he is still so pure. I want to keep him golden while he still can be, James.

Lawrence put down his pen and drained his teacup. He checked the pot for more, but only the dregs remained swirling in the bottom. He studied the two sheets of cream-colored paper he had filled with his gentle gray-blue sloping handwriting. He would not write about Cleveland, he decided. Not in this letter, at least, not now. He folded the sheets and placed them on his windowsill, where he would see them and remember to give them to James.

V   Cleveland's first kiss was on her ear. That made her shiver. His breath was loud. She arched her back, her muscles tensed, and he chuckled. He knows how scared I am, she thought.

He moved slowly around her, his face close to hers, but he did not touch her. How should she respond? He was motionless, poised in front of her, his lips nearly touching her lips, but not quite. Was he waiting for her to kiss him? She looked at his eyes; they sparkled so strongly that she looked away, ashamed that she could not find the courage to stare back. She watched his mouth as it spread into a slow careful smile. He was tilting his head; he was tilting his whole body, swaying a little from the hips, and his hair swung softly at his cheeks.

She wished for a loud noise, a clatter of plates falling in the kitchen, or maybe a scream outside in the street: something to dissolve the moment, but her apartment was strangely quiet.

Cleveland made a *mmmm* sound in his throat and pressed his lips against hers. Her lips worked reflexively against his, but she thought, I'm awkward. His eyes grew narrow, Oriental in their curve. Again she looked away; her eyes found the telephone on the table. She wished that it would ring, but it was silent. She sighed.

"*Sad?*" said Cleveland. Their eyes met. Her face was hot, and for the second time that day she felt a suspicion of nausea growing in her stomach.

I am not here, she thought. This is not possible. A fantasy cannot come true.

"*Ner*-vous, then?" She nodded yes without thinking first, and then regretted it furiously. I look like a foolish child, she thought. As if I can't handle myself.

Marina swallowed and gathered courage. She narrowed her eyes, like Cleveland's, and returned his stare. His look grew more intense, but she did not relent. She moved her face so close to his that her eyes lost focus and his face grew narrow. She drew away and saw that he was smiling.

"*Marina,*" he said slowly.

What does he want, she wondered desperately. Again she noticed the sickening feeling in her abdomen. It must have been the cognac on an empty stomach, she thought. Cognac, a difficult rehearsal, no dinner, more cognac, and Cleveland.

His right leg rested on the coffee table, his body curved toward her. His sleeves were rolled up and she imagined the veins of his lean arms pulsing. He smelled like, like . . . roses, and his odor was growing stronger.

Maybe it's the rose smell that is making me dizzy, she thought, sitting straighter. He was still smiling. Without removing his gaze from her he tossed his head and his hair fell into place perfectly. He was motionless, except for his right hand, which dropped lightly upon her right knee, and moved softly up the outside of her thigh till it came to cradle her hipbone. She started to move toward him, but his eyes stopped her. He made a *tlk* sound with his tongue, and his hand continued up, over her waist, her ribs, under her arm, and rested finally on her shoulder. Marina sat frozen. He leaned forward and kissed her quietly on the lips, and then he was on his feet, easy like a dancer.

"Good night," he whispered. Marina stood, feeling heavy and dazed.

"You're leaving?"

Cleveland nodded. The clock on the wall behind his head said 11:45. She wanted to ask him why, but she didn't speak. He raised his hand, half waved, half bowed, and simultaneously opened her door with his other hand. He left backwards, and she could see his smile until the door shut.

Marina sank back down on the sofa and found herself crying. Why had he come here, waiting for her all that time, only to act like that and leave? Had she done something wrong, broken some code of behavior she hadn't even known about? He had rejected her for some reason . . . or had he? She wasn't sure what he had done, or what had happened. Still crying she took herself to the bathroom, washed her face, and swallowed two aspirins. She sat on the edge of her bed and began to undress, and then the phone rang.

Her mother was speaking to her, fast, in Ukrainian. How strange of her to call this late at night, thought Marina, and slowly, dully, she began to understand her words. Her father, Papa, had had a heart attack that night, at home, after dinner. He'd been arguing with Serge, as he did almost constantly, and then he'd collapsed. Her mother continued, describing how his face had turned purple, how they'd pounded his chest to get him to breathe, and then the arrival of the ambulance.

"Mama," Marina kept trying to interrupt. She thought, he's alive. He must be alive or she would have said so right away. "Mama . . . MAMA! How is he?" she said in English. He was alive, in intensive care, in the Trenton Memorial Hospital.

"I'll come home tomorrow morning," Marina told her mother, in English. Her mother began to speak of saints and prayers and masses, all in rapid Ukrainian.

"I'll be home tomorrow morning," repeated Marina. Her mother continued, not listening.

"Good night, Mama." Marina hung up, with her mother still talking. Without turning off the light, she lay on her bed and closed her eyes. She fell asleep thinking about her brother Serge, wondering what they'd been arguing about that made her father's heart fail, wondering how Serge felt, wondering if her father was in pain...

An hour later the phone rang again. Marina opened her eyes to the painful bright glow of her lamp. She remembered Cleveland, her father, Serge, her mother. The phone rang three times, four, five times. She was afraid not to answer.

"Hello," she was hoarse.

"Is this Maria Kazakov?" The voice was timid, and unfamiliar.

"*Marina*. Who is this?" She could feel herself growing cold... maybe it was someone from the hospital... But there was music in the background, the start of a Beethoven movement. Which symphony? The voice continued.

"This is — you don't know me — this is Fish."

"What?"

"My name is Fish. I need to talk to you."

"What is this? Who are you? How did you get my phone number?"

"It took a while. It was hard, but I wanted to talk to you."

"Who are you, some kind of pervert?" Did he have something to do with Cleveland Arms? Marina found herself hanging up the receiver. She picked it up again: dial tone. She took the phone off the hook and turned off the lamp. She pulled the blankets up around her and shivered.

Chapter 9

I   The room was bright when Gabriel opened his eyes. It was warm, too. When he threw off the blankets he was sweating underneath, sticking to his pajamas. He slid out of bed and picked up his teddy bears, which he'd kicked out during the night. It was hot, but he wasn't allowed to open the window because Mom hadn't put the screens in yet. He found his slippers, skidded down the hallway, and ran downstairs to the kitchen.

It would have been a perfect Saturday to play baseball. It was warm enough not to wear a jacket, and it hadn't rained for three days, so it probably wasn't even muddy. Steven and Selby would be out all day until it got dark and their mom made them come inside. But not Gabriel. Aside from the usual time he had to put in practicing, there was something else. Today was special.

Mom was downstairs already, all dressed. She was wearing high heels and her black silk Indian dress. When she was wearing that dress she looked like the sorceress in Gabriel's old King Arthur book.

"You look pretty," said Gabriel. "You look skinny in that dress." He knew she liked to be told that. She smiled, but her eyes were red at the edges. He knew that she had been crying. He hugged her around the waist. She tilted his face up and smiled again. He thought she would kiss him, but she didn't.

"I'm getting a cold," she said, reaching into a drawer for a

Kleenex. She blew her nose loudly, but Gabriel knew her nose was stuffy from crying.

"Here," she said, pushing a dark plastic bottle toward him. "Take one so you don't catch my sniffles." Vitamin C.

She was cooking. She hardly ever cooked at breakfast time except when she sometimes decided Gabriel wasn't getting enough nutrition, and then she fixed him runny omelets stuffed with things he hated: mushrooms, green peppers, bean sprouts. Yick.

Gabriel lifted the frying pan lid suspiciously. French toast! Next to Sugar Frosted Flakes, that was his favorite thing to eat for breakfast, and usually he only got it on holidays or the times he stayed at his dad's house and Sylvie cooked it for him.

"Wow! I'll get out the syrup!" The syrup came in a plastic jar shaped like a lady, Mrs. Butterworth. Gabriel got to pick out the syrup at the supermarket because only he ate it.

Gabriel ate four pieces of French toast with Mrs. Butterworth, and drank Tang. His mom drank coffee. Gabriel kept wanting to talk to her, but he couldn't think of what to say. It was going to be a hard day. He spilled syrup all over one of his pajama legs and she didn't even yell at him. She didn't even tell him not to put them back in his pajama drawer.

While she was washing the dishes, he took a bath without even being told to. He even washed his hair and dried it with her hair dryer, so that it was straighter than usual and easy to comb. He put on his shirt with the cuff links, and his black winter suit, and his school tie. He found his dress shoes under the bed. He hadn't worn them since Christmas, and they were too tight to fit his feet in. Well, he could wear his school shoes. He'd worn them in the recital last week. The left one had dried mud on it, but he chipped most of that off with his fingernail.

At ten Toby came. It was only the second time Gabriel had seen him wear a suit. The first time was at Elise's funeral.

It was black, with a vest, and it made him look taller, and stiffer and older. He drank some Tang and some coffee and Gabriel's mom fixed some French toast, which he ate with butter, but without Mrs. Butterworth.

Elizabeth and Toby sat in the kitchen talking quietly, so that Gabriel, sitting in the living room looking through his baseball cards, could hear them but not hear what they were saying.

At ten-thirty they got into Toby's car and drove to the cemetery. Gabriel sat in the back. He closed his eyes and did not look out the window. Toby had the radio on, playing some trumpet concerto. Then there were some loud commercials, then Mozart piano music. Elizabeth reached over and snapped off the radio.

"Mozart," she hissed, as though she didn't like Mozart. Gabriel kept his eyes shut. The windows were rolled down in the front and the rush of air made it hard for him to breathe. They slowed down. He could feel the car turning, going slowly over gravel, and then stopping. They were there. Toby opened the door and Gabriel hopped out. Elizabeth stopped to fix her hair in the rearview.

Gabriel's dad was there already, with Sylvie and Carrie and Cory. Gabriel wanted to run up to his dad, but he didn't. He took his mom's hand and walked beside her. On the other side she was holding Toby's. She stumbled on a little rock.

It must be hard, Gabriel thought, to walk in high heels across a field.

This was the third time they'd been to the cemetery. Once, last year, at a memorial service like this and once before that at the funeral.

If Elise were alive she would have been sixteen on Thursday. She died two years ago on Monday, and they were having the service today, Saturday, so everyone could come. Gabriel wondered what he would have gotten her for her birthday if she were alive. The day before she died he'd picked out two presents for her: an album of Rubinstein playing Chopin and a book about horses. He had never wrapped them, but for a long time he didn't play the record, as though it would be wrong. Then one day, months later, he'd suddenly had the idea to slit open the cellophane and take the album out of the dust jacket and play it. He'd felt like he was doing something bad, but he'd listened to both sides, and then listened to both sides again. He played that album every day almost, until he was tired of it, and now he played it every time he wanted to hear

Chopin piano music. He'd played Chopin himself when he'd played the piano, but he hadn't played it nearly so well as Elise.

Their old piano teacher, Mr. Grainger, came to the service. Mr. Grainger walked with a cane, and like Gabriel's mom, he faltered a little on his way from his car to the grave. Elise's best friend, Marybeth, and her mother came, too. Marybeth had always acted like she hated Gabriel. She used to always call him names, and tell Elise not to let him into her room, and whisper secrets about him; and after Elise died she'd never spoken to him, or looked in his eyes if she saw him on the street. Now she came up to him and gave him a quick hug. She was taller than before, and less chubby. Her mom hugged Gabriel's mom, and Gabriel's mom started to cry quiet tears. Marybeth was wearing a white dress with blue flowers on it, and the blue flowers almost matched the color of her eyes. Gabriel was surprised to find himself thinking that she was pretty.

His mom let go of his hand when she started talking to Marybeth's mother, so Gabriel went to the other side of the grave, where his father was standing, holding Cory in one arm and Carrie, who was almost too big to be held, in the other. Sylvie was bent over a big canvas bag, pulling out graham crackers and plastic baby-bottles filled with orange juice.

Gabriel's dad smiled at him and shifted Carrie's weight down to his hip. His smile was a firm one, with the corners of his mouth disappearing into strong dimples. He said, "Hello, son." Gabriel ran his fingers through Carrie's black hair. She buried her face against her father's shirt. She had hair like Sylvie's. Cory didn't have much hair, but it was blond, like Gabriel's and his dad's.

"Hi, Dad." His dad smiled again, the same way. Gabriel wondered if his father was sad for Elise, like his mom was. He knew his dad wouldn't cry like Mom — Dad never cried. But maybe he was feeling all sore and bruised and unhappy inside, the way Gabriel himself was. He wanted to ask him how he felt, but he knew he shouldn't.

"Good weather for this, today, hmmm?" said his father. Sylvie gave graham crackers to the girls. Cory dropped hers and began to whimper. Quickly Sylvie stuffed one of the orange juices into her mouth. Cory stopped crying and began to concentrate on sucking the juice out of the bottle. Suddenly Gabriel was filled with disgust for her and Carrie, who was quietly munching crumbs all over her mouth and dress. He was beginning to feel sick, like the time he threw up at school, at the end of his recital. He turned and trotted back to his mother, ignoring Sylvie, who was offering him a graham cracker.

The minister who did the service was Presbyterian, like Gabriel's dad. Gabriel didn't listen to what he said. His voice was boring and he wasn't even talking about Elise. He was going on and on about the Kingdom of Heaven. Gabriel had his right hand in his mother's and his left hand on his stomach. He was feeling sick and grouchy and he was hoping he wasn't going to throw up right there, right in the middle of the cemetery, in front of everyone.

He looked across at his father, but the sun was reflected off his glasses and he couldn't see his eyes. Where was he looking? At the minister, at the grave, at him, at his mom? It was impossible to tell. His mouth was hanging open a little. Like a moron, thought Gabriel. He had never thought of his dad as a moron before. Gabriel was in a *bad* mood. The sun was shining too hot and his suit was itching. He loosened his tie a little with his left hand. Sweat was dribbling down his neck. Every time he thought of the four pieces of french toast he'd eaten, he felt sicker. The sunshine was getting brighter and he had to squint to see the minister. The minister said a sentence with Elise's name in the middle of it and Gabriel's mother made a choking noise. She let go of his hand and turned to Toby. Toby put his arms around her and she was crying in little gasps with her face against his shoulder. Gabriel was standing there alone and there was a breeze, which chilled his sweat, and he began to shiver. It was getting darker, some clouds were forming over the sun and maybe it was going to rain or maybe it was going to be nighttime now, and piano music would start to play, because, as his mom had said, that would be the best way to remember Elise, not outside in the open with some minister, and it was growing darker and colder, and Gabriel felt his knees slip and the music was loud.

When he opened his eyes again he was on a bed, in a cool dark room with the blinds pulled. He could see streaks of sunlight slipping through the slats in the blinds. He was wearing his good shirt with the cuff links and his suit pants, but someone had taken off his jacket and his shoes and his necktie. He sat up and looked around the room. Where was he? It smelled like perfume in here and everything was beige. Oh, yes, this was his father and Sylvie's bedroom. It was very modern, all the furniture the same color and lots of metal lamps, which were all turned off. He was feeling dizzy and empty. He wondered if he had thrown up in front of everyone or just fainted. Should he go downstairs now, or wait for someone to come up and get him? Carefully he stood up and went into their bathroom. On the marble counter-top were many, many bottles of ladies' face things, and the hamper was piled high with the magazines his father always had: *Publishers Weekly, Harper's, The New York Review of Books.* He flipped on the light and squinted at himself in the mirror. His left cheek had a big red blotch, etched with the pattern of the bedspread. His hair was sticking up on the left side, and on the right side it was all flat. He reached for the comb on the edge of the sink. It was filled with dark hairs, Sylvie's. Yick! Black hair made him squeamish. Didn't his father have a hairbrush? He opened the medicine cabinet. More ladies' face things, shaving cream and razors, bottles of pills, a baby cup. Well, maybe his dad used this awful comb, too. With a Kleenex he pulled out most of the hairs and dropped that mess in the toilet. There was still some gunk in the base of the teeth, but he ran it through his hair shallowly and gingerly. It didn't do much good, anyway.

Gabriel found his shoes, jacket, and tie on a chair. He stuffed the tie into one of the jacket pockets and put his shoes on slowly. He was expecting the door to open and someone to come in to see how he was doing, but no one came. They must think I'm sleeping. He took himself slowly down the hallway, down the beige-carpeted steps, into the sunny foyer. There was Toby's jacket and his mom's spring coat and some other jackets piled on a chair. Knowing that he should be with everyone else, and not wanting to, he dumped his jacket on top of the pile and followed the voices that were coming from the dining room.

People were talking more quietly than they usually do at parties. His mom was saying something to Marybeth's mother and Toby was speaking softly and nodding yes. Toby was holding a Styrofoam cup with two fingers, as though what was inside was very hot. On the table was a giant coffee urn, and stacks of cups, and rows of plastic spoons. There were also glass trays filled with little sandwiches, and piles of paper plates. No one was eating except Mr. Grainger and Marybeth, who were sitting next to the sandwiches, eating them and talking to each other. Gabriel wondered if Marybeth took piano lessons. He knew she played the trumpet in Elise's school band and that she was not good.

Toby saw Gabriel standing in the doorway first. His eyes got big and he put his hot coffee cup down on a bookshelf.

"Heyyyyy!" he said. "I was just going to go up and check on you." Gabriel thought for a second that Toby would pick him up, but he didn't: he put his arm around him and led him to where his mom was standing. Marybeth's mom was saying that Gabriel should eat something, he must have low blood sugar. Gabriel looked at his mother and made a face that meant he would *not*. His mother's lips were tight, like when she was nervous or concentrating. She held the back of her hand against his forehead, like she did when she thought he might have a fever. Her hand felt hot and dry. Her face was red and her eyes were more wrinkled than usual. But her wrinkles don't make her look old like a grandmother, thought Gabriel. She looks like a little girl, like someone Carrie's age, who has been crying. He would have liked to bury his face in the lap of his mother's warm, gold-trimmed black skirt and be hidden from everyone in the room, and maybe cry a little, but now he was grown-up and brave.

Mr. Grainger was walking across the room, asking him how he

felt. Marybeth stayed where she was sitting, looked away, looking embarrassed. Sylvie came out of the kitchen with a tray of little cakes. When she saw Gabriel she put the cakes down and came over, exclaiming something like, "Oh! Oh! Oh!" She, too, tested Gabriel's forehead with the back of her hand. Gabriel felt himself blushing from the attention. Then everyone began to remark that the color was coming back to his cheeks. He wondered if the design from the bedspread was still imprinted on the left side of his face.

They made Gabriel sit down on the sofa, and he was brought, by Sylvie and Marybeth's mother, orange juice, a cream-cheese-and-olive sandwich, and a brownie. The orange juice had pieces of pulp in it and Gabriel couldn't even think of drinking it. He nibbled a corner of the brownie to be polite. He wondered where his dad was — probably in the kitchen feeding Carrie and Cory or upstairs putting them in for a nap. Slowly all the adults went back to their conversations and left Gabriel alone on the sofa. His mom's arm was linked in Toby's arm as they talked to Mr. Grainger and Marybeth's mother. Every minute or so Toby would turn around and look at Gabriel. If Gabriel caught his eye, Toby winked.

Marybeth was sitting alone in a corner. On her lap was a plate with two brownies, but she wasn't eating them. She looked at Gabriel, and when she saw him looking back she looked away.

Gabriel put his plate down carefully on the floor, and balanced the orange juice glass on top of the sandwich. He wandered past the table of food, out of the dining room. In the hallway he met his father coming out of his study. His dad looked surprised. His eyebrows rose above his glasses. He was carrying a cigar box.

"So you're up on your feet again?"

"Yeah." Gabriel scuffed the rug with his toe. What was in the cigar box?

"I have some things for you in this box," he said, as though reading Gabriel's mind. Things for me? thought Gabriel.

"I was just bringing them upstairs to the bedroom for you, but come here." The study looked almost exactly the same as it had when it was in their house. The same furniture, the same rug, the same bookshelves filled with the same books and statues. It was the only room Dad had taken with him when he moved out. Against the far wall was the Steinway, which Gabriel's mom had never forgiven him for taking. Whenever Gabriel came into this room he had a sense that he had walked backwards in time, into his own house before the divorce. That was a long time ago, when he could barely see above the top of his father's desk. Now on the rare occasions he came in here he felt large.

His father sat at the desk and Gabriel stood beside him. This is the way they'd always talked when he was little, only now he was taller standing up than his dad sitting down. He could see the bald spot on the top of his head.

"These are things that meant a lot to me when I was a boy. I thought that you should have them." Dad was pulling off the rubber bands that held the box shut. Those must be old rubber bands if he's had them since he was my age, thought Gabriel. He hoped the box would be filled with antique baseball cards. No.

Inside was a book with an army-green cover: *Handbook for Boys*. Boy Scouts? His father had been a boy scout? How queer. Gabriel didn't know anyone who was a scout. There was also a whistle that made no sound. That was for calling a dog, his father said.

"I don't have a dog."

"Oh, yes . . . do you want one?"

"Mom wouldn't let me. Remember, she got rid of the cat?"

"I see, well. I'll keep this, then." He slid the whistle into his top drawer.

There was also a Swiss Army knife with eight different kinds of gadgets on it.

"Isn't this great?" said Dad, pulling out the corkscrew, the scissors, the tiny wrench.

"Yes." Gabriel wondered what he would use it for. He already had a penknife somewhere at home. The last thing in the box was a leather case with five different fishing baits: mostly they were made from feathers and string and small metal weights.

"I never went fishing," said Gabriel.

"Would you like to?"

Gabriel shifted his weight from one foot to the other. He wanted to say, "Not really," but instead he just shrugged.

"We'll have to go sometime."

Gabriel could tell by his father's tone that he didn't mean it. Good.

"Shall we join the others?" Dad handed the box to Gabriel, not bothering to refasten the rubber bands. Gabriel nodded and followed his father back down the hallway. He put the box down on the chair by the door so that no one would ask him about it.

Mr. Grainger and the minister were both waiting to say good-bye so they could leave. The minister shook his dad's hand but said nothing to Gabriel. He had said nothing to Gabriel the whole time.

He doesn't like children, Gabriel decided. Mr. Grainger shook hands with both him and his dad. He would see Gabriel soon around Curtis, he said. Gabriel decided not to remind him that he wasn't at Curtis yet.

Next Marybeth and her mother left. Sylvie insisted on wrapping up a plate of brownies for them to take home. Marybeth's mother gave Gabriel a big hug and Marybeth didn't. She did smile at him on her way out the door. He noticed that she had a tiny blue earring in each earlobe. She and Elise had always talked about getting their ears pierced, but they had been too afraid.

Now was something Gabriel dreaded: his mom and dad and Sylvie and Toby were together in the room without other people around to diffuse the hostility. He hoped that Toby and Mom and he would leave soon. Sylvie kept carrying utensils, trays, back out of the dining room, and his mom, who usually offered to help with kitchen things, didn't. Dad offered Toby a scotch and Toby said no, so he poured one for himself.

"So, shall we sit down?" said Dad.

"We have to leave," said Mom, sounding almost angry. Sylvie, who was holding the coffee urn, looked up at her and then ducked into the kitchen. Toby looked at his shoes, then looked at Gabriel, then looked at Gabriel's shoes. Gabriel's mother walked across the room and picked up her coat. She handed Toby and Gabriel their jackets. Everyone walked toward the front door and Sylvie came out of the kitchen to say good-bye. Just then Carrie or Cory started to whine upstairs, "Mohhhhhmmmie," and Sylvie seemed relieved to say "Excuse me" and run up the steps.

On his way out Gabriel picked up the cigar box. He knew it would hurt his dad's feelings if he left it there.

"What's that?" said Elizabeth in the car.

"Dad gave me . . ." he kicked it gently out of sight, under the front seat, "a box of junk."

There were still a few hours of daylight left when he got home, and instead of making him practice right away, Mom let him play baseball. Steven and Selby were glad to have another player, to have use of his catcher's equipment. Gabriel hit a triple into the Edelsons' yard, and he ran the bases extrafast. The running felt good.

II When Marina got home the house was filled with neighbors, her aunt from Cherry Hill, and Uncle Franz's wife, Hannah. She went straight to the kitchen, where she knew her mother would be, making food for the guests.

"I'll help, Mama," she said, sliding out of her jacket and backpack at once. Her mother hugged her and kissed her without putting down her pot holder. She shouted to her Ukrainian neighbor to get the cakes out of the oven quickly before they burned.

"You look good," she said in English, and then in Ukrainian, "You're too pretty to cook — go upstairs and see if you can get your brother to come down here and talk to everybody, and then you talk to the guests, too, okay?" She always put an okay at the end of her requests.

"Okay." She kissed her Cherry Hill aunt and her neighbors and her cousin Lucy and Hannah Kazakov hello and ran upstairs. Serge, as usual, was playing rock music, not too loudly, but loudly enough to be heard faintly all over the house. Marina knocked on his door. There was no answer.

"Come on, Serge, it's me, Marina," she said. Still no answer.

"What are you, sleeping in there?" She tried the door; it was locked. She pounded.

"Open up!" Then Serge's crackly, recently deep voice said something she couldn't understand. The lock turned and the door opened inward.

Every time she saw him he was taller and skinnier. His hair was down to his shoulders, curly black like hers, and wild. He was wearing blue jeans and a black Grateful Dead T-shirt with silver glittery lettering.

"Hi," she said, trying to push the door open enough to get inside. He didn't budge.

"So you're home." The skin under his eyes was blue-gray.

"Serge, you look awful. You look like some kind of burned-out druggie. What's the matter?"

"Fuck you." He tried to slam the door closed, but Marina threw her weight against it and pushed him backwards. He was so skinny that she was stronger than he. He stepped back, then flopped onto his bed.

"So you can force your way into my room. Bravo, superwoman."

"What's your problem, Serge? I'm just trying to be nice." The room was dark with the shades pulled down. On every wall was pasted a huge poster of a rock musician, and on the door was taped a poster of the Marx Brothers smoking a water pipe.

"It's dark in here — why don't you pull open the shades?" No answer.

"What's that smell? Strawberry incense? Yech. Why don't you come downstairs where Mom is baking? It smells good there." Still no answer. Marina reached over and pulled open the shade. Light flooded in. Serge sprang off of his bed, looking pale and threatening.

"Will you get the hell out of my room!" he screamed.

"Why don't you just calm down?" Marina knew Serge well enough not to pay attention to him when he threw tantrums. He and her father were just alike, always yelling at someone about something.

"It's like a tomb in here." Marina cranked open his window. "It stinks. If you're going to sit around smoking dope all day you might as well air the place out instead of trying to cover up with that sick strawberry stuff."

"Who asked you?"

"Nobody has to. Come on, I'm your sister. I know what's bothering you. You feel guilty about Dad."

"Shut up."

"But you shouldn't. Nobody's going to blame you. He yells a lot and you yell a lot and you both yell at each other, but you didn't make him have a heart attack. It's just a coincidence. If you hadn't been around he probably would have had one from yelling about Jimmy Carter or something."

"What the hell do you know? You weren't here. You weren't around."

"I'm only trying to help."

"What do you know? You don't know anything about it except what Mama told you on the phone. And then you hung up on her in the middle of her talking to you. I was in the room."

"Serge, I was half asleep."

"Well, go back to sleep."

"*Serge.* Serge, you're only trying to lay some guilt on me because you're blaming yourself —"

"Oh, it's from superwoman to psychologist. Why don't you just shut up?"

"Because I want to help you —"

"What do you know? You weren't here. You didn't see his face turn purple. You didn't see him jerking around on the kitchen floor."

"His face turned *purple?*"

"You weren't here when the ambulance came and they put electric shocks in his chest so strong that his whole body lifted off the floor."

"What did Mama do?"

"What do you *think* she did? She ran around and got in the way and cried a lot and talked in Ukrainian. Yeah, it was real nice of you to hang up on her that night. That made her feel real good. You're great, Rina, just great. Why don't you just go downstairs and look pretty and play your flute for the guests."

"You're being a jerk. I came up here to try to make you feel better."

"Oh yeah, well, I'd feel better if you'd just leave." Serge rolled over with his face to the wall. When she was sure that he wasn't going to say anything else, Marina left his room. As she closed the door behind her he said, "Tell Mama I'll be down in five minutes."

Downstairs, Mama was in the kitchen, sweeping up a glass Hannah Kazakov had just broken.

"I was trying to wash it," she explained to Marina. "I'm such a klutz. At home I break everything. I hope it wasn't valuable, Mrs. Kazakov." Marina's mother made a clucking sound and shook her head no. Marina knew that glass was one from a set she had brought with her all the way from Russia — a wedding present.

"Just something we picked up at a gas station," said Marina, knowing the sarcasm would be lost on Hannah.

"Oh, good, then I don't feel bad," said Hannah.

Marina's mother asked, in Ukrainian, if Serge was coming downstairs.

"He says he'll be down in five minutes."

"Good. You have such a way with him. He hasn't come down all day, poor boy, he's so upset about his father, but you are so good with him."

"Right." Marina left the room quickly and sat down beside her Cherry Hill aunt and her cousin Lucy, who was nine years old and too shy to talk. Aunt Anya was chain-smoking Parliaments. She had already almost filled the big ashtray. Marina got up to empty it for her, wishing that she could smoke, too. She was dying for a cigarette, but that would upset her mother, who didn't approve of Anya's smoking, either.

When Marina brought the clean ashtray back, Aunt Anya thanked her and asked her questions about how she liked school. When she ran out of questions, she began to push Lucy to tell

Marina about *her* school. Anya spoke to Lucy in English only, and Lucy understood little Ukrainian and spoke none. The little girl squirmed in her chair. She was uncomfortable talking with her big cousin. Marina could not think of much to say to her aunt. She knew not to ask after her husband, who was a drunk, and Lucy was her only child, so there was not much else to say.

Finally Marina's mother and her neighbors and Hannah brought out trays of food and laid them on the table.

"Why don't you call your brother?" said Marina's mother.

"He said he'd be down soon . . ." Marina dreaded the thought of going upstairs to him again. Just then Serge appeared at the top of the stairs. He loped down, two steps at a time. He'd changed into a plain white shirt and combed his hair. Everyone hugged him and greeted him carefully.

They all think he must feel guilty about Dad, thought Marina. Serge talked to Aunt Anya and his mother and Hannah and the neighbors and his cousin Lucy as he ate, but he did not look at Marina.

"You look nice," she told him as they were all putting their jackets on. In the car she sat in the middle, squeezed between him and her mother, but he stared out the window for the whole ride.

Vladimir Kazakov had been in the hospital for three days now. The nurses wouldn't let all of them into the room at once, just the immediate family. He looked old and fragile, and there were tubes emptying into his arms and tubes running up into his nostrils. His forehead was bruised — he'd hit his head on the kitchen counter when he fell. He reached out for his wife's hand and she knelt down at his side sobbing in Ukrainian. The nurse in back of her warned her to be quieter. Serge was standing back, almost at the door, with his mouth slightly open, staring at his father.

Marina looked across at her father's roommate, a toothless old black man with his dentures in a glass beside him. He was snoring softly. She wondered what was wrong with him. There were flowers on the table beside him, and candy. She wondered why no one had thought to bring her father flowers. She would get him some tomorrow.

Her mother was telling her father: Marina's here.

Marina stepped forward and took his hand. She knew he could barely see her without his glasses. Never had he looked so old to her. She thought: he's fifty-six; he looks older. He looks like an old, old man.

She asked him, in English, if she could bring him anything. He said, "I miss Beethoven. That's what I miss when I'm lying here. There's no Beethoven in this hospital."

Marina promised him that she would come back the next day with a radio for him. Then her mother said, "Serge is here."

"Should we leave them alone together?" she asked her mother. But Serge stepped forward with tears in his eyes and his father grasped his hand hard. Serge put his face against their clenched fists so his father could feel his tears. Marina stood back watching, jealous.

She did not sleep in her bedroom that night. Aunt Anya and Lucy were using it. She shared her mother's bed: the place Papa usually slept. She had imagined that the mattress would be permanently tilted toward his side, since his body was so much heavier than his mother's but the bed was firm and comfortable. She was glad not to be sleeping in her own room. She hated the pink-and-white frilly bedspread and the white frilly trim on the lamps, which reminded her of being a little girl. Serge had fixed up his room the way he liked it when he became a teenager, but Marina had moved away to Curtis too soon. Every time she came home and slept in that room she felt as though she were eleven years old.

Marina slept lightly; her mother kept sighing in her sleep, and in the morning Marina was the first one up, even before her mother. She took the first shower, careful not to use up too much hot water, and set the dining-room table for five places: herself, Mama, Anya, Lucy, Serge. Hannah had driven herself home after the hospital visit. She would come back today with Peter and Franz. Mama fixed eggs and sausages and Marina made the coffee. The neighbors had left Ukrainian pastries. Marina ate greedily, thinking that she would be fat if she lived at home. Serge didn't come downstairs until breakfast was nearly finished. He was shirtless, thin with pointy shoulders, and his chest was hairless. He greeted his aunt and cousin, but said nothing to Marina. As always he ate little.

Marina decided, it's useless to try to talk to him. She followed her mother and Aunt Anya into the kitchen and wiped dry the dishes as they washed them. Idly she listened to their conversation: This and that about heart attacks. This and that about husbands. Aunt Anya's husband, Alex, had had one two years ago, and still he drank. It occurred to Marina that as sisters they might soon become widows together.

They would have each other . . . She stopped herself.

Last night Marina had dreamed about Cleveland. She couldn't remember what had happened in the dream, but she had woken up with his face imprinted on her memory. Cleveland. He would be gone now, back to Chicago. Thinking about him made her uneasy, uneasier than thinking about the way her father had looked yesterday, with all the tubes running.

Car doors slammed outside, and her mother and Anya dropped their dish towels and ran to the front door. That would be Uncle Franz and family. Marina shuddered at the thought of seeing her uncle so soon again after the concert last week. She wondered for an instant if he knew Cleveland. No, that was impossible, because he wasn't connected with that crowd. He had something to do with the little boy on stage because the little boy was, what? The son of his boss. That was it. As Marina put the last plate away Hannah Kazakov appeared at the kitchen door holding a foil-wrapped tray.

"I made some brownies," she said, grinning proudly. "Where do I put them?" Wordlessly Marina took them from her and put them under the metal cake-tin. Hannah let out an embarrassed laugh and disappeared back into the hallway.

Poor Hannah, thought Marina. She never knows how to carry herself. Today Marina didn't feel like being nice and making her feel comfortable.

As soon as she was sure Hannah was not coming back into the

kitchen, Marina lifted the cake-tin lid noiselessly — a maneuver she'd practiced often as a child — and carefully pulled a brownie out from the aluminum foil. It was neither very chocolaty nor chewy and there were no raisins or chocolate chips, as in her mother's. What a disappointment, anemic brownies. Marina heard footsteps in the hallway and swallowed quickly. It was Lucy.

"Everybody's getting ready to leave, I'm supposed to tell you," she said.

"So soon?" said Marina, still chewing, but Lucy was gone. Marina remembered to unplug the kitchen radio and take it along. They rode in Uncle Franz's station wagon, Hannah and Peter in the front seat, with Franz driving, and Marina squished in the middle seat with her fat aunt, chubby cousin, and her mother. Serge rode in the way-back alone, stretched diagonally across.

This time they were allowed to see her father just one at a time, immediate family only. His condition was a little worse, they said. Mama went first and came out crying after five minutes. Marina was next. The room was dark and the old black man who'd been his roommate was gone. Still there were no flowers on her father's side of the room, and the other man's flowers were gone. Was he discharged or dead? Marina wondered. She started to plug in the radio, but the nurse who was stationed in the room told her to stop.

"He asked for his radio," said Marina. "He *requested* it. He wants to hear Beethoven."

"No. Not in intensive care," said the nurse. Marina glared at her and rewrapped the cord around the radio. Her father's face had a grayness to it that frightened her. He seemed to be asleep, but when she said, "Papa," he opened his eyes. He was looking at her.

"I brought your radio," she said, "but they won't let me play it." He muttered something she couldn't understand. She glanced at the nurse, who was watching impassively. His breathing was loud, raspy.

"Is he in pain?" Marina asked.

"We gave him a sedative," said the nurse.

"But is he in pain?"

The nurse shrugged. "Yes, but we gave him something that should help."

Soon the nurse asked her to leave.

"That was five minutes," she said. "That's all you can have today. We don't want to exhaust him any more."

"Is he awake or asleep?" asked Marina.

The nurse craned her neck over to look at his face.

"I guess he looks like he's sleeping."

"Well what difference does it make how long I stay, then?"

"That's the rules. I didn't make them."

"Why is his face so gray today?"

"You're going to have to leave the room. You can ask questions in the hallway." Marina kissed him carefully on the cheekbone. His skin was warmer than she'd expected it to feel.

Next was Serge's turn for five minutes. Aunt Anya, Lucy, Hannah, and Peter weren't allowed inside since they weren't immediate family. Franz, being his brother, was. When he came out his face was oddly pale against his beard. Marina decided that Franz and Serge, with their powder-white skin, which was bluish under the eyes, and their bluish-black hair, looked very much alike. Like brothers, almost. Papa had boot-polish black hair, too, before it turned gray. I look like them, too, she remembered.

Marina's mother wanted to stay at the hospital, in the waiting room. It was Anya who finally convinced her to come home.

"You have guests," she told her in Ukrainian, "you can't just stay here all day and abandon them. And who is going to cook supper?" With that Marina's mother was ready to go back home for a few hours. Anya wrapped her thick arm around Mama's waist and supported her on the way to the parking lot. Everyone was silent until Peter began to whine that he was thirsty, and Hannah whisked him off to the nearest fountain.

"I'm not thirsty for that. I want a soda."

"We'll get you one at home," said Hannah.

"But we're not going home. We're going back to *her* house." Peter pointed at Mrs. Kazakov's back as she walked slowly in front of him.

"Hush, Peter," said Hannah.

"I bet she doesn't even have sodas."

Marina saw her brother scowling at their cousin.

"Goddamn brat," he mouthed, noiselessly.

"Yeah, how old is he anyway?" she whispered to Serge, who did not respond. Franz, who had heard her, glared, first at her, then at his son. Marina caught his eye and looked away. Franz tapped Peter on the shoulder.

"That's enough," he said sharply. Immediately Peter was silent.

"We'll get you a soda, honey," said Hannah, putting her hand on Peter's shoulder. Peter shrugged her away and pouted. He has the same pout as Franz and Serge, thought Marina. For an instant she hated them all.

In the car, Peter picked a fight with Lucy. This time the two children were in the way-back and Serge was sitting up front between Marina's mother and Franz, who was driving.

"She keeps putting her feet on me," announced Peter to the silent riders. Lucy said nothing, just quickly pulled her legs up beside her. The car rounded a corner and Lucy was tilted toward Peter.

"She keeps touching me. Fat thing."

"Peter!" said Franz, but it was too late. Lucy was already crying, from the embarrassment of what Peter had said, the embarrassment that everyone had heard him and that his father had corrected him, and from embarrassment that she was crying. She put her head down and sobbed in little hiccups.

"Peter, I think you should apologize to your cousin," said Hannah. Lucy, more humiliated by the attention, sobbed harder.

"Aw, Jesus, what a baby. I'm sorry," said Peter. "She kept touching me, though. She wouldn't stay on her side."

"That's enough," said Franz.

"It's okay, Lucyna," Anya was telling her. "You'll feel better when we get back to Aunt Sonia's and have some lunch."

"Yeah, stop crying. I'm sorry," said Peter. "I didn't mean to call you fat." Lucy made more miserable hiccuping noises.

Marina's mother and Serge ignored all of this. Marina strained to see her brother's face in the rearview, but the angle was wrong. He was motionless except for his hair, which flapped in the breeze from the open window. Marina's mother was resting her weight against Serge's shoulder. Is she asleep or crying or what? wondered Marina.

The minute they walked in the door, Serge stormed over to the refrigerator, pulled out a can of Pepsi, and tossed it to Peter, who caught it like a baseball.

"Great, thanks," said Peter. "Only now you shook it up. It's gonna explode." Serge stomped up to his room.

Three hours later the phone rang. Serge was in his room with the music going; Marina was in her parents' room, practicing; Franz and Peter were playing chess in the living room; and the women — Sonia, Anya, Hannah, and Lucy — were in the kitchen. Anya answered and handed the phone to her sister. Her wail brought her children running, Marina still holding her flute.

Their father was dead, of a second, massive heart attack. Serge ran to his mother and her arms folded around him. Marina pressed her cheek against the cool white plaster of the hallway wall, conscious of Hannah's hand on her shoulder. She closed her eyes; there was shouting and talking and weeping all around her. Flute still in hand, she slid cross-legged to the floor. She was eye-level with Anya's hem. Anya was wailing and hugging the wailing Sonia, who was holding Serge. Someone (Hannah) handed Marina a glass of water. She sipped from it with clenched teeth, not moving from the floor. Anya, Franz, and Serge gently led her mother into the living room and sat her on the sofa. Marina followed them with her eyes, ignoring Hannah, who was trying to get her to stand up. Finally, Hannah joined the others comforting Sonia in the living room. Marina, glass of water in right hand, flute in left, buried her face in her knees, not weeping. Peter and Lucy sat wordless, side by side, on the steps. Peter passed his Pepsi can to Lucy and she took a gulp automatically and handed it back. There was the strong, sweet odor of cakes burning in the kitchen.

III   Lawrence's mother suffered her first stroke in 1957, a few months after his accident. It was James who found her there unconscious on the floor one evening when he returned from a long practice session at the rented studio.

After her son's accident Ann Frost Chattarjee had begun to care for Lawrence daily. At first James resented her frequent visits to their home, but soon he grew to appreciate them, knowing that she relieved much of the emotional responsibility that had been suddenly thrust on him. Gradually he came to respect the angular, energetic woman. He began to think of her as a friend, and then as a substitute for his own mother, the heavy, luxurious Pearl, who had died before he became Lawrence's lover. It was Pearl who had first fought for James's career, pushing him always to succeed.

Ann Frost Chattarjee had done the same for Lawrence, James realized, and slowly he began to notice the samenesses in the two women. James had thought that Pearl was the only woman he could ever love, but Ann was different, and his admiration grew into a kind of quiet emotion that he had never experienced.

He knew Ann had accepted her son's homosexuality from the moment Lawrence told her about it. Lawrence said she had been prepared for such news from him: many male musicians she knew were homosexuals; it was part of that world. In his final year at Curtis, Lawrence had grown close to an older student, Maurice D'Artoit, a black violinist from the Dominican Republic who hoped to become a conductor. Maur, as he was called, was in his early twenties, a straight-backed, mustached, polite young man who oiled his hair back in the manner of a Spaniard. Lawrence brought him home frequently for dinner and frequently they went out together in the evening. Some nights Lawrence did not come home until sunrise, but Ann said nothing, quiet and watchful. It was Lawrence who spoke first.

"Mom, I'm eighteen years old. It's time I moved out of your house."

She reminded him that he was still a student; he had no money.

"Maur has asked me to live with him, in his apartment." Maur's father was a wealthy liquor merchant.

Ann let him go, not mentioning to him that she would be left alone. Lawrence was filled with the same youthful selfishness that had caused his mother to abandon her family and her career for Rajesh Chattarjee twenty years earlier. Still, as he explained it later to James, he was more constant than she had been. He called her every evening and they spoke of her daily life, her students, and his career plans. He was flourishing at school and was about to graduate. He asked her to go to New York City with him, at William Kinkaid's recommendation, to the Bernard Thorn agency, where he signed a contract for management.

Five months after Lawrence moved out of Ann's house he moved back in. Maur had won a competition and was off to spend the summer conducting a festival orchestra in New England; he had graduated and, not sure he would be returning to Philadelphia, had had the entire contents of his apartment shipped to his new home in Maine. Lawrence settled back into his old room. He wasn't looking for an orchestral position, and he had just signed with Thorn Associates — too soon for any engagements — so he had some time just to practice, do some jobbing, talk to Ann, and think.

He told her he didn't miss Maur. He hadn't liked living with him. He hadn't liked using his nice expensive apartment and his nice expensive things. He had no affection for Maur's linen suits and fancy cigarette lighters. All he had acquired from Maur was a taste for cognac. He bought Ann a bottle of Martel for her fortieth birthday, but she didn't like it. It was strong and bitter, and she had not tasted any alcohol since the days of Rajesh, so Lawrence went back and bought her a necklace with a single pearl and drank most of the cognac himself.

At first Lawrence played for small community orchestras, did recitals in towns he had never heard of, and his paychecks barely covered his travel expenses. He grew restless.

"You're doing *fine* for your first year under management, kid, are you crazy?" Bernie told him. "You're just a novice. I know flutists twice your age who'd give their eyeteeth to be doing the dates you're doing already. Relax, leave it to me."

Lawrence did not relax, and neither did his mother. "This is not just any talent," they told Bernie.

Bernie shrugged. "I know. But wait."

Lawrence and Ann pondered what to do. They knew that he was ready to perform with major orchestras. Finally, without telling Bernie, and without even warning Lawrence, Ann telephoned William Kinkaid and asked him to help. Lawrence knew his mother was terrified of Kinkaid, who was the most important flutist in the United States. All the time Lawrence had been his student, she had listened eagerly to stories about him: he wore his hair this way, he wore a tie clip with the theme for *L'Après-midi d'un faune* engraved on it. All of her flute students used his method and exercise books. Lawrence knew Kinkaid was her hero, but she had never spoken to him except to shake his hand as his best pupil's mother at Lawrence's recital receptions.

Ann Chattarjee was a shy woman, loquacious only with Lawrence, who knew that she had no female friends and that she had not dated a man since his father left her. She was not close to her students or their mothers; she was an orphan — an orphan who had been estranged from her parents before they died. Lawrence knew it was not her habit to force herself on strangers, and yet she found Kinkaid's number written on the back of one of Lawrence's old notebooks and dialed it.

"Mr. Kinkaid? This is Ann Frost Chattarjee . . ." Lawrence imagined the conversation, her heart's flutterings, her hesitation, his politeness — kind refusals?

But three weeks later Bernie called, saying the NBC Symphony had contacted him about an audition.

"Tell them I don't want to play in an orchestra. *Any* orchestra. You know that."

"No," Bernie shouted. "This is for a real date! A concerto."
Someone had mentioned Lawrence's name to Toscanini.

It was a nonsubscription concert, not on the regular radio series, a benefit for polio. But it was with a major orchestra; it was in New York; and it was reviewed. Bernie took over from there and Lawrence's next season catapulted. He had four dates with orchestras and ten recitals. That year for her birthday he gave his mother a whole string of pearls and a washing machine.

Lawrence moved out again, this time alone, into an apartment on Rittenhouse Square. He bought himself two new tuxedos and a new set of luggage. He went everywhere by airplane: no more bus trips to little towns in Ohio. Community orchestras could no longer afford to hire him.

For three years they lived like this: Lawrence's fees got higher and higher and he was able to take his mother along with him to hear his concerts. They stayed in hotels nicer than they had imagined existed, and in the summer of 1954 they went to Europe — to England, Denmark, and Vienna. When they came home Lawrence told her he was taking another apartment, this time in New York.

"It's impractical to live in Philadelphia when New York is the mecca for everything. You can come, too, you know. I'll find you a beautiful place, maybe even in my neighborhood."

But Ann Chattarjee refused, saying that her life and her students were in Philadelphia, saying that for the second time she would let him go. He did call her frequently, even when he was on tour, and when he wasn't touring he'd visit her regularly on Sundays. He bought a shiny red car from England, a Jaguar, remembering how his father had always fantasized about owning one. When he visited her it gleamed in the driveway next to her rusty Chevy.

He had a new lover, Tony, whom he called his secretary. Tony didn't travel with Lawrence. He stayed home and took care of the apartment and answered Lawrence's correspondence. Lawrence knew that Tony was jealous of his affection for his mother, so he never brought him along to meet her. It wasn't important, since he knew his affair with Tony would be a short one.

One day Lawrence drove up in the red Jaguar with someone in the passenger seat. It was James, seventeen years old and boyishly thin; James was also a flutist, Lawrence explained. "I'm going to be his mentor."

Ann nodded, said nothing, and set a third place for dinner.

The first thing James noticed about Ann, after his initial surprise that as a white woman she looked so much like his exotic lover, was that she wore a single pearl at her throat — the one Lawrence had given her on her fortieth birthday. Pearl, like his own mother. He learned later that she wore this pearl every day, except when she went to Lawrence's concerts, and then she wore the string of real oyster pearls he had given her the next year.

James was instantly jealous of Ann because Lawrence loved her, and he was jealous of Lawrence because he still had his mother. Pearl had been dead for less than a year when he moved in with Lawrence, and James knew that she would have approved. His father, Sam, would probably disown him when he eventually learned about Lawrence; but no matter. James was not interested in his father or his little sisters.

Sometimes James had thought he hated Pearl. He hated her loudness, her way of telling everyone else what to do. He hated the way she looked — fat, overdressed, with a hint of a mustache above her lip, but Pearl had been James's biggest support.

She'd spent all of her ample energy working toward building his career as a musician. She was constantly seeking better connections, better teachers, better summer programs. She was constantly reminding him to practice; she sat in on all his lessons and had long conferences with his teachers afterward. Like James, she had little concern for Sam or the girls, who were homely and untalented, physical replicas of herself.

At first James hated her for dying. How could she leave him alone like this, alone to live with his father and sisters in an angry household that didn't want to understand him or help him? It was her own fault. She was fat; she had diabetes; she didn't take care of herself. So she had died and left him. Once, in a screaming match with his father, he let all of this slip out — and the next day he found that his father was making him an appointment with a psychiatrist. He refused to go. He wasn't crazy, he said, he just needed to pull himself together. What would Pearl have him do if she were here? he wondered; and when he learned that Lawrence Chattarjee would be playing soon in Baltimore, he bought himself a ticket and went down alone on the train.

It worked, it worked! The best thing possible came true. If Pearl could have seen him she would have jumped for joy. He could picture her cheering him on, waving her heavy arms, shouting happily and loudly.

Being with Lawrence made him forget his sadness about Pearl. He'd nearly forgotten her when Lawrence began to take him along on his Sunday visits to his own mother. James didn't want to face the possibility that another person was important in Lawrence's life.

After Lawrence's accident, Ann began to come regularly to their apartment. She packed a suitcase, drove to New York, and took a room in the YWCA nearby. James invited her, out of politeness, to stay with them, but to his relief she declined. She came by every morning, spent an hour or two sitting beside her son, checking with the nurse who they'd hired to look after him the first month, straightening up Lawrence's bedroom, and then she left and would not return until evening, when she fixed dinner for Lawrence. She always left enough food on the stove for James, and when she was gone James would eat alone in the kitchen. She did not invite James to eat in Lawrence's room with them, and he did not presume to join them.

As much as he resented her, he was glad she'd come. Lawrence's depression after the accident was dark, severe. James was almost afraid to sit beside him in the sweet-smelling room — he didn't know what to say. He never knew what he should say. He supposed that Ann Frost Chattarjee knew what to do with her son, since she spent hours alone in there with him. When she left, Lawrence was not cheerful. But who knows how gloomy he might have been if she hadn't come? James found himself wishing that she would stay longer. The hours he spent alone in the apartment with Lawrence were growing longer and more lonely. He began to talk to Ann, to try to catch her in conversation so that she wouldn't leave as early. They began to share pots of tea, and they began to talk. They talked about Lawrence, about Lawrence's career, about Lawrence's music. And then they talked about the flute and flute technique and William Kinkaid, and one day they found themselves talking about James's life and Pearl. Ann wanted to know about Pearl. She said she had never formed a friendship with another mother when Lawrence was a boy. She'd met other women with children: neighborhood women, or mothers of Lawrence's friends, but she hadn't liked them enough to talk to them, or to explain why Lawrence was such a dark-skinned little boy. She'd always been curious about other women's motherhood, she said, since she had no sisters, and her own mother did not talk with her.

James told her about Pearl and her tubes of makeup and swirly bright dresses, and Ann wanted to know more. Why did she wear wigs? Why did she eat so much chocolate? She said she couldn't picture herself doing these things. James told her how Pearl had stood beside him while he practiced. Yes, Ann said she understood that, she had done that herself. Pearl had taken him regularly to concerts and recitals. Yes, Ann had done that, too. And while Ann had given Lawrence her own gold-plated flute, Pearl had insisted that she and Sam sacrifice their Florida winter vacations in order to buy a good instrument for James.

Ann was light and quick, nothing like James's concept of a mother. She drank her tea without sugar or milk, and if they had cookies she never ate more than one. She was healthy, far more than Pearl, who gasped for breath after one flight of steps. She did everything precisely; James jokingly asked her if she'd been trained in the army. When she cooked a stew, she prepared and arranged all the ingredients first, everything neatly lined up on the kitchen counter. The food would look too perfectly displayed to cook.

Lawrence and James had a maid, Eunice, who came in twice a week to clean and do the wash, and the hospital nurse, Marge, was supposed to help keep Lawrence's room straight and his bedsheets changed. Nevertheless, Ann found domestic chores to do in the apartment. James remembered Lawrence telling him of the confusion of his childhood household. Could this woman ever have had a cluttered, messy house? But then she'd been working to support a student husband and a little boy. Her energy had to be released somewhere, and now that she'd left her students behind in Philadelphia, it was being channeled into caring for Lawrence and James. Once James had heard her in the living room playing a flute. She hadn't known that he was in the apartment at the time, and Lawrence was asleep, drugged by painkillers. She was running through a Kinkaid exercise routine that Lawrence had used as a warm-up. Her tone was surprisingly crisp, reminiscent of Lawrence's. James stood silently, listening, until he couldn't stand it. He made a little noise, and Ann, startled, stopped, put down the flute, blushing. James blushed, too, and when their eyes met they both smiled. Something happened, something broke at that instant. They reached a wordless understanding and James wanted to cry. He wanted to embrace her, but there was no need. He crossed the room and ran his fingers along the flute.

Over dinner they talked about how to bring Lawrence out of his depression. Ann said she was as baffled as James. Should they consult a psychiatrist? Should they believe the advice people were giving them to lift his spirits? James wanted to tell her, "You're his mother; you must know what to do; you must have the right instinct," but Ann had said that she was baffled.

It was a few days later that he came across Ann lying collapsed and paralyzed on the hallway floor. Her eyes were open, but she was silent; she couldn't speak, she was choking a little. James was afraid to lift her, and also afraid to leave her alone. He dashed down the hallway to the kitchen telephone. She'd had her first stroke.

IV Marinamarinamarina. Fish is obsessed with fish is obsessed with fish is obsessed with ma ma ma ma
Ma ma ma ma ma ma
Marina.

Eric Fish lay on the floor with his head under the bed pretending he was crazy.

Ma ma ma ma ree ree ree

His nose scraped the bottom of the box spring. His eyes were open and there was pink light in his peripheral vision.

Na na na na na!

Marina, your hair, marina your ivory cheeks, marina your long fingers. Play. Playing.

She played the flute, he knew that. She was at Curtis, he knew that. He knew her phone number. Her uncle worked for Max.

Kazzzakovvvv. Zee, vee, nice sounds.

He freed his head from the dark bed-cavern. He was on his back on the Pepto-Bismol-pink shag carpet, which he hated — this had been Sylvie's room before she'd gotten married and moved out of the house — and he stared at the huge poster of Botticelli's *Birth of Venus* that he'd tacked on the ceiling. *Anadyomene.* He'd heard that word used somewhere for a Venus on the half shell. Where? In some lecture, probably.

He was wearing only underpants and the carpet was itchy. Venus. Venus wasn't as pretty as Marina. Only Leonardo had created an angel as beautiful as Marina.

Zing! The phone, his own line. When he jumped up he hit his head on the edge of the bed frame. Would it bruise? Well, what's another zit for Fish?

"Ow. Hello." It was Ben. Ben. Mr. Ben, Big Ben. Hey, man. What was up?

"Hey man, I'm pretty crazy these days," said Fish.

In what manner?

"In the manner of speaking about a woman."

The same woman?

"The same one."

Ben was playing Patti Smith in the background. *Horses, horses, horses.* Fish had that album, too, no, it was a tape. He'd taped Ben's. Fish has horses. Flying fish, Pegasus.

Fish pictured Ben sitting there, on the phone, right now, joint in one hand, paintbrush in another, now which hand was the phone in? Paintbrush resting on the tray, or joint in the ashtray. Was his hair longer, curlier, wilder now? Fish hadn't seen him since October in Chicago. He hadn't come home for Christmas. No bucks.

"Listen, man, I happened to go to this concert last week and your friend Cleveland was at it, I mean here, in Philly, and he was there with the girl . . ."

The girl?

"The girl. Would you happen to know if he's into her, or anything?"

One never knows with Cleveland. I don't know. Could be.

"Could be?"

But not to worry too much. He's back in town now.

"Back in Chicago?"

He was in the restaurant tonight.

Fish shut his eyes and pressed on them. Concentric circles of orange and green light. Ben must have his stereo on amazingly loud if he could understand the lyrics so well over the phone. *Horses, horses.*

Don't let it get to you.

"What's that, man?"

The girl. Don't let her get to you.

Do you know how to twist? Well, it goes like this. . .

Could you do me a favor?

"What's that?" Eric straightened up. He didn't usually get to do favors for Ben.

A small favor. Call my old lady. I tried, myself, earlier, but I couldn't get through. Tell her I got enough bucks together and I'm coming home for Easter.

"Oh, wow, man, okay. I could get into that, too."

I knew you would.

"Your old lady'll be glad to hear it, too."

She will.

"How are you going to do it?"

Bus, of course.

"Naturally."

Tell her I'll get there on the fourteenth.

"Okay, man, okay, I'll be glad to. See you then, Ben."

I'll call you.

C is the possibility. Dip in. Click.

Eric tried Mrs. March's number right away. He'd dialed it so much as a kid. He let it ring a long time since she lived alone and she might be in the bathroom or something. On the sixth ring she answered.

"Mrs. March, this is Eric, Eric Fish." She was quiet for just a second, but long enough for Eric to imagine that she was startled to hear from him.

"Oh, *Eric*. Hello. What are you up to these days?"

"Just the usual, Mrs. March. Listen, I just got a call from Ben. He's been trying to reach you."

"He has?"

"Yes, he asked me to call you. He's coming home to visit at Easter time."

"Oh, he is?" She sounded pleased. "How's he getting here?"

"Bus. He must have saved up enough money for a ticket. He's coming in on the fourteenth."

"Well, maybe I'll talk to him before then and pick him up at the terminal downtown. Maybe I'll call him tomorrow. Right now I'm working in the darkroom. That's why it took me so long to answer."

"How is the photography coming?"

"Oh, *very* well, Eric. I finished the course I told you I was taking at the Women's Center and the instructor thinks she knows a magazine that would like to buy some of my prints. Not for much money, of course, but to have them published would be wonderful."

"I'll say, well, congratulations. I'll have to come by and look at them soon."

"You should do that, Eric. And Eric, maybe you'd want to ride along with me to the bus station to pick up Ben."

"Okay, Mrs. March."

The March house was only four blocks away from where Eric lived, but it was not on the way to school or anywhere else, so Eric never passed it. Before Ben moved away Eric had spent more time there than at his own house. He'd been best friends with Ben since kindergarten. Back then when they were kids Ben's house was always full of children and animals. Ben was the youngest, and he had a sister Joan, who was an editor, and a sister Allison, who'd moved to California, and an older brother Toby. The Marches always had a litter of kittens or puppies, and hamsters or guinea pigs, and sometimes a lizard or a frog in a jar, and the house was usually a mess. There were no rooms off limits to children, like in the Fish house. All the rugs in the March house were worn thin and the floors were scuffed, and there were fingerprints on the door-jambs. Ben's mother was always driving kids and groceries around in a station wagon.

Eric's mother drove a Trans Am, which was broken half the time, and when it was in the shop she drove his father's Lincoln. They had wall-to-wall shag carpeting in every room of their house, and the wallpaper had velveteen patterns, so they hadn't been allowed to put their fingers on it. Eric and Nathan and Sylvie had been allowed in the playroom, and in their own rooms, and in the kitchen, but they couldn't play anywhere else. There was never a mess in the Fish house, except after Eric's dad gave a party.

Eric and Nathan had played at Ben's every day after school and all summer. Half the time they'd stayed for dinner. Eric's mom never seemed to mind.

But now the March house is strangely quiet and organized. All of the kids have left, so Mrs. March has had time to straighten it up, and when Mr. March left he gave her enough money to buy new curtains and rugs, and all the things that get ruined easily in a houseful of children. She'd varnished the floors and redone the woodwork and hung her photographs on the walls for decorations. The house seemed darker, cooler, and green plants were everywhere. Eric didn't like going there. It was so different. Like another planet, not the same place at all. How could Ben stand it, to come home and see his old house like this?

Eric flipped on the radio. *I've got the hesitation blues, hesitation blues . . .*

Calling Mrs. March was strange. Seeing her was strange. He didn't even like running into her at the 7-Eleven. After the divorce she'd cut her hair short and lost weight, and instead of polyester shorts and housedresses she was wearing blue jeans and Indian shirts. And long dangly earrings. And she took night courses in photography and art history. She was always trying to talk to Eric about painting. It was as though she were his age, some kind of peer.

How could she be his peer if all through his childhood she'd been the one who was in the background fixing Kool-Aid, wiping up puppy messes, showing them how to pitch a tent in the backyard, lecturing when she caught them smoking behind the garage. She was a mom, not a person. She must be in her mid-fifties now, and suddenly she was changing her image, her life so completely. It could make you dizzy, thought Eric.

. . . *hesitation blues, how long, baby, how long?*

Eric's mother sometimes took night courses at the high school, but those were in dancercise or tennis. She played tennis a lot. She'd been doing it ever since Eric could remember, but she wasn't very good. Eric wasn't much for athletics, but Nathan was, and even though he only played tennis a few times a year — his sport was racquetball — he beat their mom every time. Eric's mother didn't care. She was only interested in tennis to burn calories. Sylvie was like that, too. She and their mom played together a few times a week. They were two of the thinnest women Eric could think of, and all they talked about together was how much they ate, or this new diet or that new diet.

Marina doesn't have to work at her perfect body. Eric was sure of that. He couldn't fathom her in sweaty gym shorts swinging a tennis racket, or going to some exercise class, all dressed up in leotards, like his mom. Marina is naturally perfect. She must be, there is no other way.

There is no other way . . . . *singing the blues, hesitation blues* . . .

Women. What a mystery.

Eric stretched out spread-eagled on his bed. Ben always got all the women. It was his Leonardo looks. He was so cocksure; it was his style. Eric tried to copy his style, but he always lost his nerve. The Irish John the Baptist, Ben March. Ben could probably get that Marina if he wanted her. Eric grimaced. It was his style. He acted as though he had some mystery behind his eyes. But Ben wasn't so complicated, he wasn't like that, really. He wasn't even a real painter, but the women didn't know that, not at first, and by the time they found out, if they did, he had them *snared*. All women liked Ben, even Sylvie, who was so critical. Eric's mom just loved him, even after the time she'd found out he'd sold Nathan half a gram of cocaine. She still loved him. She was always asking after him, wanting to know when he was coming back from Chicago.

Marina probably would fall for Ben, but she wouldn't get the opportunity, thank God, since they lived in different cities. Eric could just imagine the frustration of having Ben take her away from him. Away from him? How could he think like that? He didn't have Marina. He wanted her bad, but he didn't have her. He didn't even have a chance. She would probably never even consider looking at him twice, normally, but now he'd really screwed things up, by acting like a lunatic.

Well, there was always the chance that she went for crazies. Ha.

There was something strange about her, though. Why was she hanging around that Rosen character? Eric had checked him out and found that everyone knew he's gay. Not bi. Gay. So why was she staying with him in Chicago? What was that all about? Eric didn't have anyone to ask.

Marina, marina, marina. Stop thinking about her. I can't. Don't want to . . . . *got the bluuuuuuues*. That was the end of that song. Eric jumped up and flipped the sound off.

What was he going to do? He should be doing something else, studying, maybe. Studying Titian. There was a midterm tomorrow, or was it Wednesday? He'd lost track. He picked up his notebook. Wednesday. He had another day. Still he could stand to . . . he pulled out the oversized book of prints. Fuck it, he wasn't in the mood. He opened the book, slammed it shut. A breeze.

Change the subject in his mind. Women. Think about other ones, which ones?

For years he'd liked a girl named Carla. She went to his junior high, and then they sent her to the Catholic parochial girl's high to get her away from boys and Jews, and particularly Jewish boys. She was Italian, and her hair was black and straight and she had the longest eyelashes, and in her ears she wore tiny pearls. She wasn't like the other Italian girls, with tight pants and high heels and layers of lipstick. She was different, and she read books. Eric had had eighth-grade English class with her and she'd read more books than the teacher. He'd thought that she was the smartest person he'd ever met.

Her father owned Pizza Towne Steaks & Hoagies and Eric used to hang around there out of sheer dedication, eating slice after slice of soggy pizza, so he wouldn't get thrown out for loitering, and hoping that she'd come out and work behind the counter. But she rarely did. She was always upstairs studying. Her father wanted her to go to law school, and he didn't mind if she didn't work in the shop. Her brother, Vince, did most of the counter work, and he was always throwing Eric dirty looks. He must have known Eric had a crush on his sister, or maybe he just hated all Jews. When Carla did appear behind the counter, Eric's heart would beat so fast he'd sweat. He could never bring himself to talk to her; the most he could do was ask her for a napkin or how she was these days and she'd say fine and then go on with what she was doing.

When Eric told Ben about Carla, Ben came along with him to Pizza Towne to see for himself. He couldn't remember her from junior high. There'd been four Carlas in their class, he claimed. After they waited around for an hour she came out. Ben pronounced her cute but nothing special, and went up to chat. His charm worked instantly. Carla kept talking to him, even when another customer came up to her and even when the other customer cleared his throat and looked annoyed. Carla's cheeks were flushed, and she watched Ben as he walked away. The whole time they sat there she kept glancing at their table.

Eric could feel his ears burning with rage. He knew Ben would go out with Carla and she would fall in love with Ben, and he would be left outside in the cold. Oh, how could that happen? After all the time and concentration he'd put into his pursuit of Carla? He'd done things like look up her home telephone number and then call, and when someone answered hang up. Sometimes he even got to hear her say hello. He imagined that she was saying hello to him. "Hello, Eric." Could she say that with tenderness? No. Because now she'd be in love with Ben.

"I'm really not that interested," said Ben for the third time on the way home. "Besides, I *have* a girlfriend." He was going out with a girl who was older, who was out of high school already, who went to art school downtown, Fay. Fay was the one who got Ben interested in painting. She lived in her own apartment downtown. Ben took Eric along once to visit her. The place was full of plants and the smell of turpentine. Fay had an enormous collection of water pipes that took up three shelves in her bedroom. Eric was fascinated by her bedroom; Ben had already told him she had a waterbed, and Eric kept sneaking little glances at it, to see what it was like. It just looked like a regular bed in a big wooden frame. It wasn't bouncing or anything. The sheets were plain white and all rumpled.

Ben was only fifteen then and he already had an eighteen-year-old girlfriend with her own apartment and a water bed. Ben was like that, he thought. Eric, at twenty now, was still a virgin. That was his biggest shame. Even Nathan probably wasn't a virgin anymore.

Women. Recently Eric had heard that Carla got pregnant and married some law student. She was still going to college. She still wanted to be a lawyer. And she was going to have a baby soon.

"Lots of luck," said Eric out loud. "Women."

There was his mother Myrna, and her mother Ida, who was senile, and his sister Sylvie, who married a Protestant and caused a brief scandal among his aunts, Rose and Esther and Marsha. And there were Cory and Carrie, whom, no matter how hard he tried, he couldn't bring himself to like or to be interested in, and there was Mae, the cleaning woman (scraping bottom here), and Mrs. March, whom he'd just talked to, and Joan March, he hardly ever saw her, and who else? From school there was Phoebe Gelesnik, his favorite art-history prof. Period: Early Renaissance. There was the woman behind the circulation desk of the Furness Library, the one with the red hair and glasses, he liked to talk to her, and there was the Greek girl at the food truck he bought his lunch from. She had the most perfect, muscular arms. And there was Page Allen, with her neat blond ponytail and plaid skirts, sitting beside him in Twentieth-Century Japanese Art, and there was Lisa Smith, who was black, who was really a friend of Ben's from high school, but he liked to get high with her sometimes after sociology class, and they'd gossip about what Ben must be doing in Chicago, and there was Debbie Chen, the graduate student who'd tutored him in chemistry to get him past his science requirement. She was so precise and quick, and now and then he'd see her walking on campus, exotic in her purple clothes, holding hands with her Chinese boyfriend. And there was Monica Something, with the big nose and punk haircuts and bright pink canvas shoes. She liked him a lot, he knew, but no thanks, and there was Jill Klein, whose name he learned from a class list. He'd sat in back of her every day for two semesters of Persian Painting, and when he felt like falling asleep in the lecture he'd wake himself up by concentrating on the tiny black mole on the back of her neck. Every day, for two semesters, she'd worn her hair up in a bun. He wasn't sure what her face looked like.

And there was Cheryl Silverman, who'd been his girlfriend in second grade. What had happened to her? There was Janine French who used to beat him up at day camp, and there was Sally, who'd been Nathan's girlfriend in tenth grade. There were all of Sylvie's girlfriends, all named Debbi or Sue, they all blended in together, and there was Faye Dunaway and Mia Farrow and Jessica Lange and Jessica Savitch, Patti Smith, Beverly Sills,

Phoebe Snow, and Venus de Milo, and the Birth of Venus, *Anadyomene*, and Mona Lisa, who was not at all beautiful really, and Madame X and the Odalisque, and the Angel from the Virgin on the Rocks. Angel, angel, angel. Marina.

"Angel," said Eric. He picked up the phone, thinking, I don't like what I'm doing. He glanced at the clock; 11:06, not even too late to make a legitimate phone call. She answered on the third ring.

She must live alone, he thought. If anyone answers it's always her. No roommates. Good.

Her voice was tired. Had she been sleeping?

"Hello, Marina, this is Fish."

Who? Who is it?

"You don't know me, but I've been watching you for some time."

Who is this?

"Fish. That's my name. Really. Marina, don't be nervous or anything. I'm not dangerous, I just really like you a lot. I know this sounds weird —"

Who are you? What do you want? How do you know my name?

"Don't get upset. I can explain everything. I'd just really like to see you —"

Who are you who are you who are you

"— in person. I'd like to talk to you. It's not what you think. I really *like* you. I want to see you —"

Click.

"Please." But the line was dead. He held the phone to his ear till the dial tone came on.

"Shit," said Eric. He tossed the receiver onto the floor.

He fell asleep with the lights on and the music off and in his dream the Angel, Marina, poised on the rocks, was frightened. Fish was wrong. He was a monster, a horrible gargoyle with hair like snakes, Medusa, he moved toward her and she shrunk back, no! he wanted to tell her, no, I'm just a big dumb lumbering harmless monster. I'm Yogi Bear, and then the background was a bright cartoon and Marina was turning her head, she was turning and the clouds were coming and the sky was real, not the cartoon sky and Eric was saying, why isn't this a painting, why not? And the trees were real now and she was on the rock, but she was changing. Locusts and Wild Honey. Her chin was long and her eyes were like slits. Why was there so much red? She was becoming Giovanni, locust and wild honey, Salome, head on a plate. Salome, why wasn't she Salome, the woman? She was John the Baptist, she was, she was the Angel, no she was Ben. Ben. Baptist Ben. The Locusts were singing so loudly, their voices rising and rising in pitch and behind them was the drone, sound of the drone, tambourine, now drone, male bees doing all the work, making all the wild honey, and she was he, and the sound grew more intense, and the colors grew bright till they exploded in a flash and the image was gone.

Chapter 10

I

PURITY	Gabriel.
OBSESSION	Myself. James. Cleveland. Gabriel's mother.
INNOCENCE	Gabriel.
MYSTERY	Marina. Cleveland.
LOVE	James.
FEAR	Myself, for Gabriel. Myself, for James.
PROTECTION	Myself, for Gabriel.

Lawrence made notes before he began a difficult letter, just as though he were about to write a chapter of his book. He wrote them on long lined yellow legal paper, and for his most important letters, he wrote out first drafts on this paper also. He had written James last night, but it was not enough. Now, at eight A.M. he couldn't work. There was too much inside him, he needed to unleash a whole symphony of thoughts. He needed relief. He had to write again, more completely, right now.

The chapter was pushed aside, into a corner: notes, typed sheets, Xeroxed references, draft sheets, all in one pile. He mouthed the name Gabriel. Where should he begin?

James,
    When I first made love to you years ago I knew that you were not pure. Not at all. There was the tinge of the world already in your eyes,

though you were only a boy, only seventeen. It was already there, James, and though my love for you was strong, it has never been pure.

It is in your music, that tinge, and of course that is a good thing, for one grows quickly tired of listening to a boychoir. You are of the earth and the water, not the sky. It's good, James.

But James, I am drawn to the sky. I am always looking out my window, across to the sunrise, across to the clouds, or the lack of clouds, or the wall of clouds, or the stars.

None of these things I can touch. Not like the pedestrians or the trees below. Not tangible, not reachable. Not again. If I came from something high and untouchable, I cannot go back. I can be brilliant. I can be lofty, but I can never be pure.

James, for us there is no further sublimation. We are humans; we crawl, we walk on the dirt, we eat dirt, ingest it with our food, we cannot rise above where we have sunk; there is no purging, no sanctification, not from our humanity, not for us. Not us, not you and me. Not anyone. No one can be uplifted.

It's good. We hold our weight well, half risen, half fallen; you, your music, your art, so swelling with the voice of a man, any man, any woman, people, what we are, the way we sing, the best of us, worst of us, how we breathe and eat, and sleep and make love, and how we hurt ourselves, how we hurt our own bodies, what we do, and do again, what we can't escape or deny, what we know because we have learned it from centuries of pain and searching and why it gives us guilt. Why we are obsessed.

James, I'm obsessed. With nothingness, with air, with atmosphere, with pure oxygen. It makes me dizzy. I want to inhale a cloud, whatever it's made of. I want those vapors. I want them because they're white, the purest, cleanest, white: angel wings, and at night they're gone, and in between, when the sun sinks and rises, they are rich or pale with color. Hue. Never, never, are they stained, however. Always they return pure. I want to inhale a cloud, be inside of one, make it part of me, never let it dissolve, break down, disappear, go wherever clouds go when they are gone. Never.

James, it's his pure mathematical music. Gabriel's. I don't want it to change, and it's my task as his mentor to develop it. He has to learn to play with expression of life, expression that he will learn with his adolescence, his approaching adulthood. There is so much that he must learn, and he must learn to transfer it into his music. That's what makes an artist great, not the technical prowess. You know that. Pyrotechnics, competition-winners. Boring. You know that they never last unless they learn to reach, to be tainted with the tainted. To be human.

I know this. I know what is good, what is human, what is art, because it's part of us, part flesh. Connected. I love flesh, skin, breathing people. Sin, failure, hope, experience. I love the world, so why am I so drawn to his innocence? His music, which is only an equation of sound and silence? He knows so little yet, and what he has felt he is unable to translate. I like this. I am drawn to his inability, his impotence. He will never be the same; it is my job to deflower him. I must despoil his sanctity. I must help him mature. I must or he would be a eunuch forever, a castrato. It would be an act of cruelty for a talent such as his never to mature. It has happened to others, James, count those cold technical prodigious genius failures. I have been chosen for this most delicate operation, this surgery, and I cannot escape this duty. I could never trust another teacher with Gabriel. I must teach him, but, Oh, James . . .

Nine A.M. and the traffic noises had quieted down outside. Lawrence walked across the room and began to roll the windows open one by one, ending with the bay window in front of his desk. He'd had the original ones removed and these put in at his own expense. He was planning to stay here for years, and the management had refused to pay for such alterations. But sliding windows were too painful for him to open and shut regularly. He chilled easily. Cool spring air flooded the room. Fresh, recently-rained-on smells with only a hint of auto fumes.

Lawrence went into the kitchen and turned on the light under the kettle. He would make a pot of tea. Nearly out of Earl Grey. Must remember to stop and get another tin.

Spooning the leaves into the pot, he stopped to sniff. They were so evocative. Smells worked well to bring him back to the past. For a second he was back in Oxford, in Arjit's rooms. He had Persian carpets on the floors and real oil paintings by artists even

Lawrence had heard of. He had three rooms and in one of them lived his manservant, a wiry little Hindu who wore a white dhoti, even in the wintertime, and who called Arjit "Sahib." Arjit ordered him around in Hindi. The servant had no English. He made Lawrence think about Sujita, wonder what had become of her.

He could just picture Arjit's dark, slanting eyes and the sensuous curve of his upper lip. His mustache. Had he had one? Lawrence couldn't remember.

Earl Grey with milk. They'd drunk that together often. Arjit never went to the Indian restaurants, never drank Indian-style tea. Lawrence's father used to make Indian tea at home. It was the only cooking he ever did. First he put a pot of water on the stove, then threw on the flame. He dumped the loose tea right into the water, then added sugar, cloves, cinnamon sticks, and something else Lawrence couldn't remember. Then when it was boiling he poured the milk straight into it and cooled it down. This he brought to a boil once again and it was done. He poured it through a strainer into cups for himself and Lawrence and Sujita when she was with them. He always spilled at least a cup's worth all over the counter and some on the floor. Ann would complain about this bitterly. She refused to drink the tea herself. Said it was too sweet, said it made her sick. Lawrence secretly loved it, but never asked for it unless it was given to him. He didn't want his mother to know that he liked so much something that disgusted her.

James, it is so good to talk to you this way, through the letters, and you know it doesn't bother me that you're not a letter-writer yourself, but sometimes I wish, no, I want there to be something more. I wish I could know you more. I've felt I haven't really known you fully, not ever since I left for Oxford, so many years ago. I lost you then, that's when you got your mystery. (That's how I refer to it when I'm thinking to myself.) You've been a little closed to me ever since then, and I have always felt it. You are resistant. There is a corner of you that is private, and of course I respect it, but, irrationally or not, I resent that it is growing, yes it is, it is growing larger. I cannot understand more and more about you as we grow older.

Should he really be writing this? Did he want James to see it? Well, this was just a draft. He'd decide later.

I look at you and I look at the girl, Marina, at your side. Such dark, strange involvements. What could they mean? I ponder your movements long after you are gone, you know. I picture your hand easy on the small of her back. Your shoulder inclined in her direction while you are in conversation with me. I know what it means, but I wonder, what could it mean?

Why?

It is like this with Cleveland, too. What is it you see in him, is he the same as the girl? Is it that glint of jewel in his eye? The way his glance reflects every available light? Is it his manner, the way he holds himself? We used to have a word for that, you know. No, I know he's a whore and I know you know it, but he's intriguing to you. Deeply intriguing. I can feel it in you. What is it you want? What do you want with that girl? What do you want, James? You are clinging to everything, you have him, the girl, you have me, what do you want?

You don't want Gabriel, I have no fears of that. You have no interest in purity and what is chaste. I speak in a metaphorical sense, of course. You don't want Gabriel and I'm glad of that. You probably just skimmed past the first part of this letter until you got to the part about yourself, that's how concerned you are about it all, damn it.

Damn it, why am I drawn to you? I'm as possessed by you as I am by Gabriel; two such extremes! Oh, that he doesn't slide too far to your end! How could I love you both if you were the same? My heart would break, well up so big with grief. I couldn't bear it, James, why did you change? Where are you going? I love you and I don't believe that you love me anymore. Was it ever love, James, from you, or was it only selfishness? Have you ever loved me at all or was it always you? You, you, you. You never questioned that everything wasn't for you. You'd use anyone like a whore, but it's you who is the whore. That damned mother did it to you, turned you into one before you left your diapers. Everything for you, for your career. You caught on to it so well, too. You did an excellent job for yourself. Oh, Pearl would be so proud. You damned slut. You never loved me. You may have said you did; you may have told yourself you did, but you never did.

Well what do you want out of me now, broken down old man Lawrence? Why hang on? What can I give you? I can't give you anything anymore — your career is set. You took that from me. (I'm being unfair, I know. Let me.)

You took everything you needed, and now it's all just for appearance' sake. Just to look good. Look, everyone, see how nice James Rosen is to the ruined old cripple, just see. I can see right through you, all but that little corner, you're as clear as glass, transparent. Even trite. It's only that little corner of myself that sustains your musicianship! No wonder you keep it private! If I could see through that, too!

He could never show this to James. How ridiculous he was. He'd been writing so furiously he'd forgotten about his tea, and now it was unpleasantly lukewarm. He dumped that cup down the sink. What was left in the pot was still hot.

Oh, James, I'm so afraid. I don't mean those things, and yes, I do mean them, and I'm so afraid they're true and I know they are and I don't want to lose you. I don't want this to be true. Oh, if only it were simpler and we were all like Gabriel, so precise and perfect. A measure, a bar or two at a time. Quarter notes, half notes, triplets, all senseless and perfect. No pain. No loss, no feeling. Only sound and silence.

If only I could protect us. No, it's too late for us. If I could protect HIM I would. I would keep him safe forever in a perfect room, crystal, acoustically sanctified. A chapel for sound. No, a cathedral; I can see him there now, in his choir gowns, he is an angel, the Archangel . . . I know so little about the Catholic church, but I know there is an Angel Gabriel, and that angels have no bodies. They are metaphors for goodness, and they are safe. They have wings, they fly; they can transport themselves through space in an instant, and they are the guardians of our lives.

James, I have not thought of this before: Guardian Angels. Perhaps Gabriel will save me.

Lawrence read what he had written. He had followed his outline, but he'd said everything differently than he'd planned. It was this way frequently when he wrote: he discovered things he hadn't thought of, new ideas. He put the yellow sheets, three of them all filled with his handwriting, into his bottom drawer. He wouldn't be recopying this, no, not without substantial deletions. He hadn't even known he was angry until just now. Was he really, or was that just a fleeting feeling? Don't think about it anymore, he told himself. He pulled the notes for the chapter over to him, began to reread what he'd done yesterday: a most thorough outline. Now all to do was fill it in, do the actual prose.

He glanced at the clock: 9:30 A.M. At 11:15 he was due at the club for a squash game with some lawyer.

II   Marina took her phone off the hook after the seventh call from that Fish person. She didn't have classes this morning. She was trying to practice and the phone was driving her crazy. But she kept thinking: What if Mama tries to call? What if she needs me, or what if Cleveland tries, or what if my teacher wants to cancel the lesson?

She'd called the police, but they didn't seem to care. The man had taken down her name and address, but told her that the telephone-company business office handles telephone harassment. That office was open from nine to five. "But I'm getting these calls in the middle of the night," she'd insisted. No matter, they didn't care. It was eight now. He'd stopped calling at three, started again at six. In an hour she'd report it and for now she was safe, it was off the hook. She was going through her warm-up exercises.

Who could this guy be? What could he have to do with her? He sounded so young. Did he know James? Did he know Cleveland? He didn't talk about them. He didn't talk about anyone, only her. What did he want? She was so jittery. Every stray noise in the apartment made her jump. *Flick-flick-flick.* That was just the shade tapping against the windowpane. She stopped playing and went over to the window. Her apartment faced Seventeenth Street on one side and the alley on the other. Down below were hundreds of people on their way to work, the street was full of cars, the sidewalk full of pedestrians, mostly everyone dressed nicely for

business, some bums, some students. There was Mrs. What's-her-
name, the building manager, arguing with some deliveryman.
There was a policeman ticketing cars.

All the activity down there made her feel safer. Not safe enough,
though. The water pipes rattled and she gasped, startled. Maybe
she should get a dog, a Doberman pinscher. Of course they didn't
allow pets in the building. Maybe she should have her number
changed. That would cost money, but it might be worth it. Maybe
she should move. No, that was silly. This was one of the securest
buildings in the city. They hadn't even let Serge and Papa in the
time they were in the city and came to see her, not until she came
down and identified them. Serge and Papa. She'd found them staring around in the big old dusty entranceway, looking at the huge
dingy old painting of Miss Clara Armstrong, the bust of Sir William
Pepper, whoever he was, examining the fine woodwork. Serge and
Papa. They were wearing work clothes then; they'd been in the city
to pick up some fixtures to build Mama's special sewing closet. She
remembered she'd been a little ashamed that Papa was wearing an
undershirt (white, with yellow stains under the arms) and that his
shoes were flecked with paint. Serge looked like an average
teenage hood with his black glitter T-shirt and skinny white arms.
She'd been ashamed of them, she probably would be again if they
showed up now, oh, shit, she was going to cry.

She cried noiselessly. There was no one to hear her. At the funeral she'd wept uncontrollably. She'd been so embarrassed, thought
she'd be more composed, but no, she couldn't stop, couldn't help
herself, kept thinking in the back of her mind that she was being
just like Mama, a hysterical woman. All of the women were crying. Anya was almost as loud as Mama with her wailing and Lucy
was sniffling and even Hannah had big tears leaking out from
behind her glasses and Marina was so ashamed of herself.

The women were all weeping together, and Serge silent the
whole time, hating her, she knew it. He made her feel like such a
piece of shit, oh, how had this all happened, they used to be such
good friends, it was all over, oh, shit, shit, shit, she'd lost him,
she'd lost Serge, she'd lost Papa, she'd never get them back, Serge

might as well be dead too, he'd never forgive her, oh, how could she have been so rotten, how could she have been so ashamed of them and let them know it on top of everything else, oh, she'd been so contemptuous, she'd let them know that she was ashamed of their accents, their language, their food, their taste in furniture, in clothes, their little square house, their poverty, shame, shame, shame, how many people at school knew she was Ukrainian? Not many, they all thought Russian. Marina is Russian, exotic, beautiful. Oh, shame, shame, shame, she'd let them know she was so glad not to be living with them. She never called them, never went home, she was such a little shit, and Papa died knowing it and Serge knew it and he'd never forgive her, and Mama knew it, only she was such a saint she'd never let on, never say anything, but she knew it and it must hurt her so much, oh, Marina, you're such a lousy shit, crying and crying and feeling sorry for yourself, and you know if you'd call Mama right now you'd get impatient with her and want to hang up as soon as you started talking, and why do you always insist on talking to them in English, never Ukrainian, when that's your real language, the one you knew first, the one you used to fool the other kids with when you and Serge could talk to each other in front of everyone and no one knew what you were saying and it was special then, so special, like magic and it was fun to be different, why won't you use that language anymore, you won't let yourself think in it, it only comes to you in your dreams when you can't help it, you're so glad when Mama's talking to you and you find you've forgotten a word. Marina, you're such a shit, crying, crying, crying, sitting on the edge of the bed feeling sorry for yourself, you deserve it all, Cleveland, this Fish person, anything that could happen to you, you shit.

She could see her face across the room in the mirror, all red and ugly, eyes small, squinting. She looked like Serge after he'd been fooling around with drugs. She blew her nose. Serge. She went over to the mirror and examined her face. Serge. Same eyes, similar nose, only smaller, more like Mama's than Papa's. Same mouth, almost, but fuller bottom lip. Same chin, exactly. Same pale, pale, almost blue-tinged skin, same redness around the nostrils, but that was temporary. Serge — they were so much alike when they were kids that people often asked if they were twins, and he was two years younger, almost. Now he was taller than her by nearly a foot and he still looked her age; they could still be twins, fraternal ones, hatched from different eggs. When they were kids they used to say that yes they were twins, that made them special, and it seemed to please grown-ups. They'd played together alone mostly. They had a civilization they'd invented. The population was made of small plastic animals that they'd collected. He had his, half of them, which he controlled — and that was his town, Sergecity, and hers was called Elyria for a reason she couldn't remember now, and sometimes there would be wars, but usually they were very cooperative. The rugs were the grass and the wood floor was the river. Her kingdom was the dining room and his was the living room and the kitchen was the Forbidden Forest because Mama wanted them and their toys to Keep Out. Marina had a jail in her kingdom and that was mostly for the little orange tiger who was always causing trouble, and once he tried to kill the king of Sergecity and Serge stuck him in *his* jail, but it was all right because at the end of the game he gave him back, it's not like marbles where you keep the pieces you win. What had they done with all those little plastic animals? They were probably still in the house somewhere, in a bag in her room in the closet, maybe. When was the very last time they'd picked them all up and put them away? Had they known it would be the last time? When had they stopped playing with those things? She couldn't remember anything about that. It mustn't have seemed important at all at the time.

She was daydreaming. It was after nine, time to call the telephone company and report this Fish person. First she washed her face. She always felt tired after crying. She'd like to lie down, take a nap, but that might be dangerous, she could be late for her lesson, or even sleep through it if she wasn't careful, and with her poor attendance record that was a bad idea.

The man at the phone company told her to write down the exact times of all her problem phone calls, and to hang up on the caller right away. Then in a few days she should call back the business office with the times of the calls and they would try to trace it from the computer. That should work, said the man, provided the caller was using the same phone every time.

"But what if he's not?" said Marina. "And what if he just comes over here and kills me in the meantime? If he has my phone number and he knows my name, then he probably knows where I live, too. Isn't there a faster way to trace the calls?"

The man at the phone company assured her that most obscene phone callers are not dangerous.

"Most!" shouted Marina. "And what about the other ones? Besides, this guy isn't obscene, he's perfectly polite. He just scares the shit out of me." Oops. She shouldn't have said *shit* to the telephone man. Now he'd probably be offended and uncooperative.

He seemed not to notice, however. He just repeated his assurances that she would probably be all right and suggested that she call the police if she noticed anyone suspicious loitering around her residence.

"Thanks," said Marina coldly.

On her way out to her lesson the phone rang. It was Fish again.

"Hello, this is Fish . . ." he began. Marina hung up, wrote *10:47* on the pad she kept by the phone.

III The phone rang while Elizabeth was doing her exercises. It was long distance.

"Please hold to speak to Sue Levin," said the secretary's nasal voice. Eight-ten in the morning. They start early, thought Elizabeth with approval. What a change for Sue Levin to be calling her.

"Did you get the quote from Rosen?" said Sue Levin, not wasting the time to say good morning.

"No, he's on tour now," Elizabeth began.

"Never mind, worry about that later, what I wanted to let you know is that I think I found a manager, a good one, topflight."

"What? That's fantastic! Who is it?"

"Myra Davidov, she's looking for a prodigy. She wanted violin, but she's interested. She doesn't want an Oriental, and that's all that seems to be around. She's been looking for a few months now and I hear she's ready to consider another instrument."

"What are our chances?"

"I'm having lunch with her tomorrow. Let you know then."

"Oh, I'm so excited —"

"Listen, I'm late for a meeting. I'll call you tomorrow."

"Oh, of course. What —" The line went dead.

Elizabeth bristled with energy. She was too agitated to finish her exercises. She began to wash the breakfast dishes. Whom should she call? Toby would just be annoyed. He didn't approve of the agent business at all . . . but who else could she tell? Gabriel was in school. She dialed Toby's house. No answer. Oh, yes, it was Tuesday morning. He'd be at the paper by now. She dialed the sports desk.

"Of course I am not thrilled," he told her, "but I'm glad your day was made a little brighter."

"Oh, do you have to be so sarcastic? You have to admit this is pretty important."

"Well it hasn't happened yet, so don't get your hopes up too high. This could fall through."

"You only wish."

'You know I do. You know how I feel about it, but we can discuss this later, I have to —"

"I know, get back to work. I know you have a deadline, but I had to tell somebody."

"Just don't tell Gabriel."

"Why not?"

"Because if it doesn't work out he'll feel rejected, and that would be an unnecessry burden to dump on him."

"I hadn't thought about it. Okay, you're right. I won't tell him unless it works out."

"See you tonight for dinner?"

"Please. We're having stir-fries. Come around seven."

"It's a date." He made a kiss sound in the phone and hung up.

Why doesn't anyone say good-bye anymore when they hang up the phone? wondered Elizabeth.

She called Max to tell him, but his secretary kept insisting that he was in a meeting, wouldn't put her through. She refused to leave a message.

"Just have him call me," she said, knowing that he would not. Max never returned her calls, never had, even when he was married to her. She wondered if he returned Sylvia's calls.

Myra Davidov! Elizabeth pulled out her copy of *Musical America* and looked up the Davidov roster. Not bad. Two major pianists, then three she hadn't heard of, a major violinist, a major organist, a cellist she'd heard of, an important string quartet, a woodwind ensemble that sounded familiar, a chamber orchestra from Poland, lots of singers — Elizabeth didn't know opera, so she couldn't judge those — two conductors she recognized, and an established composer. *No* flute soloist at all. Excellent. She left the book open on the table — she'd show it to Toby when Gabriel wasn't listening — and danced around the room. She had so much energy. What could she do? What could she do?

IV Hmmm. Hmmmm-hmmmm. Hmmmm-ing.

Ann Frost was sitting in her room in the nice rocker that Raj had brought her. The sun was dancing on the windowpanes. There was dust on the window and it sparkled like diamonds. There were ivy vines growing up the window, too, and they seemed almost yellow in the strong light. Should she clean the windows? But she had no rags, no, not here. She looked around the floor for a bucket of soapy water, but there was none, so she would have to do that later, besides, it was nice to pretend that the windows were sprinkled with diamond dust. Raj had given her a real diamond, just a tiny one, when they got married, but she'd lost it down the drain when she was giving the baby a bath and Raj had been so mad, he'd hit her. No, that was wrong. Raj never hit her, he'd said it was okay and that he would get her another one, that's right. She looked at her fingers. When would he bring her new ring? She must ask him next time he comes. Her fingers were looking a bit wrinkled today. She must have been holding them in soapy water, oh what had she done with that bucket? Her fingernails were getting very long and she must remember to clip them. How annoyed her teacher would be if she didn't! She must remember to practice after clipping them. Must remember to use the pads of her fingers, close the holes completely, oh, she'd been a lazy girl with her closed-hole flute, but now she knew better, and she must remember. Where had she put her flute? It must be somewhere in the room. Yesterday she'd known where it was, but not today. Where was the nurse? Did she move it? Probably. When Raj came again she'd tell him about that nurse. The nurse probably had her bucket, too, but that was all right, she didn't feel like cleaning just now and she had a good excuse not to, with her bucket missing. Besides, her fingers were so wrinkly she really shouldn't. Let the nurse wash the windows, the lazy thing! Always wearing that white suit just so she wouldn't have to clean. Doesn't want to get her dress dirty. That's how it is around here. She'd tell Raj about it and maybe he'd take her away, like he really ought to. She wasn't too fond of this place and they would never leave her alone, always rearranging her things, hiding her books. and what had they done with her flute? And they were so disorganized, never remembering to bring tea when she asked for it, and always making her take pills, pills, pills, probably all the wrong ones at the wrong times, they were so mixed up. If she had a car she'd leave. What had Raj done with the Ford? Where did he park it? Maybe when he came to visit her and he was in the bathroom she could steal it and escape, she still knew how to drive. But the keys. She'd have to get them from him, unless . . . of course, she had her own set of car keys and she'd use them. If she could get them from the nurse. Where was that nurse now? It must be time for tea.

Here they bring you things. They don't let you get it yourself.

She hadn't fixed dinner for a long long time now, and she couldn't understand why since she was a much better cook. It was strange, and she had mentioned it to the nurse and the doctors, too, but they didn't seem to understand.

It wasn't bad having people to wait on you if they'd only do it right. But they were so disorganized. They never remembered to bring her tea, or bring her the bedpan when she needed it. If someone would only help her up she could do it all herself. It was just this business of getting back on her feet that was so hard these days. Raj should help her. Raj should come and help her walk; they could walk home, that's where they could walk. And the baby would be there. He must be taking care of it, feeding it that hot curry stuff probably. Where was the baby? Why didn't they bring it to visit her? She would try to remember to ask the nurse about this. Hadn't she asked her before? She was such a lazy girl, that nurse, they were all so lazy, never doing any of the housework, always pretending not to hear her questions. They hid her flute, probably because they didn't want to listen to her practicing, and they were stupid. Didn't they understand how she needed to prepare for her lessons? What would her teacher think when she showed up without even practicing all this time? What a disgrace! She should consider skipping the lesson — why, she couldn't even find her flute. She would have to hide somewhere in case they came looking for her. Where could she hide? How could she find a hiding place if she couldn't even get out of her chair? Maybe the nurse would help her if she explained it to her. But the nurse was such a silly girl, how could she make her understand?

V It was a half-day because of exams and Gabriel was sitting on the wall waiting for his mom to pick him up. Today he'd had Math, which was easy, and Spelling, which was a big mess. He hadn't studied for it and he'd told his mom he had because he'd thought he could fake it. Now he was going to be in big trouble because he was sure he'd gotten half of the words wrong. He reached into his blazer pocket and pulled out his baseball cards. Today was a rotten day — he'd lost four valuable cards, including a Pete Rose, flipping in the recess yard this morning!

"Yo! Hey! Gabe!" It was three girls from Sanborne School walking up the hill. Sanborne was the girl's school next to the Wolfe School, the one Elise and Marybeth had gone to. Sanborne and Wolfe School had dances together and shared the same swimming pool and squash courts, and smart Sanborne girls came over to Wolfe School for the accelerated math classes.

One of the girls coming up the hill was Cheryl Smith — Gabriel knew her from Math. One was Heather Burns, who was famous for having a big chest, and the third one Gabriel didn't recognize.

"Gabriel! Hey!" Gabriel waved limply in recognition. He looked around quickly to see if anyone was watching. Back by the elm trees was a group of seventh graders from Wolfe. Gabriel's heart beat a little faster, but he tried to look bored.

The girls walked up to him.

"Hi," he said, pretending to study his baseball cards.

Cheryl did the talking. She was in charge, since she knew Gabriel best.

"You know Valerie Bender?" Gabriel nodded, slightly surprised. Valerie Bender was supposed to be the cutest girl in the sixth grade.

"She likes you," said Cheryl.

"So?" said Gabriel. He knew he was expected to say that, sounding as bored as possible.

"Do you like her?"

"I dunno. Why should I tell you?"

"Would you go out with her?"

"Why?"

"She wants to know, that's why."

"Oh?"

"Yeah. Well? Would you?"

"Okay." Gabriel shrugged to show that he didn't care too much one way or the other. The three girls, their mission completed, ran back down the street giggling. Gabriel glanced over at the elm trees, but the kids who'd been standing there were gone.

This is how it worked: if a girl liked you she'd get her best friends to find out whether you liked her, and if you did then you'd go out with her. It was the same if you liked a girl: you'd get your friends to ask her for you. Going out with a girl meant that she was your girlfriend, but you didn't have to see her or call her if you didn't want to. Two months ago some girls had asked Gabriel if he wanted to go out with Arly Stein and he'd said yes, but he'd never called her once and at the mixer he hadn't talked to her or danced with her. As a rule he didn't dance with girls. And Arly, he had never even been sure of what she looked like. Then her friends had come back and told him she was mad at him for ignoring her and she was breaking up. Gabriel had said that was okay. According to the other guys, Arly wasn't supposed to be pretty, anyway.

But Valerie Bender was a different story. Everyone in his class all seemed to think she was the best-looking sixth-grade girl. Gabriel had gotten a good long look at her when she sat across the aisle from him on the field trip to Harrisburg. She had blond curly hair like his own and she was a little fat, which made her look bigger up top. As far as Gabriel knew, she was going out with Peter Kazakov, who was supposed to be the best-looking sixth-grade boy. She must have broken up with Peter, or else she was trying to make him jealous. Peter would be mad when he found out that Gabriel had agreed to go out with Valerie.

Gabriel's mom's car appeared, puttering up the hill. He jumped off the wall, pulling his book bag with him, and climbed into the seat next to her when she stopped.

"How were exams?" she asked.

"Math was fine. Spelling was — not so good." He braced himself for further questions.

"Oh, really? That's too bad," she said. Gabriel glanced at his mother. She seemed to be smiling from behind her sunglasses. What was the matter with her? Why wasn't she grilling him about his Spelling exam?

She switched on the radio, but, as usual, only static came out. Sometimes, on the rare occasions that the car felt like it, they got to listen to the music, but not now. She began to hum the melody of one of Gabriel's warm-up études. Something was distracting her, putting her in a good mood. Gabriel wondered what it could be. Did it have to do with Toby? With Dad? With himself? He started to ask her, but stopped. He wasn't going to take any chances on starting a conversation that might get her thinking about his Spelling grade.

He leaned back in his seat and looked out his window. They rode past the three Sanborne girls standing at the bus stop. Valerie Bender. What a pain. He should have said no, even if she was supposed to be so cute. That was just her reputation. She wasn't pretty, really. Gabriel knew perfectly well that the only reason her chest was so big was because she was fat. He should have said no but those girls had taken him by surprise and he hadn't had a chance to think. Peter was going to be furious when he found out and he'd probably call Gabriel out for a fight, which would be awful since he was stronger and faster than Gabriel. Even though he was short. Peter was the only sixth-grader who'd made the junior varsity football team this year, and he was a good soccer player, too. The more Gabriel thought about it, the more nervous he got. Maybe he should call up that girl Cheryl and tell her he didn't want to go out with Valerie after all. She wasn't worth it.

His mom was humming all the way home, all the way up the driveway. She got out of the car and skipped up the steps to the house. Why was she acting like this? Gabriel followed her inside, and she didn't even yell at him when he dumped his books on the chair in the hallway.

"What's for lunch?" he asked.

"Lunch? Oh, whatever you like."

"Can I have peanut-butter-and-marshmallow?" he asked cautiously.

"If you want."

Strange. She hardly ever said he could have peanut butter, let alone peanut butter with marshmallows. He ran into the kitchen to make his sandwich.

"Can I have Kool-Aid, too?" he yelled, pressing his luck.

"Mmmm-hmmm."

"Wow," said Gabriel under his breath. Maybe she would even let him play baseball with the other kids this afternoon instead of making him study for his exams. Tomorrow was Science and Social Studies.

That night Toby came over and after dinner he and Gabriel's mom sat in the kitchen talking in low voices while Gabriel practiced downstairs. They weren't listening to what he was doing Gabriel tested this by experimenting with playing the trills in the wrong places. His mom still hadn't told him what was going on, why she was in such a good mood, and she and Toby stopped talking every time he went into the kitchen for a glass of water or a Kleenex. He was running out of excuses to go into the kitchen and he still didn't know what they were talking about. Either it had to do with him, maybe his getting a manager or something, or it was a personal thing with them. Maybe they were going to get married. If they got married Toby wouldn't be his dad, since you can't have two dads, but it would seem like he was. That would be fun, to have Toby living here all the time. Once he'd asked his mom why she didn't marry Toby and she'd blushed and said he wouldn't understand; he was too young.

Just as Gabriel was getting ready to go to the kitchen again, this time maybe sneak up so they wouldn't hear him coming and wouldn't stop talking, the phone rang. He heard his mother pick it up, and then she hollered, "Gabriel! It's for you!"

For him? He never got phone calls except from Steven and Selby to play baseball, but they never called at night. Gabriel put his instrument down and ran upstairs to the kitchen phone.

"It's a girl," whispered his mom. Gabriel felt his face going hot with embarrassment.

"I'll take it in your room," he mumbled, turning around and running upstairs. That would be Valerie calling to talk. What a pain. And how embarrassing in front of his mom and Toby.

But it wasn't Valerie. It was Peter. His voice was high and squeaky with anger.

"I heard you wanna go out with Valerie," his voice cracked.

"So?" said Gabriel.

"So, she's my girlfriend, and you're gonna have to fight."

Gabriel was tempted to say, "Then keep her," but he couldn't. If he didn't fight, Peter would tell everyone he was a faggot.

"So?" said Gabriel.

"So meet me tomorrow on the soccer field after exams let out, turkey."

"What if I don't?"

"Then you're a faggot, turkey."

"Oh, yeah?" said Gabriel. "I'll be there."

"Okay, good-bye," said Peter.

"Bye," said Gabriel.

Two weeks ago Brad Schuster had fought Henry Oppenheimer over Sally Miehaus and Brad had broken Henry's glasses. Henry's mother had called the school to complain and the headmaster had announced that any boys caught fighting on school grounds would be suspended for a week. Last week Lawrence White beat up Roland Guest for insulting him at gym class, but they didn't get caught, so they didn't get suspended, even though Roland had had a black-and-blue eye ever since.

At least Peter had the sense to pick the soccer field. It was far enough away from the main buildings that probably no teachers would be around. No one used the field during exam time.

Gabriel walked slowly down to the kitchen. This time he really needed a glass of water. His mouth was dry.

"Who was it on the phone?" said his mom, nosily.

"Just some girl," said Gabriel, trying to sound bored.

"What did she want?" said his mom.

"*Elizabeth*," said Toby. That meant, Mind your own business. Toby was the only person in the world who could get away with telling Gabriel's mom what to do. Gabriel looked at Toby gratefully, finished his water, and went back down to his practice room.

That night he dreamed he was on the soccer field at school, only it was huge, ten times bigger than in real life. There was an audience in the bleachers: Valerie was there in a princess costume, like in a Monty Python movie. On her head was a hat like an upside-down ice-cream cone and bright scarves were tied to the tip, fluttering in the wind. Beside her was the King, who was Mr. Shaffee, the headmaster, and Miss Hahn, the music teacher, was the Queen. Beside them was his dad and for some reason his dad wasn't with Sylvie; he was with his mom, and Toby wasn't there either. But beside them was Elise and her friend Marybeth and then Gabriel realized that they were telling him that Elise wasn't dead after all, that was all a mistake, they'd been mixed up.

It was time for the fight and Gabriel was having trouble putting on his armor. No one would help him. He asked his mom and dad and they kept saying he was a man now, old enough to fight for a girl so he was old enough to dress himself. He wished that Toby were there, somehow he knew that Toby would know how to fix the armor. There was a zipper on it and the zipper was stuck, and the harder he tried to pull it up the worse it was. Peter was approaching from the other end of the field and the audience was cheering. Peter was wearing black armor, all spiked and pointy and his helmet and visor was snapped shut so you couldn't see his face. He was riding a horse, a great big black one, and coming at Gabriel fast. Gabriel looked around. He didn't see his own horse anywhere. He picked up his sword, but then he noticed it was made of plastic. It was the toy sword he'd had when he was little. Gabriel looked over at the audience and his mom looked angry at him.

"I told you to find a better sword," she was saying. Peter came at him fast and swung his sword, but Gabriel ran between the legs of the horse and he was all right. Peter swung again and Gabriel ducked. How long could he keep dodging Peter? He tried to run away, but he tripped on his armor and fell. Peter was approaching him on his horse and there was no escape. He was going to be trampled. He covered his eyes with his hands and suddenly he was flying. He'd figured out how to fly. He was high up, above the field, above Peter, above the audience. He zoomed out above the school, over the trees, the streets, the rooftops, over fields and roads he didn't recognize. He kept flying and flying, not sure how he was doing it, but it was working. He was flying. There was no danger. He'd left all that behind.

But then he remembered Elise. All these years he'd thought she was dead, and it turned out that she was alive after all. He turned around to fly back to the bleachers where she was sitting. He wanted to see her, to hug her. He felt so sad. Where would she be in those bleachers? There were so many bleachers. How would he find her? The crowd was enormous, like the stadium at a baseball game, and there were so many heads, so many faces.

He woke up crying, remembering everything. At first he thought that Elise was somewhere in the house, and then he realized: it was a dream.

It was so early that the sun wasn't completely up. He had to squint in the grayness to see his clock: 6:15. His mom usually woke him at 6:30. He climbed out from under the covers, his legs shaking from the nightmare, and took himself to the bathroom. He peed for a long time and brushed his hair. His mouth had a nasty morning taste. Yick. He brushed his teeth.

He was already dressed in his school clothes, sitting in the kitchen, eating Froot Loops, when his mom came downstairs. She was excited about something — singing, making coffee, skipping back and forth from the refrigerator to the toaster to the stove — and she didn't ask him why he was up early. She didn't remind him to make his bed.

The Froot Loops swam around in the milk, getting soggy. Gabriel had a knot in his stomach.

"I have a tryout after exams," he said, "so don't pick me up early today. I can probably get a ride home from another guy."

"Well, call me if you need me," she said. She didn't even ask what kind of tryout.

VI "James." He said his own name, slowly, the first words he spoke that morning. His voice was not hoarse. His head was surprisingly clear after taking three Valiums last night — what a headache he'd had.

James, never Jim or Jimmy. No one ever got away with shortening it. Pearl hadn't let them when he was little, and now anyone who tried got the most wilting look, enough to stop the offender instantly.

He was staring at the slow, revolving fans on the ceiling. They were only decorations. The room was air-conditioned, even cold. He'd slept under blankets.

Rehearsal was soon. He'd have to get up.

There was so much to do. The orchestra, very second-rate, was still struggling through the repertoire. He'd be lucky if they managed to stay with him rhythmically, more or less, and hit a good percentage of the right notes. It wasn't Guido's fault entirely, though he did seem to be slipping a little, from frustration and laziness. The orchestra simply couldn't be that good. They were poorly trained, unmusical — what? slobs, idiots? How unkind would he be? It was a poor country with a poor orchestra. All the best native musicians escaped, of course, for the United States, to play for good money. These men were bad because they were poor. Poor because they were bad. They had to struggle, they lived in bad housing. Their instruments were awful. They were grossly underpaid, probably. And he, James, was getting a lot from this trip. Government money. It was his second tour here, thanks to Guido's influence. He stayed, courtesy of the government, at the best hotel, the Hilton, ate at the finest restaurants with diplomats and politicians. The government men dressed military-style. They were uneducated in everything but politics and economics and even their concepts of those were peculiar. They knew nothing of music. To them James was important because he was North American. They were cautious with him, but he was not uncomfortable. United States citizenship, he knew, was an invisible shield of armor. He was totally safe.

It was late. He stretched, did his knee bends, shaved and

showered carefully. No time for breakfast. A car was waiting for him at the door of the hotel. Ten A.M. and ninety-five degrees outside. The brief interval between leaving the air-conditioned lobby and entering the air-conditioned limousine caused his pores to open beneath his suit with a flash of sweat. He sat in the back, enjoying the chill, flute in his lap, watching through the windows as they raced through the dusty white modern city, a quick lapse past a neighborhood of shacks and fruit-vendors, and then into the garage of the modern cement building that housed the concert hall. Armed guards raised the electronic gates manually. There were guards everywhere, even at the entrance to the symphony hall. The orchestra members wore identification badges. They were waiting there, quietly assembled, Guido giving them some kind of instruction in rapid Spanish. James went backstage to warm up. A guard stood fifty paces away from him, staring unfocused ahead. Last night at the hotel there'd been a party. Some rich North American businessmen and their wives, Guido, James, politicians in their elaborate uniforms, a fat man not in uniform who was clearly a native — he spoke the dialect, joked with the politicians. On his left index finger glistened a huge blue diamond. He wore dark glasses, though it was evening, and at first James had mistaken him for a blind man. He was not blind. He read the menu. He beckoned the guard from across the room and whispered something in his ear. The guard nodded, then disappeared for the rest of the evening. Later James saw the man whispering to a waiter in the same way and a drink was brought to him immediately. James was not told who the man was — and he did not ask. In this country he asked nothing unless it was related to music. He was American, safe, uninvolved.

When his warm-up was finished he looked up. The guard was still there, unblinking. James went out to the stage where Guido and the orchestra were waiting for him.

The rehearsal went badly, but James struggled with himself and kept his temper even. The performance opened tonight, but, he kept telling himself, *it doesn't matter.* There was no one in this godforsaken country, except Guido and himself, who knew anything at all about music. No one would know the difference if they played wonderfully or like a junior-high-school band. He would simply grit his teeth, metaphorically, and bear it. He was doing this for the money, only, and perhaps for Guido's friendship. No, that wasn't enough to entice him here. He was here for the money. Why the government was paying such a sum to bring him down here was something to wonder and speculate about, but not to question. James was quite content to keep his mouth shut and enjoy it. The government of San Joachím must want to impress its big friends up north by hiring an expensive Western musician for a few weeks. And for this kind of money and publicity James was happy to be an ambassador of culture.

The first performance would be eight o'clock. There was a luncheon at two, in the same building, with some uniformed men, and Guido, and the same man who'd appeared last night, the fat one with the huge ring. James never questioned the typed itinerary he was given for each day; he simply did what he was told. He'd be given the afternoon before the performance to rest, he knew, and that was all that was important to him.

Lunch was difficult, for no interpreter had been supplied and only Guido spoke English. James ate sparsely. The cuisine, as usual, was French and rich. He had tasted almost no native food the entire time he'd been in the country; they were constantly trying to impress him with their French-trained chefs and French wine cellars. The politicians and the ringed man spoke to James in strained, embarrassed English, then, as they relaxed and drank more wine, they lapsed back into Spanish, speaking to each other, ignoring James and Guido. Halfway through the meal James felt something rough and dry pressed into his palm. It was Guido's paper napkin. Instinctively James stuffed it into his pocket. He did not look in Guido's direction. While they were waiting for dessert, James excused himself and headed toward the men's room. A guard followed him to the door and waited outside. In the stall James uncrumpled the napkin. The words were large, unsteady —

Guido must have written the message under the table, without looking at it: FOREIGNERS MUST GET OUT. IT'S GOING TO BE BAD. CAN YOU HELP ME?

James blew his nose on the napkin and flushed it down the toilet.

"Foreigners must get out." How soon? Rumor did say that the regime was a bit unsteady — yet there hadn't been a coup in five or six years. There was revolutionary activity, some terrorism, but that was all easily quashed by the government, which was pro-American, pro-Western.

James watched Guido slowly eating his crème caramel. Guido smiled politely at the conversation of the others, his tiny Mediterranean mustache quivering. Guido was an old lover of James's — they'd lived together briefly in Manhattan after Lawrence left James for Oxford. He was a Bronx-born Italian. He had wanted nothing but to conduct opera, but he hadn't been able to find a good one. He'd taken the job in San Joachím four years ago, hoping to get a better symphony, or better still, an opera company, as soon as possible. But he'd stayed and stayed in San Joachím, complaining about the poor orchestra, the intense weather, the odd government . . . he could have left, but he hadn't. He was secure. He was making money, accumulating wealth that he could use later. He had no reason to leave just yet, he'd told James last year. He was living well for now, and when the time came to move on, he would.

Guido rested his spoon beside his half-eaten dessert. He was making a joke in Spanish. The politicians were laughing. James watched, isolated, not understanding. The laughter continued and Guido looked up, met his eye, and for a second his expression changed: he flashed James a look of panic.

Time must be running out, thought James, something was going to happen.

Back in the hotel room James rested on his bed. There was no need for him to go over the score. It wasn't worth it, not with this orchestra. He was thinking about Guido. Guido must know about an approaching coup, something secret, something you couldn't talk about in the open — and they'd been given no time together alone. Would it be safe for James himself to finish out the week at San Joachím? He had an urge to talk to Lawrence, as he usually did before a concert in the States. He'd tried to call a few days ago, but it was impossible to get through. Bell of San Joachím was clearly a haphazard operation. Perhaps he should try again . . . no it wasn't worth the effort. He'd be home in a week. Everything would be fine then. A week. Surely the government would be stable for a week. He'd be safe after that.

The hall was not even one-quarter filled, as far as James could tell. Dark heads, dark bodies. He marched out on stage, glancing at the orchestra members in their collection of ill-fitting tuxedos. He would do his best to keep them with him, that would be all. No attempts to bring them to artistry tonight. Guido was a model of Mediterranean elegance. He bowed coolly in the sparse applause, but each time their eyes met during the performance, James imagined that he could detect Guido's hysteria, masked, readable only in his eyes.

Four more days of tension. Tense lunches, tense cocktails, tense dinner parties. Guido passed no more notes, they had no opportunities to speak in private. James was annoyed. Didn't Guido have the influence, or at least the daring, to arrange even one conversation between the two of them. He kept flashing James those meaningful, imploring looks, but there was no other communication. What did he expect James to do for him? James was a musician, not a diplomat. How was he supposed to help Guido? He didn't know anything about politics, especially in South American banana republics. The best he could do is report what Guido had written on the napkin to a State Department official when he got home — but what use would that be? The State Department must already be on top of things. They probably knew more about the situation than Guido.

James packed a little more quickly, a little less carefully than usual. He was distracted. He wanted to leave. One more lunch with Guido and some politicians. They were becoming familiar to him now, as individuals, the men in the uniforms. He even knew some of them by name. He wanted to forget them. He wanted them to all jumble in his mind again, like when he'd first arrived — he wanted this all to be behind him, to be unimportant again. One last lunch and he'd be driven to the airport and in hours he'd be back in Philadelphia, arranging tomorrow's tea with Lawrence, or dinner with Marina, falling into his own bed, sleeping off his jet lag. One more lunch to sit through. He hoped that Guido wouldn't hand him any napkins today.

They were all there, the usual politicians who'd been at the other lunches, plus an important visitor from the President's cabinet, Señor Sánchez, who spoke no English and ignored James after their introduction. The fat man with the dark glasses and the diamond was there, too, at the table with Señor Sánchez. It was all the same as the other days, the same foods, the same wines, the same waiters. The same constant conversation in Spanish, of which James could understand nothing. He watched the way he would watch a foreign movie without subtitles. His attention wandered. He daydreamed about his upcoming recital tour — in two weeks he'd be doing engagements on the West Coast: San Francisco, San Diego, Los Angeles, Seattle . . . The same program in each hall, it would be fun, like a vacation . . . Guido was looking at him again. No napkins in the lap, though.

"What do you *want?*" said James. Guido's eyes widened.

"Pass the salt," he said, alarmed. James passed him the butter dish.

"Help me, amigo," said Guido hoarsely. The fat man was watching them, salting his meat, staring in their direction from behind his dark glasses. James shuddered. Tomorrow he would be home.

VII   Gabriel went straight to the soccer field as soon as the exam was over. Peter wasn't there yet. He rolled up his sleeves and took a drink from the fountain. He could hear laughter in the distance. Valerie Bender and her friends were coming over the hill, taking the shortcut from their school. They waved to Gabriel and climbed up on the bleachers. Gabriel turned his back to them. He felt a chill descend through his spine, though it was hot in the sunshine. Here was Peter.

"What took ya so long?" said Gabriel. "God. I thought you chickened out." Peter had dark stains under his arms. The air was heavy with the smell of spring grass.

Gabriel had meant to take the first swing, but Peter was faster. He got Gabriel in the stomach and knocked him backwards. Gabriel kept his balance and swung at Peter. Somehow he missed and Peter grabbed both his wrists. Gabriel tried to wriggle free, but Peter twisted him around and pinned one arm behind his back. The other hand he grasped tightly. What was he doing? Peter worked intently, unclenching Gabriel's fist. He freed the index finger. Gabriel was too confused to resist. He heard himself scream in pain and terror as the bone snapped.

"You jerk! You — you — *bastard!*" he yelled. Peter was grinning.

"Break your finger, turkey? Now you can suck on your thumb!"

Instinct and rage gave Gabriel the strength to straighten up.

"You jerk!" he repeated. He kicked Peter hard in the balls.

Gabriel gathered his books with his good hand and walked across the field. He could hear Valerie Bender and her friends giggling as Peter howled in pain. When Gabriel got to the goalpost, he began to run toward home, the long way, through the woods. He didn't faint from the pain. He didn't even feel dizzy. The echo of the girls' laughter rang in his ears for a long time.

They didn't understand what Peter had done to him. But Peter knew the importance of Gabriel's hands. How could he have done that? Gabriel was filled with dread. How could another musician have hurt him this way?

That night, when they were back from the emergency room, the phone rang: it was Valerie Bender. He hung up.

Chapter 11

I When he was sure that James was safe, deep into a long, drug-induced sleep, Lawrence called a cab and rode out to the home. Angelthorn, such an odd name. It reminded him of his mother. Angelthorn Manor home. It was inside the city but away up in Chestnut Hill, far enough to be a double-digit taxi ride. It saddened him a little to think he visited her infrequently enough that the expense of the cab was not even a problem.

Near the entrance to the expressway was a child selling flowers on a traffic island. It was a little boy of ten or eleven, racially ambiguous as he himself had been. Lawrence made the driver pull up to the boy's stand and he bought from him a bunch of three lilies, slightly wilted, three dollars. Lawrence handed the boy a five. The boy hesitated, focusing on Lawrence's hand, then produced two crinkled singles. Lawrence took them, then handed one back.

"Keep it for jelly beans," he said gruffly, embarrassed by his gesture. The cabby drove off before Lawrence could see the expression on the boy's face.

"I wouldn't of bought them flowras if I was you," said the cabby.

"Why not?"

"Everyone knows they gets them used from hospitals an' funeral homes an' graves, that's why. That's why they always look a little *dead*, if you know what I mean."

"Rather morbid," said Lawrence dryly. "Well, I've heard that story before, and it doesn't bother me. It would be a shame to waste the flowers — nothing wrong with a little recycling."

"Just tellin' ya what I know."

"Thank you," said Lawrence. He rested the flowers on his lap. The petals were brown at the edges, like the vanilla cookies his mother used to give him after school. As a child he had always preferred sweets to the food he was supposed to eat. He could remember his father, tall Rajesh, telling him he would never grow if he filled up on vanilla cookies and ate no dinner. His mother had always avoided sweet food — it made her sick, she said. But there was one kind of candy she did love without reservation: white chocolate. White chocolate was rare except at Easter, when all the candy shops were full of huge chocolate rabbits, white and dark. Every Easter she'd give him his own basket of jelly beans, marshmallow chicks, robin's-egg malted balls, chocolate footballs, and a huge coconut egg, and he and his daddy would go to Woolworth's and pick her out the biggest solid white-chocolate rabbit they could buy. The rabbit would last for weeks. It would get eaten downward, ears first, and everyone would help, especially Lawrence, and even Sujita, who usually ignored Western food. But the rabbit was bought for and belonged to Ann. It was hers. Good God, he'd forgotten all this for so long.

"Do you know of a candy store that would be open on Sunday?"

"What, in Chestnut Hill?" said the cabby.

"Yes."

"Beats me."

They drove around through the main street, past scores of closed shops until they came to a drugstore with the inside lights still turned on. Lawrence got out and tried the door. Locked.

"We're closed," said a man, through the glass. He waved Lawrence away. Lawrence tapped again. The man opened the door.

"We're closed," said the man again.

"Please," said Lawrence. "This is important."

"Emergency?"

"Well, of sorts. Yes."

The man opened the latch and Lawrence walked in. There it was, displayed prominently: the Easter candy.

"Do you have any white chocolate?" asked Lawrence.

"What are you, some kind of a nut?"

"It's for my mother. She's in a home. Every Easter I bring her a white-chocolate rabbit, but I left this year's on the airplane. Please. She's not quite right in the head, you know, and it's important to her. It would be such a disappointment . . ."

"Oh, Christ. All right, since you're in here anyway. We have rabbits and chickens. Which do you prefer?"

"The rabbit would be nice."

"It's two ninety-five. Oh, Christ, I'll have to open the register again. Pain in the ass. I'm late already. Look, just take it."

Lawrence pulled out a five-dollar bill. The man, bending over some account books, did not look up.

"I said take it. It's more trouble than it's worth. Take the rabbit and get lost."

"Oh, really, I couldn't."

"Will you get the hell out of my store?"

"Well, thank you very much, sir."

"Get lost."

"Thank you. Happy Easter."

"Jesus Christ," Lawrence heard him say as he closed the door behind him.

Lawrence peeled the price tag off the rabbit as they pulled up the long drive to the home.

Angelthorn. Angel of Mercy. Angel. Guardian Angel.

Angel of God be at my side. To light. To guard. To rule. To guide. That was a poem he'd learned in the Catholic school his mother had thought was trying to convert him. A prayer. To a saint. Saint Ann, mother of the Blessed Mother, wife of Zachary. Was that right? The car jerked over a curb and they were pulling into the Angelthorn Manor driveway. He told the cabby to wait. He wouldn't be long. His mother had little memory left, and the lengths of his visits did not matter.

II First the crocuses. She had photographed them while there was still a light layer of snow on the flower beds: that was when they had bloomed. Then the hyacinths — they were still with us — and now the tulips.

Flower-gifts, black-and-white prints in frames she had made herself, perched carefully in the baskets she had saved and used every year. Toby's had always been the largest one, which was lucky, because she'd been able to fit an extra print in it for Elizabeth; and Joan's was the green one; and Ben's was the small, bright one with the psychedelic patterns. He'd picked it out himself when he was nine. Allison's was there, too. Pink straw. She fixed that one up for Gabriel. Besides the prints, she'd put in jelly beans and marshmallow chicks and chocolate footballs. She'd meant to dye eggs, but somehow there'd been no time. Of course, they were all grown up, except little Gabriel, and his mother probably had him dye his own eggs, so no one but Mary herself would miss them.

At the last minute she remembered that Ben had said he might bring Eric back with him for the dinner, so she had to improvise. She took a melba toast box and covered it with green wrapping paper and made a little handle from the paper, and that was the basket. She pulled some plastic grass out of each of the other baskets so she had enough to fill that one, and she redistributed the candy. She selected one of Joan and Douglas's prints, the one with the slightly lopsided frame, and put that in Eric's basket. There. Something for everybody.

Joan and Douglas arrived first. Douglas had baked three kinds of bread, and he'd bought a tape of his String Quartet No. 2 being played by some friends. Joan put the tape on the stereo and poured some drinks. Douglas went into the kitchen and started making a salad without being asked. He made the best salads in the family and that was his regular job any time they had dinner together. At home, it seemed, he did all the cooking for Joan, who got back quite late each night from the Press. Mary admired her daughter's life so immensely. Why couldn't she, Mary March, have lived like that? Joan had given in on no account, had not even taken her husband's name. Douglas cared for her. He worshiped her. But he did not burden her with a house full of noisy kids, endless laundry baskets to empty, meals to cook, rooms to straighten or paint or wash or coax angry children from . . . How different. But was Joan any happier with gentle Douglas than Mary had been with Dick? She'd never know. To ask Joan would be meaningless. How do you compare? How could you measure?

They were drinking scotch and soda in the living room when Toby drove up. Mary winced a little as she watched his Toyota wheels squash two of her tulips. She shouldn't have planted them so close to the driveway. Elizabeth was stunning in blue — she still walked like a ballet dancer — and the little boy was wearing a blue suit several shades darker. Toby was wearing blue jeans, new ones, though: she could see the crease all the way in the distance. He walked stiffly in the unbending fabric.

Douglas had the door open before they could ring the bell. Elizabeth and Mary exchanged hugs. Douglas shook hands with the boy, who showed him his finger splint proudly. Elizabeth and Joan kissed each other's cheek and Douglas hung up the jackets.

Soon they were all sitting around the coffee table exclaiming over their baskets. Mary's eyes kept wandering toward the picture window, searching for Ben's figure stalking up the path. When he arrived the group would be complete.

Joan poured Elizabeth a scotch and Douglas went to the refrigerator and found a beer for Toby. He also brought out a ginger ale for Gabriel. He'd poured it into Ben's old Yellow Submarine glass.

"Oh, wow!" said Gabriel. "Beatles!"

"How's the finger doing?" asked Joan, cross-legged on the couch. Gabriel made a face, but said, "It doesn't hurt too much now."

"When does the splint come off?" asked Mary.

"Two weeks," said Elizabeth. "Then he can practice again."

"It's a pain in the drain," said Gabriel.

"But he's lucky," said Elizabeth. "The orthopedic guy said it should heal as good as new."

"So the only setback is lost practice time?" said Joan.

"Yeah, and I can make that up easy," said Gabriel. "I've been practicing solfèg, and Mr. Chattarjee's been teaching me theory. I don't have to do any recitals for a while anyway."

"Three months. He has a student recital in three months," said Elizabeth.

"Oh, we should all try to make it, then," said Mary absently. Joan sank back into the sofa.

"Max tells me Gabriel has an agent," she said looking at Elizabeth. Elizabeth's eyes sparkled: Joan was a compatriot, despising Max. She wanted to say, "So, now that Gabriel's done something important Max has finally noticed him." But no, not in front of Gabriel.

"Yes! Yes, Myra Davidov is supposed to be fantastic. At least everything I've herd about her has been positive. I think she could do great things for him."

Gabriel was blowing bubbles into his ginger ale with his straw. When he looked up, all of the adults were smiling at him. At least they weren't going to ask him to perform, not with a broken index finger.

"Too bad you can't play something for us," Mrs. March was saying.

"I'm working on a piece for flute and piano and soprano," said Douglas. "Maybe when your hand is better you'd like to read through the flute part."

Gabriel nodded. He looked at his mother, who was smiling dreamily out the window. The afternoon sun looked like fire in her hair and her eyes were the color of her dress. Bluer than anything. Blue enough that you would stop and stare even if you didn't know her. She was squinting from the sun, but her eyes looked like jewels. Like diamonds. Soon the grown-up conversation got to politics and President Carter. Gabriel's mother, who didn't read the newspapers much, kept staring out the window with a little smile. Toby's arm was draped over her shoulder.

If Toby married his mom, then Mrs. March would be his grand-mom, which would be fine, since he didn't have a real one, and Joan and Douglas would be like his aunt and uncle. Toby had another sister, named Allison, but she lived far away. Maybe she would come for the wedding. Would his dad come? Probably not. Gabriel had gone to his dad's wedding. He'd been the ring boy, but his mom had stayed home and painted the bathroom. She'd driven up to the reception to pick him up and walked into the hotel wearing her old painting clothes. This had made Sylvie very mad, but Gabriel had thought it was hilarious. He knew she'd done it on purpose. Normally she never left the house looking like that: baggy jeans with paint all over them, and an old sweat shirt of Dad's and broken floppy tennis shoes. She smelled terrible. Gabriel got into the car beside her and they giggled all the way home. During the ceremony he'd felt confused and sick and ready to cry, but in the car he was laughing so hard his stomach hurt. It would be nice if they got married, Toby and Mom.

Toby already acted like a dad, anyway. The night of the fight, when it hurt too much to hold it in anymore, he'd gone to Toby first, not his mom. But Toby had been as furious as his mom anyway, and he'd lectured him all the way to the hospital, though he knew Gabriel was in pain. And then together they'd nearly embarrassed Gabriel to death by going to see Mr. Shaffee to complain about Peter.

Peter didn't get suspended, though, and since he was such a screwball, Gabriel felt sorry for him, though he couldn't forgive him for breaking his finger.

Gabriel had told the whole story to Toby later and Toby had said, "I hope you learned a lesson from all this."

Gabriel had nodded.

"And what was the lesson?"

Gabriel thought for a moment. "It's better to take a chance on being called a faggot than to have your finger broken?"

"Well, that, too, but what else?"

"Um, if you do get into a fight always keep your fists closed?"

"What else?"

"I give up, what?"

"Watch out for women. They're real troublemakers."

"I'll say."

"But they can be quite irresistible."

"Not these girls. Not Valerie Bender."

"Wait till you're fourteen."

There were jelly beans in the basket Mrs. March had given him for a present. He had already eaten the ones on top and now he was searching through the plastic grass for hidden ones. His mom wasn't paying attention to him — otherwise she'd be saying not to eat the candy till after dinner. The sunlight had moved a little so that her hair was not so electric bright. Her eyes were still clear blue. Now the sunlight was strong on Toby's beer glass, making it a sparkling amber. Toby was looking through the sections of the Sunday *Times*, which he'd found in the magazine rack beside his chair.

"Hey," he said suddenly. "Look at this!" Everyone leaned over to see the headline he was pointing to:

BOMB RIPS SAN JOACHIM AIRPORT

and the smaller headline read, AMERICAN FLAUTIST UNHARMED.

"My God," said Elizabeth. "That's James Rosen."

"He's dead?" said Joan, who couldn't see the paper clearly from her seat.

"No, he's fine. He escaped the whole thing. He was in a men's room when his whole flight-gate blew up," said Toby. "Hmmm. Seems to say here that they think the blast might have been aimed for him."

"But why?" said Elizabeth.

"What was he doing down there?" asked Douglas.

"He was on tour," said Elizabeth.

"In *San Joachim?* That place has been a tinderbox for months," said Toby.

"I had no idea," said Elizabeth.

"Oh, yes, I'd read about it," said Joan.

"James Rosen," said Mary. "Now is he the famous flutist who lives on Rittenhouse Square?" Nobody answered her. Gabriel slid out of his seat and stood behind Toby to read over his shoulder.

World-renowned flautist James Rosen escaped without injury yesterday as a pipe bomb exploded in the Pan American Airlines concourse at the San Joachím National Airport. Fourteen persons were killed in the blast and 36 others were hospitalized. The San Joachím Liberation Front, an avowed terrorist organization, has claimed responsibility for the bombing.

Among the dead were Guido Campani, the American-born conductor of the San Joachím Symphony Orchestra, and Salvador Alteros, Assistant Vice-Minister for Cultural Affairs in San Joachím.

The airport incident is the fourth instance of terrorist activity reported in San Joachím this month.

Mr. Rosen, the 41-year-old flute virtuoso, was leaving the South American republic after a two-week engagement as soloist with the San Joachím Symphony. After being examined by medics, he was flown unharmed to New York by private jet . . .

"Who's Guido Campani?" asked Gabriel.

"I don't know," said Elizabeth.

"Never heard of him," said Toby.

Joan shook her head, "No." Gabriel sat back down. Toby put his hand on the boy's shoulder.

"Gets you shook up, doesn't it?"

"I'm not shook up," said Gabriel.

"It's disturbing to read about someone you know in the newspaper," added Douglas.

"Don't think about it, Gabriel," said Elizabeth.

Mary March was just about to say, "He can't help but think about it," when in the corner of her eye she noticed Ben and Eric Fish starting up the front-yard path.

"Hey, guys," she said, waving, and then remembered that the sun was behind them, they could see only their reflections in the picture window. Douglas opened the door.

Ben March had cut his curls shorter than chin length, but left them long enough to cover his ears. His high-boned cheeks were ruddy with the mid-April breeze and his eyes glistened. His eyes were green-brown, like his mother's, the color of pond water. He greeted the entire crowd at once with a detached smile and his stance was a blend of ease and excitement. His jeans were tight, and around his neck was a white silk aviator scarf. Douglas took his scarf and leather jacket, and Eric's blazer, and hung them in the closet. In one swift movement Ben was in the middle of everything, seated between his mother and Elizabeth on the sofa, talking and sipping the scotch that was handed to him, exclaiming over the framed prints in his Easter basket, laughing infectiously. Eric, embarrassed, plump, clumsy as usual, tripped on Toby's shoes and knocked his shin into the point of a coffee table. There were no more chairs so he sat himself on the floor, eye-level with Ben's knees. Someone passed him his basket and he blushed, thanked Mrs. March for the photograph, and began to chew on the jelly beans.

There were seven places set around the dining-room table and Mrs. March added an eighth for Eric. This was the first time since Christmas dinner that she'd had all the extensions in the table. When the kids were growing up they'd used it every Sunday, not just on holidays. It was always Dick's parents or her parents (now both dead) or friends of the kids or, rarely, friends she and Dick had known in college. She didn't have any new friends at the time, so far away from Vermont, where she'd grown up and gone to college and met Dick, and the mothers of her children's friends had been so much older than she: strange, dull Northeast-Philadelphian housewives. Eric and Sylvia Fish's mother was a case in point: nothing concerned her but her wardrobe and the measurement of her waistline. Mary simply could not talk to the woman. Her daughter, Sylvia, had grown up to be just like her and her insecure, dull sons, you could see where they came from. The March children might have their problems, but they were all bright, talented, fascinating people. For a second a vision of Allison's face flashed through her mind. No. She must not think of that now. In her immediate field of vision were the other three: Toby, a successful writer, about to marry an intelligent, beautiful woman with a talented little boy. Joan, an editor with a publishing career and an uxorious husband. And Ben, her favorite son; the most talented, the most alluring, the most loving and beloved child a mother could have. Mary blew the dust out of the wineglasses, one by one, and set them at the corner of each place. Don't think about Allison. Not now.

Toby walked into the kitchen loudly complaining that he'd accidentally bought the kind of wine that doesn't have a twist-off cap. Where was a corkscrew? Mary handed him her best, a fancy Japanese one called Ah-so. Ben had mailed it to her from Chicago. It was guaranteed, he'd written, to keep all cork fragments out of the wine.

"Goddamn it!" yelled Toby. The cork had lodged itself deep in the bottle neck. Douglas helped him push it inside with a knife.

"Tastes better this way," said Toby.

"Wow," said Gabriel, fingering the price sticker on the bottle. "You paid six dollars and forty cents for a bottle of wine?"

"I'm a big spender," said Toby, hugging Mary, who was trying to transfer the ham from the cutting board to the serving tray, "when it comes to my mom." A pineapple ring slid to the floor.

"Look what you made me do," said Mary.

"Can I pour?" said Gabriel, reaching for the bottle.

"No, this one's tricky," Toby said. "Only an expert can pour when the cork's still in the bottle."

Elizabeth burned her hand getting the bread out of the oven.

"Mom, you should use a pot holder," said Gabriel, but Elizabeth's look told him to be quiet. Douglas broke off the tip of Mary's aloe plant, which made Elizabeth's fingers sticky but didn't help the pain. Mary took the potato casserole out of the oven herself. Gabriel was given the job of putting fruit cup around at everyone's place, and it was time to sit down.

Dinner on Thanksgiving or Christmas or Easter at Mrs. March's house was the closest Gabriel ever came to having a big family meal. Being here was different. It felt — warm to have all these people around him. Everyone liked each other and they were always joking around. Besides, everyone liked him. He was the only kid, the youngest, so they paid him a lot of attention. It wasn't like at his dad's, where all you could talk about was Cory and Carrie and how one of them had said a whole sentence, or the other was starting on Suzuki violin. People cared about him here, and they didn't talk down to him or treat him like a baby, the way Sylvie did.

When they passed him the ham he took a big piece and a pineapple and three cherries. His mom looked at him sternly and said, "Someone else here might like cherries, too."

"No, it's okay. There'll be enough," said Mrs. March, just as he was about to put one cherry back. He also took lots of potatoes, since he liked those, but avoided the broccoli and the string beans and the salad. Since it was a holiday his mother didn't say anything about that. When they passed the bread around he took the heel from each of the three loaves. The heel was his favorite part of the bread, since he loved crust. He expected his mom to tell him not to be piggish about the heels, but she didn't say anything. He looked at her plate: one tiny piece of ham, no pineapples or cherries, no potatoes. She never ate anything fun except ice cream, and whenever she ate ice cream she moaned and groaned about the calories when she was through.

Everyone was talking again about James Rosen and the conductor in South America who'd gotten blown up. They were explaining about it to Ben and Eric, who hadn't heard the news. Ben told them how he and Eric had gone to see James Rosen in Chicago, and Eric, who'd been looking at Gabriel the whole time as if he thought he should know him but couldn't remember how, said. "I think I know you. Did you play the flute at a recital at Curtis last month?"

Yes, yes, everyone said, and that was the recital that James Rosen had come to.

"You were great," said Eric, looking down at his plate.

"Thanks," said Gabriel, wondering why Eric looked so embarrassed.

"Cleveland was at that concert," said Ben slowly.

"Cleveland?" said Mary March.

"A friend of mine. I wasn't there, but my friend was in town. I didn't realize that Gabriel here was one and the same as the magnificent flute prodigy he described."

Gabriel flushed. Ben had a way of looking at people and making them feel special, singled out. He was older, important enough to live in a different city, but he was still a boy. Not one of the adults yet. Gabriel, who had never had an older brother, was nervous around him, and when Ben praised him or smiled at him his heart leapt.

"I've heard a lot about your virtuosity," said Ben.

Toby groaned under his breath. His brother's speech affectations and annoying mannerisms seemed to have only worsened in Chicago.

"What a little phony," he muttered to Elizabeth. He'd been complaining to her about Ben all week in preparation. She kicked him gently under the table, and commented on Douglas's homemade bread to change the subject.

Everyone agreed the bread was delicious, and Elizabeth asked Douglas to explain how he'd made each kind. Ben interrupted regularly to tell how he made bread, or how it was done in the restaurant he worked in, or what he'd read about that particular bread in Craig Claiborne or James Beard.

When they discussed the wine, Ben told everyone all about that vintage and that vineyard and that particular appellation, and then proceeded to talk for five minutes about wines no one else at the table had heard of.

"How did you learn all this, Ben?" asked his mother.

"At the restaurant," said Ben modestly.

"You know so much," said Toby, "for a waiter."

"*Toby*," said Mary. Ben looked down at his plate for a moment, then looked back up.

"You're just not as impressive as you think you are," said Toby.

"Not now, Toby," said Mary. "Not during dinner. Save it for later if you *must*." Elizabeth elbowed Toby's ribs, gently, to express agreement. Toby shrugged.

"All right," he said, and reached for the potatoes.

Ben gritted his teeth.

"I have an announcement to make," he said. Everyone looked at him. He put down his fork and looked around the table. Mary put her fork down, too.

"Yes?" she said.

"I want to announce that I will be moving back East" — he looked quickly to his mother, "not here — to New York. I am going to be living with my lover."

"Oh, Ben," began Mary, happy and confused.

"I'm going to be applying to art schools," he added.

"I'm so glad, Ben," said Mary. "Who is the girl, though? You haven't mentioned her before."

"It's not a girl." Ben looked directly at his mother. "My lover is a man." Mary March's hand trembled as it held her wineglass, but she did not spill a drop. Eric's jaw dropped. Toby threw his fork down and it clattered on the plate.

"Damn it, Ben!" said Toby. "How could you do this to your mother on Easter?"

"Toby," said Mary. "Calm down. He hasn't done anything to me. Let's just eat our dinner peacefully. I'm glad to hear that Ben will be coming back East."

Ben held his chin high, poured himself another glass of wine.

"What — what does he do?" began Mary slowly. "This man?"

"He's a musician," said Ben, glancing around the table. "A violinist. He just accepted the second violin position with the Allegro Quartet. That's why we're moving to New York."

"The Allegro Quartet," said Mary. "I've read of them in *Newsweek*."

"What's his name?" said Douglas gently.

"Cleveland Arms. Cleveland Arms — right now he plays in the Chicago Symphony."

"*Cleveland*," whispered Eric. "God." His face was white and his ears flushed. Why hadn't Ben told him? Why had he waited until now, until they were in front of all these people? Cleveland. He should have guessed. Of course, it was all right there, right in front

/ 271

of him. He should have known. What a fool he'd been. What a damned idiot. He was beginning to feel too hot, sweating under the arms and at the neck. His plate of ham and vegetables suddenly looked nauseating. What was he doing here, anyway? This was Ben's family, not his. This was Ben's holiday, his family, his life, and he, Eric Fish, was an outsider. God Damn it. And he hadn't even known it. What a fool. He pushed his plate away. Pork. He wasn't even supposed to eat pork. His stomach was churning. He looked around the table. Gabriel, the little boy, was staring at his mother, Elizabeth, who was staring at Toby, Ben's brother, who was staring at Mrs. March, who was staring at Ben. Ben was looking at his wineglass. Eric felt alone. He pushed the slimy plateful of ham farther from him and it upset his wineglass onto the tablecloth. Suddenly everyone was looking at him, and he felt himself jumping up, dabbing his napkin on the stain, heard himself apologizing to Ben's mother, saw himself knocking clumsily against the table, nearly upsetting all the other wineglasses, heard himself saying that, really, he didn't feel so well, something had come over him. Next he was reaching for his coat, refusing offers of rides home, rushing outside into the cool afternoon breeze, walking briskly, almost running, until he was sure he was out of sight of the March house picture window. He slowed down to catch his breath. He could feel tears on his cheeks.

Eric's abrupt departure from the dinner table and the house disrupted the mood. Everyone was talking loudly and nervously, trying to clean up the spill, to set things back to normal. Everyone except Ben, who stared pensively out the window at Eric's vanishing figure, and Gabriel, who wanted to ask his mother a hundred questions, but knew this was not the right time. He would have to wait until they got home. Toby began to cut himself another slice of ham, and Elizabeth, too jittery to eat, offered him hers. Gabriel reached for another pineapple ring and his mother told him to finish his meat first. He almost said, "You didn't eat yours," but stopped himself in time.

Mary March tried to pass around the potatoes for seconds, but nobody wanted any.

"I wonder if he will be all right," she said, meaning Eric. No one answered. "He looked so upset," she added.

Soon everyone would stop eating and she could clear the table and bring out the dessert and coffee, and then that would be finished and they could talk politely for a bit while they washed the dishes . . . and eventually this day would be over and they would all go home. She could hardly wait, she felt so drained. She wished they would all leave just the way Eric had. No fuss, they'd just up and be gone. She'd have the house to herself again, except for Ben, who was still in town for a few more days. She wanted to be alone, without the pain company brings, even the company of her own children — even Ben brought her pain now. Even Ben. She wanted some Tylenol. Six years ago she would have been reaching for a Valium, but now she knew better. She excused herself and went into the kitchen, to the cabinet where she kept the familiar red-and-white, over-the-counter, nonprescription, safe, child-proof bottle, and drew herself a glass of tap water. As she swallowed the tablets she felt a hand on her shoulder. Ben? Ben had followed her silently into the kitchen, recognizing her pain.

"Mom . . ." He'd come to comfort her. It wasn't Ben. It was Toby. She pressed her face into his warm sweatered shoulder and released a long, shuddering sigh.

III Marina tiptoed down the stairs at eight A.M. but she was the last one up. Serge was at the kitchen table holding a coffee mug in his right hand and sliding the Sunday paper out of its bread wrapper with his left. Mama was putting sweet rolls into the oven to heat.

Marina sat at the table and began to poke through the newspaper. She and Serge spotted the comics section at once and dove for it simultaneously, tearing it halfway down the middle.

"Jesus Christ, Rina!"

"What are you, ten years old?"

"*Children*," said Mama in English.

Marina dropped her corner of the paper. "Go ahead," she said.

"No, you go ahead, since it means so much to you."

"Serge, I said you go first. Look. I know. We can read it together."

"I hate you reading over my shoulder."

"Serge, I'm trying. I'm really trying." Serge looked at her through shaggy black bangs.

"Okay. Truce." He creased the paper down the center fold with his thumbnail and tore it carefully. He handed her half.

Yesterday they had worked together at the kitchen table, side by side, making Ukrainian Easter eggs. Mama had stood at the counter pounding bread dough. It was the first time they'd painted eggs since they were little kids. It had been Marina's idea. She's bought the eggs and gathered the materials. Serge had surprised her by cooperating. They were both trying for the first time in years, and for the first time since Papa had died, a month ago, Mama was singing again, and smiling, and hustling around doing household chores.

Last night, after Mama was asleep, Marina had gone into Serge's room, and for the first time ever he'd offered to share a joint with her and she'd accepted. They'd talked for about two hours, mostly about Papa, and about Mama's depression and how to work her out of it, and Marina, though still cautious, relaxed with Serge for the first time in years. Several times she was even on the verge of telling him about her problem with the Fish person, but each time she lost her nerve. She would tell him tomorrow, she decided, on Easter.

For breakfast she ate three boiled eggs, four buns, and two cups of coffee and a glass of orange juice, and when Mama fried some bacon for Serge she had some of that, too. It was more than she'd eaten all week.

"You little pig," said Serge, watching her. It was the first time in a year he'd teased her out of fun, not malice.

"Oink, oink," she said, shuffling through the newspaper sections. She was finished with the comics. Serge was reading the magazine.

Where was the Arts & Leisure? She wouldn't mind reading the concert reviews . . .

"Oh my God," said Marina. Serge looked up startled. It was the front page. James's picture was on the front page.

She'd known he was going to San Joachím. He went on tour to lots of places. But she'd had no idea the place was about to erupt in a civil war. Guido Campani, his friend, the man who'd arranged to bring him there, was dead. Blown into a million pieces. And James was fine. James was alive, but the newspaper said the bomb was planted for *him*.

"I can't believe this."

"*What?*" said Serge impatiently.

She explained, saying that James was one of her teachers. She hadn't told her brother that her lover was a forty-one-year-old bisexual.

"This is pretty heavy stuff, huh?" he said, reaching his hand across the table, grasping hers. His knuckles were bony, red, and dotted with freckles. Marina started to cry, and her brother, explaining to her mother in Ukrainian all the while what was bothering her, gathered her up in his arms.

"I feel sick," she gasped, after a minute. Serge pulled her over to the kitchen sink and held her hair back while she vomited her breakfast into the drain. The smell of fresh coffee grounds, in the strainer beside her face, rose into her nostrils.

He helped her into the living room and sat her on the couch. Mama brought her a glass of ginger ale to wash away the bad taste.

"It's been a hard month," said Serge. She started to cry again. She wanted to tell him about Eric Fish. She wanted to tell him how frightened she was. She wanted to tell him about Cleveland and about James and about how confused she was. But she didn't. She couldn't tell him those things.

IV When Eric got home there were no cars in the driveway. His father was probably out playing golf, and his mother was probably playing tennis or shopping or at a Tupperware party. Good. He didn't feel like dealing with them anyway. He reached into his pocket. Shit. No keys. What the hell had he done with his keys? They were probably down by the pond where he and Ben had gotten high that morning. The last he could remember he was using them as a roach clip.

How could he get in? Climbing through the windows was out ever since his mother had installed the new burglar alarm. He went around back and tried the kitchen door. That was locked, too. Shit.

The sky was growing dark and it was starting to drizzle. That meant his father would be home soon. He couldn't play golf for long in the rain. Eric started toward the pool house. At least it would be dry in there. He could wait inside until someone came home and let him in the house.

It was dark and he tripped over the diving board on the way in. He cracked open the door enough to let in some light without letting in the rain, which was starting to pour down, and sat down on a still-inflated raft. His shelter was dry and windproof, but rather dark. He shuddered, imagining how many spiders were sharing the pool house with him. How long was he going to have to stay in here? He reached into his pocket for his papers and bag of grass and started to roll a joint. He was good enough to roll even in pitch dark. He smoked slowly and by the time the first joint was gone rain was beating down hard on the roof. He rolled another, and still it grew darker outside and there was no sign of a car in the driveway. By the time he finished the third joint he was getting sleepy. He flicked his lighter onto the longest flame and held it out at arm's length. He examined the little house: nothing but porch chairs, flotation devices, the diving board, pots of chemicals, and some forgotten bathing suits. No spiders, as far as he could see. He leaned back against one of the rafts and closed his eyes.

All he could see was Ben's face. O Paraclete, what could this mean? Ben, Cleveland, this was so confusing. What had been going on? He tried to remember all past conversations with Ben about Cleveland, about himself. What could they have meant?

What had been happening all this time that he hadn't noticed? He was such a fool. He'd thought that was so wise, so cool, but no, no. Not him. No.

Ha. Had he been on the wrong track. Worrying that Ben would be stealing Marina from him, when Ben wasn't even . . . wasn't even on the same track. Jesus Christ.

Cleveland. The violinist. Marina had been with them, Cleveland and James Rosen at that recital, and now James Rosen was in an explosion.

What did this have to do with Ben? He remembered when he'd first seen Cleveland, during that visit to Chicago last fall. Ben had worn such tight leather pants to the flute concert. James Rosen. The concert where he'd first noticed Marina. Ben had tight leather pants and a ring like a snake swallowing its own tail. But he wasn't wearing that ring anymore, Eric had noticed that. At least he had noticed something. God. John the Baptist. How it had haunted him when Ben's leg had pressed against his leg that day on the hammock. As though he'd guessed that it meant something. Ben was a homosexual and he loved Cleveland. He did not love Eric. He did not love the Fish. The Baptist. The desirer. Who? Whom did he desire? He desired Cleveland. Not Fish. Could it be that Fish desired the Baptist? Undoubtedly in the most fraternal of ways, but . . . oh, shit, what was this all leading up to?

He was hungry. Fish was hungry. What about some Fish food. None in the pool house, though. He creaked open the door farther. There was not a single light on in his house, and outside it was pitch dark. Where had his parents gone? He was cold and hungry. He rolled another one. Reefer tended to kill his appetite.

Fish, Fish, you're so alone. What was Marina doing now? Probably beside her man, the old faggot, in some hospital. Was he hurt in the explosion? Eric couldn't remember what they'd said. He pictured James Rosen swathed in bandages with only his prominent Jewish nose — somewhat like the Fish's own — exposed. And Marina at his side weeping silent tears. No, not weeping. Smiling. Maybe laughing. God.

Occasionally Fish thought he heard car wheels swooshing up

the street, but no headlights beamed into his driveway. He thought he could hear the phone ringing deep inside the house. Would that be Ben calling? Calling to explain all this. The Paraclete calling. This is John the Baptist. Head on a plate, please. Yes sir! Coming right up.

Who could it be on the phone? Marina perhaps. Yes, yes that would be good. Hello. Hello, Eric. This is Marina. Hello. Her voice calling him. Because she wanted him. Him. Fish. No, not Fish, Eric. Marina calling Eric. It scared him to think that. She could call him by his first name. In this world there was no reason why they couldn't be equals. They were both young. He was younger than James Rosen, and no worse looking, though, true, not as rich, and he didn't play the flute and wasn't famous or even much more than a Fish and she was the whole Marina. He could never have a chance. In this world they were not equals. No chance.

If there had been a phone in the pool house he would have tried her number, but she was a Christian. She wouldn't be alone in her apartment on Easter. She'd be with her man and he'd take her out to some fancy Gentile ham dinner in a fancy restaurant, or she'd be at a concert or a party, or anywhere but alone in the dark and the cold like Fish was now. How ridiculous, Fish. How stupidly ludicrous. Lude-a-crous. In his pocket he had five Quāāludes, which he'd bought from Ben for four dollars apiece. He swallowed the first and waited for what seemed like a good time. The wind grew a little quieter and nobody came. It was dark. He swallowed the second and did not wait long before he swallowed the next. There was only the delicate patter of rain on the roof and the mild drone of traffic far away on the highway, and nothing more. He swallowed the fourth, nobody saw him. It was dark. What had he done with his lighter? He couldn't remember. It had gone the way of his keys, perhaps. He wasn't going to waste the fifth — he'd paid for it, hadn't he? He'd never thought of taking them all at once. Kind of like eating a whole box of Whitman's Sampler. His head was beginning to whirl, swim a little. Fish swim. Perhaps he should put an end to this game. Time to induce vomiting? He stuck his finger down his throat, then remembered how he hated to throw up. Most revolting. Oh, God, what was he going to do? If only he had a teaspoon of mustard or some syrup of ipecac. None of that out here, though. What did they do to induce vomiting in the wild? Locusts and wild honey. The Baptist.

Some of the pool chemicals, perhaps. Chlorine. Was that a — what did you call it? — purging agent. Was this chlorine? Perhaps, or whatever. It wasn't hard to pry open. There was a measuring cup inside like it was some kind of laundry detergent. He scooped some out. May I borrow a cup of sugar, Mrs. Fish? This was too powdery, not at all palatable. He would have to add water. Add water, then serve. Presto. He was out in the wet universe with a leap. In the center of everything. Puddles, the smell of trees. Birds calling. Mud and wet cement. He was very sick. He crawled to the pool, like a desert-man to a mirage. Water, water. It was a winter-pool, still, now, full of leaves and the bodies of dead animals. Sticks, garbage, the carcasses of housecats and raccoons. Fish, too. He needed a drink. Where had his cup gone? Somewhere. No matter. There might be another one there. It was only a few feet away, but the going was slow. Such a wet, wet desert. So much moisture, but nothing to drink. How did the poem go? He was dying, truly dying. A Fish, dried out and searching for water, yearning for the ocean. Closer and closer. Closer. Ah. On his face. He could feel it on his face, so very cool and thinly caressing. Such warmth on a cold rainy night.

Chapter 12

I It was dark by the time the train pulled in and she hurried out of the terminal into the street. The city was awash in a yellow light. It was raining slightly.

The temperature had dropped, and at first she was chilly, but she walked so briskly that by the time she reached her building she could feel herself beginning to sweat inside her raincoat.

The guard at the desk looked up, but said nothing. She had lived there for eight months, long enough that she didn't need to show identification. All the guards recognized her face.

Once in her room she hung up her coat, kicked off her stiff shoes, and dropped her good clothes into the hamper. Just scrambling into her jeans and a sweat shirt made her relax a little. She thought of practicing — she had a lesson scheduled for tomorrow and wasn't prepared. She was jittery and she wanted a cigarette. There were none in her backpack. She checked her drawers. None.

She put her sneakers on. It would be pleasant to walk a few blocks to the 7-Eleven and buy a carton of Salem Lights. As she was putting on her anorack the phone rang.

No. Don't answer. It's probably just that Fish person again, calling to harass her. The phone had probably been ringing all day, the whole time she'd been in Trenton.

Six, seven, eight rings. She'd let it ring off the hook, but she wouldn't pick it up. Nine, ten, eleven. It stopped. Good. She opened her purse and pulled out some dollars. These she shoved in her pocket. No need to invite muggers to steal her pocketbook.

One foot out the door and it started ringing again. Damn it. Just close the door behind you and forget it. But what if it was Mama calling, or James?

Who cares? Let it ring. She'd call Mama later. Then she remembered the explosion. James in the airport, not getting killed by a bomb intended for him. God. She felt the morning's nausea sweeping over her again. God. She'd better answer it. It could be James or someone with a message from him. Or it could be that awful Fish.

She picked it up on the fifth ring.

"Marina!" Serge.

"You sound upset," he began.

"Oh, no, just out of breath. Um, I had to run for the phone."

"I called because Mama fell asleep on the couch after you left. You know, how she drifts off in front of the TV."

"And?"

"She woke up hysterical. Something about you. She had a nightmare. I just called to make sure you got home safe, so I can tell her you're all right."

"I'm fine. I — Serge —"

"What?"

"Never mind."

"What is it?"

"Nothing."

"Okay, be like that."

"Be like what? Oh, never mind. Tell Mama I said I'm fine and tell her good night."

"Okay, Rina. Catch you later."

"Right. Bye."

The second she hung up it started ringing again. Now *that* would be the Fish. She left, slamming the door shut behind her.

It was raining harder. She pulled up her hood; tied the chin strings. Her hair was hidden. No one could tell who she was, or even that she was a girl, since she was using her special bouncy walk designed to imitate a young boy. She was asexual and anonymous. She didn't undo her hood even when she entered the store. Too much trouble. She'd only be there long enough to pay for the cigarettes.

Eight dollars for a carton of Salem Lights! Very expensive. She checked the prices of the other brands. Also eight dollars. Everything was eight dollars for a carton. She checked her pocket. Good. She'd brought enough to pay for a pack of Life Savers, too.

Slosh, slosh, her sneakers were wet. She could feel her feet wet inside wet socks. The floor of the store was scattered with wet brownish puddles, which she stepped over to avoid skidding.

There were four people in front of her in line. An old black man with a glass eye and shaky hands. A rough-looking man in his twenties who asked for razor blades. Two nurses in white dresses and white stockings, which were streaked with mud. One held a package of Pepperidge Farm gingermen, one held a cup of frozen lemon yogurt and a can of baked beans. On the counter beside the cash register was a display box of Tiger's Milk bars, a canister of hard pretzel sticks, a canister of Bic Lady Shavers, and a jar for Jerry's Kids, which was empty. The counter was wet and pushed to one side were some wilted lettuce leaves. Marina moved up in line as the black man staggered out of the store.

Someone tapped on her shoulder.

Someone tapped on her shoulder and she jumped a little.

She did not turn around immediately.

It was a youthful black face, one she did not recognize. Male. With a hint of beard at the cheeks and chin, but still too young for real whiskers.

"Hey, baby."

Fish. Is Fish black? She had never thought that he might be, but he could be. Fish.

She turned away, clutched her carton to her breast.

"You got any money, baby?"

She did not turn. The man at the register did not look up. The nurses left quickly with their purchases and Marina was next. She handed the clerk her money.

"Hey, I'm talking to you."

She reached her hand to her pocket to put the change in and she felt a certain violence, her arm jerked from the direction she'd intended it.

He made her look at him. He was dressed like she was, wet jeans, a parka. She looked at his hand. He held a black object, which he shook angrily.

"White bitch."

"I don't have any money." She held her head up, trying to give him an arrogant turn of the cheek. Her heart was racing. She had never seen a real gun before.

She caught the clerk's eye as she turned away. Pure fright.

"Jesus Christ," she heard the clerk say.

"White bitch." The floor was dirty, white-gray, wet. Awash in red. Her cheek went down on cold linoleum. Fish? she thought. No...

A bullet also shattered the glass of the front window, another smashed a jar, sending pickles sliding to the floor, and a third whizzed past the clerk, lodging itself in the shelf, above the cigarettes and razor blades. No one else was hit.

II   The cleaning woman was leaving as James arrived. He met her in the hallway and she let him in, speaking to him by name.

"I heard about your accident, Mr. Rosen. Glad to see you's on your feet again." She pronounced *accident* "ass-ident." James nodded, pursed his lips. He couldn't remember having met the woman before. How did she know who he was?

It was four-thirty and the southwestern bay window was filled with spring sun. Sunlight slashed in on the furniture, illuminating random pieces of wood, glass, carpet. In the kitchen there were clinking sounds, and in seconds Lawrence was there in front of him, holding his best teapot, the Dresden one, in his good hand.

"You're exactly on time," he said. He wasn't wearing his glasses. His blue eyes were moist and faint-colored like skylight. His eyebrows drooped into a squint.

"Yes," said James. "I thought I might be early." His voice shook, and this made him wince. His knees were shaking, too. He felt Lawrence's arm lightly on his waist and let himself be led to a soft chair. He sat and listened to the sounds of Lawrence preparing tea in the kitchen.

The walk, five blocks, down two streets and through the park, was the first he'd taken all week since he'd arrived. He wasn't in pain, just weak. The force of the explosion had thrown him down, against the foot of a urinal, and his knees had been so badly bruised that at first he'd thought the kneecaps were broken. But it was nothing, a minor contusion. He was only *shaken*, as one doctor had explained to Lawrence in his presence. Emotional strain only, nothing physical. Why did he feel so weak?

Lawrence had out the Chinese teacups Freddy had brought back from his trip. He'd never used them before, they were that special.

"You don't have to go to all this trouble," said James.

Lawrence made a click sound with his tongue. He brought out a tray of cucumber sandwiches that he had prepared. There was cake for dessert: cinnamon, James's favorite.

"I didn't make it," said Lawrence nodding at the cake. "That girl did. What's her name. But I sent her home a while ago and I did the tea myself. She breaks everything, you know." Lawrence's eyes glistened. They were moister than James remembered them. Was he developing cataracts?

The sandwiches were tasteless, a little soggy, but James ate carefully, conscious that he was pale today and that he had lost weight noticeably in the past week. He did not want Lawrence to accuse him of lacking appetite. He took his tea milkless, and in the sunlight it assumed a brilliant orange glow.

Lawrence was going to suggest that James stay with him for a few weeks, until he felt better again. James knew this and didn't

284 /

want him to. Lawrence knew James would object, but he had made up his mind: he was going to insist.

"It's not fair for you to be alone now," he said after a silence.

"I'm fine," said James. He took a quick hard nip at his sandwich.

"Too much has happened," said Lawrence. "No. You shouldn't be by yourself."

They sat not talking, knowing what the argument would have been. From somewhere outside, through the open window, came the sound of children singing. James, plate on his knees, glanced in that direction.

"I say it because I have been there before. I have needed you. I could not have recovered without you. And now it's you who needs me. I can help you."

"It's not like that," said James. "No, I'm fine."

"Too much has happened."

"No."

"I need to help you."

"No. You can't Lawrence. I don't want help. I'm all right. Nothing happened to me at all. I'm the one who was spared."

"You've had a big shock."

James shrugged. He looked at his lap, where the tea saucer had tilted and a round spot of warm tea was slowly spreading on his flannel trousers.

"Oh damn," he said weakly.

"I'll get a rag," said Lawrence, before returning with a roll of paper towels. "Gray pants. You're lucky. The stain might not show."

"I'm lucky," repeated James.

Dried off, changed, and sitting in the same chair, this time face to the window, James saw a girl crossing the square in quick, short steps. No, she was taller, chunkier, her hair was not so long or so black; and yet the sight of her filled him with instant horror. He could feel the color vanish from his face. Oh, that Lawrence would not come in the room!

And he did.

"I see you've found the good one," said Lawrence, motioning at his favorite bathrobe, which James was wearing. "It's the most comfortable." James looked up.

"God, you look awful," said Lawrence. "What happened?"

"No, it's very comfortable. The bathrobe."

"James, your face is white. Are you ill?"

"But just because I'm wearing it doesn't mean I'm going to stay here. Heh-heh."

"*James,* what just happened?"

"Oh, Christ, Lawrence. You must know me too well. I looked out the window for just a second and I thought I saw Marina. That's all. I'm seeing ghosts."

Lawrence set the cake down on the parson's table. "You loved her?" he said coaxingly. James kept his eyes on the window. He did not turn toward Lawrence, only gave him his profile.

"You did not love her, but would have liked to?" suggested Lawrence. James exhaled loudly a long-contained breath.

"Why are you talking about love?" he said. "I haven't thought about it."

Lawrence poured himself more tea, and the dregs from the first cup fluttered up to the top. He said, with caution, "I'm sorry." James did not reply. "Marina's death was an impersonal one."

"Imagine dying in a grocery store at the hands of a perfect stranger. For no reason except you happen to be there at the wrong time."

James trained his eyes on the wooden crossbeams in the bay window, not looking an inch beyond them.

"And Guido," said Lawrence. "How horrible for him. Imagine being murdered as a pawn in someone else's game."

James grimaced into his tea. What was unsaid, and what he knew Lawrence was thinking, was that the explosion was intended for him. Everyone knew it; it was even in the newspaper, the *Times.* The explosion was intended for James because he was the famous American. Guido had just happened to be in the way. A failed musician, Guido had finally made the *Times.* He'd been a pawn. James, too. He sipped slowly.

"And on top of everything," said Lawrence, "there's the suicide of that boy." He paused.

James turned and looked at him expectantly.

"The boy," repeated Lawrence. "You've heard, haven't you? Max, my publisher — his wife's brother drowned himself last week. Pity, he was only nineteen or twenty. He'd been drinking scotch or something and took some drugs and threw himself into the family swimming pool."

James looked away again. "I don't remember him."

"I was worried about Gabriel. Apparently he'd seen him right before the drowning. They'd all been together at an Easter dinner, and the boy left the house in a huff about something that had been said and went home and did that. Gabriel's mother told me the story. I was worried that Gabriel might have been traumatized. He's such a sensitive child, but no, he seemed to understand. He accepted it, the way he accepts a lot. His mother's ambition, his parents' divorce, his sister's death. He seems to have a mystic understanding of such situations. How can I explain it?"

James glanced at Lawrence, half-listening. He was going on about one of his students again, the prodigy. James sighed and touched his tender kneecap. He did not want Lawrence to think he was not paying attention. He closed his eyes, pretending to concentrate.

"Three deaths in two days, James. A random murder, a political murder, a suicide."

James shrugged. He was sipping his tea, eyes closed.

"What's missing is a crime of passion," said Lawrence. James smiled, eyes still shut.

Lawrence cleared the plates away and James thought for a moment that he had taken the saucer out of his hand a little roughly. Of course it was just his imagination. Lawrence was such a gentleman that he would never express annoyance in a physical manner. He placed all the precious glassware carefully on the Ethiopian tray and walked steadily into the kitchen. The water was running, and then there was a tinkling sound, pleasant at first, until it became clear it was the sound of shattering glass, the delicate sound of a most precious teacup smashed.

"Oh dear!" said James loudly, hoping at once to sound sympathetic and jovial. There was no reply, and in the kitchen Lawrence swept the tiny fragments onto his dustpan, a tear brimming, then trickling from the corner of his eye.

III   They wouldn't use the photographs Toby's mother had taken. Well, maybe for one of the shots on the inside of the brochure, or on the back of a herald, they were adequate for reproduction. But what they needed was professional work.

"Professional." Myra Davidov talked funny and Gabriel's mother explained that she had a New York accent. Her hair was frizzy and she wore a cape, even indoors, and her fingernails were painted the color of blood. Gabriel was afraid of her. She looked like one of the characters from his bad dreams: a witch. She had a large nose with a hump in it and he kept imagining a wart growing out of the end.

They were going to have to spend a whole day taking pictures at some studio *she* recommended, and that meant it would be in New York, so there would be another long trip up on the train. And Gabriel was going to have to wear a tux, which meant going out and being fitted for a rented one, and wearing it all day long in a hot studio under hot lights. He could just picture himself itching and sweating all day. Yick.

His mother was sitting up straighter than usual and taking notes on things Myra Davidov said. He knew his mom didn't like Myra Davidov because she'd made fun of her voice on the way to her office, but now she was being so polite and nice to her you'd think they were friends.

Gabriel slid down in his chair and stretched his toes out as far as he could. He just touched the leg of Myra Davidov's desk. The whole desk was made of some transparent material, maybe glass. There were no drawers; it was a big table. Where did she keep her things? She had an intercom on the desk, just like Gabriel's dad. She leaned over and started talking to her secretary on it.

"Hazel, bring in those sample brochures and heralds and some posters, and bring in the artist's contract, and get me a cuppa black."

While she was saying this Gabriel's mom nudged his elbow and hissed, "Sit up straight." Hazel was black and very tall. She was wearing a silky dress that looked like scarves sewn together. Her hair was cut short, like a man's.

"Hazel used to dance with the Joffrey," said Myra Davidov as soon as the door closed behind her. "Till she ruined her knees. Three operations."

"How awful," said Elizabeth.

Myra Davidov shrugged. She sipped from her mug. "Oh, I'm sorry," she said "You want cawfee too?"

Gabriel's mother shook her head no.

"You?" said Myra Davidov nodding to Gabriel. It was the first time all morning she'd spoken to him directly. He jumped.

"Coffee?" He'd never drunk coffee. It wasn't a kid's drink.

"No, we're fine," said his mom.

While his mother looked over papers, Myra Davidov talked to Gabriel some more.

"So, Gabe. I'd like to get to know you. Tell me, what do you like to do besides play the flute? Do you like sports? Do you play anything?"

Gabriel looked cautiously at his mom, but she was busy reading the papers.

"Yes," he said.

"Yes, what? What do you like to do?"

"I like baseball." His mom still wasn't looking up.

"You like to watch or you like to play?"

"Both, I guess."

"You on a team?"

"Uh-huh."

"School team?"

"No, Little League."

"Little League. Do you practice on days you play baseball?"

"Uh, yes." He looked desperately at his mother. What was he supposed to say to this lady? His mother still didn't look up. She was reading the little print on the contract.

"I'm catcher," he volunteered cautiously.

"What? You mean you catch the balls?"

"Yes —"

"No."

"No?"

"No, you're gonna have to stop that."

"Stop being catcher?"

"Too dangerous. Mrs. Van Allen, take him out of baseball, *please*."

"Make him stop playing?" said Gabriel's mother, paying attention at last. "Why? He loves it."

"Too dangerous. He could damage his fingers. He broke a finger already this year, didn't he?"

"But it wasn't from baseball."

"Yeah, I was in a fight," said Gabriel. He felt his mother kick him quickly.

"I don't care," said Myra Davidov. "You wanna be serious? Take him out of baseball. Don't fool around with that stuff." She must have caught the look of panic in Gabriel's eyes. She continued: "Hey, that's not for all sports. He wants to do a little swimming, let him do a little swimming. He wants to play a little tennis, okay, but not too much and watch he doesn't get hit by the ball on the head."

"What about soccer," said Gabriel's mother. "They don't even use their hands when they play soccer."

"I don't know much about that," said Myra Davidov. "Maybe it's okay, but don't let it interfere with his practicing. That's the thing with prodigies. They turn fourteen and all they want to do is fool around with girls or play sports. You're not gonna do that to me, are you, Gabriel?"

Gabriel shook his head no and lowered his eyes. He was thinking about baseball.

He would not stop playing. He knew his mother would not force him to. She would not allow that. She loved him. She would lie to Myra Davidov for him, say that he'd quit, and all the same she'd drive him to the games and the practices and let him play in the yard with Steven and Selby as long as he'd finished his practicing. No, that would not happen.

After the Myra Davidov meeting, his mom took him to the coffee shop downstairs in the same building and bought him two hot dogs on hamburger buns and a large root beer. She had a large coffee ice cream to celebrate and when she was finished complaining about the New York menu prices she talked about Sue Levin and how they should stop by and see her, only four blocks away, but they didn't have much time before their train, and Sue Levin was probably busy anyway and she could easily drop her a thank-you note or a postcard. Gabriel wasn't listening; he watched the people walking by the window and thought about Friday's game. He was catching and it was his last chance to qualify for the All-Stars. He was nervous.

"Don't worry, Gabriel," said his mom, sensing his worry. "I won't make you quit baseball."

"Oh, I know that," he said. Of course not. He was just worried about catching a good game.

Chapter 13

August 6, 1979

Gabriel,
These long yellow pages won't reach you, only my quiet voice, but this is where I come to find my words. I gather them from paper.
What shall I say to you? You've had your first disaster. It must seem so large to you. I called it a fiasco out loud and saw the shame in your eyes. No, we'll have to talk about it again. I'll have to show you it was a mistake that will help you learn and that will be forgotten by the public, which has a fickle and short memory.
You weren't ready, but you couldn't have known. You'd had only success with all of your other attempts on the stage — how could you have known this one was too ambitious?
I suppose I could have stopped your mother. I could have voiced stronger objections. I could have absolutely insisted that she call the whole thing off, cancel it, but then she would have tried again. She would have found another hall for your father to rent, another recital to underwrite: another fiasco. She would have tried until she got her inevitable disaster.
Now you have an unpleasant memory and two reviews, one coolly disdainful, the other mocking. (Yes, I read them, too, though I did not mention it. They called you "jejune and unimaginative." I picture you at the dictionary looking that word up.) What did you do with them?

292 /

Paste them into your scrapbook with your old programs and your James Rosen autograph? Your mother says you did not cry. I know you did not cry in front of her. Your tears must be more private.

I will have a word with your mother and tell her all this must stop. Now that you have done her precious Tully Hall recital, which she thought would catapult you into the international concert scene, we have proof that you're not ready to become a professional. I am going to insist that she get rid of the agent, the publicist, the brochure, and all that other nonsense. If she does not, I'll tell her, I will drop you as a student. (A harsh threat, son, but I make it knowing that she will do as I say.)

I will make her promise that from this moment it will be I who directs your career. I will decide whom you are to play with, what you will play, what recitals you will give, and which competitions you will enter. And in six or seven years, when I feel you are ready, I will introduce you to my old friend and manager Bernard Thorn, who runs a far better, more prestigious agency than the Davidov person whom your mother found.

I smile to myself as I write this because I can make you mine; I can arrange things so that you will not fail. I trust your great intelligence, your talent and sensitivity, and I know that with the guidance I will give you, you will mature. You will become an artist.

Gabriel, you are a gift. You are a gift for me to tender and pass on, the music of my winter. I can make it safe for you to grow. When you blossom and leave me I will know that my own art is not incomplete. Gabriel, you will answer my unfinished measure.